"*The Word for Woman Is Wilderness* is unlike any published work I have read, in ways that are beguiling, audacious… rises to its own challenges in engaging intellectually as well as wholeheartedly with its questions about gender, genre and the concept of wilderness. The novel displays wide reading, clever writing and amusing dialogue."
—Sarah Moss, *The Guardian*

"This is not reconciliatory prose. It doesn't seek to please. It's not asking for your acceptance or the benediction of this review. It is far stronger than that. It is a quiet, sardonic, funny, fluid text, a visionary book, that shows us the future is in fact already here."
—Nick Hayes, Caught by the River

"A gripping feminist reimagining of *Into the Wild*." —*Elle*

"A thinking woman's adventure story… [Andrews' prose has] grace and reflection… beautiful, thoughtful, and often humorous."
—Lucy Scholes, *The National*

"The many-colored themes and ideas in the book are themselves painted on complex and overlapping canvases—of feminism, in an age of wilderness, but a wilderness that has been warped as it becomes embedded in the Anthropocene." —*The Ecologist*

"A good book is one that makes you think about your own life. A great book is one that challenges your thinking. But it is a truly remarkable book that changes how you think, and *The Word for Woman Is Wilderness* had that effect on me. I can't give it higher praise than that." —Bookmunch

"[*The Word for Woman Is Wilderness*] is immersive, thought-provoking, and a unique reading experience." —Jenny Colvin, Reading Envy

"Refreshing and funny and unlike anything else. I feel as if I've been waiting for this book for a long time." —Daisy Johnson, author of *Fen*

"Clever, funny and thoughtful."
—Will Ashon, author of *Strange Labyrinth*

# The Word for Woman Is

a novel by
## Abi Andrews

*Two Dollar Radio*
*Books too loud to Ignore*

# Two Dollar Radio
## Books too loud to Ignore

**WHO WE ARE** Two Dollar Radio is a family-run outfit dedicated to reaffirming the cultural and artistic spirit of the publishing industry. We aim to do this by presenting bold works of literary merit, each book, individually and collectively, providing a sonic progression that we believe to be too loud to ignore.

**TWODOLLARRADIO.com**

*Proudly based in*
**Columbus**
**OHIO**

@TwoDollarRadio
@TwoDollarRadio
/TwoDollarRadio

*All Rights Reserved*    COPYRIGHT → © 2018 BY ABI ANDREWS

ISBN → 9781937512798    *Library of Congress Control Number available upon request.*

Published in 2018 in Great Britian by Serpent's Tail, an imprint of Profile Books Ltd.

**SOME RECOMMENDED READING LOCATIONS:** Pretty much anywhere because books are portable and the perfect technology!

AUTHOR PHOTO → Abi Andrews

PHOTOS & ART → Abi Andrews

COVER IMAGES → FRONT: CAJC: in the Rockies, *Marcellina Mountain, Hwy 133* BACK: Dr Mary Gillham Archive Project, *King penguins. South Georgia Island Murphy copy Macquarie*

dedicated to
Tilikum (Tilly) the whale
who perhaps had his own name in whale language
1981–2017

The Word for Woman Is
WILDERNESS

## PASSING THROUGH THE HELIOPAUSE

The space probe Voyager 1 left the planet in 1977. Any month, day, minute, second now it will enter interstellar space and become the furthest-reaching man-made object, and the first to leave the heliosphere. This will be one of the biggest moments in scientific history and we will never know exactly when it happened. Three things would signify that Voyager 1 had crossed the border of the heliopause: an increase in galactic cosmic rays, reversal of the direction of the magnetic field, and a decrease in the temperature of charged particles. Voyager 1 reports show a 25 percent increase per month of cosmic rays. But its signals take seventeen hours to travel back to Earth at the speed of light.

When did my journey begin? At the moment of its conception? When I left home in a delivery van with a friend of my dad's who was going north with some furniture? My parents waved me off with the dog; I filmed it, my mum cried. That felt like a beginning. Or was it the moment the freighter pulled away into the mop-bucket waters off Immingham on a grey day in March?

It came about like this: I was watching a film about a runaway called Chris McCandless, who ditched his ivy-league-trust-fund life and travelled all across America to get to Alaska and live the Jack London dream, where he ate some poisonous potatoes and died. This was 1992, the year before I was born. I cried and promised myself I would start a savings account to fund a trip to

Alaska, where I too could live in the wilderness in total solitude. Then I went through the film step by step and analysed how it would have been different if the guy had been a girl.

Really, it would have been a completely different film. Not just in the sense that there were situations in it that would likely have different outcomes for the different sexes (e.g. when he got beaten up by a conductor who finds him stowing away on his freight train) but more fundamentally because a girl wanting to shun modern society and go AWOL into the wilderness to live by killing and eating small animals and scavenged plants would just be considered unsettling.

Wood-cutting mystic Henry David Thoreau shares some of the blame for this. He said things like 'chastity is the flowering of man; and what are called Genius, Heroism, Holiness, and the like, are but various fruits which succeed it,' as though even having sex with a woman would ruin your transcendentalism. 'Man' is used to refer to humanity as a whole. When 'Man' is pitted against nature in a dynamic of conquest, nature is usually 'she.'

Wildness in women does not mean autonomy and freedom; their wildness is instead an irrational fever. Simultaneously, in survivalist terms we are the weaker sex and cannot prosper individually outside of the social sphere or without the protection of a manly man. Women both are excluded from, and banished to, nature.

Even on those documentary channels that do programmes on whole families homesteading in the wilderness the woman is always Mountain Man's wife, never, ever Mountain Woman, just an annexe of the Mountain Man along with his beard, pipe and gun. In *Coming into the Country: Travels in Alaska*, the writer John McPhee describes lots of Mountain Men in careful detail and a few mountain women in passing comments. One of the Mountain Men tells John McPhee that he wanted to be utterly and totally alone, cut off deep in the country, with only three daughters and one wife, or his 'womenfolks,' as he liked to call them.

There are exceptions to the invisibility spell, of course. There is Calamity Jane the cowgirl. Nellie Bly, who did a trip around the world in seventy-two days. Freya Stark, the travel writer of the Middle East. Mary Kingsley the explorer, and that old lady who went over Niagara Falls in a wooden barrel. But the problem is exactly that there are exceptions. It is as though there is something significant to learn in the wild but it can only be accessed by men. In the wild, men carve out their individual and manly selves, as though women are not allowed individual and authentic selves. The story has the exact same plot, but 'a woman alone in wilderness' means something totally inverted. So I had this idea for a journey to Alaska.

Maybe I have read too many *Lord of the Rings* quest-type fantasies, but I cannot shift the notion that to be deserving of a destination that is really far away you should have undergone some sort of expedition to get there, like how people make a pilgrimage out of piety. So the other element of its ethos came from an aversion to aeroplanes, a combination of carbon-footprint guilt and a suspicion towards the paradox of crossing time zones in a matter of hours to exist suddenly and indifferently in a place you should not naturally be. Not just flying to a place and kind of congregating like these 'all-inclusive sun, sand, sea, collect your tokens in the *Daily Mail*' package holidays.

We were one of those families that always went abroad, apart from years when Dad was out of work. By the time I left home I had travelled to nine different countries. If asked to describe those countries I could have told you that beaches in Spain are busier than beaches in Greece, that in the Caribbean you are advised against going onto beaches that are not owned and segregated by your hotel, and that Disneyworld is too far away from the shore to go to the beach but you can go to a pretend beach at the parks anyway and one even has a slide that is a tube going underwater through a tank with dolphins in it.

Living in a technological era means that in an abstract sense the other side of the world is just a few clicks away. Everywhere on Earth has been explored and put in an encyclopaedia. And the internet has brought all of those encyclopaedias together and ordered them into a messy but functional directory. There are no more enigmas. But it also means that passage of travel has become a lot less elitist. I can utilise the internet in the same way that a man of old might have clutched a quill-written recommendation allowing him passage on his father's tobacco-merchant friend's ship.

It is very easy to feel nowadays that humanity has saturated everything; that we have conquered the world. If you were to watch a time-lapse of Earth from the beginning of its history up to the present day, for a very, very long time not a lot would happen. The continental land masses would gradually drift, asteroids would impact intermittently, and you might catch an erupting super-volcano, tiny button mushrooms of smoke diffusing. Earth would remain a relatively tranquil marble, its atmosphere pearly eddies and swirls. Then, in the eighteenth century AD, you would see a metamorphosis: cities growing like bruises, fertile soil turning to desert, debris gradually accumulating in a dull metallic orbital constellation.

There are now satellites in the sky that will far outlive us, as big as football fields, suspended in the Clarke Belt, 22,236 miles above sea level, at a distance that means they rotate in geosynchronous orbit. They experience little to no atmospheric drag and because of this they will not ever be pulled back to Earth. They might cease to exist only when everything in proximity to Earth is swallowed by our expanding sun. Until then these will be one of humankind's longest-lasting artefacts, and a legacy of the twenty-first century. Our civilisation will be immortalised by these grey exoskeletons, usurping the Egyptians, the Mayans, the Māori, etc.

Earth is around 4.5 billion years old. Anything that is living on it 6 billion years from now will be vaporised when the sun dies and will be as far from us as we are from those little fish that jumped out of the sea. But we are myopic. In the scheme of things, the rate of change over the past one hundred years is just a blink to the universe, and yet *shit*, it took so long for me to get to nineteen years. I want the trip to remind me that I am small and getting smaller. (I am stood on a dot on a balloon, all the dots are evenly spaced, as the balloon gets bigger the other dots seem to get further away but it's only because I am standing on a dot.)

Alaska is the place to feel this. It figures in the collective psyche as the Land of the Mountain Men, the Last Great Wilderness. It is big and vast and mostly unpeopled. The British Isles would fit inside it seven times and about a seventh of Alaska is set aside as protected wilderness. Its entire population is ten times smaller than London's.

I saved up £2000, the approximate cost of a return plane ticket to Alaska, after a few months of working full-time post-A-levels and living scrupulously. This is to be used for travel expenses only, and must get me from the UK to Iceland to Greenland to Canada and across into Alaska. Any money I need to exist will be made along the way. All of the above will be summarised in a tasteful voiceover on top of some sort of video montage of all the places I go looking mysterious and cloudy.

Travelling by sea and land, it will be an Odyssean epic, only with me, a girl, on a female quest for *authenticity*.

## HAUNTED BY THOUGHTS OF AN ELSEWHERE

I have a cabin on a corridor with all the other cabins; each cabin has two bunks, two lamps, two lockers and a porthole. The cabin doors do not have locks and next door keeps walking into my cabin, mistaking it for his. From what I gather he works in shifts, engineering things. Most of the employees are Icelandic but speak at least partial English. I get by with a kind of pidgin formed from their rudimentary vocab and my pocket phrase book.

There are also two students: Kristján and Urla, a guy and a girl from Manchester and Leeds Universities who use the freighter to travel home to Iceland cheaply in the uni holidays. They live in different cities and only met on their first trip. They now make their trips home coincide so they can keep each other company, and they have a rapport with the regular employees. Everyone seems to be under the impression that they are, or are to be, in love.

I am trying to capture the 'essence' of life on board *Blárfoss* for the documentary. Can I do that by filling a memory card with pictures and videos of every inch of the ship, enough to make a 3D mosaicked replica? As though to get at the essence of something is to cover its every angle, like a method of scientific inquiry, exhausting its possibilities? Probably not, because the memory card is nearly a quarter full already. I have also interviewed just about every English speaker afloat. Urla especially thinks the documentary is 'totally cool.' Everyone was taking part as a way of alleviating boredom but it has evolved into some strange kind of fame-ritual, because in the tiny world of the ship the interviewee becomes something akin to a celebrity. At first I was worried about this tainting the documentary, but I suppose I can make it a case in point.

The ship's interior is functional and plain, with dull and unengaging shapes and cold pastel colours that work to intensify the inside of the lounge, the colours of the board games and the humming of the heaters. Aside from the ubiquity of the ship's engine, which can be felt more than heard, outside the lounge there is rarely any sound apart from the intermittent tannoy presence of our captain (who we have nicknamed Capt. Oz). We have all found ourselves taking an unusual interest in food and meal times, which are almost always the same. *Plokkfiskur*, it is called: fish stew, in all its variants. Then underpinning the whole experience is a feeling that I would tentatively call weariness or dreaminess or, combining both, dreariness. A kind of suspension, being both still and unstill, wonky, caused by the weird sensation of movement when nothing visible is moving, the force of gravity contending with the swell of the ocean. Being on an object that is floating makes you more conscious of gravity. With time to think about this, I have come to an arbitrary decision as to what zero gravity might feel like.

In outer space I figure you develop a stronger sense of proprioception, which is the sense of the body parts in relation to each other. (I read this in one of the only English magazines from the lounge, *Pro Bodybuilding Weekly*.) The brain can adapt the senses to compensate each other, so a blind person might feel and hear better. In outer space, with minimal stimuli of sound, sight, smell, taste and touch, perhaps proprioception becomes enhanced. Weightlessness makes any body movement effortless. Forces would radiate from the inside of your body, your pulse would throb through your limbs and you would feel 'embodied' in the most literal sense. This is all just boredom-speculation. I also like to think I can imagine what it would feel like to not have an arm, or to have a third arm, or a penis.

# LAND OF THE ICE-QUEENS

Every star is a sun. Every sun has its own planets. Every planet has its own constellations. The 3D world is a hologram of a 2D world projected from the edge of a black hole.

## OUTER SPAAAAAAAAAAAAAAAAAAAAAAAAAAACE

We do not make enough of outer space. The only remaining frontier and it is no longer of much interest to most of the public. I suppose that is a good thing, and practical. Things would be trickier if everyone was ultra-conscious of their infinitesimality. My mum does not believe in space. I asked her once when I was young if she believed in aliens and she said don't be silly, Erin. I said it seems far more likely that there are aliens if space goes on forever. She said she had never really thought about it. I asked a bit more because I wanted to know what was past the blue sky in her head if she did not think about space. She told me to shut up, she had more important things to think about, like working overtime to make money now that Dad had lost his job at the Cadbury factory because it got bought by America.

Having busy parents meant spending a lot of summer holidays in kids' clubs and eating mainly breadcrumbed/fun-shaped frozen foods. Our domestic life was founded on convenience. Remove foil before heating quickedy-quick Micro Chips I feel like Chicken Tonight like Chicken Tonight. Only modern convenience did not bring the liberation they said it would because Mum still had to work a job *and* vacuum as well, thank you, Mr Dyson. So really she can be excused for not stopping to think about infinity.

I have been standing out on deck and looking out to sea. The sea that goes on unbroken to the horizon. There is nothing, no things but gulls, and you think, how do the gulls fly without tiring? Do they not feel panic that there is nowhere for them to rest their wings apart from actually on the ocean, and here they might get eaten by something big that comes from what to them must seem another dimension? No place to rest their eyes and sleep? The empty space makes me think of a diagram in a physics book of a ball on a plane of Newton's, a single arrangement of matter rolling on a grid of space, the loneliest object in the world. We are the ball and the sea is the grid. I have only been on an unbroken and empty plane like this on a P&O ferry to France once, and that was only for a matter of hours. By day three I feel like the Ancient Mariner.

Urla likes to read and we got along quickly. We have formed a kind of two-way book club where we swap and then discuss. We have been dipping into Ursula Le Guin's *The Left Hand of Darkness* and Elizabeth Bishop's *Questions of Travel*. Urla says she likes Le Guin; the book's world Winter reminds her a little of her own icy home, but she is not so keen on Bishop, maybe because some of the intricacies of language are lost on her, maybe because her BA is in Business Studies. I have read a little of her book, *Lean In*, by her hero Sheryl Sandberg. It is all about how women in business can help themselves to succeed in a male-dominated workplace by learning to be more like men.

Part of the trip obviously had to be about personal growth, and I have resolved to take the extended opportunity to make myself a more well-rounded human being. The five-point plan goes like this:

–Read lots of insightful books
–Know rough history of every place before visiting
–Immerse self in culture of each place
–Learn important phrases in each language
–Write. Every day

Urla's parents are separated. Her mum is Icelandic but her dad is English. He lives near to her in Leeds and she has split her time between England and Iceland since she was ten. I was planning on staying in a cheap hostel in Reykjavík but Urla's mum has a spare room that I can stay in for free for as long as it takes me to figure out how to get to Greenland. So instead of having to infiltrate my first foreign city with the blunt ram of a tourist I have Urla to show me around and she has an SUV, so we can even go see the best bits of the landscape of Iceland, something that would have taken some logistics considering my budget. Urla talks like everyone should listen and has a way of draping herself over everything like a languid cat. I think it would be fair to say that I have a girl-crush on Urla, a kind of feeling of affinity and admiration that is completely free from jealousy.

## WOMEN'S INTERNATIONAL TERRORIST CONSPIRACY FROM HELL

INT. MESS ROOM — *Urla reclining on sofa with dog-eared copy of* Moby-Dick *in hands — room is large with three sofas arranged in square and coffee table centre with books and magazines — small television with VHR mounted to wall — bookcase with videos, CDs — CD player on top of bookshelf — bookshelf modified with balconied shelves to stop books sliding off with sway — outside wide windows ocean — white ocean birds — wall of ocean rises, falls, rises, falls with motion of boat — one other sofa occupied by two men — legs splayed, reading magazines —*

**Erin:** (BEHIND CAMERA) So maybe you could just talk a little about feminism in Iceland

**Urla:** Okay, sure

*— sits up and turns to men on adjacent sofa —*

**Urla:** Do you wanna talk about feminism in Iceland with me?

*— the men look up from their magazines, shrug —*

**Urla:** They speak little English. So. There are many surveys say Iceland is the best country in the world in which to be a woman. Because it is the best country in the world in which to be a person. We have no army. We run on renewable energy. People are mostly very happy apart from those that get sad of the darkness in winter

*— the man on the left is reading an Icelandic magazine on 4x4s — he is watching Urla over the brim of the page —*

**Urla:** Let me think, so, in nineteeeeeen seventy-five 90 percent of Icelandic women went on strike over equal pay and then they got equal pay. We elected the first female president in Europe in 1980. Finnbogadóttir. She was a divorced single mother like my mum and she was re-elected three times until she retired. And then our prime minister was the world's first openly gay prime minister and she started out as an air hostess. The state church bishop is a woman. And we are the only country in the world to make strip clubs illegal for feminist reasons

*— 4x4 magazine man makes a semi-discreet 'humph' sound — Urla turns to him pointedly — he looks down and flicks the pages of his magazine straight —*

**Erin:** Do you think that has to do with nakedness being starker because in the cold climate you have to wear so many layers on a day-to-day basis? Kind of an anonymising of the human figure that might take away some issues of sexualising the body. Like in *The Left Hand of Darkness*, where cold and androgyny made a society with no misogyny and no war?

*— 4x4 magazine man shakes his head disbelievingly — Urla does not notice — she looks down at her body in high-necked woollen jumper, thick grey joggers tucked into woollen socks —*

**Urla:** I don't know. Probably (PAUSE) what else. So women do not have to change their surname if they marry. And when a baby is born its parents get equal leave. BUT

*— she raises her right index finger in a scholarly manner, holding the book to her chest with her other arm —*

**Urla:** Even in the best place in the world in which to be a woman it is still better to be a man

*— she looks at 4x4 mag man, who is leafing through his pages with a look of nonchalance —*

**Erin:** Nowhere has completely got rid of gender inequality and the attitude of some people here now is like, Okay, we get it. You have everything you want now. You have it the best in the world so stop being so righteous. Other women don't have it so great. You can give it a rest now. Although it's totally cute when you get all angry

**CUT**

## HOW TO BE A GROWN-UP IN A POST-FEMINIST SOCIETY

You are fourteen years old and you have just started your job as a waitress in a small restaurant owned by a family, each member of which fills a role in the kitchen and also deals drugs. Having never had a job you take everything here to be archetypal of the working world. You are not a feminist because feminists are lesbians and hate men and you don't. You like boys more than girls, girls are lame and preoccupied and bitchy and you'd rather hang out with boys and skate and mess around. The only girls you do like want to be boys too.

Stuart is the father of the family and the manager of the restaurant. He is short, fat, bald, and has buggy eyes. When you are introduced from across the worktop he grabs your hand in his stubby, sweaty hands and kisses you up your arm with his fat wet lips. You squeak and recoil and the other girls laugh at you. When you are outside the kitchen one of the older girls tells you you get used to it.

You do get used to it and after a time you manage not to squirm when Stuart strokes your pubescent arse, which is taut in those tight-fitting Tammy Girl trousers he makes you wear because he likes it when you squirm. When he creeps up behind you when you're standing behind the till counter on the restaurant floor and kisses you on the neck, making a squelchy sound, none of the customers ever say anything and some of them must catch him sometimes.

You watch a seventy-year-old man dine an escort while he strokes the downy hairs at the dip of your back and hips, while you tell yourself 'the dip of my back and hips is merely the concave of a crescent in an assembly of matter which is a body in which I reside.' When your mum asks how was work you say yeah, fine, because if you told her it'd be embarrassing. She'd call the police or something. None of the other girls have told anyone, the customers never say anything, so what makes you so special you call the police? It's something you're mature enough to ignore. It's a part of being a woman. When Jodie the new girl starts you even get a bit annoyed when she keeps going on about how Stuart likes her because she's prettier than you.

It's an easy job and you don't want to lose your job cuz then you won't be able to go to the cinema or anything. If you quit you'd have to come up with a good reason for Mum and you can't think of one. And you're lucky to have this job because you're really shit at it, they tell you that all the time. You do everything wrong and you're really slow and clumsy and you never smile. And the other girls are always saying he's good to us, he looks after us, he gives us free food and he's like a dad really.

You let Stuart do it because it turns him on if you don't. When you are in the cloakroom one time he calls your bluff and puts his fingers all the way down your underwear, which are the ones with ducks on them. You don't tell the other girls because they'll just think that you think that you're something special. Nobody else is complaining, don't be such a crybaby. When you close your eyes to sleep you can see clearly the spittle on his fat wet lips.

## SYMBIOSIS OF ALGAE AND ANIMALS

Urla's mother's name is Thilda. Her house sits behind Reykjavík and from it you can look out over the backs of all the buildings looking out to the sea. It is spring and the trees and parks are very green and the water and sky very blue. The buildings get so close to the sea that in certain lights, when you can't see the horizon and the harbours and the lakes are filled with sky, it can look as if the city is sitting on the edge of infinity. The sun sets but seems to sleep just out of sight, and I had to buy a sleep mask to convince my body it was night-time. Although it is getting warm for Iceland it is still cold, and whenever outside I wear my ski jacket.

Leaving *Blárfoss* had the potential to be emotional, but because for most of the others it was more of a suspension of the experience rather than an end — because most of the others would be repeating the journey again and again with slight variations in crew — it wasn't. I will have to learn not to get emotionally attached to transitory places, seeing as a journey is entirely transition. Even Urla and Kristján treated their good-bye with admirable stoicism. She says that their relationship is *Blárfoss*, that they have agreed not to see each other outside of it before university finishes, and she does not think it can even exist independently of it. I think it is very sensible.

She seems to be able to look at their relationship with a manly and objective clarity that I admire. She seems totally indifferent to Kristján, in fact, spending most of her days on the boat with me, aside from joining him in their shared cabin at night. If they were together and I approached them, Kristján would make any excuse and leave, which became an ongoing joke to Urla; she would laugh and shout, 'Bye, Kristján!' after him. I got to feeling really bad about it and started to leave them be, but then Urla took to abandoning him for me.

She says as soon as university finishes she wants to do a trip like mine, that the trip is brave and important. She made me swell up, as if with her approval I become a little bit like her. She is sure of herself in a way that I envy, in the way that she talks and holds herself. You can tell she was one of the girls at school that everybody wanted to be friends with, or wanted to at least not to be not-friends with, to be in the focus of her dislike, which I imagine to be conducted with precision and ruthlessness.

At school I preferred to be on my own. I would ride my bike places on weekends, with my rucksack — an antidote to the typical feminine handbag — full of practical stuff that I would find use for even when it was tenuous, just for the sake of being able to cut everything neatly with my pocket knife even where I could use my teeth, nursing the smallest of wounds with my first aid kit, using my compass even when I knew the way just for the reassuring comfort I found in knowing exactly where north was, its orderliness and its simple truth, comfortable in apt autonomy like Thoreau.

There was one place in particular that I would cycle, an hour by bike, across the river and down empty country lanes, to a tree that I used as a hide that looked out over the top of an abandoned limestone quarry, and it was here that I would sit with my binoculars and bird-watch. In the town the only birds you ever saw were little common backyard birds like tits and chaffinches and sparrows and wagtails but out in the quarry and away from the town there were birds that prey on other things, other birds, predatory and exciting.

I had myself an *Identification of British Birdlife* book and would sit still for hours just to collect the sight of them and the sound of the name of them like talismans. There were plentiful buzzards and kestrels that would slip in and out of the area on their hunting routes, sliding on the warm air to hang and observe like snorkellers at the water's surface, periscoping their necks then locking still before the dive, limiting any movement to the final flurry. Or the thrill of the goshawks that would sometimes weave and dip in and out of the trees either in the valley beyond the quarry or on the opposite ravine. Sometimes the goshawks display-danced, spreading their tail feathers like splayed fingers and falling through the sky like grabbing hands.

But what I really held out for were the days when I got to see one or both of the rare pair of peregrine falcons that nested somewhere in the trees around the quarry. They would always fill me up with the magic of hope, their tiny defiant bodies wheeling against the sky so small against the big, so dark against the blue, and so free. In their sky-dance they revelled disobediently against their declared local extinction.

To be able to tell the difference in these birds by their shape and their movements and to point at them and call them by their names has always been to me an affirmation of the solid truth of the natural world as a system that can be described with taxonomy, and a reminder of my place in it. It is also a reassurance; it shows me that these things still exist because I can collect them. That there are still places to watch and be a part of a realer order outside of severed civilisation.

I do not know if Urla can tell that I was the kind of person to spend my lunchtimes at school in toilet cubicles with my feet up so no one would recognise my shoes. My parents can't reconcile this sudden bid for independence and shrugging off of domesticity with what they think of as my nature; introverted and docile. They are confused by my surety and think that instead this impulse must stem from some malady; that I overthink things, that I feel too much, that I should not watch the news if it scares me so much that it makes me want to leave what I must see as the train wreck of modern society.

What they could not seem to see was that this limiting aspect of me is in part the drive for my leaving, that I want to learn how to be without it. To prove to myself and everyone else that solitude is as much mine as any Mountain Man's and that I do not have to be relegated to loneliness and displacement just for being female. It is rational and deliberate and it had always been part of the plan. I have always been obedient, the model daughter. Mum and Dad said finish school and try hard at it so I did. I kept my nose clean and I always ate my vegetables (frozen for goodness).

Already I feel something changing. I look at Urla and the way she oozes and I think, does doing this project make her think that of me? Am I that person, even if only from certain angles? Is it having a camera and a plan that gives me that authority? Or actually, just being nineteen and female and travelling alone, does it do that? It is possible that Kris's discomfort around me came from a place of awe, like the awe he shows for Urla in never talking back to her.

Yesterday Thilda took us to a geothermal spring. Neither of

us remembered to pack swimming things so we had to go in our underwear and bras. It did not matter because it was raining so we only saw a few hikers and they weren't close enough to distinguish underwear from swimwear anyway.

'The best time to go to the springs is when there is rain, because the tourists like to stay dry. But in Iceland we think, if you are going to get wet, you might as well get wet, okay?' Thilda had said.

We parked the SUV where the off-road terrain offered no more leeway, still a bit of a distance from the pools, whose grey iridescence we could just make out. The sky hung low like the pelt of a sad, wet sheep, the rain fading all outlines into each other like a bleeding watercolour and the mossy ground skirting the rocks and water, luminous in contrast. We took off our clothes and shoes, slammed the doors, and ran towards steaming water, laughing and screaming. The rain stung our skin pink.

We fell on our fronts into the hot water, slipping and flailing, trying to submerge every inch from the cold and spitting and coughing and laughing at the water filling our mouths. Then we settled still and quiet with just our eyes and the tops of our heads out of the water, blinking the rain off our lashes and bringing our noses up for air like seals. Thilda started to tell us a story.

'The famous saga of Erik the Red may be called so but it is really about a *skörungur*, which is what we call a strong woman hero. Her name was Gudrid the Far-Traveller, his daughter-in-law, and she lived in the tenth century.'

Iceland is steeped in sagas and mysticism because the landscape is animated as if it is telling its own story. Glaciers walk, the ground moves and magma seeps, and geysers erupt like blowholes on the humped back of some giant. It is as though these are living parts acting out their own narratives. The Icelandic legends are shaped by the elements, because here the elements are all-pervasive.

And the landscape is volatile and fierce. Like Thilda says, the

Icelandic women are strong because they are descended from Vikings and conquerors and raised by the icy sea winds which sting their cheeks and the hot geyser steams which scald them. And in a land where fire and ice are in battle and care little for anything around them, all people must be strong.

In the landscape the elements merge like there is no limit to their pervasiveness, no clearly defined contours. You can feel it seeping into you; trading off with the algae in the water and the mud between your toes like nourishment. You can feel the shuddering of the water making everything on your body reach out in reciprocity, every hair a tentacle. Half submerged in the hot spring; in and out; half still and warm, half cold and lashed; ears under, eyes out; the patter of rain on the surface, the gasping of the spring.

Thilda's story gives me a feeling like recognition, a sense of inevitability and completion, a slotting into place. Like finding an object you never noticed was missing until you found it and realised its lack had been haunting you all along. I recognise it by knowing its antithesis; my own home and environment. See, where I am from there is not this boundlessness. The *outside* that I know is broken to pieces and scattered.

Our cul-de-sac is on a suburban estate built on the site of an old power station that had been running up until the eighties. All the houses look the same with neatly trimmed rectangular lawns and faux-Tudor beams, no weeds (there are sprays for those), and the streets are named after famous ships. Our town was typical of Midlands industry because it is well connected to the canal and river systems. There was a power station, a vinegar factory, a sugar beet factory, and several carpet factories, one of which my mum worked in as a secretary while I was in her belly. The power station was coal-fired and archaic and the factories moved to China so they knocked it all down and built the suburbs and a giant Tesco. My mum and dad got jobs a thirty-minute drive away, closer to the city, and no one could grow anything to eat in their yards because the power station left radon in the topsoil.

The outside that I know is pastoral, a grid of owned and regimented spaces, moderated for production. Some people  think the English countryside is pretty but that is the tragedy of it. It is a result of the way our small country was built, when a bunch of rich men parcelled up what was once shared land to make it easier to go about ploughing and producing more crops. Our common wilderness became a commodity. On an island so small the mark of this is hard to not see: a monotonous quilt of rectangles divided by hedgerows. Especially in the Midlands, where there are not many mountains or bogs or other bits of stubbornly unprofitable land, and where the remains of failed industry create a graveyard landscape, the stumps covered over with prosthetic suburbia.

The peregrine quarry was the one place I knew that had a semblance of wildness to it, of richness and possibility. This is an invisible kind of poverty, this lack of all of the complexity that Urla and her mother are born from.

Gudrid lived in the days of longboats and raging seas. She travelled to what we now call Newfoundland, which is my own first port of call in Canada. This was before lucky-lost explorer Christopher Columbus, and Thilda proudly points out that although the Spanish like to think that the sagas are make-believe,

Icelanders know who really found the New World. Gudrid was the first European mother in the western hemisphere.

She had a son; they called him Snorri. But with their small clan and without the guns the Spanish had, they were driven away by the natives. Or savages, as Thilda called them.

She concludes her story by saying, 'Gudrid travelled further than all of her husbands, who died one after another and proved early in our history that you don't need a penis between your legs to make you a great adventurer.' I look up at the bulking hills and think about how Gudrid personifies them, and the geysers and the winds, and the looming, enduring volcanoes, the shifting ground. And how so much of Thilda is in Urla, and Gudrid in them both. And it feels kind of feminine, all this entering. It feels like pregnation.

It is this harsh softness. Of a landscape that is fertile and *hostile*. And it takes on this significance for me and for my journey so that I have to squeak into bubbles under the water, because I feel like for the first time ever I know exactly why I am where I am right then in that moment.


## GO WEST, YOUNG MAN

Our plans for Greenland have undergone sudden and fantastic developments. Urla and Thilda had been plotting the whole time to put us on a boat with Urla's uncle Larus, who is a whale scientist. Larus has his own research boat and is intending to go out into the Denmark Strait, the channel in between Iceland and Greenland, to survey a pod of long-finned pilot whales. They hadn't told me in case it didn't work out, but it has and we leave for Greenland in four days' time.

It is against protocol because the boat is only supposed to carry two people, but Urla threatened to stow away if her uncle took me and went without her. She will come with me as far as she can before she has to get back and work her summer job, so we will be in the double cabin and Larus will sleep in the steering room on the floor. Urla will then carry on through Greenland with me until I find a way to follow in the wake of Gudrid on to Canada. It is perfect because she can translate for me in Greenland, and she said she would write up the subtitles for the Danish when I edit the footage for the documentary. Because her uncle Larus still has to do his research it will be a slow journey of five days but we get to go whale watching and learn about the behavioural patterns of the long-finned pilot whale.

It jarred how easily Thilda let Urla go across a foreign country with a stranger so soon after they reunited after so long. I suppose we will be with her uncle and then her family friends in Nuuk once we find a way to reach the west coast, so the prospect seems safe to her. Maybe also she is used to Urla leaving, what with her being at university and having spent half her childhood away at her dad's because of the separation. But the contrast to my own parents' response is stark.

*Why can't you just be simple like other girls your age, get a job somewhere in town and work your way up, or at least go away to go to university, make something of yourself?*

*What did we do to you that made you so determined to leave us?*

*We won't sleep until you return.*

*We won't sleep ever again.*

I could not make them understand that my breaking-away-from is inevitable and keeps the history of the world in motion. The young always leave. At least the male young of the species always does. My leaving would have been a casting out, an initiation ritual, had I been a boy. Women who leave always abandon. Imagine the pinnacle form of this, the mother who leaves her children to her husband. Unnatural! Monstrous! And the man who does it? My bet is he ends up smug with a younger wife, paying minimal child support.

Urla does not need to lurch away from Thilda because Thilda lets her go. The two of them are twinned in ease, in their mannerisms, in a way that makes them seem more like sisters than mother and daughter. I prefer to be definitive about my being, where it ends and what its characteristics are. I have my dad's nose, my mother's green eyes and dark brown hair. I have his stubbornness and her impulse to over-empathise, weeping easily. But I try hard to also not be like them.

Peregrine; chaffinch; woodpigeon.

Field; hedgerow; river.

Mother; father; me.


## THE CHEMICAL WAR ON THE GYPSY MOTH

Larus has given me Rachel Carson's *Silent Spring* because 'it is one of the most important books you will ever read.' In 1962 *Silent Spring* was published to tell of how different chemicals invented for killing people in the world wars were being used for killing pests on food crops and were then having unexpected repercussions, like the death of birds and children. This is in the sixties, so everyone was doubly pissed with the government for also putting them in range of nuclear weapons that might come at any time without warning and telling them they would be safe under desks.

Widespread use of DDT was stopped because of Rachel Carson's book and the US got a mainstream environmental conscience. Acceptance of the 'ambivalence' of the oppressors could be scrutinised. Women could have rights, black people could have rights, gay people could have rights, animals could have rights, even grass and trees could have rights, and if you took to the street in a crowd with billboards you could make anything happen.

Larus overuses his own coined collective nouns like 'the

nascent youth of today' and 'the ignorant herd.' He is exactly the kind of man you imagine when you imagine the kind of man who would get upset about bees. He speaks as if he is playing an internal monologue on constant reel, projecting it into the world like his mouth is a loudspeaker. Just by looking at him I can tell he probably actually weeps at the mention of Arctic drilling.

There are certain stereotypes that fit with giving a shit about the planet, and funnily enough these are generally in some way feminine. To be a socially acceptable environmentalist you have to be female, a child, or an eccentric (which itself entails being kind of effeminate, if you are already a man). I have come to the conclusion that this is because environmental issues are perceived to be melodramatic and melodrama belongs to the feminine because women are of course by default hysterical, 'in touch with nature,' and so easily brought to tears by images of seagulls stuck in Coke cans in conjunction with sad piano music. Melodramatic because there are more pressing issues like terrorists and fascism and the looming employment crisis of the robot workforce, never mind the bees. Women just like animals because they are cute and summon their maternal instinct.

It is a vicious circle because there is no way of talking about the issues without evoking a whole discourse that is by now tainted by this idea of melodrama. Caring about the environment is lame, Greenpeace is run by scaremongers and weirdo conspiracy theorists, and the bees have gone somewhere, but it is a boring mystery.

Can YOU give just one pound a month? JUST ONE POUND A MONTH?! One pound could feed cats like Maurice for a whole year and provide shelter on wet nights and windy days and buy the love he so cherishes. Maurice loved his owners (cue sad piano music, image of wet Maurice sat in a box at the side of a road) but one day they took him out in the car and just left him at the side of the road because he had fleas and he smelled.

We must protect animals like Maurice, the furry little creatures that god gave us to steward.

But bees do kind of pollinate about everything we eat. So really, though, Larus, where have the bees gone?


## I USE SONAR TO EXPRESS MYSELF

We have found the pod of long-finned pilot whales. There are over one hundred of them and it is incredible to look at, their bodies rising smooth and bulbous from the grey water like bubble wrap, blowing air from their blowholes, spraying water like saliva from a blown-up balloon let loose. After two days of tailing them I am reassured that they are not going to rise up as one and overturn our little boat. I was pacified by realising that they also hang around with dolphins. Dolphins are an animal I can trust. In our pod there are a group of Atlantic white-sided dolphins; Larus says they herd the fish together with the whales. The dolphins are curious about us and come right up to the boat to play around in the foam that comes off our propeller. Their faces and noises are the epitome of happiness, just pure unbridled joy at this strange thing chopping up their water and making it foamy. So simple and pure, like the joy of children.

I have won the tolerance of grumpy Larus. He was moaning about how it is 'people like me' who have ruined Bali by thinking they are all spiritual and swamping the place with their yoga mats. He sees this as something flawed in the psyche of the youth of today. I asked him how many children he had and he said he has five from three different mothers because that is just how it was in the sixties. I asked him if Bali's overcrowding was not just the inevitable outcome of overpopulation and that there were the same annoying yoga mat tourists in the sixties, but in the sixties there were fewer people so there was less yoga mat crowding and that maybe it is actually his generation's fault for breeding so much. He grumbled some stuff but since then has been actually quite amicable towards me.

On top of his research for the Ocean Association, Larus is conducting his own. The pod is particularly interesting to him because of the dolphins. He uses the equipment on the boat to record and plot their sonar and by measuring patterns he hopes to be able to crack their language. The graphs in the office already prove that the dolphins are talking; Larus has plotted the quantified appearance of each distinct vocalisation in descending order across a horizontal axis, the times occurring across a vertical axis. The plot of a graph where information is being communicated always results in an angle of 45 degrees because all languages have units that range on a spectrum from frequent to infrequent. If it is not a 45-degree angle then the noises are random and uncommunicative. This is the same for any language, Icelandic, English, Dolphin.

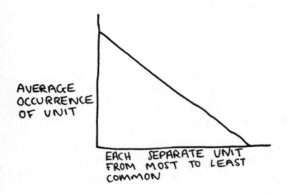

AVERAGE
OCCURRENCE
OF UNIT

EACH SEPARATE UNIT
FROM MOST TO LEAST
COMMON

Larus says he can apply this method to any long piece of sound data. His other focus is noise picked up by dishes aimed at outer space. A friend in America has built his own dish behind his house in the desert and he and Larus work on the data because the only government-funded dish used specifically to listen for aliens, the Big Ear radio telescope in Ohio, was taken down in 1998 to clear space for a golf course. It ran for twenty-two years and it actually picked up the kind of thing they were looking for. It appeared to come from north-west of the globular cluster of M55 in the constellation Sagittarius. It lasted for seventy-two seconds and they called it the Wow! Signal because that is exactly what astronomer Jerry R. Ehman wrote on the computer printout.

But the signal it picked up only occurred once, so after searching for it they eventually presumed it was some sort of fluke, the logic being that any *intelligent* civilisation would keep on sending a signal over and over to make it more likely to be heard. A three-minute-long radio signal was sent from Earth to a cluster of stars at the limits of the Milky Way one time in 1974 and never again. By the time any hypothetical civilisation had got it and then sent a reply it would be around about AD 52,000. The sustained attention span of the average human ranges from between five to twenty minutes.

The guys that sent the signal referred to themselves as the Order of the Dolphin. They called themselves this because one of their members, the marine biologist John C. Lilly, used to take hallucinogens and climb into tanks with dolphins to explore interspecies communication. John Lilly found that dolphins can process linguistic syntax. He taught them to differentiate between commands such as bring the ball to the doll and *bring the doll to the ball*.

He would talk about them like he thought they were people. Larus played us a track by a lady spoken-word poet that I liked. She imagined what a whale might say to John Lilly if it could speak telepathically to him, and what the whale asked as it swam circles in its ceramic-tiled prison was whether every ocean has walls.

Because of the difficulty of relaying a message through both deep space and deep time, Larus thinks we also need to consider that aliens might have come to Earth billions of years ago and encoded a message into our DNA, in the genes that do not do a lot apart from sit around. He says that some decoders are looking for mathematical patterns because intelligent civilisations must understand pi and prime numbers and things as universal truths that transcend language. What Pythagoras said: *the whole cosmos is a harmony and a number.*

Some of the guys from the Order of the Dolphin, like the turtle-necked celebrity cosmologist Carl Sagan, also worked on the Golden Records that were sent into space with Voyager 1, which by now could be outside the solar system and on its way to somebody else's. The Golden Records were a kind of time capsule. In it they sent pictures of a whole range of cultures and creatures, sounds from Earth like screaming and laughter and greetings in lots of different languages. President Jimmy Carter left a written message for the aliens inside the time capsule:

> 'This is a present from a small, distant world, a token of our sounds, our science, our images, our music, our thoughts and our feelings. WE ARE ATTEMPTING TO SURVIVE OUR TIME SO WE MAY LIVE INTO YOURS.'
> — President Carter

The time capsule is President Carter's baby. With it he has conceptually colonised the future.


## THE CEILING IN THE SKY

I nominated myself to help Larus while Urla fished for dinner because I like to sit and listen to him talk about space. I am helping group all of the sound bites that Larus has from the dolphin recordings into categories that are similar sounding. He plays them from the computer and we decide which of seven folders to put them into.

When I was little I wanted to be an astronaut up until age thirteen, when at careers day I sat with my parents and told my head of year about how I wanted to be an astronaut; they all laughed as though it were cute and he signed me up for work experience at a paragliding centre on the basis that I must have liked the idea of flying.

Larus was at Kennedy for the lift-off of the Apollo 11 mission. He was there to protest, stood in a line with its back to the launch pad, holding a sign that read 'Meanwhile in Harlem,' but as soon as he heard the roar from the propulsion engines he turned around and could not take his eyes away. There is a photo somewhere of the group with him turning and gaping; he did not ever cut it out of the newspaper because he had spoiled the integrity of the group's statement. He told me this confidingly and made me promise not to tell Urla because she would never let it go.

My being an astronaut was something I did not ever doubt as a child because Mum always told me *the whole world is your oyster* and until that careers day I had no cause to doubt her. It did not matter to me that all the cartoon astronauts were men. I think I always positioned myself as male without actually being aware of it. Whenever I watched films or read books with a male hero I totally imagined myself as that hero. Call me Ishmael. Call me Ralf, call me John McClane. It is not fair that only the boys get the fun parts.

I said this to Mum and Dad about fun parts when they started protesting at the idea of me doing this trip after college. It took a while to dawn on them that I was being serious and had come of legal age to do it without their permission anyway. Mum said, 'Your father and I have decided that we can't help you financially with this trip because we are not behind it.' I told them that was fine and I could fund it myself. 'What if you are in an unsafe place and have one of your spells?' (By this she means my propensity to kind of faint for no apparent reason sometimes.) Of course I have not told them the *real* tundra-wilderness plan and the full extent of the 'survivalism' experiment, because, well, that would just have been cruel when I know they would suffer for it.

When America shot a rocket to the moon, even with the sexual revolution in full swing, it was still too soon to let women have a cosmic one. Larus was telling me about an independent programme called Mercury 13 (which he agreed to talk about to the camera), which took accomplished female pilots and put them through the testing that NASA did on their own astronauts, the Mercury 7 programme, the theory being that for various biological reasons women were actually better suited to space flight. It was a success but NASA just could not have ladies on the moon before men, so they kept the requirement that all NASA astronauts be a member of the air force, and women were still not allowed to join the military. So none of the Mercury 13 pilots were taken on, although they had more air experience than a lot of the men at NASA (some of whom secretly did not have all of the requirements anyway). When Larus told me this I remembered how bitter I felt at the paragliding centre while two boys in my year got sent to Leicester Space Centre on 'limited allocation' work experience.

Maybe America sent a man to the moon to undermine Russia's female cosmonaut Valentina Tereshkova. She was ten years younger than the youngest NASA astronaut and had spent more time in space than all Americans combined, orbiting the Earth forty-eight times. Man astronaut Neil Armstrong did not go for all of mankind and he certainly did not go for women. America only went to space in the first place to show that communism could not be more progressive than capitalism. Tereshkova worked in a textile factory before she became a cosmonaut. Her mother before her worked in the textile factory and her father was a tractor driver. What if Apollo had crash-landed? Would Russia rule the world now?

But Tereshkova was a human propaganda pawn: the Russian female programme was dissolved the year of the Apollo moon landing. Cosmonaut Yuri Gagarin's official birthday was moved a day so that there were no records that he was *really* born on

International Women's Day; Russia could not have had him as a national hero if he were born on International Women's Day. That would make him a sissy.

## MANNED SPACE FLIGHT IS THE
## TROPHY WIFE OF THE SUPER-PHALLUS

INT. BEDROOM CABIN — *Erin and Urla sit on opposite sides of the bed, facing each other — on her head Urla has a cone with wings coloured with felt-tip pens to look like a rocket — on its side it says NASA under a penis with flames coming out from beneath the testicles — they are talking into walkie-talkies —*

**Erin (Jerrie Cobb)** (PUTTING ON AN AMERICAN ACCENT): Oh hey, NASA. It's Jerrie Cobb from the Mercury 13. So I did everything you said I should

**Urla (NASA)** (BAD AMERICAN ACCENT. DEEP FOR MALE): Mm-hmm. What's that?

*— Erin bursts into laughter —*

**Urla** (IN HER NORMAL VOICE/LAUGHING): Hey. What? Are you laughing at my accent?

**Erin:** Sshhhh

*— Erin clears her throat and resumes her serious-American tone —*

**Erin (Jerrie Cobb):** I did all the tests like all the guys did. And hey, it's funny. I actually kinda blew them out the water

**Urla (NASA)** (ACCENT) (THEATRICALLY SUSPICIOUS): What tests?

**Erin (Jerrie Cobb)** (LAUGHING): You know. All the secret tests you make the guys do so they can go into space

**Urla (NASA)** (PAUSE): I don't know what tests you're talking about

**Erin (Jerrie Cobb)**: I'll remind you then. I put freezing water in my ears to see what it feels like with no balance. I spent days alone inside a box. I ran on a treadmill till I thought I might die. I drank radiation

**Urla (NASA)** (SCOLDING): How'd you find out about the secret tests? They're secret

**Erin (Jerrie Cobb)**: Er, well now. We have a scientist friend. He invited us to do them. He said you didn't have your own programme for ladies so he made one to show you that you should have

**Urla (NASA)** (THEATRICALLY CONDESCENDING): And why's that?

**Erin (Jerrie Cobb)**: Because all his evidence suggests that it is way more logical to put a woman in space than a man

**Urla (NASA)** (GRINNING): There is no NASA-led evidence to prove this

**Erin (Jerrie Cobb)** (WHINING): Oh please, NASA. I promise I won't let you down. I coped just as well in the physical tests. I've got a higher pain threshold. I beat all the guys in the psychological ones. I'm so small you'll hardly even notice me, I swear. I won't take as much food or oxygen. I could even go up there in a smaller shuttle. And all of my reproductive organs are inside of me so I'm less likely to have radioactive children

*— the girls both laugh then recompose themselves —*

**Urla (NASA)**: That's all very nice but we won't be taking the female programme any further

**Erin (Jerrie Cobb)**: But why? We worked so hard. Some of us lost our jobs or our husbands

*— Urla/NASA waves her hands dismissively —*

**Urla (NASA):** There are many reasons

**Erin (Jerrie Cobb)** (SMIRKING): Give me one good reason

**Urla (NASA):** Er. I'm, er. I am not authorised to divulge that information to third parties who are not associated with any official NASA programme

**Erin (Jerrie Cobb)** (LAUGHS/MOCK ANGER): Well, why the hell not?

**Urla (NASA)** (DRAWLING): Let it drop now. You're like a dog with a bone. Do you have a husband? Think of how you're making your husband feel. If not think about your daddy. You know your daddy wouldn't want you up there

**Erin (Jerrie Cobb):** But gee. All the tests show I'd do just fine

**Urla (NASA):** The tests are not fully conclusive. You might well get up there and just faint or something. And what if you got to space and got yourself raped by an alien? Imagine if you were the courier for an extraterrestrial being back on our planet

*— Urla straightens up and wags a finger on her free hand pointedly — continues in her best pretend-self-righteous voice —*

We will not continue the female programme because of the risks it would bring to the American public. My word is final

*— at this Erin/Jerrie Cobb screams in frustration and throws her walkie-talkie into the duvet — Urla jumps and her rocket hat falls off — both the girls are laughing —*

**CUT**

# NOT THE WHITE BULL JUPITER SWIMMING

INT. CABIN — MORNING — *Erin is sat on the bed with laptop — Urla has camcorder — zoom in — Erin's face — zoom out — sudden noise from outside —*

**Larus** (SHOUTING): GIRLS — GIRLS COME — SHI—

*— Larus bursts into cabin, knocks into Urla with camera — Urla turns — camera focuses on Larus — excitement —*

**Larus** (WHISPERING): Girls. Come quickly. Outside

**Erin:** What? What is it?

**Larus:** You'll see. Come quickly. Quietly.

*— girls follow Larus into corridor — Urla is in front with camera — Erin out of shot — out onto deck — Larus looks over deck — girls gather round — water slaps against side of boat — Greenland is faint on horizon — iceberg — no whales/dolphins —*

**Erin:** What are we supposed to be looking at?

**Larus:** Shush. You'll see

*— the group stands silently for fourteen seconds — four metres away from the boat the water breaks — gush of air from blowhole — ridged back of sperm whale breaks surface — Urla shrieks —*

**Erin** (YELLS): OHMYGOD—

**Larus** (SHOUTING): CHRIST. It's nearer than before

*— boat rocks —*

**Urla:** Is it safe?

**Larus:** Jesus. Sorry. It took me by surprise. Yes, we should be safe. Just no more screaming, girls

**Urla** (LAUGHING): You screamed loudest. I have it all here.

I can play it back to you

**Erin:** It's so big. I've never seen anything so big. Is it a sperm whale?

**Larus:** Yes, it's a sperm whale. We will be safe, they're not that curious. But it's very close

*— creature resurfaces further from boat — Erin jumps —*

**Erin:** Oh god, it got me again

*— nervous laughing — group stand and watch the whale resurface twice more before sinking into the calm water, its mass leaving its imprint in tiny bubbles —*

## CUT

## THE COMMUNISTS ARE IN THE FUNHOUSE

KULUSUK: looks pretend. It is a tiny island 'settlement' with only five hundred people in it, which is, apparently, quite large for Greenland. The houses look like they were erected from a flat-pack box, as if they could be neatly folded away and taken with the people if they migrated. They are painted block primary colours: little toy houses, stage props. They are set into the rocks at jaunty angles. The slopes sit vertical against the still water, as if the island is built on the tips of a mountain range that lies just below the surface. The water must not get stormy because some of the houses sit just metres from its edge.

Urla is glad to be back on shore. She was short and restless and pacing in her catlike way, flitting between being happier reading on her own in the bedroom cabin and coming into the wheelhouse to sit with us but not saying anything, as though to remind us of her presence before slinking off back to her book.

I can't sleep now, my womb feels like it is full of acid and lined with tar, and I can't flail around like I would in my own bed because I will wake Urla. One of the nearby houses has huskies and they have been howling all night at the moonless sky. My eye mask itches, my Mooncup is uncomfortable and I am scared of leaking on the sheets on our last night with Larus.

This is the kind of period that requires a big fat nappy towel but I am trying to be good to the environment. I am still so glad to have my periods back that I feel no resentment towards it. The pill had stopped them and I went without for the whole time I was on it. I went on it like a lot of teenage girls do, because my periods hurt a lot and would interrupt that steady forward march to the drumbeat of patriarchy, making me take time off work and school. As though being female is an ailment to be cured with medicine.

I have been staring at the first ever picture of Earth for about an hour now. The one taken from the Apollo mission where they flew around the moon to take pictures of craters, the mission before they actually landed. They went up there to take these pictures of the moon's craters but the astronauts decided to turn the camera around and film Earth rising from behind the moon.

At that moment, for the first time ever, images were appearing on the screens at NASA of Earth from outside Earth. They were watching themselves watching themselves almost in real time from 238,857 miles away. Right then, they reached a new level of self-consciousness that will probably never be recreated outside that room and moment ever again. A Copernican Revolution.

In the 1960s, the space race expanded the human psyche to incorporate a concept of deep space and deep time. The Earthrise photo made people stop and think about Earth more holistically. Maybe that is why people of the sixties cared more about each other and the future.

It is the most reproduced image on Earth, and has become more and more abstract until it has been reduced to an icon for human achievement in the twenty-first century, its significance totally inverted. I am starting to feel a bit strange about it. Because I have been exposed to it so many times that it has numbed me to what I am actually looking at, I am staring at it to try and really see it. It stays on my retina when I blink hard, so when I open my eyes it bleeds into the image on the screen and I can kind of imagine it rising.

They gave a name to the feeling astronauts get when they look back at Earth; they call it the 'Overview Effect.' When they are going round in orbit and they are trying to put it into words and it is all cauliflower clouds and dancing green ribbons of aurora and lightning like flicking modem lights and any way they put it sounds so stupid, they get frustrated with their words because it is the most earthly thing on Earth but at the same time it is outside our earthly logic.

It is the same in parts of science that deal with a reality that evades our logic. The scientists have to simplify things using a language we can all understand. Three guesses whose language they use!

But they have to use one language to talk to other scientists, and to distill their complicated theories until they make sense to us laypeople. But in so doing they make them into something nothing like what they wanted to say in the first place and we believe in this end product because it came from the mouths of scientists. They talk about *quantum soup* and *quark flavour mixing* and you wonder if it looks more like a minestrone or something smooth like pea soup. And they call their instruments things like THE SUPERCONDUCTING SUPER-COLLIDER, so you wonder if they left the naming jobs down to earnest five-year-olds.

My favourite example of this is physics king and wife-manipulator Albert Einstein's name for non-local faster-than-light interaction of atoms that are separated in space. The particles were created in the same instant in space but then got widely separated, but they can still be said to be the same particle, and if you measure one it immediately affects the other. I do not understand it fully but I just like what he called it. He called it *spooky action at a distance.*

And astronauts say things that seem so obvious and dumb, like, 'You realise that the whole world is interconnected,' and you snort at how obvious and dumb these clever astronauts sound, but then you think about it and actually maybe they are on to something. They say things like, 'You realise that we are all already in space, on a giant spaceship, spaceship Earth,' and you think they are just saying that in a condescending sort of subterfuge to everyone who is not *really* on a spaceship, until you realise that you had been thinking of yourself as on this anchored point from which they send rockets to space, when you have been out there the whole time. There is nothing underneath you and nothing above or either side for a very, very long way. The moon rolls around a groove in the space—time fabric created by the gravity of Earth.

There should be a flight about every five years that takes all of the current world leaders into orbit so that they can look down at Earth. If the UN wants world peace why have they not thought of that one?

## MUSH QUIMMIG MUSH MUSH

Urla has taught me how to say: Hello, my name is Erin, thank you, yes, no, and the food was very nice. There is a Kalaallit Inuit family from the settlement that were travelling today to pick up supplies from Kangerlussuaq (gan-ker-schloo-schooak) on the west coast, where there is a DIY shop that has something specific that they need, and a family member that needs ferrying, and various other menial things which all seem insane to have to travel FIVE HUNDRED MILES for.

They intend to return with a heavy load, so the family are sending the dad and son out with two almost empty dog sleds. The dogs can run between forty and sixty miles in a day, so the thing should take us thirteen or fourteen days. It is too mountainous to get into Nuuk from the east side, but the ferry that goes from Kangerlussuaq to Nuuk only goes once a week. If all goes well, I should get into Kangerlussuaq the day before the ferry.

The dad is called Amos and he loves his dogs. When Amos put me on the sled with his son Umik he made things awkward from the offset by explaining that he might be a bit shy with me because he did not get to meet many girls in the village. Umik is about fifteen, does not say or smile much, wears a beanie with Miley Cyrus on it and a pair of neon orange-framed sunglasses which he never takes off.

Urla switched her mood as soon as we started moving again. She seems erratic, as though a cloud passes its shadow over her but lifts and then sunshine again. I was a little worried that maybe she had become bored with me; she seemed frustrated by the conversations that me and Larus had. It was the only way to keep time moving through the days at sea, but she would groan 'boooringggg,' Larus would throw a small object at her, and then she would leave the room.

When we left, Urla hugged her uncle aggressively. I was sad to leave him, but it feels like he has a place in my future as some kind of surrogate uncle or something. He gave me a pile of books and a badge that says *Save The Bees* which I put on my rucksack, and a knife for gutting fish. He also gave me his Skype and his mobile number, saying that I had to keep in touch weekly, and that he would worry about me once I had left his niece behind. This paternalism irritated me a little.

Urla is riding with Amos and I am with Umik and Genen,

the lame dog who refuses to be left back at the house without the pack. He is sweet but a bit much. He has taken a shine to me and is keeping my legs warm but cutting off their circulation intermittently. He also smells, all of them smell, from being fed almost entirely on preserved seafood.

I have tried talking a bit with Umik using the Greenlandic phrase book but I am appalling at pronouncing the words. I think he resorted to putting his iPod on to stop me trying. I thought it would be nice of us to try Greenlandic in case they are sore about still being a colony. I got the phrase book from the harbour office in exchange for my Icelandic one and eight Danish krone. It is a thin thing and useless for actual conversation. I can only pick from utilitarian phrases that are laid out in this odd way that falls into accidental narratives at points:

Please
Thank you
How much does it cost?
This gentleman/lady will pay for everything
Would you like to dance?
I love you
Best wishes
Leave me alone!
Help!
Call the police!

I enjoy the narratives of phrase books. They always seem to follow a haphazard protagonist who is forever getting lost and bothering the emergency services. Oh, our hero is at a bakery. Now they are at a flower market. Oh, now they need an ambulance, holiday over! The phrases are like the names scientists come up with for things, almost useless but better than nothing, I suppose.

I am starting to really need a wee. I have asked Urla how to broach the subject and tried to convince her to tell Amos she needs to go so that we both can because I do not want to. I am just going to hold on until we stop, whenever that is, nightfall, which won't actually fall but just become a state that we suddenly find ourselves in at some point in the unforeseeable future. By midnight the sun will just about disappear for a few hours.

## THE GREAT WHITE SILENCE

The command to make the dogs stop is extremely satisfying. They say 'aaahhh' really loud just like that, like letting out a massive sigh. The dogs lose momentum and the sleds come to a prompt but smooth halt, proportionate to the length of the sigh/command. Aaaaaaahhhhhhh. We did not head off until the afternoon today so we have had a full seven-hour stint without breaks. It was about eight in the evening when we stopped, very hungry and sore. I was almost definitely sure my period had leaked in my salopettes but no one could tell through the thickness so it was fine. Bit of a panic as to what to do but we have now figured out the toilet situation. One of us holds up a piece of tarpaulin while the other goes, but we have not yet found an explanation for Umik and Amos for the hysterics that Urla goes into as I try to take care of my Mooncup discreetly.

It makes me think about the Inuit relationship to the land, how consciously gentle they are to it, how aware they are that every single human being leaves an imprint, a mark on the land behind itself. Out on the ice with no plumbing and no soil this becomes stark. Every time you have to expel your waste a mark is left in the sparkling white snow and that impact is made so very concrete. Starting from our beginning anyone could track us right to where we end no matter how hard we try to leave everything in this place as we found it, could follow our paw marks and scratches and dug-up snow and buried bones.

The two tents Amos has look so tiny and bright against the vast white of the ice; accidental, futile, defiant, out-of-depth. Like a single plant clinging to the side of a cliff. We are sharing a one-man between the two of us, which at least guarantees maximum body heat exchange. Without the swooshing sound the moving sleds make, and with the dogs all asleep and huffing, this place is eerie-silent. Apart from when the wind makes the tents crackle, their taut skins whipping frantically. The quiet is ominous; we all feel it, the act of writing this itself feels like pathetic fallacy. But there is nothing but us for miles around, the nearest town is the one we headed off from. Urla says polar bears never come this far south, so not to worry too much about attracting them with my blood. It had not occurred to me to worry until she said.

Urla got a really great interview with Amos today. She did all the speaking, of course, with me filming. We watched it back and Urla translated it for me. He talks about being out on the ice, especially alone (he does most of his trips without Umik but he brings Genen).

I took it so that he was sat cross-legged on the ice with Genen, with nothing else in shot. It was almost perfect, like it encapsulated this ethereal feeling we have both tried and failed to describe: something just less than emptiness, a white collage.

What Thoreau said: in wildness is the preservation of the world. He is often misquoted as having said wilderness, but he meant pure wild-ness. Not wilderness in the sense you usually conceive it, a space set aside to be chaotic or fierce or biodiverse. He meant it in the sense of 'wild' as in 'self-will' in the past participle. Like looking out over the ocean, or into space, a blank and human-void place, and feeling tiny; this is what Thoreau meant. The very opposite of culture or civilisation.

It is an overwhelming feeling because it reminds you of how you are not like it; vast, indifferent, unfathomable. The ice will erase you. When you and everything living here leave, the ice will swallow up all of your traces. No symbols at all. You. Not you.

The ice sheet refuses human cartography utterly. It is an empty and markless expanse with nothing to anchor the lines of a map to. Well, probably there are glaciologists who can map it in some way, density of ice maybe, accumulation of atmospheric particles perhaps, but this can only be seen with a very specific kind of vision. An esoteric landscape does not help a person to find their way if they are lost; you could walk from the centre of here and never find your way again.

It makes me feel light-headed, this nullification, if I stand and look out into the expanse. But it is not like a paralysing onset of agoraphobia; instead it is the jolt of a sudden release, the severing of an anchor. It is so not at all like home, where cartography is inescapable, knitted into the soil, and there is no chance to get lost, not really. *This is a place for walking, this is not: Welcome to the County of Worcestershire, Private Property, Do Not Walk On The Grass.*

I asked Amos if he thinks we are on course to get there in time for the ferry. He just said, 'Immaqa,' which kind of means maybe and is the catchphrase of Greenland. Bodes well. Most methods of transport here only happen on a weekly basis.

## ON BEING OF GREAT ADVANTAGE TO MY SEX

Sledding across all this snow it kind of feels like we are doing an antithetical version of messianic explorer Robert Falcon Scott's Antarctica expedition. I watched the Herbert Ponting documentary for inspiration before we left England. At the beginning there is a slide with a quote from King George V along to some jolly colonial-era trumpeting. King George said, I WISH THAT EVERY BRITISH BOY COULD SEE THIS FILM FOR IT WOULD HELP TO FOSTER THE SPIRIT

OF ADVENTURE ON WHICH THE EMPIRE WAS
FOUNDED.

I wanted some of that spirit, even being of the 50 percent already excluded by KG. Positioning myself as male again; my masculine counterpart who lives in my brain, appending a fraud penis so I can traverse Scott's Antarctica in my imagination.

We hunt and shoot some seals, but we have to feed the dogs that way so it is not too bad of us. And then they start to anthropomorphise the seals, which is kind of sweet, oh, nice guys, right? But we get all fond of this one seal and her pup, who is too fat and small to clamber out onto the ice when some killer whales chase it because they are hungry. Then we harpoon the killer whales to rescue the baby. Then we sit down to a bowl of seal stew.

Scott and his men died to put a flag at the South Pole. This is where the fine line between exploration and imperialism was crossed. The expedition was not an exercise in curiosity and adventure but a race of nationalistic pride. Men just love to stick their flags in places. North Pole, South Pole, on the seabed underneath the North Pole, on the tops of mountains, on the moon. Like territorial animals pissing on things.

Annie Smith Peck was a mountaineer who beat Indiana Jones to the summit of Mount Coropuna and stuck a 'votes for women' flag on the top of it. She was one of a handful of female explorers to be recognised for her success. Okay, ladies, Annie Smith Peck can have that one, although she is a 'superwoman' so don't you mere mortal women go getting any ideas.

People go mad for that stuff still now, this boyish British Peter Pan nostalgia for exploration and empire. Scouting and wilderness techniques and Bear Grylls, the zealous Christian outdoorsman on the Discovery Channel. When it came out *Scouting for Boys* was only beaten as a bestseller by the Bible. It actually came out after the imperial age of Scott and Shackleton when British masculinity was feeling threatened by the waning strength of empire and the rise of the women's rights movement. The emasculation of men. Which is maybe what the current resurgence of Mountain Man documentaries on television is all about. And they made Bear Grylls the new Chief Scout.

I want my documentary to be the opposite of colonial exploitation. I want it to explore, quietly, without imprinting. To be porous to all things without contaminating. I want it to be conscious of its tracks in the snow (I did get footage of this to use to that purpose).


## THE RESURRECTION OF RACHEL CARSON

Today I ride with Genen again. I go to the furthest places at times like this, when I am stationary in transit and alone with just my own head. I fell asleep and had a dream about Rachel Carson. I was in the 'woods' that are near my house, which really is just a square of lank trees they did not cut down when they built the estate. It is also laced with radon. It is kind of a recreational area for the housing estate, where everyone walks their dogs. It stinks of dog shit. Mum told me not to play in there when I was young in case it somehow got in my eyes and I got blinded by the shit.

I was in the woods, standing in the woods and being very still because I could hear buzzing and I was trying to figure out which way not to walk. Then next to me what I had taken for a very ordinary mound of undergrowth started to move. It began to rise in the horizontal shape of a human body. The human shape pulled up all the turf around it as it began to sit up, plucking the plant roots out of the soil like snapping violin strings. They made a noise like that, pluck pluck pluck. When the human shape had sat up it started to brush itself down, its clothes caked in mud and its skin smeared with dirt and dog shit. I recognised

Rachel Carson even though I don't know what she looks like and her face was just a smudge with lichen for eyes.

'Pigeons are suddenly dropping out of the sky dead.'

I was not sure if she was addressing me. It was hard to tell what way her lichen eyes were facing, but her head was turned away from me anyway. Then I woke up from pins and needles because Genen was sat with his femur digging into my shin.


## FIRST FOOTPRINTS IN THE FRESH SNOW

Every day here is just a slight variation on the first, differentiated by switching sledges, sluggish topics of conversation, and a sky that will sometimes bleed dramatically pink to orange like the belly of a rainbow trout. Sometimes there are strong winds. The constants are the smell of the dogs, wincing at the whip-crack, tensing for the snowdrifts, pins and needles, and the white nothing. I am trying to stay proactive and read but I am kind of too bored to concentrate.

A THOUGHT: This nothingness is going to be a very prominent part of the trip. Lots and lots of sitting around, waiting on things, being in transit, but out on the ice like on the ocean this is intensified, your own small contours marked out against the vastness of ether, so that you look at your hands out in front of you and follow the line of your fingers up and down and think, *I end here, all of me fills up this container that is my body.*

Like proprioception. I keep on thinking that this is the closest I will ever come to moonwalking. There are parallels: the same bulky outerwear, the same being-in-emptiness. Yes, it is almost like moonwalking.

All day I was with Urla and we did not speak more than ten words. Today is day nine, entries are sparse because, mostly, I had nothing to say. It is hard to think with no stimulation. Doing nothing is exhausting. We have slipped into this kind of mental hibernation, except Umik and Amos, who have their tasks to occupy them. Mostly I have been sleeping lots and dreaming vividly. And the ice has saturated my dreams. After a while nothingness becomes potent and textured because of the sense of what is absent. Things are evoked more than if they were actually there: colours, heights, depths. Slight changes in the monochrome landscape come out in relief. When the ice-mountains precipitate onto the horizon they appear as a whisper and disappear as quietly. The horizon is the only spatial marker and it is always on the horizon. We are perpetually at the centre of nothing.

It feels like trespassing to be alive in a place that is not dead but is inexistence, negation of potentiality. Anything alive is only ever passing through. I cannot put a word on it and when I try I can only think 'primordial,' but that word entails potential because a beginning initiates a narrative. The one I want is the very opposite of origin.

Words are getting harder and I am starting to think like the ice; without contrast there is no definition. The ice is self-referential and there is no way into the tautology. I cannot get my bearings if there is nothing to grasp.

## THESE ARE SHINING PARTS

I was sorry to leave Umik behind to look after the dogs and sleds. We all hugged goodbye awkwardly, which made him visibly uncomfortable. It felt strange to be walking, and to be walking off the packed snow. I thought permafrost was a permanent frost that kept the ground crispy, but Amos explained it is underneath the ground, and keeps the water up so everything is actually wet and boggy. It was a difficult walk with all the sucking mud, and the weight of our rucksacks. It got a bit warm, even with the wind, so we had to take our coats off, but the wet brings all the insects out and some of them were biting through our thinner sleeves.

I had managed to walk all that way without looking up much from where my feet were going and what insects I was slapping into my skin so it did not even occur to me that the ice was gone until we started driving. Amos was so excited to be in a car, he drove the whole way with the window down and his arm resting on the door, which made it cold in the back but neither of us wanted to say anything. He was talking to his brother, who picked us up in his 4x4, all animated, which suited me because I like to zone out when people are talking a language I do not understand.

Then I started to look out of the window and it hit me how colourful everything was. Not really objectively, but in such contrast it nearly hurt my eyes. All this space just mossy and vaguely pink and it just went on and on and on. It hardly changed for the whole journey, flickering on in muted colours, and in front and behind the road was a thin wisp existing through it. The only shape to change was the twisting spine of the mountains.

Wilderness, vast open spaces untouched and just left be. Not a reserve portioned off as a space where you are supposed to go and be recreational. It made me think of Alaska, and how much left I have to see, and how out here it is easy to imagine yourself alone and happy in it.

As I watched the landscape thaw I thought I felt my spirit thawing a little with it. As if there was something deep inside me that was frozen and had maybe always been frozen and like an Alaskan wood frog frozen dormant for winter it was beginning to wake up to the world again with the spring.

A RECURRING FEELING: getting excited like forgetting something and then remembering you already did it, like I was waiting for a phone call from Mum asking me what the hell I thought I was doing, young lady, and to come home right now, but realising, nope, she was not going to.

Amos was really apologetic about leaving us at the hostel and seemed genuinely distressed that he did not have room to accommodate us, which was very sweet. We gave him money, which he took with some sort of feigned coaxing; he kept saying, 'Lovely girls, lovely girls.'

Kangerlussuaq was only built quite recently by America for the airport. The hostel seems like it is made from slotted-together foam board, partition walls. Like knocking into it would just make it collapse. All of the furniture looks like it was bought from Staples and the mattresses are made from foam.

There is a television with American cable and the Discovery Channel. I am taking notes from Bear Grylls for the documentary, both for handy tips and for a character profile of the kind of idea of 'man and wild' I keep going on about. As though modern feminism is more ubiquitous than ever before (or so it seems to me, as maybe it does to each new generation) and in backlash, with renewed fanaticism, a strain of hyper-masculinity has occurred. Compensating; which men have always liked to do!

## THE ULTIMATE GUIDE TO ENDURING
## THE MOST DRAMATIC HARDSHIPS
## YOU CAN IMAGINE

INT. — *Erin sits on the corner of a bed with a notebook and pen in hand, facing a television — outdoor survivalist show with presenter Bear Grylls — interior is sparse: desk, table, chair, window, rucksacks and possessions spilt on the floor — Erin turns to notice camera and snorts — zoom in on her face — then on television screen — Bear Grylls is hoisting himself up a waterfall —*

**Bear Grylls** (ON SCREEN) (YELLING): SURVIVAL can be summed up in three words (PAUSE) Never. Give. Up.

*— camera pans back to Erin —*

**Erin** (PUTTING ON AN IMPRESSIVE IMITATION):
I have penetrated every crevice of the planet and conquered the
WORST nature can haul at me. There is nowhere I haven't taken
on. I'm going to show you the skills I invented that you need to
be as man as I am. And survive anywhere on this unforgiving
planet

*— Urla is laughing behind camera — camera back to TV screen
— zooms in and out erratically on presenter struggling against
onslaught of water —*

**Erin:** If you're stranded in the wilderness you need a weapon.
Ideally a rifle. If you don't have a rifle nature will sometimes
throw you a rope in the form of a makeshift weapon. Behold.

For example

*— Erin flourishes her pen to the camera —*

**Erin:** This thousand-year-old arrowhead I found on the floor.
I will tie it to a stick with the cord from my parachute. If you
don't have an arrowhead or a parachute cord, use your initiative.
Initiative is man's best weapon

*— she winks — Urla laughs —*

**Erin:** I am on a journey of SURVIVAL. (THROWS BACK
HER HEAD AS SHE SHOUTS) Every step of this
journey is me. Man. Surviving. Not dying. Never succumbing to
the weakness that is death

## CUT TO —

INT. *— still in same interior but props have moved — belongings
piled in corner — Erin has T-shirt tied to her head turban style and
is brandishing a broom handle like a scythe —*

**Erin** (GESTICULATING BROOMSTICK ON EMPHASISED WORDS): The tropics are home to most of the plants and animals in the world, most of which are trying to KILL YOU. Not every creature in the jungle wants to kill you. Instead these ones want to EAT YOU ALIVE. Sometimes in the jungle it can feel like everything is out to get you. BECAUSE IT IS. Man must reassert his dominance in the jungle. I flick the tarantula off my leg

*— Erin mimes flicking her leg —*

**Erin:** Petty bug

*— pan to television — presenter is in a desert, talking with spear-clad barefoot gentleman who is holding up to him the corpse of something furry — pan back to Erin, who is looking at the screen —*

**Erin:** If you are stranded in the desert you can expect a visit. FROM DEATH. It would take years to learn all the skills of the San Bushmen but I have done it in a matter of hours. They eat every morsel of the desert hare and respect its soul. I will bite out its liver and leave the rest because its liver contains a vitamin that is vital for preventing something bad I mentioned earlier

*— onscreen presenter passes the carcass back to the San Bushman —*

**Erin:** Take the rest of the carcass. I have no use for it. No, you may NOT have one of my adventure-sports-sponsorship power-bars, San Bushman

*— camera shakes with laughter —*

**CUT TO —**

EXT. FROZEN LAKESIDE — *Erin in snow next to a body of frozen water — she is now brandishing a large stick —*

**Erin:** Here in the Arctic there are fish under the ice. I have a frozen deer leg so that's what I'm going to use to smash through the ice. If you don't have a frozen deer leg, use your initiative.

# HOW TO CONVEY
# INVISIBLE DEATH

## CONTAMINANTS THAT CAUSE ADVERSE CHANGE

I was back standing on the ice sheet in a blizzard. There were two figures in orange jackets with their hoods against the blizzard and goggles on, glaciologists. They were peering over one of those big drills they use to get ice core samples. As the core came up its gradation changed, from glowy green like a nuclear ore on top down to pure white. The glaciologists conferred.

'Witnesses described huge bonfires on which the bodies of the birds were burned,' said Rachel Carson from beside me.

I could hear clearly what the glaciologists were saying even though they were very far away.

'The core shows residue,' said the one.

'Hmm, yes, they also found it in the underground rivers,' said the other.

'When some of the Eskimos themselves were checked by analysis of fat samples, small residues of DDT were found (0 to 1.9 parts per million).' Rachel Carson always spoke with no lilt of emphasis in her voice. Not to me or anyone really. Maybe to herself.

'It's much worse than we thought.'

'Much worse.'

'The fat samples were taken from people who had left their native villages to enter the United States Public Health Service Hospital in Anchorage for surgery.'

I asked, 'Where have the bees gone, Ms Carson?' But my voice was lost to the wind.

'For their brief stay in civilisation the Eskimos were rewarded with a taint of poison,' she said instead.

'Quick, empty it and let's go.' The glaciologists emptied their lab pockets into the core hole. There was a pause as they leaned and peered into it, then a succession of plops like pebbles in still water. Then they replaced the core.

The noise took me back home to the cul-de-sac between the two lamp-posts that marked the boundary of where I was allowed to play when I was little, where Mum could still see me from the living room as she did the polishing and listened to Boyzone. There is a wall, the side of Marge and Graham's house, where Charlotte from next door was sat facing it, making the noise, crack crack crack, that the snails made when we would throw them against it if we were bored so their shells burst and their guts spilled out. We would have to kick them down the drain in time before Graham would come out to shout at us when he guessed what we were doing to his wall. Down into the underground sewage, plop plop plop.

When I was little I was fascinated by the sewage system. To get rid of anything all you had to do was flush it down a drain. In the yard there was a drain lid, and if you lifted it you could watch all the things coming through the drains in the house on the way off to wherever they were going. We used to put the dog poo in it then flush the downstairs toilet to send it away. If there was ever any evidence of something bad I had done I would lift up the drain lid, put it inside, run in to flush, then run back, in time to see it being washed into oblivion.

One day I sat on the toilet and I jumped up because something had tickled my leg. A snail was sliming its way out of the sparkly white basin. It had come from this elsewhere place and made its way through the plumbing inside our house to the top-floor toilet. This changed something fundamental about how I saw the drains from then on, my own miniature Copernican Revolution. Suddenly the philosophical implications of flushing into the black-hole-void needed to be scrutinised because drains were now not the portal to the place-of-no-return I had thought them, a bit like how Jerry R. Ehman who got the Wow! Signal must have felt, like, *'I am not alone something has come out of the void to me wow!'*

Maybe in the dream of the glaciologists on the ice sheet I am realising the similar always-there-but-not-appreciated thing that haunted Rachel Carson. That sometimes there are things that need to be spotlit against a stark white backdrop for you to perceive them because when ever present you do not interrogate them.

The Eskimos did not invent the invisible death. We did. The ice sheet is not-so-pure wilderness. You and I can't see it but the glaciologists can. They can read the core samples like testimonies to our guilt as geomorphic agents, as ushers of the Anthropocene. And of all the corruptions we will leave behind us there is one that will outlive them all. We are the first civilisation on this planet to have made an invisible death that will outlive all relics of all civilisations ever. We made nuclear waste.

With this comes a responsibility, but how to convey invisible death to the future is a problem unique to our age. Larus told me that some of the guys from the Order of the Dolphin and the Golden Records also worked as part of the Human Interference Task Force. The Task Force was set up to solve the Forever Problem, the problem of relaying warnings at nuclear waste sites to possible future civilisations, possibly as far away as the half-life of plutonium 239, some 24,000 years into the future.

They could not use a single language because language is always dying, so they tried to come up with universal symbols: a monolith with warnings in multiple languages, cats that glowed when they got close to nuclear waste sites, invented fables for the future, majorly complex booby traps, and an Atomic Priesthood cult who would pass down the dark secrets to each new generation within their elite.

The waste will survive us. It is our most enduring time capsule, our ugly baby. What does it say about us? What did we do when we discovered its power? Of course we went and made a superweapon.

Since the Cold War the world has existed in equilibrium and this equilibrium is still enough for us to have almost forgotten that it is holding us up. The Nash Equilibrium is the concept that once all sides are armed with nuclear weapons, none has the incentive to disarm or to use their weapons, based on the premise of MUTUAL ASSURED DESTRUCTION, the idea being we are at a point where if one country attacked another, we would all be fucked, so it benefits nobody to do so. But to keep the equilibrium each side's defences must be taken into account. If one side has more fallout shelters than another, and more of the population could theoretically be spared, then they are unfairly favoured, and the balance is tipped. Because of this there could not be nationwide plans for fallout shelters built by the government during the Cold War. Covert shelters were built, under town halls, in people's yards. There are secret underground time capsules all over the Western world. What would a future archaeologist make of them?

For the Nash Equilibrium to work each country has to look as though it would blow the shit out of its enemy in retaliation for an attack on the homeland. America has adopted the policy that any attack on America would be responded to with all-out retaliation under any circumstance. Russia takes this one step further with their 'Dead Hand,' which automatically releases all their warheads as soon as an attack is detected by seismic sensors.

I was on Skype talking to Larus about this and told him that Britain has a peculiar response. We have the Letters of Last Resort, to be opened and read at the end of a chain of events. The British government has been destroyed and the prime minister and the 'second person' to the prime minister have been killed. Our submarines float deep in the Atlantic and almost no one on board knows where they are at any given time. The submarines presume the homeland to have been destroyed if a) there have been no naval broadcasts in four hours or b) BBC Radio 4 has stopped broadcasting. In this event the four submarine commanders open the safe inside the safe and read the four handwritten letters from the now-dead prime minister, written the very day that she/he assumed office. Then they have to follow the instructions, which will be one of three things:

1. blow the shit out of the buggers
2. spare the blighters
3. your call, commander

The letters are destroyed when each prime minister leaves office, so history will never know what was written by them. Larus said that is the most British thing he has ever heard.

I think given our colonial record the submarines probably have on board their own carefully designed time capsules, for the preservation of the nation, something that says WE ARE NUMINOUS AND NOT ERASABLE. Our submarines are called *Vanguard*, *Victorious*, *Vigilant* and *Vengeance*. (And who came up with those names?) So, floating portentously in the Atlantic right now, the decision has already been made.

A paradox: what is the point of retaliation if you are dead and gone already and have no way of knowing any better? What is the point of causing immense suffering to the innocent civilians of the enemy?

The point is, apparently, *you can't exist when we do not*. It is *we will be remembered*. It is WRATH OF THE EMPIRE.

I asked Urla if she knew about the Letters of Last Resort and she said no so I told her. She just looked a little confused.

'Didn't Uncle Larus ask to talk to me?'

I paused to think about it, and said no, he didn't mention

it, although he went in a rush, which when I thought about it then did seem a little unusual. She looked at me strangely and changed the subject.

## WOMEN INTERESTED IN TOPPLING
## CONSUMER HOLIDAYS

I stood at the bow of the ferry, watching the water and eating very continental-tasting biscuits. It became surreal if you watched it long enough with your chin on the handrail. Like a glassy Rorschach Test, all the icebergs twinned in the water, which was a sky itself, obscured only when a floe passed, or when ice fell from one of the cliff sides and shattered the mirror. There was a cracking sound when this happened, like the noise an ice cube makes when it cracks in a tepid drink.

NUUK: a surreal city. Like Kulusuk but bigger and denser. Buildings are still toy houses but multi-storey and apartment style, set at angles to each other so that they sit in the rock like a doggedly arranged model village, a Playmobil city. Slate grey is the base of everything, it is the colour of the cliffs and the colour of the boulders and the pebbles. Everything in blocks of colour, as if cut and stuck from sugar paper. For the first hour or so in I could not put my finger on what was missing. There are nearly no trees or plants apart from the wiry grass.

There is a new mall, apparently a point of contention for people, usually dividing the old and the young. Some of the older people see it as Nuuk becoming too 'European.' Greenland is a country in the midst of change, not least because global warming is melting the ice sheet. Complete melt would mean that resources that were hidden by the ice before are revealed to be reaped. If they could be more self-reliant then they would be able to manage independently from Denmark, which would make them the only Inuit country in the world. But looking further ahead in time there is a chance that the amount of water it would create could turn Greenland into an archipelago. Their Inuit culture would have to change beyond recognition. Could they then be called Inuit?

Of Urla's family friends: the daughter, Naaja, is about Umik's age, she speaks quite good Danish, is a bit shy with me but she looks at Urla with adoration whenever she talks. The dad, Klas, is Danish and the mum, Kalistiina, is Inuit. The inside of their house is interesting because it is like a museum for their hybrid cultures. Lots of fish- and whale-based ornaments, and a cupboard full of weird votive figures that Naaja tells us are made by the family when they have bad feelings, to dispel the feelings. They are eerie, but apparently customary. Some of them are made out of bones and teeth, and what looks like Kinder Egg toy parts. I also keep noticing extravagant fake flower vases in the windows of houses we pass, I suppose because the flora in Greenland is so limited and this makes them a novelty.

## MANKIND'S MOST NOBLE GOAL: THE SEARCH FOR TRUTH AND UNDERSTANDING

From Nuuk, Klas drove me, Urla and Naaja twenty miles into the tundra with a tent, some of Kalistiina's seal-fur blankets, a gas stove, our bags, canned food and lots of bottled water, and will return to pick us up in four days' time. Some Danish hikers found Naaja on the tundra already. She went off from camp on a walk on her own just because she likes to do that. She took her phone in case she twisted her ankle or anything. She came on in the afternoon and said she was with two men. She asked Urla to talk to them and tell them she was camping out with older friends and that she was okay because the men would not take her word for it.

They walked Naaja back to the tent even though it took them an hour or so. They must have been bored with their afternoon of dramatic hardship, so bored that they were ready to transcend it already and instruct us on how to be in communion with it successfully (as many Mountain Men are prone to). When we came out to meet them, they conferred conspicuously out of the sides of their mouths, and told us we were too young to be camping out alone. They said it was very dangerous to be out because a polar bear had been spotted in the area and that the ranger had told them this on their way out. As though by avoiding this abstract and likely non-existent danger they had already conquered wilderness and were in a position of authority on the subject by now.

Naaja would not believe them, and asked them what they were doing out without guns or flares if they knew there was a bear. Naaja has spent her whole young life knowing this place, but these men on a walking holiday of course boasted superior knowledge just by virtue of being older and being men.

They asked us to pack up and walk back with them and we declined as politely as we could. They were pissed off and said they would tell the ranger we were out, and that the ranger would be angry that we wasted his time in worrying over us. We promised them we had the number for the ranger saved in our phones and we would call him if we needed rescue. I got this all on camera without them seeing. They walked away, disappointed that their damsels had repudiated them.

Naaja assured us when they had gone that polar bears rarely ever come this far south, and besides we were too far inland. The hikers were either too stupid to realise their lie was almost impossible, or else they did not know what they were talking about and would believe anything they heard from any wise Greenlandic tundra man with a sense of humour that they might have met.

TWILIGHT THIS MORNING: I went to sit outside for a bit because I was feeling restless. It was probably about two but I am finding it difficult to sleep. The light through the tent is like a red lamp and gives me headaches, makes everything inside strange colours. The tundra was waking up with all the subtly hopeful colours of a new day: rust and pink from the tiny coarse flowers that blanketed the soil but still shadowless, the sun still just below the horizon and no stamp of cloud shadow, no elongation to the small and lonely trees. It all just stood, luminous and itemised like a child's non-dimensional painting. I walked away a little to sit on a rise so that the tent was below and chalky red in the half-light. My home that will shape-shift into each new space I stop to sleep. A compact and portable idea of home. It was so pretty that I cried a little bit.

## THE PILL REFUGEE FORUM

Urla got an interview with Naaja where she told us that lots of her friends (Naaja included) had had abortions. It was in Danish, of course, so Urla had to explain. She asked and Naaja did not mind at all, did not seem fazed by it as long as I promised to cut it out of the film. Of course I promised to, but I struggled a bit with coming to terms with it. I managed to convince myself that it would be dishonest of me as a documentary maker to cut it out, mostly because it would have been such an interesting and relevant sequence.

I asked if they did not have the pill in Greenland. She said no one ever talked about the pill or sex or anything, so no one really thought to use it. Her sex education at school was to have a doll that had a chip inside and could tell at the end of the week if it would have stayed alive, had it been a real baby. She said that mostly it just made her classmates think it would be fun to have a baby. They were thirteen when they did the exercise.

From what she said they seem stuck between two cultures. The Inuit leaners go back to the villages and have babies, but there are fewer and fewer of them, and the modernisers abort their babies and stay in the towns. But still living with traditional myths of transmigrating souls means the soul of the dead fetus can go on into a tree or a rock or an animal or another baby. So what is there to moralise about?

Naaja's grandmother, her mother's mother, teaches her Inuit myth. I wanted to know about the transmigration. It is a concept that underpins the myths of Inuits through Siberia, Alaska, Canada and Greenland. It holds that not only animals and plants but also inanimate objects and landscapes can have souls. Anything can be viewed as 'spiritually charged.' The souls transmigrate between vessels. When such radically different vessels can be chosen by any soul, and a male vessel can take on a female soul and vice versa, is there as much of a concept of gender? Are they a queer culture?

They do not see humans as different from the animals; there are not separate taxonomical categories of being. A person can become a man or a woman, a tree or a stone. All life is a continuum and a horizontal one. For Inuit all soul vessels are equally important no matter if they talk or not: dolphins, rocks, women. In fact they are all talking, they have something to say, just maybe not in words.

Naaja's dad is a Christian. She told us he came to her mother's town with the town planning service, to talk to the council about telling the village people the benefits of moving to the city. The government wanted the villagers to move out because it was costing them too much money to send supplies, it being the only village for miles around. They knew if they could get the young to leave the old would eventually die out and the village would not need to exist.

We told Naaja how the pill is handed out like sweets in Britain. I told her it is great that not many of my friends got pregnant but it is not so great that it makes lots of girls numb. That it makes some of us so numb sometimes it is countered with anti-depressants. That it can stop you menstruating, the feeling of which is like an ever-absent *something* that I could only compare to displacement, to homesickness, as though homesick for a body. But it does not make you as sad as having a baby would. For this we must be grateful. The pill is progress.

Naaja's mother followed her dad to Nuuk because she loved him. They married two years later. Naaja's mother's parents did not come to the wedding. They stayed in the village until they had to be evicted. They will not talk to Naaja's dad, but she goes with her mother to visit them in their new, bigger village on the coast. When her dad hears her mother talking to her about myth, he tells her to stop telling fairy stories. Mostly they talk with her grandmother. Her dad wants Greenland to melt so that the resources can be got at and it can be rich like Denmark.

*What do you want, Naaja?*

*I want what you want, of course. I want to see the world and make a life for myself. I want to leave Greenland and its small way of life.*

*But somebody has to stay and be Inuit!*

*Why should we stay when others do not? Where does it come from, this obligation? Where is yours?*

*We aren't so different. You could come with me.*

*But we are very different. You are so free.*


## DO PELICANS LOVE TO SOAR?

The others are sleeping. Outside, the tundra is putting itself together for us. Yesterday we spent the day walking and filming, trying to find something for the documentary. We walked inland through the mountains against the meltwater of the glacier as it found its way to the sea. It was urgent, dense and grey;

panicked like a jar of paintbrush water knocked onto a meticulous landscape.

I'm looking for something but I am not sure what. An idea, perhaps, that I had of the place before I was here. Of the trip before I was on it. I am actually here now, I have arrived. But where am I really? It is hard enough to actually be there, let alone convey it with a hand-held camera.

In the morning we startled a herd of reindeer. Must have smelled us and bolted. They ran fast, even the tiny babies and the heavily pregnant ones. A unified movement like a cloud of starlings, all the more magical for its silence. All of our mouths made O's and we let out a kind of wistful sigh, simultaneously. And after we laughed disbelievingly about where we were and what had just happened and how awake we were.

We hadn't seen them until they started to run. In the evening we saw them again but this time before they noticed us. Must have been downwind. We had climbed to the top of a low peak to see what was on the other side and found the reindeer in a valley with a small lake down its length. We crawled on our bellies to a vantage point where they could not see us. The mosquitoes found us quickly and lying still very soon became difficult. There were more of them because of the lake. I watched the small animals through the pixellated window of the camera, which shook whenever I tried to swat away the flies with my other hand. The reindeer were tormented by them as well, shaking their heads every few seconds to keep them out of their ears.

Reindeer lope, as if they are always tiptoeing. These movements, so secretive, made me feel dishonest, like a voyeur. The footage was achromatic, as though there only to record the novelty of the experience itself. But it is more than that.

I am finding it difficult to separate things that say something from things that do not. It is also hard to find things that say what I want them to. I went over what I have so far and I can't decide if I am saying what I set out to say, or if I am saying

anything at all, or if I just have lots of records of my own sentiments. Unsure if the things themselves are saying things or if I
am projecting this on to them, in the way that there are feelings
evoked when you look at a postcard image you are very fond
of; these might not translate when you show the postcard to
someone else.

I guess I am taking what I see and making it iconographic but
I am finding it difficult to translate the feeling of being present in the moment, which is itself the thing left untranslated in
the nature documentaries and encyclopaedias of exotic species
which have been my only prior experience of nature on this
scale. Or maybe not left untranslated, but translated back and
forth until really it has disintegrated, like the Earthrise photo.

I do not want to imbue this film with empty codes that seem
talismanic to me. But then maybe it does not matter, maybe it is
a vessel for me and I am just now waking up to see the sea. And
we have to try to translate or else no one would ever understand
anyone. We have to make icons of faraway unexperienceable
animals or else people like me would not know to care about
them.

I watched the reindeer film over and over. One reindeer I had
not noticed before is muzzling a rock around the floor. You can
only just make it out, but it goes about muzzling this rock on
its own for the entirety of me filming it. After a while watching
I felt something new about it that I had not felt before. Maybe
even empty moments are never really empty. I am beginning to
wonder if this is part of the documentary making itself.

## *DOG VOICE* NOW YOU MUST LEARN
## HOW TO SAY GOODBYE

We etched our names onto the smooth patch of a rock, where
it was bald of moss, next to where we pitched. It felt very

chapter-defining, one of those things you always remember, like it could be a figurative scratch that etches out some more of what will one day make up my fully formed soul.

We asked Klas soon after we started to drive out of the tundra, and there was no polar bear. There have not been any sightings for months. I feel very strange about going on without Urla and Naaja. It would be nice to go traipsing round the world in a girl-caravan. But as integral as they seem now (and especially Urla) we need to go our separate ways, just like we did with Larus.

Really, though, it is amazing to me that just by chance of circumstance and necessity two or three quite different people can begin to exist in a kind of *symbiosis*, what in ecology is termed a mutually beneficial relationship between two dissimilar organisms living in close physical proximity, and somewhat defies Darwinian ideas of evolution as purely competitive. Like a cleaner wrasse that eats only the ectoparasites from the lips of the sweetlips, a larger fish. The wrasse gets fed and the sweetlips rids its itchy lips of parasites. One must feel a kind of relief at least when encountering the other in the wide expanse of the ocean. And maybe in their own way you could say, taking this a little further, that these fish are also *friends*.

Sometimes, in the literature, it is acknowledged that symbiotic associations between species can be so integral to their individual biology and identity that actually their individual biology and identity have little meaning outside of the relationship anyway.

I think that being real friends with someone is a kind of integration like this. In the way that you let that person know every detail of you in order to get close, even the horrible little things that mostly only you know and that make you an individual by virtue of their small uniqueness. You share all of these with only this person of certain closeness so that the contours of both of you are chipped away, you are porous and receptive and there is almost nothing left to define where you end and where they begin. Intertwined like trees grown together and fused. Inosculation, that is what this is called. Trees that grow together and then apart.

It might seem portentous to say this of someone I have only known a short time but that seems to be what happens when your situations are so transitory. They are on fast-forward because really you might never see this person again. So you are simply the most visceral version of yourself.

I am going to really miss Urla. I did a lot of crying when we said goodbye. I think she was alarmed and misinterpreted a little; she said, 'Hey, don't be scared, you've got this.' I laughed and said I know I've got this, I am just going to really miss you. I smiled resolutely and thought to myself that this is the thing I can't get caught up in, this is the noose of homesickness. I am doing this journey alone by and for myself and this tug is the over-socialisation expected of women which traps us, and is precisely what I am striking against.

Naaja says she looks around herself in the village at her friends and their lives and she feels so different to them. I understand that because sometimes I would do the same, would look around me at the vacant expression of the cashier in Tesco, the foundation faces of the girls with arms heavy with bags at the shopping centre, the tired faces in the ill-yellow lighting at the bowling-cinema complex, tired from a week's work and a weekend not to be wasted. I did not recognise myself in these places and tried very hard not to.

But I know my own mum would love for me to go back to my home town and get married and never leave, and sometimes I feel very sorry that I do not want to do this. A lot of girls from my school had their babies and never left and seem genuinely happy for it. If all the girls were to up and leave like the boys can then how would any culture preserve itself?

But is it not just the inescapable itch of youth, its bore-dom, its listlessness, that makes you want to up and leave? The youth are always and always have been churning. Fields must be ploughed so that planted seeds will germinate: a period of customary churning prior to the germination of adulthood. Why do the girls suppress it?

I had a worry before I left, that I would get out here and just pine for home. When I was little my favourite film was *Homeward Bound*. In the film two dogs and a cat get left on a ranch with minders while their human family go on holiday; they think they have been abandoned but instead of feeling betrayed they presume something is up and decide to escape the ranch and just walk home. But this takes them through the Californian wilderness and the whole thing is about their treacherous journey home through this forbidding place full of wildcats and porcupines.

Sometimes when I was little I wished I was an orphan because they always had the fun lives in the stories. They had no familial ties keeping them bound with guilt. Most of the good adventure stories are about grown men or boy orphans. I planned to run away from home just for the adventure, wade down the river until I got to the sea because the sniffer dogs could not follow your scent through water. But I would get down the road to the lamp-post boundary marker and my mum would poke her head out and offer me a piece of carrot cake or something and I just could not break her heart.

I worried that *Homeward Bound* might have brainwashed me into losing my sense of adventure once the journey was under way, because really what the film says is pets are pets, not wild animals, same as humans are not wild animals, and do not go into the wilderness because it is bad out there. That it had ingrained this static idea of belonging and origin and the *outside*.

*You will leave me behind.*

*Please go to university.*

*I am too headstrong not to.*

*But also after, go back to the village. Fight for your culture!*

*We won't ever speak again.*
*We will stay in touch.*
*We don't even speak the same language.*

It is a shame that Greenland wants to move away from its old ways in order to keep up with the rest of the world. But how can we say they should not, that we want to keep all the wealth for ourselves? What do we want? This idea of its beauty and uniqueness, as culture-porn for ourselves too? Soon all I will have of Naaja are these memories and our footage of her. Then I will carry her with me if she can't go.


## THE RIGHTS OF NATURE

Back on a boat again. This one is the *Modet*, a commercial fishing boat. The wonky feeling from *Blárfoss* is worse here, what with the boat being much smaller. But I have got my sea legs now. There is an animosity, or it feels like it anyway, because all of the men are really superstitious in a hit-one-knee-got-to-hit-the-other-or-the-boat-will-sink kind of way, and the oldest guys especially believe it is very bad luck to have a woman on board. The aversion gets gentler down the age range. Logan is the oldest, older than Jon, who is Uncle Larus's age and older than the rest of the crew by at least two decades. He has not spoken to me once.

He reminds me of a seafaring Ted Kaczynski, the Unabomber. Ted Kaczynski posted letter bombs from his cabin in the Montanan wilderness. He was called the Unabomber because for years no one knew his identity, but bombs kept appearing via the mail in universities and airliners around the United States. He posted bombs to universities because he wanted to destabilise The Machine, symbolically at least if not literally. To punish The Machine for oppressing him and encroaching on his wilderness. For him a university was a hub of intellect, which really means 'symbolic culture' and the very opposite to his wilderness, a place devoid of human impositions. He must have hated the Golden Records.

Before he went to the wilderness he was a genius mathematician at Berkeley. He is worshipped as the God of the Mountain Men by some. Uncle Larus is a Kaczynski sympathiser; he even gave me a copy of Kaczynski's story 'Ship of Fools.' He says he is a misunderstood environmental defender and not a terrorist.

When he looks at me it is as though Logan is trying really hard to post me letter bombs, like his squinted eyes could be sending out envelope bomb blades, like those chakra disk weapons the Hindu god Vishnu uses, if only he could just squint hard enough.

I have my own cabin, which is a store cupboard with a camp bed in it. There is a spare bed in the dorm cabin with the others but the captain seems to find the idea of me cohabiting with them indecent. Probably I won't dwell on this too much since I quite like my little cupboard. It does not have a working light but it is quiet and I have a head light.

It transpires that *Modet* used to be a whaling ship. I did a little interview with Jon, which somehow became a defensive rant. Greenland always hunted whales for subsistence. Why should they not hunt them for subsistence? Now it is illegal to hunt them. Since the whaling ban they fish haddock. Sometimes they catch whales and they die and they have to throw the dead whales back into the ocean or they will be fined. The problem that came about was simply one of crowding. Fisherman and boat crowding. Ratio of whales to fishermen unbalanced. For him there was no issue of morality. No sympathy for the souls of the whales. A direct quote from Jon: 'The money was good. It is hard to think about the future when the money is good.'

Jon speaks like an echo of the whalers of old times. They needed to understand whales as swimming hunks of meat and oil because they were very, very valuable commodities. It would not do for commodities to have feelings. Whale blubber and especially the oil of the sperm whales were our main energy source before fossil fuels. They were instrumental in the beginnings of the Industrial Revolution. Traumatised by the slaughtering of their species, whales began to attack whaling fleets and therefore became monsters to us. They were nearly driven to extinction by the nineteenth century. Then we reached peak whale oil. The sperm whale was saved by the alternative invention of kerosene and the expansion of the fossil fuel industry. They do not attack ships anymore.

*They aren't sentient. They are fish. Fish are there to be eaten.*

*Whales are not fish.*

*What next? Haddock have feelings too? We can't eat the haddock? Then what do we eat?*

*Maybe one day whales might be classed as non-human people and this whole conversation would be considered highly offensive, like how we look at the times before the women's rights movement.*

*Ha! You can't say that as a woman. That is comparing women to animals. Very unfeminist.*

*Maybe that is what people said about the idea of women's rights before the suffragettes and in the context of the abolishment of slavery.*

*That is not a comparison.*

I think about saying these things but they would make for an even more uncomfortable ocean passage. I figure I should keep my mouth shut for now. It is fine, they don't hunt whales anymore.

But that is not the issue. The issue is that the bad seeds are still there.

When I found out about the whaling, I thought, how can Larus be friends with these people? He comes to help them if he is nearby, if they have caught a whale. He helps them place the whale back into the water and he tags the whale. He tries to educate them on the whales, so that they might understand them better, and in understating, develop some kind of empathy. He is not their friend. He is just cavorting with the enemy to further his own agenda.

## THE SUPER-TRENDY SPONGE CLUB

Whales have now become the mascot of environmental stewardship, our very own symbol of empathy for other animals because they represent the idea that humans are not the only self-conscious creatures on Earth. We only recently started to acknowledge this and it has led us to wonder if there are other animals, especially cetaceans, who are so emotionally sophisticated that they might even be more emotionally sophisticated than we are.

In the limbic system of orcas or killer whales, for example — that is, the emotional processing bit — some parts are much bigger and more complicated than in the human brain. Something evolved there that has not evolved in humans. Because they have so much social cohesion scientists think that this part of the brain could be working on something crazy like a *distributed sense of self.* Like they can kind of transmigrate into each other in real time, like mega-empathy, or telepathy. Which is really bloody sad if you think about mass strandings: they just can't imagine living disconnected from the social group because of their innate collectivism. Like women!

Were Scott and his men beached whales, dying in sacrifice with the rest of the pod, laying down their life for their kingdom, fundamentally collectivist, subsuming their 'selves' into the identity of the British Empire?

I would say no because what I think they had in mind when they kept pushing on into the obliterating snow was not death, as the end of self, but rather *immortality* (which is the conceptual opposite of a whale giving up any individualised notion of self in its suicide, dying with the colony because without the colony there is no self). The men on Scott's expedition were demanding to be individualised; honoured; glorified; remembered forever. (In a bee colony, around twelve males get to mate with the queen and pass on their DNA. Male bees explode after impregnating the queen, but it is not just anyone gets to say they impregnated the queen.)

Think of Lawrence Oates of Scott's mission, who left the tent saying *I am just going outside*. Maybe what he had in mind was some kind of cryogenic freezing. Maybe he was really going outside to make a time capsule of his body.

According to the International Time Capsule Society based out of Oglethorpe University in Georgia, the dawn of the millennium saw an intense increase in the amount of time-capsulisation around the globe. Perhaps because the millennium is a marker of deep time. Perhaps because of our sense of infinitesimality in our new view of our place in the universe, perhaps because of the prospect of nuclear dawn.

What could be more representative than a fully formed and cryogenically frozen self? The desire to be reanimated in the future, a whole human self projected into the uncharted future. Maybe Lawrence Oates was really doing a President Carter.

In Shark Bay, Australia, a group of dolphins has formed a little clique that you can only get in to if you are what they call a 'sponger.' It is called the Sponge Club. It was started by a dolphin they called Sponging Eve, who showed some of her girlfriends how to hold a sponge on the end of the snout so as not to get grazes when shuffling in the grit for food. Spongers only really hang around with other spongers, or dolphins that want to learn to sponge. This is what we describe in humans as *cultural transmission*. All but one of the dolphins in the Sponge Club are female; they seem to be better at keeping up relationships and therefore cultural transmission. Probably while the males hang out around the fringe of the group, hassling other males and being macho.

The realisation that things like culture that we once thought were distinctly human are being found in other animals is blurring the rankings of our very meticulous taxonomies. But New Age idiosyncrasies are obscuring the science. Where it is being discussed, it is quite often hampered by mystical and totemic portrayals of these animals by people who think they are magical.

John Lilly has to answer for some of this. His maverick experimentation with hallucinogens and his obsession with decoding dolphin language in order to talk to them has tarnished dolphin study as pseudo-science. Plus he was still looking at it the wrong way. John Lilly was ranking language as the highest form of intelligence, as though we are ahead of the animals on a scale of progression, as though animals have not just adapted themselves as we have to the skills most required by their environments. He was still setting humans outside of the rest of nature and looking for the next best contender to invite into our elevated realm. John Lilly was Narcissus looking for something that reflected John Lilly back at himself.

The understanding that humans are just animals is maybe already there in children, who feel a kind of empathy towards animals because they see them as furry, scaly, feathery people. But of course children's understanding of animal experience is not perfect because they take human-like responses to mean what they would mean in people.

When I was little I went to SeaWorld and loved every second of it. I thought the whales were happy and had a genuine best-friendship with their human trainers. You expect a super-friendly place like Florida where they invented orange juice and Mickey Mouse to be really good to their animals. And they are in the biggest pools you had ever seen and they really love what they do — look at the way they leap and smile and splash, all obvious expressions of joy and excitement.

YAAAAAY, goes the internal monologue of the dolphin. And the whales are far from home but they have each other and they love to be a family. They get the tastiest fish and the best care and fun toys and stimulation from people that they would not get in the wild and they are safe from those nasty Japanese poachers. Shamu has been alive forever so they must have long, happy lives in captivity.

You would never guess that the big one they get out at the end to do the big splash is not really called Shamu and would go on to kill lots of people because he is so emotionally traumatised from being masturbated by humans so his sperm could be sold for millions and being stuck in a concrete box with strangers who do not speak his dialect of whale and who rake him with their teeth for being different.

Cetaceans are intensely social. They have coded clicks that they use around each other. We can't decode what they are communicating, but they seem to be repeating a pattern. These clicks seem to be social affirmations. If they are saying anything it might be HELLO HELLO HELLO in their specific dialect. The sad whales of captivity could just be repeating HELLO HELLO HELLO in mutually unintelligible dialects.

Cetaceans are women's allies in the war against patriarchy because patriarchy holds the cetaceans down with us. Orcas travel in matriarchal pods. The root of the word dolphin, *delphus*, means womb.


## SO LONG AND THANKS FOR ALL THE FISH

Either I won Jon over or he invited me to watch the second haul because he was worried I would tell Larus they neglected me on the boat. He was hesitant in everything before I got out there, though, taking ages over giving me a bright orange anorak that drowned me already in case I fell in the water. He pointed out where the whistle was built into the collar and made me blow on it.

It was obvious as soon as I followed him out why he was being so cagey. A couple of the guys swore blatantly, one of them being Logan, who came straight from the other side of the deck and pushed past me back into the cabin, to go into his quarters, take his shoes off, put them back on again and masturbate in frustration over my pillow or something.

When the netted fish break the surface of the water they seem to be dead already and the gulls appear from nowhere to hover over and peck at them until they realise they can't lift them from inside the net. All pouched up inside the net, they spiral jaggedly but still quite mesmerisingly into each other because they are slippery and they swirl from the squeeze of the net and the pull of the water. It is the kind of movement that if you concentrate seems self-perpetuating, like a siphon flow, and you can't imagine how it might have started or when it will stop. A perpetual motion machine. (But this is an illusion. A perpetual motion machine is an epistemic impossibility; energy always dissipates. Second law of thermodynamics.)

AN ANALOGY: Once upon a time a bunch of people were on a ship too and they went hubris crazy from their own seamanship and they steered their ship into more and more perilous waters in order just to test their ever more brilliant feats of seamanship. Then the people on the ship started to argue amongst themselves, complaining about conditions on the ship. A lady on the ship complained that ladies do not get as many blankets as men. A Mexican on the ship complained he did not get paid as much as his Anglo counterparts. A Native American on the ship complained that he was owed compensation for the theft of his ancestral lands. A gay man on the ship complained at being called names for sucking cock. An animal lover on the ship complained that the dog on the ship was frequently kicked.

A lowly cabin boy piped up that everyone should stop arguing because really the issue was that the ship was headed for wreckage in the more perilous waters and that none of their problems would matter if the ship was wrecked, but nobody listened to him because he was just a lowly cabin boy. They called him a fascist and continued to argue amongst themselves about their personal issues, and nobody turned the ship around. Meanwhile the captain distracted them with condolences (an extra blanket for the lady, for example) that were always slight enough to placate but never for long, in order that they would not revolt and the ship could keep steaming ahead.

The ship went on sailing north until it was crushed between icebergs and sank to the bottom of the sea.

This is an analogy of civilisation written by Ted Kaczynski, the Unabomber. Obviously it has some major flaws. Why is the captain suicidal? Is there really one malicious captain steering the helm of civilisation? If we sabotage the ship, like he wants us to, then wouldn't we drown in freezing waters? But mostly my issue with it is that he does not seem to see that the problems of the people on the ship stem from the same place that built the ship badly (hint: patriarchy!). That to address the root of all their problems is to also steer the ship responsibly. As though the people on the ship were separate from the ship, as though the ship were sturdy and eternal, not contingent and always in the process of being reconstructed. I decided I should demonstrate this to Logan when the guys finally broached the subject of my presence on the ship.

'We thought you might be a spy that Larus sent to try and dig up the dirt on our whale data,' said Jon.

'I just need to get to Canada, and Larus said you'd take me. I can't say I disagree with how he feels about the whales, though.'

'That's exactly the sentimentality a woman would come up with,' Logan piped up from nowhere.

Everyone paused for a second with cutlery midway to mouth because it was the first thing he had said directly to me the whole trip.

'I'd kill a whale catch if I had my way. I'd stab it in the jugular and let it bleed out slowly. It's how we've always done it. No amount of squeals from folk like you will stop it, as much as you like to think it does.'

Thinking I would meet him on his own territory, I said, 'A curse on you and your boat,' which I thought was quite funny. I did not think he would take it so seriously. He called me a witch, said something about how the catch had been bad and the boat was headed for doom now and slammed out of the room.

There was a big old awkward silence until Ethan, the warmest to me, said, 'You really shouldn't have said something like that,' and a few of the guys exhaled loudly and let out low whistles.

Logan is like Ted Kaczynski in that he does not realise it is his own issues with me that was sending his ship to imaginary doom in the first place. It comes from inside him. It is a thing they have both imposed but are thinking is an *essential thing*.

The 'curse' will be lifted, so I suppose I did cast a spell on the boat in a way. Because when Logan realises it is *he* who is cursing the ship he will have to change his views on women (although there my own analogy falls down; Logan and the Unabomber are not synonymous because Ted Kaczynski would never kill whales).

I am partially onside with the Unabomber on the green issues, but like a lot of primitivists he believes in a Darwinian world of individual strength and combat where women have a subservient role because that is just *essential human nature*. And he really does not like feminists.

What he says: *feminists are desperately anxious to prove that women are as strong and as capable as men. Clearly they are nagged by a fear that women may NOT be as strong and capable as men.*

What Charles Darwin the sexist Victorian naturalist said: *the chief distinction in the intellectual powers of the two sexes is shewn by man's attaining to a higher eminence, in whatever he takes up, than can woman.*

What is 'strong'? Why is it 'good'? They are as superstitious as

Logan. They believe in the perpetual motion machine, without seeing that something started it, something gives energy to the machine. What the Unabomber needs is a feminist revision.

*What YOU need is a feminist revision.*

*Get off my ship you witch-whore.*

# THE RECEDING HORIZON

## GO CAREFULLY BRAVE SPACE PROBE
## FOR MY DREAMS GO WITH YOU

I had to steer clear of the northernmost mainland of Canada because it is sparsely populated and so logistics would have been difficult. It made more sense to go south to Saint John's, North America's oldest city. It's on the bigger-sized chunk called Newfoundland just off the bottom tip of Labrador, near where they excavated a Viking settlement that could have been Gudrid's. Means I have to ferry over to the mainland again across the Gulf of St Lawrence.

Thank god for the Trans-Canada Highway. I can use it to get all the way across the country to Yukon near the border with Alaska. You can get the whole way using Greyhound buses but they are way too expensive, so I am hoping to be able to do most of it with carpools and just a couple of coaches.

If I get completely stuck I suppose I will just have to hitchhike. I keep bringing up pages on the computer about women going missing while walking near the highway. A guy got beheaded and eaten on a Greyhound from Winnipeg, though, so none of my options are perfect.

The whole dynamic and landscape of the journey is to change now completely. Physically, it is all so lush and green and so many trees, such big trees! So weird to not be on rolling water. I think for the first few days the sensation will carry through, like how liquid that has been shaken about carries on sloshing even when its vessel has stilled. And it is also strange to think that now for the first time I am really on my own, because all the way so far I have been with Urla or kind of passed between adult guardians. Now it is just me and the whole of Canada, each leg of the journey a level to complete, bonus points carried over to the next level for novelty and amount of budget spared. And something else as well. Perhaps *velocity*. Because I have a vast space to cover and not much time or budget to do it in.

The internet tells me that Voyager 1 has left the solar system after all. It is now 12 billion miles away from Earth. That is 121 astronomical units or 121 times the space between Earth and the Sun. There has not been much fanfare to accompany this, maybe because it does not fit into our dogma of linear time, there not being a point where NASA could sit cheering and giving high-fives. They figured it out by comparing the number of protons around it this year with those around it last year, and from that estimated that it must have crossed the heliopause in around August last year.

So before I even left England it was already gone. In retrospect we will slot it into the history of our progressive forward march. Like when Columbus accidentally discovered a world that had already been discovered, several times over. Convinced it was India, he called the people he found there Indians, but more embarrassing is that we still preserve that mistake in our speech today. Europe did not hear about it until he got back afterwards and then the spread of the news would have been slow compared to our instantaneous world. It was an event that set into motion the beginnings of Western world domination, so from our perspective I suppose we are bound to distill it. Is this the drive behind time capsules? Are they a way to feign control over time by chronologising, a way of saying I MARK TIME THEREFORE I AM in order to assert existence?

It is cool that something made in the 1970s is still sending us signals from so far away when you consider what computers looked like in the seventies. On his way back from the New World, Columbus threw a bottle overboard with a message inside addressed to the Queen of Castile, detailing what he had found in case he drowned in a storm (I MARKED TIME THEREFORE I WAS). Voyager 1 will carry on sending messages for maybe ten more years until its plutonium runs out, after which it will carry on into interstellar space without us for a billion years before disintegrating.

In Port aux Basques I found a cheap hostel. I was invited out to drink with two obnoxious American boys I met in my dorm but I passed because they were obnoxious and because I was tired and had arranged already to Skype Larus.

## WOMEN'S BLOOD MYSTERIES

I had decided to ask for a lift just to Truro so that if I ended up in the car with a weirdo I could get out in plenty of time before it got too late, then if the driver happened to be taking the route on to Moncton I could decide to stay with them or not to. I won't pretend I was not uncertain as I stood with my thumb out at the side of the road, feeling small. When she pulled in for me she did it almost erratically as though on seeing my small uncertain self up close she could not sail past and just leave me there. I am very aware that in this context my youth and gender will be a blessing and could also very easily be a curse. As it happened, Jules was driving back from seeing friends in Sydney to her home in Riverview just outside Moncton.

Jules: long brown hair speckled with grey and a denim pinafore with a roll-neck sweater on underneath. A big voice and a way of asking questions that makes you think she genuinely wants your life story, as though she collects them. I told her everything about the documentary, about the journey so far. She told me to go ahead and get the camera out if I wanted to ask her anything, she would love to be a part of it.

She told me about how when she was a bit older than me she had done the entire Trans-Canada Highway from British Columbia to Newfoundland with her boyfriend. She spent some time after that living in a commune near an Indian reservation learning about Native American spirituality under some white New Age spiritual leader reborn as Raven-Wildheart or something. Then when she was hiking back home to BC alone afterwards she took a ride in a van. The guy was jittery and kept licking his lips, which were cracked; she had a bad feeling from the offset but his was the only vehicle she had seen in hours because she was in backcountry. It got dark fast and she had no idea where they were when he pulled over and took his cock out for her to suck.

She got out of the car but it was prairie land and she had nowhere to run or hide. The flat, indifferent plains lay out before her on every side. She started to walk as fast as stoicism allowed but she heard the gears crunch into reverse and he rolled down the passenger-side window to ask her 'where ya goin', little lady?' as he crawled her. She ran back off the road so that he would have to turn the car around to chase her.

The moon was behind a cloud. She was out of the beam of the tail-lights, and by the time he had aligned the car to the way she had gone, he could not see her running. And besides, his eyesight was bad, she had seen him squinting at the road signs. She turned and could see the car had stopped from the still of its lights, stiffening to the sight of his figure hunched in the car under the weak glow of the interior light. He took something out of the glove compartment and straightened up, holding it out ahead of him. The flashlight stammered feebly, he tapped it on his palm and it flickered out completely. She heard faintly the clunk of its loose parts as he kicked it into the dark.

Jules did not know which way to head. She had tried to aim

herself away from the road in a westerly direction, but in the opposite direction to which they had come so as not to stumble onto a road he might still be following. After walking half the night she curled exhausted into a dip in the ground and let the grasses wash around her. She lay awake all night, whispering to the prairie dogs for comfort and listening for the sound of an engine, until it was light enough to make out a farmhouse not too far away. The people inside were sympathetic to her, giving her breakfast and then a ride all the way home, a three-hour drive.

The pervert had a generic van and for years afterwards when she saw a similar van she would go clammy.

'But all the other amazing journeys I had apart from that one stupid one… I never let it stop me. It's the kind of thing that just happens sometimes. You gotta roll with it. Assert your freedom!'

Yes. Like Sylvia Plath said in her journal, why should women be relegated to the position of custodian of emotions, watcher of infants, feeder of soul, body, and pride of man? A consuming desire to mingle with road crews, sailors and soldiers, barroom regulars — that is what Sylvia Plath had. To be part of this scene, anonymous, listening and recording. We can't because we are females, always in danger of assault and battery. Oh, to be free to sleep in an open field! To travel west! To walk freely at night!

Looking out of the window and thinking, in this part of the world there are so many spaces between people that are just for trees. Conifers tower over the highway, making flashing striped shadows, and eagles are in the sky above them. Grass creeps back into the rubble fringing the asphalt. Lakes start to appear as flashes in gaps between the trees, like looking inside a zoetrope. There are spindly top-heavy trees that stand twice the height of the tips of the conifers. We are entering taiga land now, boreal forest.

'You know if you just drive through this you miss it all?' Jules said. I told her yes but I have to get all the way to Alaska before half of my money runs out, then head back on the rest. She asked, 'Why've you got to do that, sounds like a lot of pressure?' I told her I have to do it for the project, and that it is constructive pressure.

'Why Alaska? What's Alaska got that New Brunswick doesn't?'

'Gold fever. The mythology of gold rush country. Frontiers land. Jack London land. I don't know what it has but that's what I'm going to find out.'

She laughed. 'You going to disappear into the wild, then?'

I told her about the wilderness plan. She smiled and laughed and grimaced and seemed altogether perplexed about her feelings towards it all. Like with the story she had told me, I could not tell if she was being encouraging or cautionary. I asked her why this was.

'I don't mean to patronise you, but you're so young! And I surprise myself. See, you remind me of a younger me, I was around your age when I did similar things and was sure of them while I did them and when I look back on them now even. But you also remind me of my daughter and that makes me worry for you. Of course I worry for her because she is my daughter. Isn't that messed up? You'll understand one day when you are a mother. Where is your mother anyways?'

And from out of nowhere and without hesitation I said, 'She's dead.'

Maybe because I thought she would not press anymore after that, but in her uninhibited New World way she said softly, 'And what about your dad?'

'He's dead too.'

I stared right ahead after that but could see her taking snatched glances at me, searching my emotionless face to find the vulnerability there. When she could not find it we sat in silence a while, between us the sombre reverence of the orphan, so young and so blameless and yet wizened beyond years.

After some time had passed she said, 'Won't you get lonely out there?'

I asked her did she think Henry D. Thoreau was ever lonely. He was not, he was in a state of solitude. And besides, even that state was not ever pure. I will bring the camera with me, and this presumes an audience. Thoreau meditating on solitude by conversing with a diary is a paradox if you think about it. There is never solitude, only degrees of separation. You have to know something to know it is not there.

No man is an island, not even Ted Kaczynski, the man-island of all man-islands. When Ted Kaczynski was a boy genius at Harvard he was used as a subject by Henry Murray as part of the CIA's secret illegal MK ULTRA mind control programme. The aim of the programme was to find methods and drugs that could be used in interrogations and torture, to weaken the subject and elicit a confession. They chose geniuses because in theory their minds would be more resilient to intrusion. His code name was 'Lawful' and he was seventeen years old. Murray used 'vehement, sweeping and personally abusive attacks' against the child Unabomber's ideas, beliefs and his ego.

After such an attack on his idea of his self and his place in the world, is it any wonder he subsumed himself into something bigger (nature) and so different from the institution of Harvard (civilisation)? Ted Kaczynski was no island. He was another product of the Cold War.

After Jules dropped me in the city centre and I walked away feeling her tear-filled eyes on my back I found a bench right away and rang my parents because I felt so bad that I killed them like that. I have been keeping my promise to email weekly, but that was the first time I have heard their voices in fifty-two days. At the start they texted almost daily, like a check-in to make sure I made it to the end of the day; it would come always around 9 p.m. They must have adjusted based on my time zone so that they would always catch me just before I settled down. But they are becoming less and less persistent with it.

'Oh, there she is!'

'I'm sat on a park bench in Moncton in New Brunswick.'

'Where's that, love?'

'Canada.'

'She told you before she's in Canada now.'

'Well, I never heard of New Brunswick! What can you see, lovely?'

'Lots of tall buildings, a neat little park, no pigeons.'

'What time is it there?'

'It's about 6 p.m.'

'And are you on your own?'

'Yes.'

'Oh, love.'

'What time is it in England?'

'It's one fifteen.'

I skirted around the hitchhiking aspect of the journey and told them I had been getting coaches and, yes, my budget was doing all right, it is pretty cheap out here actually. We chatted for a while about things at home, how one of the neighbours had got a new dog that seemed to disagree with our own dog, how the weather had been especially hot for May and how the house was empty without me. And then there was a long pause with lots of little gasps that meant she was crying.

'Don't go getting all upset, she's fine. Listen! She sounds so happy! Aren't you happy, Erin?'

'Yes, very happy.'

'You see, she's doing just fine.'

I went to wrap it up then because I was about to start crying too and if she heard me cry, well, that would just be it, she would set in with her mantra that I had made a terrible and malady-driven mistake. But then she said in a very small voice, 'Yes, I know she's doing just fine, of course she is,' and that did me in.

I waited until we were off the phone and then I sat and wept quietly alone on that park bench in Moncton, New Brunswick, for a full minute until I had exorcised those cumbersome feelings from me and I got up to find a hostel for the night.

## THE POLLINATOR HEALTH TASK FORCE

QUEBEC CITY: This whole couch-surfing thing is really novel. All Lucie gets out of it is someone to show her city to, and I suppose a little cultural exchange. Seems to run on a backpacker mentality that sees meeting new people and sharing as the ultimate human rewards. I keep thinking of it like outside your customary social sphere you do not have any prerequisites and can be yourself more than you are yourself at home, become a really exaggerated version of yourself or whatever self you choose to accentuate for a short while.

It feels so natural that the strangest thing about it is that there will be a point in just a few days when it is all undone and I am a stranger to these people again. That we will stop existing to each other apart from in rare and passing thoughts.

She and all the friends I met identify as 'Pure Laine'; of pure French descent. We did not stop at the Citadelle, the massively serene City Hall or any of the other strikingly majestic/oppressive buildings of the British colonial era, but she lingered at anything built before the British took Quebec in the Seven Years' War: the Notre-Dame de Quebec, the cobbled architecture of the Haute-Ville and the Basse-Ville of the Old Town. The ramparts are the only fortified city walls north of Mexico. It is like the architecture itself is vying for prominence, a physical manifestation of historical egos. But a thought kept bugging me: it forgets that the sparring ground was appropriated and the fighting was imperial on both sides.

Lucie told the story as if it began with France and that is how the exhibition at the Musée de la Civilisation told it too, which I suppose it did in terms of written histories we can understand.

Cultures indigenous to the Americas had no written history before Europeans came and Latinised (or in some nicer cases invented a new syllabic alphabet for) their speech. Writing is the time-capsulation of language, pinning it so it can't float away on the wind. (An airborne language is the kind of which Ted Kaczynski would approve.) Their history is oral, is 'prehistory.' So in a way it is as though they did not exist.

Museums are time capsules. Sometimes they are time capsules of the other but by what taxonomies do they become 'of the other'? The Golden Records time-capsulised different cultures and species under the umbrella of 'life on Earth.' It could be that the relics of past civilisations that we sanctimoniously preserve and curate were meant for the future anyway. Maybe this is the most basic human impulse. (I mark time therefore I am, I marked time remember me, this is how I marked my time.)

At the time-capsule museum in Oglethorpe University, Atlanta, Georgia, there is an underground chamber sealed in 1940 by the founder of the university, the 'father of the modern time capsule,' Thornwell Jacobs. It is called the Crypt of Civilisation. It contains all the great literature, voice recordings of Hitler, Stalin, Mussolini, Roosevelt, Popeye, objects like a toaster and a typewriter, scientific instruments, the contents of a woman's purse, a black doll. By 'our civilisation' they meant 'the United States and the world at large during the first half of the twentieth century,' according to the inscription on the door. Next to this is a 'language integrator' based on the Rosetta Stone, for teaching a subset of English called 'basic English' in case it is not spoken anymore (a gesture towards solving the Forever Problem).

This is taxonomy of sorts; an order to say this culture is different from that culture. They are because I have known them. A discovered animal exists but an undiscovered one does not.

Divided they can be ranked. And if not denying the existence of native cultures we are at least able to say, they are behind us, primitive, not-quite-there-yet like animals.

It bothered Thornwell Jacobs that there was so little preserved of ancient cultures. He wanted to make future archaeologists' jobs easy for them. He thought of it in 1936, and figured that date to be the halfway point to the future, 6,177 years after the Egyptian calendar had been established at 'the beginning of history' in 4241 BC. So he set the date for the crypt to be opened at AD 8113. And he based the idea of the crypt on the 1920s openings of Egyptian pyramids and tombs. (But still he was the father?)

The crypt is an old underground swimming pool built in the bedrock underneath one of the university buildings. Buried in the bedrock underneath Eurajoki in Finland is the world's only deep geological depository for nuclear waste. It is called Onkalo, which means cave. There are tunnels excavated from the bedrock. The tunnels will be filled with nuclear waste and sealed with concrete. Then the sealed tunnels will be marked with warning signs, or maybe they will not be marked at all; Finland has not decided yet. Because surely to mark them with symbols that will die is only to draw attention to them. And if a future civilisation digs up the Crypt of Civilisation then they might expect Onkalo to contain similar archaeological delights.

At the Musée de la Civilisation there was an exhibition on the very first French settlement in Canada, which had been excavated in 2005. The settlement burnt down but they have not figured out whether the scorch marks told of accident or arson. The exhibition does not speculate much about the arsonists. I got so caught up in Lucie's turbulent history that I forgot that it erased thousands of years of culture, indigenous Canadians killed or cultivated or penned up by Europeans as if they were livestock or an unfortunate feature of the landscape.

## AND LIVE ALONE IN THE BEE-LOUD GLADE

Sat in a diner eating on my own, waiting for the coach to Ottawa. I am thinking about how the small autonomy of just being alone in public for a woman is also a right that needs to be claimed and kept on being claimed until it is a given. In order to do away with the anxiety that is shaping you from outside, like the deer in the glade that twitches its ears as it grazes, looking up and behind itself always in anticipation of predatory eyes. Women can't eat alone unless we claim it, can't go to a bar and sit alone, be in solitude in social places, as though always the female body is a lonely body, an invitation.

But tonight I sit in a diner on my own and nobody has looked at me. There are not many people in here, granted, but nobody has questioned or tested my being there with their looks. The waitress brought me a complimentary basket of bread and a jug of water without me asking, and smiled, as if to say, you are welcome here, this table is your own.

Growing out of the girl and into the woman sitting in cafés alone, libraries alone, anywhere alone, really, without feeling the itch of the out-of-place, displaced, mistaken. With the self-assuredness of the intentionally-put-in-place. I am starting to feel that now. A body that says, before they think to ask, no thank you, I am where I intend to be.

## IS THERE WATER ON MARS CUZ
## WE'RE THIRSTY

I have showered and put my least dirty clothes on, and looked at my reflection properly for the first time in weeks. I looked different, perhaps just dirty or tanned, or perhaps I have forgotten myself a little.

Now that I am not on the ice sheet or the ocean or moving in a car it is like I am back in real life and that before was unreality. It feels uncomfortable. Like the velocity is gone and now I am at standstill. I feel restless.

I have been on the move now for two months so I need to get to Alaska ASAP but I am about on target. So far I have spent about £470, just under a third of my original budget. I also have an extra £200 I won in a travel-writing competition for a thing I wrote about sledging in Greenland, so I am doing all right, but it still makes sense to stop and work while I am in the more populous part of the country and work is theoretically easier to come by, before I move back up north and west. I found a job in a hostel in Ottawa city on a helpshare website so I will stay put for a few weeks and come up for some air.

A girl called Jackie who is hitchhiking to the West Coast of America, following in the steps of serial narcissist-road-trip-writer Jack Kerouac, keeps a blog I have been following closely. She has a big following, and some of them are other girls doing similar things, an online-feminist-adventure-blog-vanguard. It is exciting to feel like I am a part of something bigger. I reckon feminism would have worked a lot faster if Annie Peck could have connected with all the other unnamed women who were taking on man-roles, mountaineering and shit, and realised she was not as remarkable as her male counterparts said she was. I think she would have liked that. What Annie Peck was missing was the internet.

Benny runs the hostel. He takes on backpackers because they attract other backpackers and also work for a pittance because they mostly don't have work visas. I cover shifts on the bar, reception, kitchen, wherever there is work, for about £5 per hour. On top of this I get my own single room, food and drink. I have to work eight-hour shifts every day so that is £200 per week with a couple of days off. If I keep it up for two weeks I can make a little bit of money to tide me over.

Everyone who works at Benny's is under thirty and the hostel is full with travellers. You'd almost call it a melting pot if it weren't so homogeneous. Maybe let us say it is a bunch of at-least-one-time-Europeans but some of them speak differently.

An Ottawan guy, a friend of Benny's called Tom, has stayed at the bar talking to me every night I have been here. Tom is quite attractive, I would say. He has deep-set eyes that bore in a bit in a sexy way when I am talking. So far, though, even though he has had opportunity to try it, he has not suggested coming back to my room. I am glad about this. I have a few weeks and it is more fun to be stretching it out, but also should it be an ill-suited pairing then I have less time left to dwell in the regret of it.

I did do a few interviews with people around the hostel. I got onto this topic that everyone seems to bring up without really knowing that they are. Lots of the interviews come back to the same elusive thing and this is coming from people from all sorts of nationalities. It makes you think that the world is really a very small place after all, if everyone can be saying the same thing that is not really saying anything, without knowing it. It has something to do with what *freedom* feels like, and how it is always just ahead of you, a bright little light like an orb, but if you run hard enough at times and in places like this, you catch it up and you can float it in your hands.

Otherwise I suppose everything documentary-wise is on the back burner because I am keeping the laptop in a safe and there is hardly ever time to get it out. It is making me agitated; some-times instead of sleeping I am thinking of all the things that are waiting to be captured. Like gathering butterflies, and butterflies are really slow and plentiful so I won't run out or anything, but I might miss a good one while I am not looking. And maybe there is someone else out there butterfly-gathering, gathering them quicker and better.

It makes me empathise with the anxiety that must have been felt on both sides during the space race. The not knowing where the Russians were at, and oh my god, what if they get there first, what if tomorrow even they announce it, we made it here, the moon is ours. This panic drove them, it rushed them into cutting corners they should not have. Russia had many people die in the process. A fire burned up over one hundred spectators in a launch-pad accident. This was kept classified until the nineties. But what else do we not know? Maybe Yuri Gagarin was not the first cosmonaut. Two Italian brothers with a home-made radio claimed they were picking up transmissions from other, abandoned, cosmonauts. They thought maybe Yuri Gagarin was just the first to return alive.

But besides what we don't know, we *do* know perhaps the most heart-breaking best-friend-sacrifice story in history. When Yuri Gagarin inspected Soyuz 1 he found 203 structural problems and he urged his superiors to delay the mission but they would not. Scheduled to fly the mission was his best friend, co-pilot Vladimir Komarov, and Vladimir Komarov would not back out of this mission he knew to be a suicide mission because his back-up was Yuri Gagarin. On the day of the launch Yuri Gagarin tried to halt the mission, demanding that he go in Komarov's place. Of all the design flaws Komarov overcame, it was the very last hurdle that got him. After surviving the multiple perils of space he died as he hit the ground in Russia when his parachute did not unfurl.

And then even where they pulled it off, if you look at the minute details they are embarrassingly botched. Like when cosmonaut Alexey Leonov became the first human being to spacewalk, he nearly could not get back inside because his spacesuit was badly designed and it inflated. He went up in a spaceship made for only one person, with co-pilot Pavel Belyayev. When they had to calculate re-entry it was so cramped in their shuttle that they could not go through the motions in time and their orbital module did not disconnect from their landing module when it should have and they ended up landing 240 miles from where they intended in a forest on a mountain in the taiga, where they had to spend two days fending off bears and wolves frenzied in mating season before help arrived on skis.

America had the Apollo 1 fire. Neil Armstrong and Buzz Aldrin reckoned they had a fifty-fifty chance of coming back alive and President Richard Nixon had two scenario speeches prepared for him. The worst-case scenario speech said very noble and chauvinistic things like THEY BIND MORE TIGHTLY THE BROTHERHOOD OF MAN and THEY WILL BE MOURNED BY A MOTHER EARTH THAT DARED SEND TWO OF HER SONS INTO THE UNKNOWN and EVERY HUMAN BEING WHO LOOKS UP AT THE MOON IN THE NIGHTS TO COME WILL KNOW THAT THERE IS SOME CORNER OF ANOTHER WORLD THAT IS FOREVER MANKIIIIIIND.

So really they did not have much of a clue and they were just going for it and hoping for the best. How the hell did they even pull off the moon landings? I mean, imagine having almost no deep space technology and then setting the task, guys, you have eight years to put an actual human being on the actual moon, okay, great, thanks, Mr President Kennedy, sir, we'll get on it. How did they even test the rockets before using them? I suppose they just pointed them at the sky and crossed their fingers. And they had no clue what would happen to people if and when they got up there. Maybe they would spontaneously combust. Maybe their organs would be sucked out. Maybe they would bring flesh-eating alien microbes back to Earth with them. So maybe I should not freak out too much and it is best not to rush the project.

Considering all this I wonder a bit when Larus teasingly says he thinks they faked the moon landings. You were there, I say, you saw it happen. Yes, but maybe they just flew around the world, maybe they never made it past the Van Allen belt where the radiation gets too much, is it really more far fetched to think that it could be the whole thing was a scam directed by Kubrick so they could have one over the Russians and become Kings of the World than to think that they really risked the lives of men and the whole planet live on television, sending them up there in a little tin can propelled by explosives, all the way to the moon, which is a very, very long way? And that almost all seven of the landing missions went without a hitch of the death-causing kind? And then we never went back there? Why does the flag wave? Why no impact crater? Where are the stars? The rock with the 'c' on it? And besides, Watergate?

## WOMEN INCENSED AT TELEPHONE COMPANY HARASSMENT

I took it upon myself to make the moves on Tom because sufficient anticipatory time had passed. This being week two. He said, 'I knew you wanted me, I was just making you work to get it,' or something equally arrogant, but he was drunk and I know he was just saying it to try to be alluring.

Today he took me around Ottawa because we both had a spare day. I think we are not compatible but it does not matter under the circumstances. For one he is boring on his own, and also he tried to insist on buying all my drinks and then he just did not get it and we had to agree to disagree so things did not get awkward.

In physics the Zone of Middle Dimensions refers to physicist Isaac Newton's world of falling apples, where the physical rules Newton laid down still apply to an extent and the progress made in modern physics that undermine all of Newton's rules is kind of put to one side just to make more of an easy and livable life for everyone in 'the zone' of everyday life. Sometimes I think of my everyday life as a zone of middle dimensions where it is best to not always be a precise and righteous feminist even when you know you are right. Sometimes you have to do that for the sake of simplicity; suspend your indignation like, yeah, if you say so, Newton. But I did try asking Tom why he thought he should buy my drinks, which he thought about quietly for a while, then came up with, 'It's just what guys do.' He said, 'You're an idiot anyway, if guys were always offering me free drinks I'd just take them.'

I tried to explain to him that accepting a drink is like agreeing to buy something that does not have a price on it and if something does not have a price on it is usually very expensive; that it is like that story about making a deal with the devil when the devil says, 'I get to have whatever is in your yard,' and you think he can only mean the tyre swing but really he meant your *yard*.

Tom did say something very suddenly illuminating and not in a good way. We were sat looking over the confluence of the rivers Rideau, Ottawa and another one I don't remember the name of (that is three rivers all colliding, picture it: one large body of water rushing into another, undulating. At what point does one river become another river?)

'I think Benny's kind of pissed that we are on a date.'

I asked him why he said pissed, rather than something less angry, like sad, or disappointed, but I did not get why Benny would be that either. He asked if I thought everybody got the same special treatment, their own bedroom. And I realised for the first time that, yes, the two other backpacking girls who worked the bar had beds in a dormitory.

It is so stupidly transparent, so unassumingly obvious and self-assured and so without deviousness, that I failed to notice. But I guess they think I have been playing their game all along.

I didn't react because, well, I bet Einstein, after he disproved Newton, did not just bumble through life coming to loggerheads all the time having to explain fundamental physical laws to people who were just completely ignorant, I bet most of the time he just got on with things. There is being a good feminist and then there is not having any friends. I had told myself two weeks and had made all my next plans accordingly, so I have to make it work for a few more days. But I did make a point of not inviting Tom back to my room tonight.

## WOMEN STILL APPRECIATE CHIVALRY FROM MEN ACCORDING TO STUDY

I packed up my stuff and quickly left this morning without anyone seeing me, even as I got my things from the locker in the common room, where Benny was passed out on the sofa asleep. The keys were still in his hand. I took them gently and opened the safe behind the reception desk to get to the moneybox, and took the wages he owed me from last week. Then I took a hundred more. And then I put the hundred back.

Last night after my shift I had been in bed maybe half an hour without Tom, who I jilted at the bar, and I heard a knock on my door. The first was soft, but when I didn't answer he knocked louder to try to wake me. I kept quiet, feeling indignant, and then thought, no, I don't want him to think I am asleep, I want him to know that I am sending him away. So I said, 'Go away, Tom.' And a really slurred voice said let me in but it was not Tom's.

Then I heard metal scratching metal where he was trying to fit the key inside the lock. I jumped out of bed to stop the door opening fully and Benny leant into the room leering. He said, 'Hey, let me in,' and leaned heavily on the door. He is a lot bigger than me and I knew he would be able to force his way in so I stood back and let him fall on his weight and I stood straight and spoke loudly at him so everyone would hear.

'No, you can't come in my room, Benny, now go away. You're drunk.'

Next door's dorm had opened up at this point from the

banging and two of the guys came out to ask if I was okay. Benny turned around pitifully from the floor.

'It's fine. She's fine. I'm leaving. I was just... checking on her.'

He dragged himself from the floor and wiped his arm slowly over his mouth to try to be inconspicuous, calling me an ungrateful bitch as he left the room. I mouthed thank you to the others, who nodded and one gave a fingers to eyes signal, to imply he would keep an eye on me. After that I did not sleep too well even with the chair wedged firmly under the door handle.

The guys would not say anything today because Benny shelters and feeds them, and why would they jeopardise their comfortable situation? I wonder what else he gets away with; that makes me angry.

One thing that Kerouac Jackie does on her blog that is really interesting, she is deadpan about all the people she has slept with along the way. The thing that makes it interesting is that her blog is pretty big, big enough to have attracted trolls. These trolls sit and write petty things, mostly calling Jackie a slut. I don't know if the trolls have read Kerouac or not, so I don't know if they condone male sexuality and lusting over thirteen-year-old girls and wife-beating. I bet Benny likes Kerouac.

Anyway, I am away and on a coach to Sault Ste. Marie on some of the money I earned because I can afford it and because I wasn't really feeling like jumping in a vehicle with a stranger right away. It is a ten-hour coach then I have a room booked the other end. I have a lucky last-minute carpool tomorrow all the way to Thunder Bay and from there I will figure out how to get to Winnipeg.

Larus has sent me not one but two follow-up emails to an email that I have not had a chance to see let alone reply to. The first one being a catch-up and a how's things, here, look at some stuff I found for you to read. The second being a follow-on to the first with an enquiry into why I did not reply and some inane stuff about what he has been keeping himself busy with. The third is a little parental, chiding me for 'going off the radar.' I think he is enjoying living life through me or something, or it is some weird kind of deflected paternalism. Urla would have thought of some great way to enact revenge on Benny. I wish she had been there. I wrote her an email to enlist her in effecting Benny's karmic retribution, but she hasn't replied to me in a while now.

## OF THE SHINING BIG-SEA WATER

Trees clear for a diner and some cabins, then the trees clear altogether and we hit the lakeside. And suddenly a whole new perspective, a landscape with depth and a horizon instead of a belt of evergreens. It is so blue and glittering and vast that for a second I am thrown. How did we end up by the sea? But the water is still and we are so near that I can make out the pebbles in the shallows, like the lake is clear plastic in a miniature replica, and for a second the entire world feels like we have been shrunk to thumb size with this model landscape that is simultaneously tiny and proportionally huge to our new tiny selves. Low concrete bollards separate the highway from the water. My mind is surprised into silence. Lake Superior.

From back behind our green conveyor we arrive at a break in the trees again and the coach slows to elongate our passing it. The driver says, 'Over there is America,' and there it is, the stretch of the lake unbroken, America so far away and blue with distance, like Calais from Dover on a good day. I know from the map that if we were looking directly south we would be looking at Hiawatha National Park.

We pass some holiday condos. The lake now must feel very different from when Henry Longfellow, the old poet, wrote *The Song of Hiawatha*. You can write about a lake and a landscape but then when something is worth writing about this usually leads on to something beyond admiration, reduces it to something people want to come and see for themselves. Then everyone wants to get touchy-feely and build their condos right there so that they can own their lake-view property. Now Longfellow could do away with his birch canoe with paddles and circumnavigate the entire lake in his pick-up in just a few hours. It was because fancy new cabins kept creeping into his lovely wilderness that Ted Kaczynski retreated further and started to send the letter bombs.

Looking at the glassy surface of the lake I remembered that the micro-beads from your facewash are not biodegradable and they leave the sewage system to collect in constellations on the surface of all of the Great Lakes. I squinted and imagined I could see them glinting.

This morning, back to hitchhiking. I settled for a short ride out of Thunder Bay to where the road forks off at Kakabeka Falls to ease myself in with a quiet businessman I could not have spoken more than ten words to. I set up after the turn-off where the highway stretches on to Dryden in an area with thin traffic, in view of a lonely reservoir, and where the aspens bled the landscape yellow and lethargic. Small insects hummed around me as I slumped on my bag and half-dozed, sitting up to the sound of any approaching traffic. I was not making good time but the sky was milky with cloud and the air thick with warmth and pollen. If I wanted to do it for free or cheaply, I was going to have to travel the 450 miles to Winnipeg at whatever pace the day or days decreed, and the character of this day was languid. I was thinking this and just laughed out loud.

It is interesting to watch the faces of people as they pass me in cars. If I am stood with my thumb out then nobody drives by without noticing. The majority avert their eyes, as though to look at me would pull them in out of guilt, I guess because I must look the furthest from threatening, a cute siren on a rock. Those that realise they are going the wrong way to take me seem to take absolution from theatrically signalling they are going the wrong way, with big sorry mouths and shrugging shoulders. Some stare and pass, some shake their heads disapprovingly and some, inexplicably, just honk.

At around eleven a car pulled over and offered me a ride to Dryden, an old man who seemed concerned for my welfare. I watched time peel away through the window. There was a speck of bird poo on the window and by moving my head up and down I could jump it over the conveyor belt of variable treetops like in a 2D video game. It felt good to watch the world flicker by as though we were still and it was moving around us, and the  illusion would be crystallised when a train would appear on the railway where the road and the rail were adjacent and the train would converge with us in speed, making it and us appear static.

My driver dropped me at a service station. Touchingly, he was projecting vulnerability onto me; the kindly chauvinism of an old man towards a young woman. Irritating, yes, but also he is just old and sweet and well-meaning and of-his-time. He tried to give me money, which I refused, laughing. But the look on his face as he drove away really did make me feel alone and vulnerable for a moment, as though I had transformed into his idea of me. I felt pangs of guilt for this stranger who I would never see again and who would probably worry about me from time to time, wonder if I found my way. God, not even orphans are free of the guilt of people, are they?

I found a cardboard box in a bin behind the building and broke it down to make a sign, then positioned myself conspicuously with it on an embankment at the exit, where anyone about to leave could pull over for me or had to sail by my imploring cherubic face. I thought how Urla would probably say I should use my feminine powers to my advantage, so I unzipped my hoody to show a little cleavage. Then I thought, that's not very feminist, is it? Then I decided that either way it made me feel weird, and I zipped myself back up.

Traffic coming through is so thin that I only see someone pass every fifteen minutes or so. There are some semis parked and drivers mill to and from them. The sparrows have got used to me by now and are pecking around at the crumbs I am throwing to them. I managed to get one so close that I touched it gently with my foot before it flew away to a small sapling, where it sat scolding me.


## THE INEXTRICABLE WEB OF AFFINITIES

The semi's cab had two seats in the front and a raised compartment behind with a mattress for sleeping. It was very clean and neat. There were no pornographic photos pinned to the dashboard. There was a little meter up where the rear-view mirror goes in cars and he typed something into it before we started to pull out of the service station. He was very particular that I sit up front next to him, which did not seem too out of the ordinary, just in fitting with his extreme orderliness. The bed compartment behind, where he showed me to put my bag, was out of his range of vision, so I put the camera hidden just behind, where he could not see it on, and it could witness everything.

He offered me little cakes from out of a cool box under

his seat in a way that made me nervous about eating them. I declined and patted my stomach to show I was full. I figured I had better stay alert just to be safe rather than sorry. I sat saying things about the landscape at awkward interludes and he nodded and said something or other in another language and stared at my legs a lot.

The journey went on so slowly and so uneventfully at semi speed that now and then I would feel the exhilaration again at my distance to Alaska getting smaller and smaller while I sat still, and that pushed my suspicion and paranoia out of my mind for a while. Even the Stanley knife on the dashboard had become benign by virtue of its sustained uneventful just being there. There was the meter which said how far there was to go and he had checkpoints and a schedule so he could not just take me out into the middle of nowhere and do something bad. A semi was the most sensible place to be, if I thought about it.

We pulled in at another service stop at which he managed to communicate to me without English that he was going to go have a cigarette. We were in the semi-designated area of the services, where regular vehicle paraphernalia like petrol pumps and parking spaces are upped to semi scale, and men stand around leaning against their wheels, smoking and talking. I thought of Plath mingling with truckers. The driver got out and went over to the nearest group for a few minutes; they were talking and looking over to me and smoking their cigarettes and they all laughed together, then he came back to the semi. He said something to me, half-turned round in the driver's seat and laughed a little spittle out of his mouth, and then he pinched my leg. Between the thumb and forefinger, the part of my leg that indents where the muscle meets the fatter bit of thigh.

The group of men outside were staring in. They stared as we pulled away. As we passed them he held up his hand in salute to them. We rolled back onto the road. I was too caught up unravelling the situation to realise until we were moving that I probably should have got out of the semi at that point.

Later we passed a road sign that showed a turning up ahead for the road to Winnipeg — +207 km — but we passed the slip road and he did not even glance at it.

'That was our turning.'

He looked at me.

'That was the road to Winnipeg.'

'What?'

'Why didn't you turn?'

'Sorry, no understand.'

I stabbed my finger to the right.

'That was the road for Winnipeg.'

He smiled and shrugged.

'Winnipeg,' I said slowly, stabbing my finger again.

'Ah! Winnipeg,' he said, motioning forward.

I did not know what to do. I must have looked forlorn and he smiled, said, 'Winnipeg,' cheerfully and motioned forward again. I did not believe him but what could I do, jump out of a moving vehicle? Was I certain enough to tell him to stop and leave me at the side of the road? It was going to start to get dark soon and it might be better to presume we would end up in a floodlit truck stop than to risk the side of the road at night. He had to stop somewhere legit, another service station with other semis and people. You can't just go off-road and incognito with a semi.

'How far?'

I tried to act out distance with my hands.

'How long until Winnipeg?'

'Ah! Winnipeg soon soon. Yes, soon,' he said.

'Soon?'

'Soon.'

We drove on; the yolk of the sun spilt on the horizon and the sky got inky. He turned his headlights on and with the dark I began to feel panic really set in. I could see a reservation coming up to our left. An indigenous woman stood at the side of the road in a very short skirt. He pointed at her and laughed like a hyena. The woman winced when the headlights and the sound of his horn hit her face.

A little later, as the headlights breached the trees, you could see the land where the forest had been clear-cut. It stuck in your throat how it was so dense and dark and enclosing then, suddenly, barren, the sky bursting through, the weak light of it pooling out over the feebler trees they left behind, scattered like redundant matchsticks. It must have stretched for miles, naked and vulnerable like a head shaved for neurosurgery. In the far distance a town sat lit up like a cluster of glow-worms. The tick-tick of his indicator started up and we steered onto a gravel path, up towards a closed diner cabin and a portaloo where one other semi was parked with its lights out. No floodlights.

We ground to a halt and he tapped something into the meter, which played a triumphant little jingle. He said something and patted then shook my knee, grinning, and there was the spittle again. I pulled away and asked where we were. And he said something else with his hand back on my knee. I said, 'Winnipeg,' really resolutely this time. He made the universal sign for sleeping and nodded up to the bed.

'Winnipeg tomorrow.'

'No. I'm not sleeping here. I need to get to Winnipeg now.'

'Winnipeg tomorrow.'

'No, I—' I started to say through gritted teeth. He said something very firmly, then grabbed my thigh and ran his hand up to my groin.

I pushed then kicked his arm away from me. We faced each other for a few seconds, each waiting to see what the other would do next. I had to move closer to him to move around the seat so I snaked my body without breaking eye contact so that I could see where his hands were. I grabbed my rucksack and camera strap with one hand, pulled myself back over with the other and, panicky, wrestled with the stiff door handle.

Meanwhile he sat back into his seat, saying things between his jerky hyena cackles. As I pried the door open and threw my bag out he lurched for me. I threw myself down from the tall cab on top of my bag as I felt his hand tighten on my ankle, lose grip, and clutch at my shoe. My foot slipped from it as I fell.

I scrambled up, swung my bag on my shoulder and put the camera strap around my neck. Then at a safe distance, I glared back at him. He held my shoe in his hand, laughing, and I was filled with so much furious hatred for him I wanted to take a stone and smash his greasy head with it. I wanted to wrestle my shoe back out of his hands and slap it on his face. I thought maybe I would, maybe the danger had passed now, maybe the danger was only ever his violating hands, which were no longer on me. But then he lurched towards me again, making a mocking sort of animal grunt; I started to run.

I ran flat out back down the gravel path towards the dark highway. On the road I headed the way we had come, back in the direction of the reservation, I suppose because taking the road towards the town would have meant running parallel to the park, where he could have scrambled down the slope and intercepted me. The ground where the trees were cut was littered with stumps and amputations. I ran hard, away from the truck stop and the distant lights of the town and towards the blotted darkness of the forest.

I was running running running and everything hurt, but blind panic kept me moving forward and clouded the jolts in my left heel, the one that had no shoe. I had been running for about ten minutes when the pain of it got too much and I limped to a halt, bent with my hands on my knees, looking behind.

*Can he see me?*

*No, can't see the park now.*

*But he would have seen which way, following the road.*

I started to walk forward, trying to keep my heel off the ground and looking behind me. I stopped, remembering my boots tied to my bag. Brushing the bottom of my foot, I squinted at my hands. It was too dark to see much properly, but I felt stickiness between my fingers. My heel was bleeding.

I did not want to stop so I shoved the boots on and kept pressure off the heel, abandoning the other shoe in the scree by the road. Eventually I decided that probably he had not followed but I could not turn back, had to carry on ahead, just keep moving.

I felt really suddenly like I wanted to scream and hit myself. How could I have been so stupid? And look at me now, stupid and limping and alone in the dark on a road god knows where at night being what I set out not to be reduced to, fulfilling for everyone who worried and foresaw it, and what now? This is not my world to walk in. Compulsively, I wanted the phone from my bag. I needed a voice to be with me. I rummaged inside and brought out the flashlight.

*Don't put the flashlight on!*

Fuck! I scrabbled to turn it off. I hugged the rucksack to me and started to shake and whimper pathetically. Who would I call exactly? What could they do from the other side of the world? I told myself out loud *this is your mess*, sniffled into my sleeve and started walking quickly onward. The weak moonlight was strobing through the moving canopy, lighting things up in jolts like club lighting.

*Into the forest?*

*I don't want to get lost in the forest.*

*But it's so risky to keep to the road.*

I decided to carry on up the road to the reservation. Sit behind a building where I was not in the open. Find a shed or something. Until the morning. I broke into a little trot again. The indifferent trees spun, they were so high above me; the tough long grass lashed against my legs from the roadside. The road itself was lit up like a silver beacon by the moon, leading up and on and on. The trees were hush-hushing, but the sound of panic beat on my eardrums. I had to keep stopping to get my breath and readjust my rucksack. Then at some point I remembered the camera.

*I need something to complete the sequence.*

*You and that fucking documentary!*

I took a bit of footage of the road, shaking with my running. Then I noticed the figure on the road up ahead. I stopped running but carried on approaching at limping pace because there was nowhere else to go, and besides, they had already seen me. They raised their hand. They were just ahead of the reservation.

I put my hand in the air. The figure put theirs down. As I got nearer I could tell it was a woman, which made me feel easier. Nearer still, the woman from the headlights. Then I was stood in front of her, gasping.

'Are you all right?' she asked in a soft voice. I could not answer from panting. 'I saw you running.'

'I ran from. The truck stop,' I managed.

'Why were you running?'

'There was a man. In the semi—'

But then I do not know because the sky dimmed to black and some sirens started and my knees buckled under a huge pressure that came both from above my head and out of my body at once, and I fell to the floor. The woman went to catch me, I think, because when I came to I was half on the ground and half in her arms, but my leg was twisted under me and she had got on her knees to scoop me into a sitting position. My knees were gashed. It struck me how lost and young I must have seemed right then to this stranger. I feel embarrassed now at this image of me like a broken doll but I did not feel embarrassed right then, because I felt too much relief that the sick pressure was gone from my stomach, that the loss of consciousness had come on me like an anaesthetising sleep that takes pain away and the sweat all over my body was now a cooling balm to the heat. It is a familiar feeling, and by now I am used to the loss of control, and feel less disempowered just letting it happen rather than struggling against it. It makes me feel Victorian and weak.

'Oh no. All right. All right. Will you be okay here for five minutes? I can go and get my truck. You're exhausted. I'll go and get my truck. I'm Rochelle. I'll be right back.' Then she got up and ran up the path into the reservation. As she left, I wanted so badly for her not to go and leave me to be enveloped by the darkness. I sat and tore at blades of dry grass and shook, from adrenaline or shock, or something.

After a few minutes Rochelle came back with her truck and drove me to her caravan, where she picked out the gravel from my foot and put a brown ointment from a jam jar on it then bandaged it up with plasters. She gave me this thing called 'frybread' to eat and a savoury tea, telling me the history of the bread. It was made from flour and lard, invented in 1860-something by the Navajo people, who were given the ingredients by the US when they were forced into a 300-mile relocation from Arizona to New Mexico. She told me her mother was Navajo and had died of diabetes from eating too much frybread. She ate it too without a tinge of irony and so I thanked her for it.

Rochelle gave me blankets and set up her electric heater next to me on her sofa. I woke up when she came into the room with the sun in the morning, wearing a full velour tracksuit and wrapping herself in a thick leather coat from the back of the door. She lit a cigarette and started making a pot of coffee without saying anything. I wondered if she had forgotten I was there, if it was even possible to miss me in this tiny space. I had the feeling I should not talk. I shifted my position so I could look out of the window.

Outside I could see the neighbouring trailer, its smashed window blocked up with a bin-liner that tremored in the wind. Next to the trailer was the exoskeleton of a car, its tyres deflated and so sunk into the ground that it looked as though it was melting. It was brown with rust, rainbowed with spray-paint, with no glass in the windows and bullet holes in its side, dark and ringed at the edges like pockmarks of disease.

Rochelle placed the coffee on the coffee table in front of me and sat opposite on a stool that she moved directly into the beam of light from the window, even though it made her squint, and basked like a lizard does. Dust drifted past her face and caught the light like glitter. Her cigarette smoke was dense in the light, an eel curling through the dust motes. She poured the coffee carefully with the cigarette tucked in the corner of her mouth, talking around it.

She said a lot of stuff too that I did not process all of, being hazy and still reeling and replaying things as she talked. 'I suppose I should say you shouldn't have put yourself in danger like that but I guess you weren't to know any better. It happens. Sometimes girls go missing, but not usually white girls.' I remember that bit because her tone changed. 'It can happen out here because it's kind of a forgotten backwater. But anyway it didn't happen. Nothing happened. You were lucky. Or unlucky or neither, a close call. That's all.' Then she looked directly at me and I had to look away.

She was surprisingly forthcoming but in a very detached way, as though thinking aloud to herself. Nothing she said really invited participation. She looked out of the window as she spoke, at two small children who had started poking sticks into the bullet holes. Making a porcupine, she said.

Rochelle has lived on the reservation all her life, apart from four years when she lived on the road with her ex-boyfriend. They met in one of the bars, in the town I saw lit up in the distance the night before. Her ex-boyfriend was a hippy and had always wanted an Indian girlfriend, called her his Pocahontas. They broke up because he wanted to move onto the reservation with her, but it made her more and more uneasy the way he would braid his hair and wear a headband and keep pestering her to arrange a naming ceremony for him, how his favourite film was *Dances with Wolves*.

The transcendental open-mindedness of the liberal white man! So free of cultural constraints, free-spirited and open to the other! Many levels progressed from the Enlightenment specimen collectors! What almond skin, what glossy hair, I can't kill and stuff it, no no, how barbaric. I will parade it around living and glorious! We only view our animals on safari now!

She started to feel as though he wanted her as a prized possession, or maybe even just a ticket to somewhere else. As though casting off his own civilisation and shrugging on something antithetical, her culture, the uncivilised one.

It seemed to bug her to talk to me, like it made her squirm, but a silence would be too heavy with my presence inside her small home. We got on to the topic of the documentary and she asked about it. I wasn't sure if I should tell her explicitly, right after what just happened. But I decided, she will get it, I mean, the white man is her historical enemy. She laughed, not in a condescending way, really just a non-committal laugh that could have meant anything. She said, 'The freedom to roam free like a white man, hey?'

Later on she said she wanted to show me something and then she would take me to town. When we left the reservation, people were sat and stood about in groups, chatting and smoking. A couple of dark and long-haired guys loped coolly on actual frisky-spirited horses. They all stared at me. I got right into the truck under Rochelle's instruction. Someone called out 'Hey, Rochelle,' and she just called back hey, climbing in the driver's side and starting the engine before she had even shut the door. A twenty-something boy scooted up to her window and tapped on it. She let out a sigh then rolled down the window a couple of inches.

'Hey, Walt.'

'Hey, Rochelle. Hey,' he said to me, grinning and craning around her door to where I sat in the back. I said hello in response and I felt the most British and accented I have since leaving.

'Where you going, hey?' he asked her.

'Just to town.'

'What you goin' to town for?'

'Just got to drop some things, is all. Mind it.' And she pulled the truck away jerkily.

We drove a little way away from the reservation in the truck. She took us into the trees that skirt the far side. We walked uphill a little way until we came to a clearing. There were bottles strewn everywhere, tyres and large black scaffolds and needles, almost chaos but arranged in a rough circle around a nucleus, a fire pit.

'We tell the kids not to come here so of course they come. We used to put up fences but they just pushed them down. If we stand here too long you'll get a headache. They like to get dizzy off the fumes.'

She points out the still pool gathered where the dirt slopes down. There is a filmy rainbow spilt across it. A dead crow floats bloated belly up in it and I notice then that no birds are singing. There is not a sound aside from the trees swaying, and there is a tangy smell that makes your eyes sting a little. Even the sunlight seems anaemic where it reaches the pool's surface.

'The younger kids have mostly given up on the land, when they just see it dumped on like this. Nobody else wants it in their backyard so the state pays us to dump their shit here. The elders are angry at the young for trading the land for money. The young are angry with the reservation and think there's better stuff for them on the outside that money can buy. They don't speak the language much anymore. But most of them will never leave. You know, before white men came we had a matriarchy. Figure that into your documentary.'

At this point I realised that she was putting herself through telling me this even though it made her uncomfortable, because she felt it was important. I had the thought that she was telling me because she attached importance to me making a documentary, like she had found a vessel for her message to the outside world. But then I dismissed it, because it did not feel like that at all. It felt like she had a lesson for me.

The cesspool sticks with me and the smell will follow me for days. Dump waste on poor people because they are non-people and even if they shout about it no one can hear them. Indians are just layabouts and alcoholics who refuse to get jobs and live off the money they were given for their sacred lands, not so sacred if they chose to sell them anyway, hey? Somebody has to take the collateral damage, to aid progress. In *On the Road* Jack Kerouac had the foresight to say that 'the earth is an Indian thing,' right before he went to a whorehouse to purchase some Mexican Indian women.

I asked Rochelle if she knew who Henrietta Lacks was. She did not. Henrietta Lacks is a mascot of bioethics, and systematic medical experimentation on poor and invisible people. Henrietta Lacks was a working-class African-American woman in the 1950s, which made her a non-person too. Scientists sewed a piece of radium inside her and told her it was aggressive treatment for her cervical cancer. She died eight months later at the age of thirty-one. Without asking they sliced two pieces of tissue from her cervix. They called these cells HeLa.

Thousands of metric tonnes of HeLa have been grown and used for research. The cells of her lady-parts were used to find a polio vaccine and a treatment for Parkinson's and NASA sent some into orbit to see what would happen to human cells in zero gravity. Pharmaceutical companies made billions off the back of her but she is barely remembered and her family lived in poverty. They did not even know about HeLa until scientists asked them twenty-five years after she died if they could take their cells too. In 2010, fifty-nine years after she died, her grave got an epitaph.

*Her immortal cells will continue to help mankind forever.*

Her story is a sad one. But it has light to it. Henrietta Lacks is immortal, she is a time capsule, a legacy in the lady-parts of a poor African-American woman.

Rochelle said, 'What good is that to Henrietta Lacks?'

After that she hardly spoke but insisted on driving me the rest of the way to Winnipeg. She would not take any petrol money but let me buy her a coffee in a diner in town. We had a stilted conversation about my plans, where I was headed next, but it all felt hopelessly futile and I could see her thinking so as she picked at the rim of her Styrofoam cup. After the coffee I said a clumsy thank-you. She said not to mention it and swung herself into her truck. Before she drove away she leant out and said, you take care. I watched it kick up gravel as it clutched its way back onto the road, winding out back in the direction of the distant hunching conifers that camouflage the reservation.

When she had gone I felt a relief I could not put my finger on.

*You take care now, white girl.*

I don't think she meant to seem like she was helping me begrudgingly. She did not take the money and she wrapped my foot up kindly. It seemed like I called something home for her. Like probably she knows somebody that something much, much worse happened to.

*Well, yeah, duh. She was a prostitute. Probably knows a lot about it.*

For a few minutes I felt intensely sick at myself for such an ugly thought. Was I actually put out that Rochelle had not acted like what had happened was a big enough deal, for not taking me to the police or suggesting I should go?

Of course she didn't suggest it. What the hell would I say to them? Something bad maybe nearly happened to me, not sure what something. Rochelle is just a really nice lady that took me in when I was in trouble, she is an angel. When I was not, even. Because nothing bad has happened.

## THE LICHENS OF MANITOBA

Rochelle was right: nothing had happened at all. Although maybe I came close enough for it to mean something. Perhaps my abstract statistic has been accounted for now, so I am pretty much invincible. In a way, I could say that I am a real woman, a real vulnerable woman. An invincible woman.

I have been thinking probably he was not being malevolent, probably if he had known I did not want to he would have tried to make me stay anyway, that he must have thought I was up for it and been surprised when I was not or else he would not have let his catch go so easily. When he realised his mistake he let me go. I reiterate this in a way that sounds both beat and resolute, a promise no one's sure they believe in. Does he still have my shoe?

I stayed in my motel room with comfort food and watched daytime television and started to see about how I get out of here but it gets more complex now as I am leaving the Trans-Canada Highway somewhere just after Winnipeg.

## GREEN IS THE NEW RED

I took time in the motel to Skype Larus, seeing as he has been feeling so neglected. He had been explaining what has been going on with fracking in the UK while I was away. I got a bit down while he was talking, thinking about how far away from it all I am, and the area where the kids hung out behind the reservation, and how I had been avoiding checking home news in too much detail since I left. My home town has been marked out as one of the possible areas to be fracked. There are not even otters in the river like there should be, and the anglers that actually eat the fish are seen as tramps. I think they are smart. Why pay money for a fish bred in a cesspool and pumped with hormones when you can get one with equivalent danger levels of chemicals from the river, for free?

Our rivers are already lifeless and inert, so the threat of chemical contamination is met with a shrug and *well, there is nothing to destroy anyway, we need the energy!* There is no mass resistance in the UK because not enough people can see anything worth the bother of saving. The environment was smuggled off a long time ago, as far back as the Enclosure Acts, when the peasants were denied the right to graze or forage so the land could be exploited more efficiently and the peasants had to leave en masse for the cities so that they could lube up the Industrial Revolution with whale oil, and begin the colonisation of the New World. The upheaval can still be seen now where I am from, where the abandoned towering furnaces of industry still cast their shadows. They are immortalised by J. R. R. Tolkien: that exodus from the green and balmy shires of the Midlands to the fiery forges, the slags and the mine pits of the urbanised Black Country (or Mordor; elvish for 'dark land').

The Environmental Protection Agency in America is downplaying the dangers of fracking and of leaking pipelines. The EPA was started because of the legacy of Rachel Carson. I told Larus about my weird dreams about her. This got Larus on to telling me Rachel Carson's saga.

Rachel Carson worked in a very masculine field, but at home on her 65-acre family farm she was surrounded by women. From a young age she liked to write and read stories about animals and the ocean. Her dad died when she was young and she took over as the provider of the family, supporting her ageing mother. She spent all her time working in biology and looking after her ill family, who just kept dying, taking her two nieces in when her older sister died. She still loved to write and did write many beautiful and scientifically important essays and books about the ocean. She started a strong friendship, which may or may not have been romantic, with a woman named Dorothy Freeman. Dorothy was married and their friendship was mainly through letters, which Dorothy had to share with her husband to prove they were not having a lesbian affair.

A lot of the Big Dogs did not like Ms Carson because they saw her attack on Big Chemical Corporations as a threat to the paradigm of Scientific Progress in post-war America, and also because she was a woman. A jealous man scientist wrote a letter to President Eisenhower in which he said that because Rachel Carson was physically attractive and not married, she was probably a communist. After working really hard to save the planet she died of cancer at the age of fifty-six, and she never made a deal over the fact that her cancer was probably from the pesticides they sprayed over her home. She kept her cancer secret while she wrote *Silent Spring*. Rachel Carson knew very well that her body was not her own, its health in the hands of chemical corporations.

So I was already feeling emotionally fraught when Larus asked me what had happened since we last spoke. There was a big cavernous hole in my narrative so I had to tell him about how I ended up at Rochelle's. I just told him, really casual, no emphasis, and at first he found the thing almost a little funny. He asked me to send him over some of the videos from the semi. I sent them while we were talking about other things, then he opened one up and started to watch. After a minute or so he rubbed his eyebrows in the fashion of someone tired by the weight of something heavy and spherically shaped and difficult to hold.

Larus speaks a little Russian from a fleeting obsession in his twenties while trying on communism for size. The man was speaking Russian. He might have been Siberian. He most likely spoke English. How could he be driving through Canada if he didn't speak basic English, Erin? Either way Larus said he could tell the driver understood me by the way he was talking.

Then Larus ran through the clips with me and translated. *What's wrong, little sourface, are you a long way from home?* It was after that that I started to have what I think might have been a panic attack; something sat on my head and stopped me from breathing, the room went bright as though the walls and ceiling had exploded away from me and I felt simultaneously this gravity and this weightlessness, like falling and floating both at the same time and every breath empty of air.

'Erin?' Larus's voice came at me. 'I think you're having a panic attack, calm down, breathe slow, slooooooow,' and my breathing got shallower but had more substance to it. Because he could not hear me gasping anymore Larus freaked out, raising his voice, saying, 'Erin, Erin, are you still there, are you okay, can you hear me?' It was all very embarrassing.

Because he could not look at my face he looked directly into the webcam, a serious look that wavered the longer he tried to hold it. It only lasted about five seconds but that is uncomfortably long to hold a look on webcam if you think about it. Slowed down by the lag it went through micro-cycles of intensity, reasserting itself. It said, *Look into my eyes and see how serious I am. My face is saying it so hard it can't even keep it up, like it's a wet bar of soap or something. Like, we are that close now. I can be your rock.*

'Erin, I'm really concerned about you and I have a suggestion.'
'What?'
'I have some time now I've finished with the whale data. Let me come and meet you.'

Is he mad? At first I just laugh, but with time for it to sink in I get a little angry. Why is everyone concerned for me? Why is everyone stifling me? Apart from Rochelle, who maybe is trying

to liberate me with her cool indifference. TO WALK FREELY
AT NIGHT!

'You aren't infallible, Erin.'

I told him that if I were a boy he would not be dwelling on
my in/fallibility. He said that's the point. I think if I blur the
driver's face I can probably still use it in the documentary.


## INTO A WORMHOLE

I do not think the tight feeling in my chest, the struggle breathing, like my lungs were filled with tar and every breath in and
out was sucked and pushed through this viscous liquid, I do not
think it had just to do with the semi driver.

It is everything. The semi driver was just the shake that rattled like passing debris, so that I felt the shuttle's fragility. The
documentary is my shuttle and it keeps me going, it is the only
vehicle for carrying on with purpose-propulsion-direction, it
stops me from floating aimlessly into the ether, it keeps me on
track towards that shining light ahead and the feeling that comes
from it.

The rattling of the debris made me look around and realise
the enormity of this task, my journey, its sudden height and
distance. A kind of vertigo, a very sudden awareness. But this is
just a dizzy spell. Because if I do not have this project as a vessel
to move me forward, then what the fuck am I doing and where
am I going, what authority do I have being here?

Today I want very badly to call Mum and Dad, but if I did I
would likely burst into tears, and what for? Imagine how much it
would upset her. She would freak the fuck out. There was nothing she could do about it from home, so what was the point in
putting her through it?

They say in emails that I never call, that they want to speak
with me more often, but they do not understand that I can't do

it that way. We can't carry on in tandem; like the Voyagers dividing from their rocket engines I had to break away completely in order to use the break-off as a kind of propulsion too. I feel bad but it is the way it has got to be.

I checked out coaches and car shares but there is nothing any time soon. I really need to leave Winnipeg so I can catch the carpool I have arranged out of Saskatoon. Then I am staying on a farm outside Edmonton and they are picking me up from outside the town hall on Monday at 4 p.m. The only thing that seems viable is that I hitch again.

*I know this is the kind of thing I wanted to prove should not stop women exerting their right to individual freedom.*

*That is the spirit. .*


## MUSHROOM SPORES MAY FLOAT IN
## OUTER SPACE

So I stood again in a little rest area on Portage Avenue at the city limits extending onto the Trans-Canada Highway, with my thumb out. A semi breached the road; as it got close enough to see me I dropped my arm. The semi sailed past; like holding out a titbit of meat for a falcon at the country fair and baulking at the last second of its swoop to your gloved hand. I thought of Jules and her white van. I swore to keep my arm up the next time.

After half an hour another semi appeared and as it drew nearer I noticed it was slowing. I said to myself, *Come on, let's not be stupid, you just need to get back on the horse, remember.*

Roy chatted on about his home town Allgood in Alabama, US, how he had a little baby girl and had to be a trucker because it paid well and he wanted his baby to go to a good college. But he did not like being a trucker because he was sad about leaving his baby and his wife. He showed me a picture of his baby and wife. His wife was called Amelia, which he said 'Melia,' unless that was just what her name was, and his baby was called Jade. I was thinking a guy who comes from a place called Allgood can't be that bad, and I kept telling myself that. I sat awake daydreaming about how to deal with the recent events when making the narrative of the doc.

There is not much footage of Rochelle; she has been more or less the only person to not be enthusiastic and obliging. And the problem is: how do I show it so that I can make it real like it happened? I have enough that I worry I might inadvertently frame it like she had more significance to what happened than she did, something I do not want to do. I can't figure out how to use her when I edit, without it seeming like I latched on because she had said something that made her sound like a wise old Mother Willow. It was only because of an accident that she happened to me. Just an act of decency or maybe of obligation to humanity.

But I need something to tie the story together, from running in the night and onwards, a bit of narrative over the top of some of the story-less shots of her and the reservation. I thought I might as well play my feelings out with Roy, seeing as we would never meet again.

'Oh, those natives are touchy folks.'

Like he was letting me on his team in a kind of us versus them. I was not sure whose team I was more on, Woman vs White? But it made me think, do I have more of a propensity to feel self-conscious as a kind of voyeur making this film? As a woman, knowing already what it feels like to be an exhibition, to feel eyes on my body? Like the embarrassment I feel when I look in on the glass boxes of taxidermy, towards the possessiveness of 'collect and display.'

*I am doing this for you too, Rochelle!*
*You are doing this for yourself.*

Before this trip I had a pretty obscure idea of what an Indian reservation would even look like; horses, totem poles and alcoholics, based on what I had seen on a programme on the National Geographic channel once. Mum had come in with the vacuum and stood looking a little perplexed at the TV for a few minutes before saying, 'You know, I didn't realise that Indians still existed,' and I had not even thought that was very strange. I do not want Rochelle to be so much a part of the narrative that it seems like I am yoking my feminist problems with hers, even if we share some.

In the late afternoon, where the highway met Regina, I said goodbye to Roy and hopped down from his semi into a sodden rest area a walkable distance from the city. The rain had stopped but the air was damp and clung to the smells and made them sticky; cloying diesel fumes, turf, and the wet on wet of the lakes as I skirted round them.


## TAMING THE SAVAGES

I had a dream about Ms Carson again last night. She was under-water conferring with a concerned-looking delegation of fish who held in their wafered fore-fins tiny hermaphrodite fish infants. The Queen of the Fish was distraught, she wanted some answers.

In all these millions of years the ocean hasn't changed, now there is a new taste in it, she said. The taste came after your peo-ple came so you must have brought it, sour, sharp and fizzing. What is it? Rachel Carson told her that the taste that made the babies hermaphrodites was called synthetic oestrogen and her Womankind had been taking it because they were made to think it would emancipate them but what it also had done was to take their bodies from them, mechanised and controlled, warped to fit the jigsaw.

The Fish Queen did sympathise. She said, 'As fish we know of the Man tyranny that your Womankind face because we are also subject to the tyranny of Mankind, have also been subdued and controlled, but we must come to a compromise.' Rachel Carson promised to be an Ambassador of the Fish to the dry world of above. Like Thoreau casting off the sins of the flesh to attain greater spiritual purity, she swore her chastity to the Fish Queen in order to best fulfil her role as ambassador and prove her devoted kinship.

It is funny that, how a woman denying her biological breeding function is abhorrent, yet men like Thoreau or the virginal Isaac Newton denying their biological breeding functions are *chaste*, as though theirs were an admirable *choice*. What this says is that a woman's body is not her own to choose to keep from a man.

She swore she would never take the pill because it would a) cause the decline of the Fish Kingdom, which could have a knock-on effect on the rest of the underwater realm, her favourite realm, and b) ruin the integrity of the Fish Queen, and she liked the Fish Queen. Plus the pill was made by Bayer, who were disappearing the bees with their neonicotinoids. The Fish Queen swore her in as Ambassador of the Fish.

In Regina I look at a map of Canada and it reads like a pictogram of clusters of neurons. The shape is uniform; where the lines might have been pliant and organic they are neat right angles. The states of Canada are divided in horizontal strips as if Descartes or someone threw down a quadrat and declared it an enlightened territory. Illuminated and user friendly like the satisfying angularity of Enlightenment taxonomies of life; rational flow charts of stable and quantifiable kingdoms that can be pinned to a table and dissected, taken apart and reassembled.

Canadian prime minister John A. Macdonald was the father of the Canadian Pacific Railway, built from east to west in four years from 1881. The Canadian Pacific Railway Company sold the land around its railway in cheap little acred packages marketed and sold to European homesteaders as a Dream of a similar model to the American one. The Wild West was crazy and big and scary but rapid subdivision into super-manageable chunks made it easy to domesticate. Everything within each quadrat was quantified, named, tamed, land and natives included. From their new stronghold of the south-western cities, the CPRC could frontier-bust again into the north, where they built cities on the Gold Fever of the 1890s.

The dawn of railways in Britain brought about the invention of Unanimous Time. Some anthropologists think that marking time was the first step in the construction of the symbolic world, before language, before art. Because, like Einstein said, time is not something absolute. He said different observers order an event differently in time if they are moving with different velocities relative to the observed event. A seemingly simultaneous event can occur differently for other observers (also true of history). That means all measurements involving time as a constant lose their absoluteness.

But the invention of Unanimous Time in Greenwich made the world fall into our order just like the cities are order and the roads and railways are order and the animals are order and genders are order. We invented time and we have sped it up by our own making. The Clock of the Long Now is a clock designed to mark time into the deep, deep future, 10,000 years at a time. It would be built by the Long Now Foundation, in the hope of counterbalancing modern myopia and making us more responsible to the future. But it seems to me just a louder assertion, just a bigger claw reaching. (I REALLY mark time therefore I VERY am.)

In the north, where the highway does not reach, the road-veins are less tangled, like a tree spilling out and reaching all its twig-fingers to the sky in whichever way it feels to fill the space around it. In the north, where the landscape is more immutable, the settlers have been made to oblige it. In the northernmost territories the permanent villages are mostly native because the

First Nations and the Metis and the Inuit know how to bend to the land rather than make the land bend to them. And like Naaja said, they see the animal/mineral/vegetable worlds as a continuum of which we are a part in the same way that Inuit gender is a continuum.

The Trans-Canada Highway was built in the 1950s to link up the cities that Macdonald and the CPRC spawned. And all of this came to happen so that the rational concrete highway could unravel underneath me and lead me forward on my journey like my very own yellow brick road. After two hours or so a young couple picked me up and took me to Saskatoon. The journey was treeless and flat, I could see the clouds move all the way to the horizon, where they would lose their shape and amalgamate into one big haze, the blue sky stretching over me like a dome. They left me on a busy road and from there I met my carpool quickly, with a smiley man named Steve who was heading to his hometown for a cousin's wedding.

## THE BUFFALO AND THE PASSENGER PIGEON

INT. CAR — *camera in Erin's hand taking in the outside of her window — road sign flashes past, 'You are leaving Saskatoon, please come back soon!' —*

*flat plains behind a low flickering fence, stretched out as far as one can see, sickie-yellow and bleached by the sun — no glint like there should be — no pastoral quilt trimmed with hedgerows — monotonous sprawling land, dirty and dead and coaxed and quenched with rotating sprinklers, wide and uniform and on giant scales — a humming that should be insects but is diminished and croaky like an echo from giant machines that even look small against the crop desert — now and then a metal structure bent like a crouching pterodactyl butting the ground —*

**Erin:** It smells

**Steve:** Yep. Welcome to the hydraulic fracturing capital of Canada. There's been fracking here for fifty years, but nowadays it's goin' haywire. Around abouts third-biggest petroleum reserve in the world

*— Erin turns the camera to face Steve in the driver's seat — red cap, dark green North Face gilet — he turns to the camera, smiles haltingly, turns back to the road, shifts his hands on the wheel to steer from the top —*

**Steve:** Then there's your tar sands. And the forests. Half of Alberta is forest. It's all in the north. And over half of the forest is ripe for harvest. Yep. You could say Alberta runs on selling itself. Alberta is a goddam whore

*— he laughs, a short honk of a laugh — a shadow passes over his face because a cloud goes under the sun — he points to a harrier out of the window, silhouetted in the sky —*

**Steve:** That's a harrier. My pop used to point out all the birds to me. I don't remember most of the birds. But for some reason I always remember to recognise the harrier

*— he carries on glancing back at the bird from the road until he cannot anymore without craning his neck —*

**Steve:** I used to think all these environmental types were just out to scaremonger. But then when I worked the tar sands I changed my mind. And you know, I can't get my head around why I ever doubted them. These guys who just want to see the world green.

Over these corporations with big money in their pockets

*— he talks about it all with an odd kind of affection — custodial attentiveness that makes it seem as though he is talking as part of the Albertan psyche rather than out of a personal fondness or interest —*

**Steve:** But hey. Who am I to moan? Driving my car?

*— he sits quietly for a few seconds, as though waiting for her to cut the camera — agitatedly, he fidgets his hands, reaches to the glove box —*

**Steve:** You want a mint?

*— he unwraps a mint between his fingers with his wrists steering the wheel from the top — the camera shudders as Erin reaches for a mint —*

## CUT

## GOT LAND? THANK AN INDIAN

Steve drove me all the way into Edmonton to where I was being picked up even though it was out of his way. He took the petrol money and gave me his email so he could see himself in the finished product when it came about. I thought about all the footage I have, about how Steve was not really talking about what I had told him my documentary was about. But he was talking about how Alberta is a whore and even if he did not quite know it, he was talking indirectly about women too, and the significance that it took a woman with a stolen body to write *Silent Spring.*

Sam's parents left the farm a few days ago for a fortnight, to visit his mum's family on their reservation over in British Columbia. Sam is a couple of years older than me and Berry is seventeen. They both have similar chin-length raven-black hair, but Berry's face is much too soft and pretty for them to look too much alike, although they both have the same defiant jawbone. I had to do a bit of introspection and even read back over our emails to try to figure out why I had presumed they were a white family. Maybe it was the all-Canadian-sounding names.

The homestead is just north of Rocky Mountain House, a small town around two hours away from Edmonton. The drive leading up to the homestead from the main road is unpaved and winds through pine trees. Two chickens scuttled out of the way of the car as we pulled up the drive. In the clearing of the forest that surrounds their house, which is a large cabin, there is a totem pole reaching the height of the cabin and half again. I did not want to ask just yet how typical this is. There is a small shed to the right of the cabin and behind the trees fall out onto a meadow where they have a vegetable plot, paddies, a chicken coop and a shed with four yellow plastic kayaks stacked against it. At the far end a wide stream marks the boundary to their land.

Around the chicken-roost shed I counted five chickens, and more wandering around. They collect the eggs from the roost every morning and sometimes they eat the chickens. In a pen next to the roost were three speckled pigs, mucking about, two larger and one smaller. They take the bigger ones for breeding every year and raise up the piglets for market, keeping just one back to slaughter themselves for cured meat. The smaller of the three pigs was the keeper and they were fattening her up. The chickens, one pig, fish they catch from the river and the things they shoot hunting are the only meat they eat.

We grazed the pigs, letting them out from the paddy to forage through the forest for mushrooms and roots and berries and worms and things. We were assigned one pig each. I learned to move them by tap-tapping them on the flank with a stick and manoeuvring them with my legs. I followed my pig close because he kept moving and I was frightened of losing him.

The forest was awake with sound, a medley of territorial and cat calls. Now and again I would zone in on a trill I thought I knew, like picking up on a phrase recognised on a foreign street. Blackbird, wren, wood thrush, starling. And squirrels chattering at us from the trees, him digging up their nuts with his snout.

Sunlight filtered down through the canopy in diagonal beams and motes floated through them. My pig chattered happily and I was thinking to myself, yes, pig, this is what happiness is; when alone, being alone without people or people things, noticing self-acutely, and with a kind of fondness.

I asked if the chickens ever run away. Sam said they don't because they feed them and the chickens are happy here. I asked if they ever get eaten. He said Grey the dog chases away the weasels and the cats, but sometimes he misses one and they lose chickens. This just happens sometimes, and since the chickens are not exactly theirs they can't get angry about them being taken away, they just feed them and sometimes the chickens give them eggs and seem to accept that every now and then they kill one to eat. I think this is very philosophical.

For dinner we had fish that had been smoked in their smoke house, and vegetables and potatoes from their plot. I am staying put for a few weeks, to decompress before the final push. This is going to be the perfect place to go into the whole helping-out-a-stranger-in-exchange-for-food-and-board thing. Like being a Samaritan in old times, but the idea is that I learn shit about organic living.

In the documentary this will be a few weeks of time-out skimmed over in a few short clips of idyllic pastoral living, like Kerouac, McCandless et al. working on flour mills and the like to pay their way across the States. Rest time and recuperation, a big breath before the deep plunge. Since I got to Sam's I have this enduring feeling of serenity. I have caught it up for now, the thing, and its glow gives off enough warmth to bask in.

# BECOMING A RIVER AND SLEEPING
# LIKE A RIVER

Sam and I took kayaks out today. The lake was pellucid and the air barely moved. As we cut into the water with our paddles we startled fish. We could see them a metre underneath us the water was so clear. There was the sound of moving water and the feeling of being pulled away. The feeling of sitting in a little vessel on top of an indifferent intensity, the feeling of being buoyant on the skin of depth. Big swathes of time would pass where neither of us would say anything to the other, just the rhythmical dipping of the paddles and the tinkle of drips from the blades. Behind us the mountains rose, diminished into lethargy by a hazy film of distance. Above the deep green forest, black shapes hovered and dipped.

We made it most of the way back upriver but in the end, when I especially was lagging and hardly pushing back against the current, we landed the kayaks and walked the rest. Sam drove to pick them up later and I went with him for company while a friend of his who had come to stay, a guy from the town called Ollie, made dinner with Berry. I can't help but stare at Sam every time his talking gives me an excuse to. His hands are always dirty. Not gross dirty, but earthy from the farm. I might have been paying a lot of attention to him to notice that his hands are always earthy. Heavy eyelids like crescent moons.

In the truck he said, half joking, 'You're good in a kayak, I didn't know you had kayaks in England.' I told him we do, and that I was good because I had been in kayaks lots as a Girl Guide. He found the fact that I was a Girl Guide really amusing. He said, 'I hear you sing Indian songs around the campfire too?'

I told him there was a song about an Indian in a kayak we used to sing, actually.

He said, 'That's funny. We never sing about Girl Scouts.'

# A REAL MOUNTAIN

Sam said he did not know why I would want to go there, but he took me anyway: the famous Banff Park. The sky was practically cloudless and everything crisp with colour. Ollie rode up front with Sam, so I sat in the truck bed with Grey. To look out over the top of the van's roof from the back meant positioning my face in the stream of air forced over it, which stung my eyes and wrapped my hair into tight little knots. The only viable way to sit was facing backwards on the bench with Grey wrapped over me, because even though Sam said he always rode in the back I was nervous about him getting excited and bailing over the side.

Not being able to see ahead on the journey gave me a novel perspective. The Rockies started to crawl into my view. Grey knew them, his eyes twitching to them frantically. I watched the fixed point where the road disappeared at the horizon as it all rushed past and towards it, the mountains sluggishly because they had further to go.

I am getting towards the real Wild North now, like I had imagined the frontiers-land, the Yukon, to look. Not quite there yet but I can start to feel its tremor. Looking at it, you get why all the Mountain Men do not care to keep any company if they can just keep company with the mountains, so sure and majestic and other-than-you-are.

But the road rushing away underneath does something strange. Makes it feel spectral, staged, to be seen but not really felt, like how walking through an underwater tunnel at the Sealife Centre is not anything like swimming in it. Every now and then the sides of the road would rise up and show the flat innards of some great rock or crust, layers of sediment and scars where the road cuts through.

Walking through the forest, Sam chose the least scenic but most secluded route, leading through thick pine forest. Grey rushed around in a frenzy, snuffing up stories, like maybe the coyote that killed its prey dead here, or a three-year-old hare that was caught by its leg already lamed a week ago in another scuffle, that time with a wolverine, and it knew that it could not be so lucky twice. It ran some way then lay down so as not to prolong the inevitable and gave itself to the coyote.

Grey smelled its before and its death smell, then much later in the walk its after, where the coyote had passed it in its scat days after. He smelled the terror of the ground squirrel in its burrow but he catalogued the scent and left it because it was too deep out of the reach of his snout and there was much too much else to read to make time for digging. There was smell around a grand old tree with a thick trunk like the leg of a diplodocus and he ran around it excitedly yapping and cocked his leg to it. Perhaps it was a wolf smell and he was calling out to them and leaving a message in case they came back. Perhaps he was accepting the challenge of the scent of his primordial nemesis: the cat of the wild, the mountain lion.

Sam walked us through like a heritage tour guide who has been decades in the game so has all the knowledge but waning enthusiasm. He pointed out the *Polyporaceae* fungi, of the *Badius* genus, jutting from a tree, a pruned brown palm cupping water. He took a skeletal beehive, paper thin, a snakeskin doubled and redoubled, folded and helixed on itself, broke it apart in his hands to show us the chambered innards and crumbled it absently. It fell away like ashes.

He said, 'Don't you see that that is what it is? Empty? It

is a museum to itself, like someone took the whole thing and replaced it with a replica, put it aside for us to experience.' At first I thought he meant the beehive and I thought, that is very deep to get about a beehive, I am sure the bees have just moved home. But as we went along I began to think he might be talking about the park itself, like it was all a vacant symbol to him.

We walked for maybe a couple of hours and eventually came onto a lake from inside the trees. It was that opaque and turquoise blue that you can just about accept in photographs but on seeing it there in the real-world landscape I was incredulous. It had a kind of powdered texture, as if a giant had painted the blue of the sky and the white of the clouds and then swilled out their paintbrush in the water of the lake. Peyto Lake is fed by a glacier, Sam said, and in the warmer months the meltwater takes the rock flour it ground up underneath itself and spills it into the lake. When this happens the water of the lake gets called *glacial milk*.

I told them I had seen this before, in the very wildest place I know at home: my old quarry. The quarry was for limestone but it had been abandoned for years so filled up with rainwater. The rainwater mixing with the limestone dust makes a similar rock milk, although it is not as dramatic, but eerie, the hacked cliffs and flats still and blinding white like a moonscape doused with floodlights.

The quarry was fenced off because it was dangerous and also because it was a Site of Special Scientific Interest. Hunks of orange rust char it, the remains of miscellaneous pieces of machinery, but it is heavy with the presence of the fossils in its 430-million-year-old sediment. There are trilobites from the Silurian period when life was just beginning to crawl out of the sea, and as though to mirror this there are shallow pools writhing with rare newts. There is my nesting pair of peregrine falcons, which Sam says are considered particularly spiritual by Native Americans and Ancient Egyptians. Driven to local extinction in places by DDT in the 1960s, I tell them, but clawing back in this graveyard to humanity. Sometimes when I am there I imagine it is the far future and I am the last human on Earth.

But the wild of Peyto Lake is the conceptual opposite. It is modelled on life before, but really it is just a simulation. Sam made me see this. He seemed unfazed by the place and sat on the pebbled shore throwing sticks into the water for Grey. On the far shore we could see ants looking down into the lake from an overhang which Ollie told us was designated the most scenic viewpoint in Canada. He asked us if we didn't think it could be as beautiful seen from the other way round.

I was glad that being with the boys gave me a backstage pass into the park and made me different to all the other tourists, even though that was exactly what I was. Sam probably couldn't help thinking I was not any better than them either.

'It's just a spectacle to them,' Sam said.

Ollie laughed and told him to shut up, the park was beautiful, and if it weren't for all the tourists they would not have the money to keep it open and conserved.

'It's beautiful, yes, but in a different way to how it should be. Doesn't it worry you that it will end up with only preserving real mountains, picture-postcard ones? With waterfalls and snow on top and its image reflected in a lake? What about where we live? How long until the river is polluted because people have real mountains put aside to go visit in a park?'

And Sam is right. At home our quilted landscape is fully exploited and the wild is relegated to special parks. Spaces set aside for preservation are museums, and their segregation makes it okay to debase anything outside of them. Parks are time capsules and that itself seems a futile admission of the falling-apart of nature.

I chewed on my sandwich. Ollie took his time formulating a reply. 'But no one would care about mountains at all if there wasn't somewhere for them to come and see real ones.' I could not disagree with him either.

## NO PERSON IS AN ISLAND

Mum had sent me frantic messages over Facebook and to my email to say she had had a really bad dream about something happening to me and to ring her. My phone had been dead for a week at the bottom of my bag so I had not seen Mum ring. I phoned her up and she had a fit, first begging me to come home if I was going to keep on pulling stupid stunts like that, disappearing without contact, then when I promised I would not again she burst into tears.

*My only child, my daughter.*

But Mum on the phone is just a little voice, so small and so far away. She is standing on a dot and the balloon gets bigger and worse still Dad on the phone, standing on another dot, sounding tired and saying why do you have to do things like this to your mother, you know what her nerves are like. Tired in a way I have heard many times before. Tired, like you are always so far away, always have been so distant, we have always been stood on these dots getting further and further away from each other.

This is only the second time I have heard their voices since I left. I should call home more. But she is crying on the phone and yes it hurts a little, *I miss you but you know I'd never say*, but also it feels good; she is crying but she can't bring me home. The power of their summons has nothing on me now. I am becoming my own person apart from them.

Before me her name was Jennifer and she worked as a secretary and before that she was as young as I am and she had ideas about who Jennifer was and what Jennifer wanted and what she wanted was to go to Italy and learn Italian and be an au pair and before that still she was a child, a little girl called Jennifer who wanted to be a ballerina, like she later wanted me to be. She had a whole self before me and I will never get to that part of her. She is a person with a name: Jennifer. Jennifer and Brian. Not just Mum and Dad. But I have always been Erin first and daughter after. Mum, Dad, Erin. Why is it we do that?

It is a burden to have a mother that wants so much of you, but it must also be a burden to be an overly attached mother, like why can't I just shake the daughter from me? You grew out of me but you never really grew away?

*I am reminding you that your name is Jennifer.*
*Daughter; my parasitic twin.*


## THERE IS NO WORD FOR ANIMAL IN THE DAKOTA LANGUAGE

There is the bigger picture and then there is sex. Having sex grounds you and brings you out of the bigger picture. It makes life more livable and less giant and incomprehensible. It makes sense why people settle down and have babies, really. It makes sense to push an idea of love and stability to stop people from feeling so rebellious and righteous and born to save the world. I suppose that was why Thoreau and the Unabomber and all those guys took oaths of abstinence. Plus it was a handy way to illegitimise women.

Because when it suited men historically, sexuality was a thing that women had and they were above. In Greek times and in the story of the Fall, we were not allowed a say in decision-making because we were completely and utterly ruled by our sexy, lusty desires. Men could do without sex and did not see the point in dirtying themselves in such a way, and could therefore keep rational heads on their unsexy bodies.

What must have happened in recent times is that the male genome mutated like a grasshopper driven into frenzy and metamorphosing into a locust for lack of food. And now the clitoris is just a relic of that bygone time when women needed pleasure from sex to encourage procreation. Like the appendix is a relic of a time when people ate grass. No one eats grass anymore.

Sam feels heavy to lie with. He feels anchored. He feels like he bends space—time and the groove of it pulls at me. He smells like dirt, in a good way, like his skin is smoothed over with clay. We were tentative and very precious, a bit clumsy also, like children holding tiny mice. He has a freckle on his right eyelid. It is in the crease of his eyelid so that you can only see it when he is sleeping. When I pointed it out to him he said, 'Yeah, I know, my ex used to like that one,' and this made me inconceivably sad for just a millisecond.

We started on the big talks that often come post-sex. The ones you use to excavate the depths of others. I said I did not know why everyone did not take themselves off to new places, that it didn't even cost much if you did it right.

'If everyone did it then the world would grind to a halt.'

'Well, would that be so bad a thing?'

'If everyone did it how would any culture preserve itself?'

I thought of Naaja then, walking herself into the big tundra all alone, waif-small on the grey iced turf, a burden on her tiny shoulders, my own so easily thrown off and abandoned.

*And why does she not throw hers down?*

'What about places you care about? Who would look after places? Most Indians were nomadic once, but now they sit around in poverty fighting oil and mineral prospectors off land they see as sacred.'

That one stumped me. A pang of guilt for the small cold ring of protesters gathered around the would-be drill site back home.

'I just think if there's something you don't like about something you shouldn't go off in search of something better just for yourself. You should fix it, take what you have and make it better for everyone. Things don't change just by wanting them too,' he said.

*But you don't understand that is what I am doing.*

We lay awake talking and he started to tell me more and more, peeling away each layer of his skin, and in a way I wish he had not because now I have seen his innards I am going to end up really liking him. And that really will not do when I have to leave soon. He told me the story of the totem pole.

'On the bottom there is an orca, our family crest. It brings luck and will come to the help of the family when any of them are vulnerable. From my nana's house you can see an ocean cove and sometimes when they are near, in the shallows herding fish to eat, you can see the orcas arching out of the water, you can go out in a boat to meet them. Underneath it is the salmon carving, the symbol of the reservation of Salmon Water because all of the family crests are water animals in Salmon Water.

'We also have a guardian animal. This is the carving above that looks a bit like a dog but more like a bird with ears, I think. The wolf is a really charged animal and helps with sickness. Not so much physical sickness, that's more the orca, this one stands for the sickness of our family's heart, or sadness.

'And the otter is above the wolf. The otter is thought of as being mischievous and bright, happy and curious. The otter is my ma as a child because she was always sunny and laughing and hiding herself away so that my nana would get scared but my grandpa never did because he knew she would always let herself be found in the end. The otter is from the times they had before she got taken away.

'And then the thunderbird stands above them. The thunderbird is a commemoration of bad things that are acknowledged but best not talked about. It brings thunder by beating its wings and lightning when it blinks its eyes, and it is a killer of the orca. We show reverence towards it. It broke apart our family.

'My aunt and uncle carved and painted it from a cedar my

grandpa had picked out years before he died, because he knew she would let herself be found again one day even though they hadn't seen her since she was three years old. The first time they met again was when she was twenty-six, they held a potlatch feast and gave her the totem, and my ma cried herself to sleep for days in secret.

'She couldn't move back to the reservation and neither could dad to his. They didn't have the identity cards to prove their indigenous heritage, because when they were both children they were taken from their parents by Indian agents and put into adoption with white families. Dad only had his two sisters left when they repatriated. Before he got taken he was being brought up by his grandparents because his dad left and his ma died, and they are dead now too.'

He stopped talking but in a deliberate kind of way, like he was done now and that was all there was to say of the matter. I suppose he has rationalised it so well as to be able to talk it through, seeing as that is what his parents do, he says, with their speaking jobs. For the first time there was not a laughing cadence through every sentence he spoke.

This made me sad for two reasons; because it was sad in itself, and because by telling me he was signifying that he expected never to see me again after my short stay and it was therefore entirely reasonable to open up so soon about something so personal.

He said he did not know how to feel about his white grand-parents. That his mum's adoptive parents were paid to take her in and his dad's saw themselves as martyrs for saving him from the reservation where his real parents killed themselves with alcohol.

He also at some point said something really specific that I have not ever thought about before. He says they are being disappeared, but no other culture gets worn on so many T-shirts. He was being light-hearted, so for something to say I thought it would be okay to bring up Rochelle and all the things she had said about her white boyfriend's nicknames for her. I laughed and said it was kind of funny, and surely that is all you could find it now looking over it because it was so stupid.

'How did you manage to get into a reservation with a camera anyway?'

I had to tell him the whole story because I suppose that was the only credible way I was getting in there uninvited. He listened with a frown on his face. When I had finished he made me want to cry again by telling me a girl on his course at university had been researching murdered indigenous women who disappeared off the highways in Canada for her dissertation, and was murdered by two white men before she finished it. I just mumbled that it could have been a lot worse, then.

He looked redder with the light from the window on him and my own arms looked yellow. I listened to the sound of my voice as if on playback and wondered how I had ever got there, in that unfamiliar room, feeling suddenly blank and inert.


## MONOCULTURES OF THE SPIRIT

Agitations. Larus desperately in contact. Reiterated points: you've been stayed put a while, you're planning on leaving soon, right, you need to keep well ahead of winter, don't forget what you set out to do.

'I haven't. I'm still working on it here.'

'Do you not think you might be making excuses to stay put?'

'No, I think—'

'Just have a think about it. I'm surprised at you is all. Didn't think you of all people would get distracted by a boy.'

Sam could tell I was irritated afterwards. He asked what Larus had said to make me so sour. I did not tell him in case he thought I had taken it to heart. He kept asking questions about Larus, like how much we talk, how old he was, things that irritated me more with their connotations.

'I just wonder why a man old enough to be your dad, who begot five children and who probably thinks we're all "children of Earth," and that age sets no boundaries for kindred spirits, is interested in your "feminist project."'

'I really don't think that it's any of your business.'

I wanted to make it sting like I did not care what he thought. For a second he looked like a cat I had splashed with water for no reason other than to see it squirm. I should not have. It was my fault for making Larus sound worse than he is when I described him just for comedic effect, really.

Ah, the burden of being a feeling woman! But I am not about to let myself fulfil the very expectations I set out to subvert. I am fully committed to the project and ready to get on with it because winter is catching me up.

I told Sam I needed to leave because his friend Ollie had mentioned driving to Dawson Creek via Prince George to make some deliveries in his pick-up, and it would be stupid to miss the lift. He said it was an indirect route to Dawson and that I could hitch later on or he would drive me. When I said I hadn't been doing much on the documentary and I had to get on with things, he said, 'Oh, of course, for art's sake,' sarcastically.

That was just one of his momentary lapses, he was soon right back to his jovial self, only being at the same time distant with me. In the morning I could not even tell if he was mad or not.

'Well, I'm going, then.'

'Have a nice trip, thanks for stopping by.'

'It's been really nice to meet you.'

'Yeah, same with you.'

'Aren't you going to at least pretend to be sad that I'm going?'

'What, try to stop you? That wouldn't be very feminist of me.'

It was a deliberate game of trying to be the most unaffected.

So I shrugged and shouted bye to Berry and turned down the path towards Ollie waiting in his pick-up.

## TOP TIPS ON HOW TO BE A TRAVEL WRITER

The highway was empty, and our headlights pooled out ahead. For miles we would see other vehicles in the opposite lane only, and only sporadically. A hump in the road appeared, so that we could not see the behind of it as we rose and trees spilled on either side to its edge. Mounting the rise, we saw a large dark shape up ahead, maybe twenty metres. Ollie slowed the van and as our light poured up and over it we saw it was a small black bear. It stopped in the opposite lane, one paw raised limply, and looked at us. Ollie stopped the van to let it pass.

The bear stayed put, lowering its head like a dog in submission. It was small and misplaced against the wide cut of the road. It tapped the ground with its paw, hesitant, testing the cool density of the concrete, warily reading the dead-eyed, no-legged creature that stood still before it. Then it bunched itself up and bounded in front of the van, its four legs gambolling, and we watched as its rump shimmied off into the trees.

From outside Edmonton we had rejoined the Yellowhead Highway, a branch of the Trans-Canada Highway system which veers north-west, breaking off from the due westerly route and connecting Manitoba, Saskatchewan and Alberta with British Columbia. The Yellowhead is named for Tête Jaune, aka Pierre Bostonais, an Iroquois-Metis fur trader and explorer who in turn got his name from his blond hair, homage to his part-white origin.

In 1819 Tête Jaune led a brigade of the Hudson Bay Company through a pass in the Rocky Mountains, a piper with a ditty of bounties and a whole band of rats to follow. The pass now bears his name and from this the highway takes its.

I was back on the road and it felt good to see the horizon reeling in, all the temporary things staying just where I left them. The feeling that had kept me still the past few weeks was less of a captivation and more like a rabbit trap, wire noose on my leg. It was not aligned with my purpose.

*And what is that exactly?*

From Edmonton the highway slides though the Rockies of Jasper National Park fast and sure like a river. The weather was sullen, and low clouds sulked around the grey and shadowed mountains, brooding thunder. Pine smells crept osmotically through the damp air and the open windows. Breaks in the cloud cover would stream down sun in spotlights, directing me further and further on the unfolding road, enchanting, pied-pipering me like Tête Jaune with all his little rodents. Big eagles perched on telephone wires, silhouetted in the low light.

We arrived at our halfway point after Ollie had made a stop for his delivery.

'This is Prince George, where we leave the Yellowhead Highway and strike out north to Dawson. Yellowhead continues right the way into the Pacific, then by ferry onto Graham Island.'

The Hudson Bay Company drew a straight line right across Canada, not even conceding to the ocean. A branding of ownership. The other side of Prince George is nicknamed the Highway of Tears for all the unsolved murders. Sam said between Prince George and Prince Rupert at the coast, from the sixties until the last one a few months ago, something like forty have happened. Women picked up off the side of the road. Almost exclusively indigenous women.

Ollie said, 'Bet ya glad you don't have to hitch that highway.'

Could I ever have hitched that highway? I mean, could it have been the same highway for me as for them?

The next day we left the Yellowhead exactly where the designated murder zone started. Yellowhead spilled out, continuing Tête Jaune's trail through the Rockies, stalking a century and a half behind him. Him stone cold dead and unaware of his namesake (and yes, well, at least he will be remembered forever) or of the legacy of highways for indigenous women who have no namesake, only anonymous tears.

And along such a highway by 1 p.m. we had reached Dawson Creek. Ollie left me at Mile 0 of the Alaskan Highway, where Chris McCandless took a picture with the big road sign, extending 1,523 miles, all the way to Fairbanks, Alaska. Tomorrow just past Fort Nelson I will enter the Yukon, the crazy Wild North and the place that cast a spell on so many Mountain Men, where the ghosts of old miners made Kerouac wonder. The Klondike, where Jack London the wolf-man found himself.

## GOLD FEVER IN THE YUKON

From Fort Nelson I got completely stuck. Two full days to get a ride. I was not the only one trying to hitch and I had stayed down-road from the others in a long, sparse queue. There was a woman in first place who looked to be in her late twenties when I passed her in the morning after staying overnight in a hostel near the road. I wanted to interview her but she was not very approachable. She had been waiting for a lift for three whole days. Then I passed a guy who was maybe in his mid-thirties, scruffy with long, lank hair. He said he

had been waiting two days but he felt good about today and he wished me luck. I watched him stand and wave and jab out his thumb, jumping up and down, and wondered how he thought he would ever get a lift acting like a crazy person.

The girl got a lift on my first day. I only counted fifty-four cars that day. There was one woman who gave me a look that was not just judgemental, it had, considering her strangeness to me, a terrible anger to it like I had not seen before. I gave her the finger and the woman gave an even angrier honk.

I felt bored and restless but of course there would be times when I did not get picked up right away. I imagine the guy has had a much less fluid journey from wherever he came from. The next day, monotonous, feeling quite hopeless, I set myself down again at a distance from the guy, who looked like he might have stayed out all night. Then a really bad thing happened. A semi pulled in front of where I was sat on my bag. The window rolled down and the guy inside said, 'Hey, I can take you to Whitehorse.' I could see down the road that the thirty-something guy was stood with his arms out above his head imploringly.

'Don't take this the wrong way but I usually only pick up girls. You can't always trust the guys. Especially if they look like bums.'

I tried to compute the ethics quickly as I collected my things from the ground as slowly as I could.

*It would be completely hypocritical to take advantage.*

Well, if I didn't take the lift he certainly was not going to pick up the guy. I raised my hand to the guy in what I hoped was an apologetic salute, but I do not think he took it that way because he threw his rucksack to the floor and started kicking it.

'Don't worry too much about him, he's just another bum trying to get to Alaska. They're usually younger and sometimes they look sweet so someone picks them up. I reckon he'll wait maybe a week. Maybe his luck will come in and it will rain, then some old dude might take pity on him.'

The driver's name was Ron. Ron said sometimes there are ten hitchhikers at any one time trying to get to Fairbanks. He asked me where I was heading and I told him, Fairbanks. This made him laugh. I told him about the documentary.

He said, 'I like that. And why not ladies, hey? I got a little clue for you, though. You might not get a great reception when you tell the folk you meet in Alaska what you're doing. Alaskans *hate* these guys.'

'Why do they hate them?'

He said they are hated because they flock from all over North America and some from Europe too. He said they hear the call of the wild and they come running like apostles to it. Usually they get themselves in trouble somewhere and some rescue team has to bail them out.

Is that not everyone's problem the whole world over? Shall I call it *saturation*? Like Larus's yoga-mat tourists. We live in an overpopulated world now, much to the annoyance of Ted Kaczynski. There is almost not enough space left for the Mountain Men. Back when there were just a couple of hapless truth seekers then maybe they were viewed with a kind of affection. Maybe McCandless of hapless potato fame was viewed with a kind of affection, before his followers followed him.

When we crossed into the Yukon after Fort Nelson, Ron pointed out the little white sign and said, 'Welcome to Yukon!' just as I read it. I pointed the camera at everything I was seeing, not much, just a long, long road lined with tall thin trees. I think he found it endearing or something. He started to talk pointedly, like he was giving me something useful for the camera, so I directed it at him. He spoke like an overly trained actor.

'You know the *real* pull of the north has always been minerals. You know the Klondike Stampede, right? In the 1800s? Well, there's a brand-new one going on right now.'

He nodded confidingly.

'Not just gold, mind. Zinc and copper and uranium. It's all

different now, of course. Mostly the work's done by big Chinese companies, with GPS and bulldozers. Ain't as many beardy guys with pans. That's what the north was built on. Guys came seeking their fortune and the hardy ones stuck around. But a bunch came and couldn't hack it. Like these young guys now, they had this romantic idea of what it'll be like. But it'll kill ya. They went running home to the sunny south with scurvy and their toes missing.'

He paused for a bit to whistle and look out of the window. The trees to our left began to slope down and behind them a whole other sea of them rose up. Then we had a view of the mountains in the distance, the green trees blanketing right the way over them.

The first Klondike gold rush was in 1896. Adam Smith, the amoral moral philosopher, wrote *The Wealth of Nations* a century before that. Adam Smith saw the wilderness as if it were made of bricks of gold and timber, to be utilised to create wealth, and he saw the creation of wealth as a moral agenda and he reduced complexity to simple constituents as though the illusion of things could be stripped away to reveal their basic and authentic and truthful essences. But what he was doing was taking paper and cutting it to shape, saying, 'Look what shape I found when I trimmed away the excess, a chair!' when what he really did was to cut the paper to the shape of a chair.

He broke the world into mechanical pieces and put the natural world outside the world of man so as to justify a particular form of economic and political organisation (capitalism) and philosophical position (individualism) as natural. He was trying to morally justify selfishness. A sperm whale is so called because stabbing one in the head with a harpoon makes it spurt forth oil in a way that reminded whale hunters of ejaculation. And if a sperm whale is just an oil ejaculator and not an emotionally complex being then it is okay to go about slaughtering them.

'It's beautiful, ain't it? Don't it look quiet? The last great wilderness.'

He took it all in, sucked it all in through his nostrils. I am so close now and I can feel it. It feels like humming in your mouth, but masked by something loud like engine noise so no one else can really hear it but the vibrations take over your whole face and throat.

'But we got things like the Peel Watershed. Places like pristine wilderness. Mines're leaking arsenic and crap into the water. Some folk think it'll be a shame if the Peel gets contaminated. But Yukon is mining. It's kind of its soul. It's a place the little guy can make something of his lot. Cut down some trees, build himself a cabin, live a simple life. You know, still now in theory anyone  can stake a claim to mine someplace out here. It's a free country. Libertarian. And it won't stop. Them people are crazed. They're thinking, "I gotta go get it cuz if I don't then some other asshole will."'

He chuckled to himself. Then a song came on the radio and he stopped talking to half-sing to it. He sang it quietly, and only the words he knew, which were not many, and the rest he kind of mumbled. He whistled the bridge to the chorus.

While he whistled I looked out of the window. Beautiful, yes, but in a different kind of way, with a creeping melancholy to it. My first-felt elation had sapped away and left something hollowed out. I thought about the ghosts of miners that Jack Kerouac wondered about. What would they have said to Kerouac if they could have talked? Would they have told him that the emissions his exhaust was pumping, driving all over America and not giving much of a damn about anything but himself, were poisoning the air like the coal did their black lungs? That their mines had dug up uranium and mercury and cadmium, making bonds in his nostrils each breath he took? *If we'd have known then what we know now*, maybe they would have said.

And what would I have to say to the ghost of Jack Kerouac? It was all very well and good for you, Jack Kerouac, but things were different then. The not-giving-a-damn-thing is harder to get behind now. Not just because I am a woman, but because the yoke is not so easy to throw down when you know the weight just gets transferred to the many other beasts of burden.

## ARE MUTUALISMS A FORM OF LOVE?

My first lift took me as far as Haines Junction, where I had to wait only another couple of hours for a lift all the way to Beaver Creek. The roadside trees cloaked pools of water that held their own strange colours. Behind them the mountains grew again, some in the far parts ephemeral and almost-there, the snow on top like cut ice against the sharp sky today but probably gone tomorrow.

Then the road ran straight towards a big mountain, washed out by the sun, the huge long lake at its base luminously blue, bluer than the sky blue. Kluane Lake grew wider and wider as we got closer until it was as wide as an ocean and we were right on top of it. The water almost touched the road but just kept away, lapping against the gold sand for miles and miles. The road then curved over the sand towards the mountain, and for a moment there was so much of the sand that you could squint so as not to see the vague plant-life in it and pretend it was a desert and the rest was mirage.

Then the road ran brassy under the foot of the mountain and around the lake edge as if to brag about what it had tamed, as though this great feat of engineering should be lauded for its arrogance. But the mountains and the lakes do not care because they can't. And under the road the rivers flow on and on back to the sky.

Online, a little yellow envelope flashed itself at me, from Sam. I did not open it. It is best to leave it for now. Soon I cross into Alaska. There is nothing to do but feel glad that things are back the way they were always supposed to be. And this evening the mountains look rich and blue and fully dimensional.

## ENGLAND, JUST LIKE AMERICA, BUT DIFFERENT

TO REMEMBER: A deer on the road running from our vehicle, confused and running with the road, not from it. We slow the vehicle to a crawl, honking, trying to throw it off. It half-turns, its eyes bulging in fear and confusion at its entrapment. And then its epiphany; it breaks away to the forest.

From Beaver Creek the highway crosses the border and goes on a long way before it splits to Fairbanks or Anchorage. I took a lift across the border to get out where the road forks so that I could hitch with the traffic that was solely headed for Fairbanks. The geographical border had a 'Welcome to Alaska' sign and four flags erected. They were Canada, America, Alaska and I suppose the other must have been the Yukon's flag. I almost forget that Alaska is a part of America; it seems to me a far nobler place.

I caught a ride with a young couple who seemed to have had an argument about picking me up. The man at the border inspection station was wearing a blue uniform instead of the nostalgic red one. He said, 'Welcome to the United States of America,' just to be pedantic. Ahead the sign read Fairbanks 298.

After a couple of hours the road splits at Tok. I walked a little way out of Tok, where the couple dropped me, up the highway until I got to a rest area and set down my bag. Right down the road, where it shrunk to a dot at the centre of perspective, with the line of trees dragged into it on either side, real Alaskan snowcapped mountains stood still behind and waited blue and moody. The sky had dimmed grey and heavy with rain and suspense and I hoped out loud that it wouldn't fall.

It felt colder already and different, as if every place becomes itself by virtue of how it is collectively imagined. It felt like Alaska. I tried to explain this with the camera but could not figure how. There is so much important feeling to it that is frustratingly unquantifiable. Words come closer to it because they can dance around it, etch it, bring it out in relief like a lithograph. Vast, empty but full, potent and good, full of understanding and unfathomable fathoms, deep, enigmatic, but everything you want of it absolutely. It is harder with images.

The very next car gave me a lift. I swung my bag into the open back of the truck, next to some animal skins, and covered it with the tarp. We arrived in Fairbanks at around three. I rang my next host, Stan, to let him know I had arrived and went to grab a sandwich.

Stan is a guy I have been in touch with on the couch-surfing website. He had offered me a place to stay for a week while I figure out my little adventure. I am consistently surprised at the ease of finding a free place to sleep when I approach young men online. I just had to wait until the French girl he was hosting had moved on. Stan said he would come to pick me up from my spot just south of Fairbanks.

# CHIVALRY ISN'T DEAD, GUYS JUST GET SICK OF UNGRATEFUL BITCHES

Stan works in the Denali Park centre. Got the job through his uncle, who is a park warden. Told me how he would come to Alaska as a child to live with his uncle on school holidays (he's originally from Florida). He said even as a child he could not deal with the way of life down there. Said his father and he were nothing alike. He said his father has a Chevy and two jet skis and a speedboat on the lake they live on and that he wished his uncle was his father.

In the house there are trophy pictures of Stan or his uncle with big fish and stags. There is one of his uncle with his foot on a dead grizzly's head. His uncle the stereotypical Mountain Man, wearing buckskin and a coonskin cap, carrying a rifle and a scalping knife and with a big old bushy beard. Not forgetting the pipe.

It turns out that Stan is the douchey kind of Mountain Man, the exclusionary, self-righteous kind. It started when I saw Stan had Jack London on the shelf and I thought I would try to make friends by letting him know I really like London. He had a pretty reductive interpretation of him, so I bated him a little.

'Don't get offended, but *Call of the Wild* is not really a girl's book.'

'Well, whose book is it? Is it a dog's book? It's a really good imagining of what's going on in a dog's head and it works because it is eerie when dogs howl at wolves on TV. And because they do look like they are dreaming about primitive things when they snarl in their sleep.'

'Yeah, but it's not just a story about a dog, is it?'

'Well, it's about a dog that wants to be a wolf.'

'You really think a book would be timeless and never out of print because it just makes people think about what their dog is thinking? This is what I mean, you just don't get it because you're a girl.'

'What?'

'Girls are just naturally social. You could never know what it means to be called on by nature. Society is unnatural for men, it's damaging for the spirit. The call of the wild is the call of the ancestors.'

'There is nothing more primordial than childbirth.'

He thinks I can't understand what a dog feels because I am a girl! He thinks dogs and human men have analogous feelings! Stan is talking Darwin like Ted Kaczynski talks Darwin to shut up women, but Darwin was writing to justify capitalism! He wrote *Origin of the Species* eighty-three years after Adam Smith wrote *The Wealth of Nations*. They are all cutting paper into chair shapes. They are talking large organisations, interpreted in terms of self-interest and the maximisation of personal well-being, like in the free market, where firms or individuals succeed or fail based on 'survival of the fittest.' They think personal maximisation side-handedly benefits the rest of the society or ecosystem. Adam Smith called this the Invisible Hand. Darwin was channelling Smith like a medium; he was a product of his time and primed to think in terms of competitive individuals.

Russia called their automatically launched assured nuclear destruction machine the Dead Hand. The nuclear Dead Hand will automatically and amorally dish out justice to Russia's enemy. It now behaves without them. Perhaps they were saying, well, if that is how you want to play it, this is where your Adam Smith's logic takes you. Could be they were trolling when they called it the Dead Hand. (Dead hand also means an undesirable and persisting influence, which it is also.)

But there were other theories of the origin of the human species and it took thinkers who were outside the shadow of Adam Smith like *women* and *communists* to come up with them. Russian botanist Konstantin Mereschkowski came up with *symbiogenesis*,

Prokaryote
lacks membrane-bound nucleus (Karyon)
from Greek
(pro)-"before" + (Karyon)-"nut or kernel"

Eukaryote
(eu) - "true"
(Karyon)- "kernal"

the evolution-
ary theory
that complex
life came about
because of a
symbiosis of
separate single-
celled organisms.
It takes symbiosis
like the symbiosis
of ectoparasites
and sweetlips
one step further
and says that a
whole new species can
come out of the evolutionary
dependence of two or more
species. Darwin could not think
like this because he was thinking too much like Adam Smith.

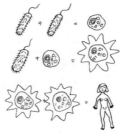

In the 1960s Lynn Margulis, the microbiologist, expanded on
Mereschkowski and revitalised his and the ideas of her predecessors like they were all the collective author (in this way she
not only lectured symbiosis but also lived it). She argued with all
the neo-Darwinists, who gave her the condescending, goddess-
invoking nickname *Science's Unruly Earth Mother.*

Eukaryotic life is organisms with larger cells that have a
bounded nucleus and organelles. Prokaryotic life is organisms
without a bounded nucleus and these are the most abundant life
forms on Earth. All eukaryotic life has a symbiotic relationship
with prokaryotic life — think bacteria in your stomach.

What Lynn Margulis said was that the emergence of eukaryotic cells billions of years ago happened because of *symbiogenesis.* That a prokaryote + a prokaryote in symbiosis = a eukaryote.

That a prokaryote + a eukaryote = a more successful eukaryote. That a more successful eukaryote x 2 = multicellular life (us). That the image of the tree of life should be reimagined to include the *inosculation* of its branches.

Lynn Margulis was Carl Sagan's first wife and they had two sons together. After her second divorce Lynn Margulis said, 'It is not humanly possible to be a good wife, a good mother and a first-class scientist, something has to go,' so it is not hard to imagine the kind of husband that Carl Sagan was. I think I have a girl-crush on Lynn Margulis.

On the Golden Records there is a sound piece that is like a load of firecrackers going off. It is a famous love story; Ann Druyan was thinking about how in love she was with Carl Sagan and now a token of their love floats forever into the void with the Voyagers and will outlive us all. Carl Sagan volunteered her when it was suggested they put an electric reading of human brainwaves on the record. Then he called her up the night before the EEG to tell her he wanted to be with her, which was very coordinated of him. What is often missed out from this love story is that Ann Druyan had a boyfriend and Carl Sagan had a second wife, Linda Salzman; a forgotten and left-behind wife of history.

To rub it in a little bit further the couple were very public about their love token. Ann Druyan said, 'For me Voyager is a kind of joy so powerful, it robs you of your fear of death.'

Note: fear of death; immortalisation; conceptual colonising of Carl Sagan to usurp any future wife he may decide to have (*our love will live forever*). They sent their love seed to pioneer into the absolute wilderness of deep, deep outer space, and it unravels this wilderness as it touches it. If Ted Kaczynski was thinking tactically he might have sent a letter bomb to Carl Sagan, who has maybe of all men ejaculated the very furthest.

Stan was not interested in any of this. I asked him if he had read *White Fang*. He said yes, he did not like that one as much. I pointed out that in *White Fang*, White Fang domesticated himself because he realised that hanging out with people was easier than living in the wild (symbiosis). Dogs live with humans for mutual aid too. There were obvious inconsistencies to Stan's dog-lore logic.

The original bona fide Mountain Men were self-sufficient trapper/explorer types who lived alone in the North American wilderness. Their numbers were highest in the 1800s during the period of western expansion and homesteading and they were mainly found in the Rockies. They were drawn to the western wild by its virgin lands and the good old challenge to their manliness. They traded with the natives and often took native wives. This was pre-Jack London.

They are thought of as honourable and chivalrous loners with a high moral code. When the fur trade began to fail, owing to over-trapping and the silk trade, many Mountain Men had to get jobs as army scouts, guides and settlers, bringing the crowds of homesteaders into the wild land they had opened up through the Emigrant Trails they had established. They initiated the corrosion of their precious wilderness. A memory of Mountain Men still lingers in the portrait of the Real Modern American Man: resourceful, masculine, hardy, provider and *free*.

My driver Ron told me that the modern Mountain Men living on the frontiers now, in cabins standing on the wilderness, get annoyed at other wilderness stander-on-ers, but they make the money they need to live as Mountain Men by working a few months a year on the pipeline. Really it does not matter if the pipeline fucks the future eventually, as long as the Mountain Men can live their lives alone in a pristine wilderness. They rely on machines like guns and snowploughs. But they pride themselves on their otherwise completely and utterly and totally unadulterated independence.

Stan is what you might call an environmental chauvinist. Like he thinks it is his job to open the door for nature. And when he becomes the warden he will become the benevolent King of Denali. Stan is a Real Modern American Man. But if running into the wild is so often a wounded retreat from societal constraints and oppressions, then shouldn't anyone *but* straight white men be doing it more?

## BUT HE'S A HIPPY, HOW CAN HE ALSO BE A MISOGYNIST?

I have had to rein in the indignant feelings I have towards Stan because, as much as I hate to admit it, I need him. Maybe sometimes symbiosis is taken up reluctantly, calculatedly. I keep him sweet by acting dumb and playing up to his idea of himself. There are ways to have covert fun with him, though. For example, I had been thinking about all the parallels between him and Chris McCandless and about what Ron had said about that phenomenon. So I told Stan he reminded me of Chris McCandless.

'Chris McCandless? Fucking Chris McCandless?'

'The guy that died in the bus?'

'I know who fucking Chris McCandless is. You think I could work in Denali and not know who Chris McCandless is? Why do you think I remind you of him?'

'Oh, I don't know. Only slightly. Just, you know, coming to Alaska from the lower forty-eight and being all resourceful and everything?'

'Chris McCandless was a suicidal idiot. A fucking greenhorn. Any true survivalist would have known to take a map and not go into the bush without knowledge. He died because of his own stupidity. And now his little cult wastes my uncle's time, they waste Alaskan taxes, and the little piece of "wild" he went into is now a well-trodden mecca. Kids drown trying to cross the river to get there. Broken kids with stupid fantasies about how the wild will complete them.'

Stan is not even Alaskan. The main difference between Stan and Chris McCandless is that Stan has had the luck to not have died yet. I wonder what the Athabaskans and the Eskimos have to say about guys like Stan.

Stan is also a lesser Mountain Man; he is a wannabe. He lives in a house! Made from bricks! In a town! There is a post office! And a health centre! The ratio in his fridge of shop-bought convenience over foraged/killed is 9:1! There are degrees, and more evolved Mountain Men get points for living in a house they built themselves in a place where, if their appendix burst, they would die.

I have made a list and am sourcing equipment for my trip from the outdoors shops in the town. Stan saw my list and tutted and added some things to it and I let him explain the particular merit of these items to me. I have to nurture his ego because he found me a cabin and he said he will lend me a gun and not tell his uncle that I am out there without a permit. Part of me wonders why he wants to help me when he does not seem to like me. The fact seems to be that he revels so much in his superior authority that he will subject me to the challenge he imagines me so unfit for, sadistically, just to prove himself right. He seems to find me amusing. He wants to see me fail.

I need to make my pack as light as it can be so I will remove all unnecessary items and leave them at Stan's, seeing as I have to come back to return the gun anyway. He is taking my things hostage as a kind of deposit on the gun.


## REGRET IN RATS, ALTRUISM IN BONOBOS

Before casting out I had to begin neatening up all of my frayed edges in order to disengage smoothly. I have told my parents that I am going to volunteer on a community project in an Eskimo village with no phone signal or internet for a few weeks

| TO PACK | TO BUY |
|---|---|
| MISC. — | string / cable ties |
| map | duck tape |
| compass | fire starters |
| Larus gutting knife | lighter / matches |
| camera | wind up lamp |
| batteries | big bags |
| solar charge | tissues |
| laptop | cup |
| books | tarp |
| penknife | trail mix |
| phone | water purification |
| notebook / paper pad | tubs |
| pens / pencils | hand sanitiser |
| rubber / sharpener | pots |
| hot water bottle | line / hooks |
| canvas day bag | Fauna / flora Denali book |
| water bottle | propane |
| binoculars | FOOD |
| toothbrush / paste | rice, oats, beans |
| spork | freeze dried meals x10 |
| first aid kit | |
| sleeping bag | |
| micro towel      gun! | Mosquito  net |
| sewing kit | Sunglasses |
| head torch | Signal mirror |
| suncream | |

Clothes — anorak, hiking boots, socks x5, leggings, shorts, trousers, tops 2x long 1x short, fleece, hat, cap, thermals, pants x5

because I do not know how else to put it to them. I sent them a link to a website that organises such excursions to make it more believable.

Then I Skyped Larus to tell him bye for now and to vent some of my pent-up frustration at Stan, but he took things in a very different direction and now I wish I had not at all. He was worrying about how we had not spoken in a while again. Then he got all strange about why he thought that was.

'Does Sam not approve of our little chats? My girlfriend doesn't like me talking to you so much either.'

It was the way he said this, like so nail-pickingly nonchalant as to be glaringly pointed. I suppose I realised the conversation was going to go one of two ways from there. I guess part of me had known without wanting to all along that this had been building, like a bird sidling over for crumbs so slowly you don't even notice until, oh, it is there.

'Your girlfriend?'

'Yes, my American girlfriend Jose.'

I involuntarily said that he kept that one quiet.

'I'm just surprised, that's all. That we've been talking for so long and I didn't know that about you.'

'There are lots of things you don't know about me.'

This made my legs twitch because I did not know what to do with myself. I turned off the webcam so he could not see me flapping my hands. Neither of us said anything for an uncomfortably long time. I was unsure how to navigate my way back out of it, before anything said became an answer I did not want to hear to a question I had not even asked.

'She finds it strange that I talk so much to a girl young enough to be my daughter.'

*Please stop talking.* I could not think of anything to say. He waited, then carried on.

'I explain to her that you're a very interesting young lady and that I enjoy helping you with your project.'

I want to cry. I try to make light. From here, maybe, I could back-paddle. I ask if she knows I am a friend of Urla's and pointedly call him Uncle Larus.

'Don't call me that.'

'Why?'

'Because it's just weird, don't you think?'

I don't dare ask why some more. I tell him I have to go because Stan is on his way through the door. I tried to make it convincing but do not remember what I said. As he hangs up the camera freezes and lingers on his face for three seconds. His left eye, no, right for him, left for me, is half closed where he got caught off guard.

I realised that it had been instinct twinging all along whenever I thought of Urla, and the way she changed so totally when we were the three of us, and how she emailed less and less. I had ignored it because I was stubborn to prove that it did not have to be like that, that two people can span a gender gap and a generational gap and have a level of understanding without any funny business, like a kind of apprenticeship arrangement.

And how Sam had put it, giving me a look like 'yeah, really' when he asked what Larus had to do with anything. And I got pissed at him for insinuating that I was being stupid and naive and that a person I held to be a friend and mentor was not just that. And Larus doing the same of him, the two of them like male narwhals clashing their horns together, telepathically. And it is like that but grosser still because he is old enough to be my old dad or even almost my very young grandfather. I got annoyed at Sam for denying me platonic camaraderie in such a reductive way, but god, he was right after all.

And thinking of Sam and how I got angry at him, well, it makes my stomach flip and it also makes me squirm, like if I think of being back there and the last day and our plain shunning of each other I feel shit and I might have done a shit thing by behaving like that but so did he and I do not want to think about it, best really just to forget about it all. It's not like we will ever see each other again anyway.

And I am trying hard not to but if I do think about it, I can't quite get my head around why it got so suddenly weird. It was after he tried to get me to stay and I did not because of course

I had to carry on. As though he was hurt that I wanted to leave and carry on without him.

Left behind during the Apollo missions were all of the astronauts' wives and children. This is perhaps more significant during the Apollo missions than on modern-day missions because they were so rushed what with the race on, all the nationalistic pressure, and so much could go wrong so easily. So the wives left behind had to go to lift-off with all their children in tow and smile for the media cameras and wave and say WE ARE PROUD, THRILLED AND HAPPY and watch their husbands and their children's fathers and their monetary means of living shoot up into the sky in a hunk of aluminium and disappear into a dimension they might not have even been completely sure existed, maybe thought of in a very abstract way like my mum does.

And if I had been an Apollo wife I would probably have thought *fuck you* in a lot of ways. Fuck you, husband, for wanting to risk giving up on our marriage bed and the beautiful faces of our children and my great cooking and our cosy life and our vows to stay together and try to see out this one life to its fullest, for some idea of eternal glory, and yeah, you will be remembered for all of history but the most you will remember of me is how I stopped sleeping at night and started getting craggy and how you eventually left me for a young fan girl and I had to spend the rest of the one life I have on this planet angry at another planet for taking you away. And maybe I would have liked to have gone up there with you too but I was just not allowed and on some level I am just jealous that you get the chance to abandon it all and be seen as a selfless hero and not a selfish egomaniac, and I do not, will not ever, I have to stay here and dress all our children for school.

Most of the marriages of the moonwalkers did not last through the strain of fame and affairs and, probably, some feeling of comedown on the part of the astronauts, a feeling of life having peaked and all nuclear-family-life-events paled in comparison; the births and the first words and the graduations and the first grandchildren, all the prototypical life-milestones. You would think they could have sent up bachelors to be fair to all the future absent-fathered children, but of course the astronauts had to be role models, they had to be figureheads of nice productive nuclear families. Even if there were other more suitable candidates (single and childless females included).

So not to say that Sam is like my sore wife but that maybe in a very small way, on a very micro level, he felt a similar kind of anger-at-abandonment. And I get that. But historically it is women that have to deal with chronic desertion (I see you, Linda Salzman) and this is exactly what I am working against so Sam can just deal with it. I am doing this for all the bitter left-behind wives of history! (Close relatives of the commonly found dragged-around woman.)

Online a little envelope flashed at me from him. Maybe I miss him and maybe I wish he had made an effort to come with me or something but ha-ha! that would not do. He did not take me seriously. Neither does Stan and even Larus didn't in the end, all that interest just feigned for an interest in something else. But it is my whole reason for being right now. And if I get disheartened then they all win and I let down all of the left-behind wives of history.


## ATLAS SHRUGGED

The more I think about the deal with Larus the more frustrated I get and the less I blame myself. I had come to see us as a kind of master and student, this is a well-established trope, and none of those guys ever had problems with sexual dynamics. Like Plato and Socrates, Harry and Dumbledore, Yoda and Skywalker. I thought Larus was in on this too.

I can't tell if I am noticing weirdness in retrospect because I am on to him or if I am seeing things where they were not because he has taken on a new face for me. Sigmund Freud, the phallus-obsessed psychoanalyst, said people cannot hear or see things that do not fit with the way they see the world or themselves. Anyway, it is going to make this disappearing into the wilderness thing all the more easy to throw myself into.

The park centre that Stan works in is Denali National Park, and within it is the Denali Wilderness Area. At the far north-east corner of this is the trail that McCandless took and where the bus he died in still is now, actually on the border of parklands. I will not be anywhere near it but it is strange to think of it existing across the tundra from where I plan to stay. As much as Stan despises him I feel a bit of a kinship with him. Like we are both allied idealists. We differ on a lot of things; for example, I will not be sending out overdramatic maybe-forever-goodbyes by postcard and phone call. I have not even told my parents what I am going to be doing because I know it would worry them sick. I do not intend to be stupid with my life either but I have read my Thoreau too, well, some anyway, and I get what McCandless was trying to find by going out there. It was a claiming of autonomy and a rite of passage that I want to go through too and I bet he died happy doing it.

The area I will go to is trail-less. I can get a lift to the visitors' centre with Stan, where I can catch a bus to drop me on the road that leads through the park. Then I can hike out from the road for a long day and hopefully arrive at the cabin that Stan has earmarked on the map for me by late evening.

Part of me says *you can't trust Stan not to tell* and another part says *you can trust his obsession to see how far you can be pushed, to see you fail* and a small part of me says *is this a girlfriend test and if I pass I become worthy in his eyes of his tolerance which for him equates to kinship?* If so, gross.

When he dropped me he said, 'So I'll see you in around

three days' time, then,' grinning in a way that was almost flirty. I laughed sweetly and he said, 'No, really, what's the limit past which if you haven't turned up on my doorstep to bring the gun back I send the search parties out after you?'

'Five weeks, please.'

'Okay, so honestly, why are you doing this? Did something bad happen to you?'

'What do you mean?'

'Well, usually that's why people do things like this, they are running away.'

'Why do you go camping, Stan? Did something bad happen to you?'

'No.'

'Exactly.'

'But like, you don't even come from a place that would prepare you for this. You don't know what you're letting yourself in for.'

'I thought you said you came from Florida?'

'You know bears in Denali maul twenty people to death every year, right?'

Then I smiled at him and passed him my *Collected Works of Jack London* with all of the feminist and socialist stories and passages earmarked and annotated for his consideration. I know he is lying about the bear statistic because I already looked it up.

What happened to me? Nothing. I think that that is the point. I need to experience something visceral to placate the hunger. And I am sick of the men that want to keep it from me. Maybe you could say patriarchy happened to me. So like a dog cast out into the rain maybe I do leave, to go cry myself a big fat fucking two-hearted river. To sleep in an open field! To travel west! To walk freely at night!

# INTO THE WILDNESS

# GOING FERAL

She stood out vivid and present in the temperature-controlled half-light of her glass coffin, upright and at full human stature, her cloak hung to give the impression of a human figure underneath. She radiated epiphany. She filled the room with a smell like the seal-fur blankets Naaja's mother gave us and an undertone of perhaps honey. It was strangely familiar and pleasant, not at all sickly. Her staff with the two-pronged antlers, still velvety with fur, sashed to it. On little fronds she had tiny bird skulls and shells. If she weren't so very still they would click together like a cartoon skeleton falling to pieces. Clack-clack-clack-clack-clack.

In the park centre where I waited for the bus, there were displays on the natural and cultural history of the park. I floated around the room; there was movement from nothing but me. Time had stopped, looking exactly about to happen. There were iridescent wings clamped open, feigning flight, above italicised names I could not get my tongue around. There were eyes, but we had taken the real ones out to put glass ones in and they stared from inside mounted skins, on placarded walls, from under glass domes, contorted majestically on rocks, on wooden plates, in awkward glory. There were tiny mottled eggs in counterfeit nests that looked as though they were about to burst out into life. And there were Dall sheep horns, a grizzly's paw pad, skulls which though dry had all once held tiny brains, capillaries and veins.

There were artefacts of the original human inhabitants too:

Athabaskan shawls, pipes and pottery. A model of a traditional toboggan and a crusty, worn dog harness. Grainy photographs of vacant-looking Eskimo men and women stood limpidly side by side with priests in robes. The plaque said missionaries won their trust with magical gifts of tobacco and medicine.

> *Prior to the arrival of Christian missionaries to the New World, indigenous religion was animistic, comprised of a worldview where humans are part of an on-going spiritual interchange between all manifestations of organic matter, often including the inanimate matter of the elements. A shaman was a human who was a seer into the spirit world.*
>
> *Both men and women could be shamans, but many of the shamans were of female form as the idea of creation was sacred and bestowed to the feminine. However men could also have 'feminine' attributes. Gender was considered fluid, and there were thought to be at least four genders approximately: masculine men, feminine men, masculine women and feminine women. People who embodied the two opposites were known as Twospirit People.*

In the rest of the world Eskimo is a pejorative term and Inuit is preferred instead, but in Alaska the Eskimos prefer to be

called Eskimos. There was a poster, a kind of family tree of the Alaskan indigenous peoples. Eskimo and Inuit are both the collective terms for distinct but similar cultures like the Yupik and Inupiat. Other natives of Alaska of separate cultures mostly distinguished by language are the Athabaskans, Aleuts, Eyak, Tlingit, Haida and Tsimshian.

The distinctions are complicated because there are overlaps between the different cultures, and although they are distinguished by language, some of the languages are maybe not entirely separate languages. And why would the indigenous people care about absolutely distinguishing cultures if souls can transmigrate to rocks, are forever in animal-mineral-plant continuum?

On the 9 a.m. bus into the park, before disembarking, I kept my eyes porous out of the window, funnelling it all in. There were just two other people on the bus, a pair of middle-aged day hikers, and I could feel them staring at the gun leant against my seat while I jotted in my notebook.

I was waiting for the mountains to begin on the left and the treeline, which I knew to be mile 52 of the Park Road and the calculated point of my disembarkation.

The scenery flickered. It was gradual, like well-thought build-up in a feel-good coming-of-age story about a girl like me getting close to something sought. It was layer on layer. Each breaching hill might have been the one to reveal the mountains like a shroud, ghostly, slipping down. Each pre-emptive revealing was excited pressure hoarded.

Finally they were there. Mountains as turnstiles, thresholds to becomings. What do these ones mark? The ground crawled meekly to them, green and a blemished kind of red like blood soaked into moss, up and up until it rendered at rusty brown and rocky tips. Behind, another sort of brown, and behind still grey and white-capped. Each row of mountains was coloured a little differently. Layered and assembled like a collage, foreground in green. But no background of sky, instead clouds that hung and panelled forward as an overlay, disturbing the order of the layers. The mountains encroached into the sky, a challenge to its separateness.

I do not remember stepping off the bus, in a way that slightly alarms. But I do remember the light and colour: dappled impressions of moss and blood. Like Monet. Up close and in cardinal parts, tiny flowers and perfect tiny tear-shaped leaves of purple. Tiny but integral parts of a bigger whole. Micro/macro and indivisible. The timid parts actually prettier, like my own lone small journey to me. At the same time whole and partial, sublime and obscure but sentimental.

A couple of hours after disembarking from the bus and I am caught. Until that point I had been plodding along absent but receptive. Then it hits me very suddenly as I stop to drink some water from my bottle and sit on my haunches and look up at the sky, where a huge bloody eagle of some kind is wheeling about. This is it. This is everything. This is my moonwalk.

After the Apollo missions lots of the astronauts would talk about a similar sudden awareness of self. After giving all their concentration to lift-off and getting up there without exploding and feeling tense and so overridden by adrenaline that they were not even that aware of where they were and what they were doing, so that when it *did* hit them the feeling was potent and alarming. Others never experienced the feeling because they did not ever stop putting all their resources into the functionality of the mission. Many of the Apollo astronauts experienced their time in space not as selves but as detached scientists.

The tundra is always whistling and it is very empty. I have enough freeze-dried food as base rations to sustain me with hunted stuff for four weeks — the ecologist Aldo Leopold said that three is enough time to get to grips with real solitude and become truly immersed in wilderness. To get into the rhythms of it. Technically past two is classed as 'settling' rather than a camping trip and is against park regulations, but I have it from Stan that no one will notice. Stan showed me how to use a radio like the one that would be in the cabin to get in touch if I need him. He has one back in his house for when nobody is in the warden's office.

It took me around nine hours' marching with only a slight deviation. Stan told me, 'If you hit the river where it leaves the forest then you are too far north,' but I couldn't see the river and had to just hope that this was because I was south of it. I was.

The cabin is everything I dreamed it would be. When I finally saw it from across the tundra I yelped and felt proud of my own tenacity. It is sat just left of some evergreens and looks out onto the tundra. There is an empty smokehouse outside and a tiny toilet shed, a collapsed and moss-covered pile of logs, and a broken pair of skis. Inside there is a mounted fox head, a row of gun mounts, where I have mounted Stan's gun, some pots, a canvas cot, a fire grate, the radio on a desk with a chair and the supplies I bought. When I move about and unsettle the dust that is uniform and thick I have a sneezing fit. I fitted the radio with the batteries I bought first thing, but I turned it off this evening and intend to keep it so.

Of course, I also brought some books to the woods, loaned from Stan's own personal Mountain Man library. Maybe he thinks his canonical texts on wilderness are the thing that might equip me to decipher it. I took Thoreau, Emerson, Hemingway, the Unabomber and a biographical book about various young male runaways. They added weight to my pack but seemed important. I figure if I hold them at arms length they could help me to see instead of clouding my vision. When Jack London went to the Klondike he read *Origin of the Species* and *Paradise Lost* (which explains a lot).

Stan didn't show me how to shoot the gun and I obviously did not ask. I have looked it over and it is pretty similar to a rifle I used to shoot with an ex-boyfriend whose family liked hunting.

He used to say he was sad about hurting all the animals, and that was why he would just be the scarer that ran into the grass to get the pheasants up. The real reason was he was a terrible shot; he just didn't want to say it to me because he was sore that I could shoot better than him. I would not shoot animals, mind, we just used to practise on targets in a field behind his house.

I am the only human being for miles around as far as I am aware. At least, that is what I was told by the bus driver, who thinks I am a day hiker too and was concerned enough for my welfare as it was that I did not correct him. He told me to look out for reindeer, caribou, foxes, pine martens, hares, wolves, wildcats and bears. Most are technically edible but I only fancy the smaller things. I have seen Bear Grylls killing and gutting many large animals and it always seems so unnecessary and superfluous. I mean, Bear Grylls obviously eats bears, that is where he gets his name from, right? He eats bears because it is essential to his identity as a *born survivor*. If he did not eat bears he would not have a job. I am only killing for one and I am only small. I think a hare a week will be more than enough to sustain me with the freeze-dried stuff.

Is it cheating to bring the 'just add water' survival packs? I had to really think about this before coming out. If I did not have them I would have to hunt for *all* my food. But people who do this kind of thing always bring supplies. Ernest Hemingway, writer of manly short sentences, took canned pork and beans. Inuits have supplies in the way of preserved foods. Modern Mountain Men buy sacks of pinto beans from Fairbanks. And if bringing supplies was cheating, maybe I should not really have technology like a gun or a radio. And that would not be survival technique, but a probable death-experiment. This thing, this authenticity, how close can you get to it? How pure can it be?

I also would not be able to make the video diary, which would undermine the entire point of the trip. The diary might seem a bit false, might add an inverted voyeurism so that it is really like

I have company out here, but I don't really know how to avoid this. When Bear Grylls cut open a camel to demonstrate how to sleep inside it I doubt if he actually stayed in there all night, snug in his authenticity, with his cameraman asleep in a tent pitched next to him.

How do you really *front the essential facts of life authentically*? Probably it is not even possible in our time of saturation. I can only try my best. Maybe writing is less inauthentic than the audience of a camera. But even then I am writing to be read, so again the 'solitude' is tainted by the inverse voyeurism. Go tell that to Thoreau and Heidegger and the Unabomber.

## THE BEARD AND THE GUNS AND THE LITTLE SHORT SENTENCES

The sun is strong enough that a full day with the solar charger in direct light will charge up a battery by half. Half a battery gives me two hours with the camera, so I need to keep on top of this. I went for a walk around yesterday to get to grips with the area in order to draw my first rough map. I had taken for granted that it would be easy to find something to eat, but after a few hours it started getting dark so I had to head back without finding anything (I did find a water source, though, a spring that is only a ten-minute walk from the hut but took me hours to find). It is difficult because I spent a lot of time singing to myself so that the bears would hear me coming and keep out of the way but that also scares away the food. When I got back I settled into the hut, arranged all my blankets on the cot, and got a little fire going in the fire grate.

I tried for about fifteen minutes, rubbing sticks together, then gave up and used the gas lighter, and cooked some instant noodles. I did feel kind of fraudulent with my lighter and my sachet of flavour, but if it is good enough for Hemingway then it is good enough for me. I sat and watched the noodles bubble, then I sat and watched them cool as I fed Stan's map to the flames in the grate, watching it curl to cinder. With it gone a pressure released; like McCandless I am alone, it is again a wilderness to me, the places I had not seen yet still to be discovered. Like vaporising Voyager 1 out of the sky with a laser beam, zap!

Today I tried again, but I headed out first thing in the morning to give myself plenty of time, thinking *immaqa*. I was awake for most of the night anyway. I had not given any thought to how it would feel the first night all alone. There was too much sound to sleep, sound I could not place, the cabin being saggy with age. Mostly I stayed awake because I had a feeling like something was about to happen, or like it had happened and I had not yet put my finger on it. Like everything for a while had been hyperreal sets and stage props but now I was in real real-life, everything with a shining core. It was so bright I could not sleep for it. It was not danger and I would not say I was scared. Just very, very awake.

Tips for being not-scared at night:

—Always sleep in tight corners facing outwards, towards the door

—Fill a rubber hot-water bottle with boiling water and curl around it like it is a live, heat-giving companion

—Hum songs to trick yourself into feeling calm

—Think of the cabin as a living guardian, then its creaks and groans will comfort not unnerve you. It affords you shelter. It is your best friend

—If you hear an alarming noise, imagine it over and over again until it no longer alarms you

—If you are still alarmed, try being just as alarming. Go outside and confront everything. Yell at it all. Send any wild animals

scurrying into the night. Look at it a while, to convince
yourself it is still and unthreatening

I went out as soon as the sun was up enough. I did not do any
of the singing this time so that I could go in stealth. First thing
I came across apart from the things that ran away before I could
see them was a caribou. She was standing behind a tree just
ahead of me and had not noticed me, but as soon as I saw her
I stopped and must have drawn in breath or something because
she looked right at me. She stood there looking at me and kind
of puffing cold air out and looking nervous. I thought about
shooting her and just living off her for the whole four weeks
so that I only had the guilt of one soul on my conscience. But
then she stepped forward slowly and her little baby stepped out
from behind the tree after her and I was shaking so bad I do not
think I would have hit her anyway. They both trotted away and
the baby tripped a bit in panic and I had to sit down for a whole
minute to stop the shaking.

After I had been out for a good five hours, although I could
not really say because I don't have a way of telling the time apart
from on the laptop, and the sun moves at a pace I am still not
accustomed to, I started feeling tired, hungry and irritable and
began to carry the gun less half-heartedly so that I could just go
ahead and shoot the next thing I saw. I wound myself up being
all stealthy and peeking round the trees and jumping out, when
I saw something dark move just ahead. I shot it before I even
had time to worry.

I had not accounted for how loud the shot would be in the
still air, how much the force would shock me backwards, how
the jolt would hurt my shoulder. After the shot everything
seemed to go really quiet, all the birds shut up as though they
thought they might be next, and I ran over to where the thing
was and got on my hands and knees by it. I was amazed to have

even hit it because I had been knocked off balance by the force, and because I had only been half-truthing when I told Stan and the bus driver that I knew how to use it. It was very dead, which I was glad about, I did not want to see it half dead, twitching or whimpering.

I had never killed a thing before and had made a pact with myself to be stoic about it, not to drop the gun and stare at my hands in horror, all 'what have I done?' But as much as I wanted to make it a point of pride *not* to cry, because a Mountain Man would not cry, certainly, I cry very easily so of course I burst into tears.

When you are a young child you cry for yourself, you cry for the attention of your parents. Growing up is feeling for the first time for the outside world, it is evolving out of your juvenile solipsism (if you are a girl anyway). I remember the moment it happened to me for the first time clearly. It was when the Columbia rocket blew to pieces over Texas on re-entry.

It was a really sunny afternoon in England. I was in the car, sat in the back behind Dad, so it must have been a weekend because I was school age. They announced it on the radio. The radio presenter's voice was all choked up. I looked up at the bright blue sky, where there was an airplane making candyfloss trails, and I cried. They played David Bowie's 'Space Oddity' on the radio and I felt like I was mourning the Columbia rocket with the whole of the rest of humanity. I remember my dad's eyes in the rear-view mirror. As I remember it he looked moved, misty-eyed, to see his young daughter cry for the first time at something so outside herself.

So girls as a very general demographic cry more. Maybe you can say this is weak. Or maybe you can say that it takes a lot of strength to admit you feel so much all of the bloody time. Like how our pain threshold is higher from tidal womb pain.

I recognised it from my fauna and flora book as a large snow-shoe hare, its blood all stark on its side and in a little pool beside it. It was pale brown and looked paler in a different way, from its loss of animation. My impulse was to cover it with dirt and leave it be. It affected me greatly to think that the blood had been making its way to its heart moments before and now it was outside it, going sticky.

I felt myself shaking, like all my feelings had turned to energy, buzzing around my body instead of turning into something I could understand. It felt like that with no causal link. Before there was a brown hare and now there is this *corporeal object*. The object is still and cold and looks like a hare, but different.

What is a thing? Is it a different thing without the essence that makes it what it is? Is an essence a soul? Before it was a hare and now it is a body and soon to be a piece of meat. This is why I have to do this thing that I am apparently going to find very disturbing. I need to know that I have it in me to live by acknowledging that I am living where living = not dead. And again for that intangible thing, this authenticity, for the documentary.

Back at Stan's I shot a video of him skinning, and I have it to watch back on the laptop. He said something snide about it but I really do not see the problem. I have never known how to do it because I have never lived in a place where I have had to learn, and it annoyed me that he was being smug when I was trying to rectify this.

The first thing to do (I will gladly be the oracle because I believe in communal knowledge) is to squeeze the animal's bladder area, for obvious reasons. Then you make a little V shape at the top of the breast to get the knife under the skin, and you cut right down its belly. When this opens up, all the bits are just there like you have unzipped a purse full of guts. I have only gutted fish before and it made me feel unusual. I was expecting lots of blood to spurt out and it all to be chaos and mess but it is not at all. You let a little blood out then it is neat, as if the hare was made just for you to eat it.

When the belly is open you just pull the guts out by running two fingers from top to bottom, which is a very odd sensation, and I don't think I will be able to get the smell off my fingers for days. Then you take off the legs and head; without a meat cleaver not as easy as Stan made it seem. After that you take off the skin, disconcertingly easy, just like pulling a tight sock off apart from a few places that have to be picked apart with the knife.

You are left with a naked, headless, pawless *thing*, which then needs the remaining entrails taken out, including the duct the poo goes through, which made me feel kind of embarrassed for the hare. I did make a bit of a mess of things but still did well for a first time, I think. I cut it into three pieces, two to keep inside the Tupperware box covered in the salt I brought, and the other to boil tonight then take off the bone and eat with some form of vacuum-packed carbohydrate. I made a fire pit for the guts and set them on fire because that is how you make sure the bears do not smell them.

I had to stop myself from using up too much of the antibacterial hand rub to get rid of the death smell on my hands. I am going out to get some firewood and then I will cook and after some reading I will be very ready for bed, I am exhausted after not sleeping last night. I feel very resourceful. Like a bird must feel when it settles into its nest that it built with its own beak and claws. Birds must be capable of feelings of sorts. When a little bird settles down into its self-built nest and fluffs up its feathers and burrows into its own neck, it is the very image of immense satisfaction.

## MORE SPACE WHERE NOBODY IS THAN WHERE ANYBODY IS

My plan is to make my map over four days. I already have my rough diagram but need to walk to each place to hone it and add finer details, like where is good for a lookout, or somewhere to maybe practise trapping. I want it to cover the area I am likely to use on a regular day so I will walk for half a day then turn back on myself. On day one I will head north, on day two east, and so on. I think I can walk about twenty miles in a very long day, so the map should cover approximately ten miles in radius from the hut at the centre.

Stan criticised Chris McCandless for the fact that he did not have an official map. If he had had an official map he would have seen that just downriver from where he could not make his crossing back to civilisation because of floodwater and subsequently ate the potato that killed him, there was a pulley system for transporting things and people across safely. But if Chris McCandless had had an official map, it would not have been his wilderness and he might as well have died anyway.

I am not in danger of that because I know exactly how to get back to the road to get the bus back to the visitors' centre, and I also have radio contact if I want to turn the thing back on. It would not take them long to find the cabin if they needed to, because they know I was headed out without camping gear. I am conceptually isolated and alone, but in trouble I could radio Stan for help. Although I had thought about going further in and leaving the radio behind, finding somewhere else to sleep. With each day I feel a little more certain that Stan will try to rescue me. Actually I am thinking about it a lot.

South of the hut the forest becomes dense and backs all the way to where the mountains start, in the south and arcing west. In the lower foothills the trees stop growing from the altitude, then just behind the mountains rise higher and are sooty black with stripes of white where the meagre snow is. Further behind still somewhere is Denali, the highest point in North America.

Mount Denali was until very recently named Mount McKinley, and is still called that by some bitter Ohioans. It was called Denali from the Koyukon-Athabaskan *Deenaalee*, which means 'the high one.' The Russians, when they owned Alaska, called it *Bolshaya Gora*, which means 'big mountain.' Then an American gold prospector came along and called it *McKinley*, which means 'President William McKinley,' bequeathed in a curious naming ritual used by colonising white men whereby the conquered entity is named after the conqueror or an adulated public figure.

The gold prospector called the mountain *McKinley* because William McKinley was a proponent of the gold standard and the prospector wanted to get one over on the silver miners, who wanted the president to be William Jennings Bryan, the proponent of the silver standard.

Then President William McKinley was assassinated by an anarchist called Leon Czolgosz because he was the 'president of the money kings' willing to exploit the poor to benefit the rich. So the name got officially etched into all of the maps in President William McKinley's memory by the American government in 1917.

Years and years and they will not stop arguing about it because for America Alaska is still very much in the process of construction. Alaskans want the name to be *Denali* from *Deenaalee*, maybe mostly because they do not want to be out-Alaskaned by the Ohioans, who keep blocking the change because McKinley came from Ohio and they want their namesake on the biggest mountain in North America. In real life in Alaska people mostly just call it Denali. The Athabaskans never stopped calling it Deenaalee and maybe do not know what all the fuss is about, because they did not draw maps.

In 2015 President Barack Obama officially finally changed the name to Denali to show honour, respect and gratitude to the Athabaskan-speaking people (as if naming is owning and he was giving it back). Donald Trump declared this 'an insult to Ohio' and vowed to change it back, so let's see how long that lasts. Does an orca care if it gets shunted from one entire species to a separate species dependent on how it hunts (which is what Larus said may be the case)? Probably the Athabaskans just shrug and say you do what you want, we are going to just carry on calling it Deenaalee under your shouting chins. The orcas say yeah, whatever, we are just going to carry on swimming and flipping seals or not flipping seals.

The tundra is always in soliloquy. Mostly it whistles and sings, but now and then the wind will die down suddenly and in the utter silence and still it feels like you are on stage. As though you did not know there were curtains until they just suddenly opened. Then the cacophony of noise again like applause.

From where the tundra and taiga meet you see right across to the east, but you do not see the road because it is too far. The sky was very blue and clouds dragged shadows over the tundra, dimming the glare of the lake.

In the forest I worried about getting lost, but heading due south-west by the compass, towards the steeper foothills, I stayed on track fine. In this area the trees were dense. This route leads to a perfect fishing spot, where the stream is shallow enough to cross and brimming with fish. I headed further on past this in order to get to the foothills because I wanted to climb past the timberline to get a better look. The ground started to slope and the trees thinned so that I had a slight vantage, and I could see what I took to be a radio mast just a mile or so away in the east. I headed there instead for no reason other than that it intrigued me.

The radio mast is really a fire tower. The foliage around it is thick overhead, and after going back into the thicker trees I could not really get a view of it until I was almost directly underneath. There was a little clearing, and when I came into it the sudden view of the tower shocked me. A radio mast was benign in my mind but a watchtower reeked too much of people. It isn't that I am hermitised already, just that I do not want to lose this game I am playing with myself so soon.

I hid back in the trees, where I was sure I could not be seen from above, and hunkered down to watch for movement in the lookout at the top. In real-life terms, I was also concerned that a park warden might ask to see my permit. Stan gave a resident permit from lost property to me, which he advised me to leave in my hut on the days I went out; that way if anyone dropped by they would leave me be, thinking I was 'P. S. Aldridge.' He did not actually explain what I should do if I met a warden while I was out, he just told me that where I was going was so far away and off-trail I would not meet one at all.

I stayed still, hunkered and watching for a good ten minutes. The tower was rusted and wind-battered. As I watched it, it gradually changed its appearance, began to seem hollower as its potential to expose me withered. But then the fire-watcher could just be sat where I could not see them, reading or sleeping or watching for fires. I decided the only way to know was to yell up. I would yell like some kind of animal from inside the trees and see if anything changed.

I yelled stupidly. Only crows noticed, lifting off from the tops of the trees and cawing at me because they were annoyed at themselves for startling so easily. Then I felt less stupid. Nobody came to the window.

At the base of the tower, with my foot on the ladder, I shouted up again just to make sure. This time, in a human voice, I asked, 'Hello?' Nothing. The steps were made of sheet metal, like the steps to a lifeguard's chair, and were rickety. They wound around the four legs of the tower in an angular spiral.

Towards the top the tower groaned against the slow wind. I came into the lookout through a trapdoor. The floor was coated with a coarse, gravelly dust, prints left where it came away on my hands. Apart from my marks it was print-less. Nobody had been up there for a very long time. I clambered inside and crawled to sit with my back to a wall.

There was nothing inside and the glass in the windows was

grimy. I looked around for a sign for when there was last a person in there. The dust was felt-like on the floor. Light came up through the boards, rendering all my movements gold-dusty and ethereal.

I had the thought to maybe check the walls for some kind of graffiti. I imagine they turn up all over the place in spaces like this. There were two; they read:

*Johnston Wills, 1952*
*P Harris, 1999*

If I had not found them I could have been the first person to set foot in there since whenever I wanted to imagine. Maybe not objectively, but that would not have mattered. Like how a scientific discovery is a discovery until a new discovery is made that refutes the original one, like how Denali stays Deenaalee to the isolated Athabaskans, who choose not to read maps. Really in this way no one ever discovers anything, they only invent things (we invented nuclear bombs but we say we discovered them because that sounds less evil). I could have invented this place as an unpeopled wilderness for myself. I sat down cross-legged and looked at them and wondered if maybe P Harris had thought the same. Maybe he wrote his name in defiance: *you can't have this place all to yourself, Johnston Wills.*

Then I remembered the rock in the Greenlandic tundra that stood to hold me and Urla and Naaja until enough rain, time and rock plants had eroded our names. I wondered what they were both doing right then. If Urla had really thought Larus and I were close in the wrong way, if he let her think that, if she hated me.

If I came back with supplies I could camp out in the tower for a few days. I did not want to cook any food and use the portable propane so soon, so I would have to bring it already cooked and cold. I only have one kind of container for bringing it so I could do maybe two nights if I filled the tub, before I got hungry again. I was brain tired, and my legs ached, and it felt safe to be so high up off the ground, rocking gently, a bird in a tree. I thought of all the canopy creatures; bees in hives, pine martens in tree hollows, porcupines sat in branches, everyone safely elevated from the prowlers, a hovering biome. I felt a comfort like fellowship, and decided to stay put until the morning.

## HEROES FOR A GIRL SCOUT

In my dream I am sat at the bottom of the mighty Mekong River talking to a giant catfish, who tells me he is one hundred years old. His eyes and scales are the same dirt-brown as the river, like over time the dirt that settled on him crawled underneath his skin and became his skin. His voice sounds like bubbling custard. All the dead men that fell in the water in the Vietnam War had sheened themselves with DDT to keep mosquitoes away. Agent Orange collected in the waters and the soil and the bodies of the living things.

The bodies got eaten by the little fish, bigger fish ate the little fish, the catfish ate the bigger fish, all the DDT and Agent Orange from all their livers built up and up in the liver of the catfish. Now the catfish is poison. A hook and line plop and sink into the brown river to where I sit with the catfish. He takes the hook in his crêpe-like fin and pops it through his blubbery lip. Above, a little Vietnamese boy reels in his dinner.

I was sleeping deeply and was jerked quite suddenly awake by a strange, long noise. A bell. I shook all over and my teeth clanked from panic. I imagined looking over the spruces like a crow sees them, stretching on and on, an unbroken sea of green and dark shadows. And then the tower.

A bell needed somebody to ring it. From a vantage of any-where over the forest, from the ridge or the semicircle of higher ground from the north, you need not be a crow. Had I lit the tower up like a beacon when I used the torch? Somebody had rung a bell.

I sat up when it came again, pealing away on the wind. It sounded distorted this time. Then right away, it came again. Only this time it sounded nothing like I thought it at all. It was unmistakable: a mournful warble as timeless and familiar as the pentatonic scale.

I grabbed the camera and scrambled to open up the window and look down into the dimly visible clearing. It was empty but the wolves were near. The howl had come so clear, and besides I could feel them. The forest was heavy with anticipation, the spires of the evergreens whispering like a crowd as the lights dim.

The howl came again, and it went right through me, could have been in the tower. It made my whole body shudder in a way that made me grin; a tingle of pseudo-fear like looking down from an airplane. My hackles raised of their own accord. Into the clearing came a dark shape, one, two, three, and then a white one, then one more black. They fanned around the base of the tower with their noses to the ground. I could hear an excited kind of whimpering.

Wolves are an animal I can trust. Their packs are hierarchical, but they are spearheaded by a male and female breeding pair, who rule together in equality. Wolf Wives are absent from *The Call of the Wild*. Two she-dogs are friendly so get killed, and the only strong female sled dog — Dolly — goes mad and has her head smashed in. Mercedes, the sole female human character in the book, spends her cameo crying and complaining. This has left a lasting impression on men-who-think-like-dogs like Stan.

For a moment of delicious fear I toyed with the vision of the wolves staying put and waiting for me. Sitting on their haunches and looking up at the tower with hungry eyes.

But they did not look up. One of them cocked his leg to the

tower then yelped, and they filed away quickly into the trees with such a purpose I knew I would not see them again that night.

## THE TIMESCALES OF HUMMINGBIRDS

When I returned to the cabin I was glad to find everything as I left it. My permit was in the exact same place on the desk, so I am pretty sure nobody came by. I will go back to camp in the tower at some other point but I need some proper food and my mosquito net. Stan was smug when he added it to my list and I had thought it an arbitrary appendage to make him feel like he had had one on me. I have to give him credit now as actually I would have been fucked without it. In the tower so high up they were not so bad, but in the cabin and outside on evenings they come in swarms. I can slap my arm and kill four at one time. I feel a little bad doing this because I know that only female mosquitoes bite and they have to do it to get enough iron and protein to make their eggs. They are only trying to feed their babies, just like everything is trying to feed its babies.

I decided to try fishing as I figured it would affect me a lot less than shooting a thing dead. I had bought some fishing line and hooks in Fairbanks, and for the rest I found a sturdy stick as my rod and tied the line to the end, where it splayed, so I could attach it around the adjoining part to make it more secure. I made the line long enough so that I could yank it out the water fast, but with no reel I can only use it in relatively shallow water.

I was stumped for a float until I remembered a redundant tampon at the bottom of my bag that I'd brought just in case I lost my Mooncup. It was still sealed with all the air in so it worked a dream. I attached this to the middle of the line before tying the hook to the end with a little ribbon of foil from a noodle packet just above it to act as the little fish-attracter thing.

Then I upturned a log and collected myself some grubs and worms for bait in a rusty tin can.

I found salmonberries (they look a little like raspberries, more seedy and juicy) and harvested as many as I could carry inside a clean sock. Along the way I managed to find lots of dandelion leaves that I washed in a stream and nibbled. There was also a plant I came across that looked like the plant the pamphlet called *goosetongue*, but it warned that it also looks like *arrowgrass*, which is poisonous. I have learned enough from Chris McCandless to know that eating anything I was not sure of would be a no-no, but it felt wholesome to be learning the things by their names just to look at and touch, their tactile truth.

Although to be fair to McCandless it does not seem he confused a lethal plant for another, it was just his own fauna and flora book did not tell him that this certain potato he was always eating actually contained lethal toxins. It was a taxonomical failing and not ignorance that killed him, as I said to Stan.

The course of the stream widens out where another joins it. The water runs clear and shallow; underneath it you can see the shadows of the fish holding themselves against the current. They hold then dart away suddenly for reasons kept from you by the mirage-making surface. I watched one fish that seemed to enjoy holding itself against the exact point where the two waters met and did not move from this meditative state for a whole fifteen minutes. Do fish feel meditative? Without awareness, just some primitive state of tranquillity?

I set up the rod to dip into the water where shadow from the trees hung over. The forest was awake to me and gave its alarm call. I made sure the rod was wedged into the ground firmly and rested my leg against it so I could feel any movement. It is like all my senses are intensified, sounds are so loud they make me jumpy and my body reacts nervously to the slightest movement. I feel like an acrobat, every body part accountable for something.

After not too much time the birds took up their usual quarrels with each other and ignored me, and the sound came thick from the trees. For some time I lay on my side with my ear to the cool, damp ground. I could feel how far down the layers of earth went below me like vertigo, with soil and crust and mantle, lithosphere and asthenosphere, all the way down to the fiery nut of the Earth. I could almost hear it, a mellow, churning grumble.

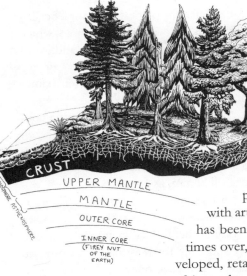

You can't feel that in a built-up place. In a built-up place the ground is thick with artificiality. In a place that has been built and rebuilt many times over, old towns fallen, redeveloped, retarmacked, returfed, that turf in ready cylinders like grass-and-soil Swiss rolls rolled out, plastered new again and again; it feels too structured to feel dizzying. This is a part of the reason I like my lime quarry so much. All its layers. At the lime quarry the earth is bare and cut open like a quiche and inside the quarry you can feel closer to the heart of the Earth, like touching the pit of someone else's scar.

The tundra is so big and open that animals are exposed everywhere, so they keep one eye on me warily, but go about doing their thing as I walk on past. How crawling with life the rough grasses are. Hares rush around and stand sentry, ground squirrels run in little bursts, stopping to gather fruits and buds in their cheeks. A weasel slinks through the grass after the voles, so frantic to gather food for the winter that they let their guard down. Summers are so short that everything is fighting against time to prepare, the predation of winter overshadowing that of everything else.

In Britain we used to have wolves and bears and lynx and bison and even elephants and rhinos a long time ago, but we are such a tiny island that we quickly killed them all and became kings of our little kingdom. Accounts for some of our colonial hubris?

The tundra is specked with water where the frost melts. The permafrost lies underground, starving the drier parts. Lusher grass surrounds waterholes, and elsewhere the grass is hardy and coarse and shrubs are dead-looking. It gives the tundra muted but multifaceted colour. The way the light plays on it from the big sky makes its depth and tone flicker.

As soon as I felt a tug I jumped up and had it over my shoulder before I even knew it and I am glad no one was around to see because the force from flinging it back brought the fish back at me and it hit my front as I turned to it, making me yell. The sound zigzagged away from me into the forest and took several birds with it. It took me a second to remember that there was no one around to hear, but when I realised I was alone, so utterly and completely alone, I laughed and laughed to myself, trying to hold the writhing fish.

And I could feel all of Jack Kerouac's ghosts of the mountain cursing at me for desecrating the art. But if the art is to demonstrate skill rather than a simple utilitarianism then I don't want to be a part of it. It is a man's sport, a battle just to collect its name, possess its specificity, like the Enlightenment exotic specimen collector (one for the collection, a big one for the wall). And to do so *skilfully*, whatever that means, probably with minimal splashing and squealing. They can keep their art.

Once I had it still against the ground I had to stun it to knock it out before I bled it, like Larus showed me on the pilot whale boat. I worried about this part because perhaps it *did* have more culpability than pulling a trigger and watching a thing drop. The fish lay still for me, looking up at the sky through the canopy with its empty orb of an eye. I have thought for a long time that anything I am willing to eat I should be willing to kill. And although I back the philosophy all the way, in practice it is as hard as I hoped it wouldn't be. I am not sure I will ever be able to kill anything without crying at least a little bit.

After it was bled I laid it out flat and took out the *Fauna & Flora of the Denali Wilderness* book to identify it. It was an Arctic grayling, I could tell easy from the fin on its back like a Chinese fan. It was quite little for a grayling, but I can make it last me two meals.

In the tundra I stumbled onto a spruce grouse sat on a clutch of eggs. It occurred to me that I could take her eggs to eat. She looked at me imploringly through one beady eye. I left her.

Other birds seen today:
Osprey
American kestrel
Pintail ducks
Snow geese
Tundra swans
Ring-necked ducks
Grey jay
Horned grebes
Plovers
Mourning doves
Cuckoo

In the south the mountains stood resolutely, still and intangible as a painting, until at one point a light aircraft cut across them, a slow and deliberate finger through perfect dust. When this happens there is a noise with it, a loud droning that I noticed for the first time while watching the first plane. It was lucky that I did because I might have spooked from hearing it without knowing what it came from. I threw myself to the ground on impulse but it was too far away to make me out. From here you could not tell the cabin from the treeline.

On the way back to the cabin I found my first bear print. It made my hairs stand on end; a first encounter. Its print a symbol of its self. A warning, a promise, a truth. But really it is just an imprint a big animal left without meaning to. How strange.

## LITTLE HOUSE IN THE BIG WOODS

It confuses me to have nightmares about a thing I can barely remember now. I had thought it over so many times before that I could no longer tell what was memory and what got added or taken away. Then I stopped remembering it at all, but it came back last night in a bad way.

In the nightmare I found myself cold and dark. I was in an ice cave. In the Arctic. The walls were blue and jagged. It smelled like damp old fish and dead things. My breath billowed in silvery wisps in front of me. Then it would crystallise and fall to the floor in tinkles. On the back of my neck I felt my hair brushed to the side and hot sticky breath ran across it slowly. A hand came from behind and clasped over my mouth, a stubby, sweaty troll hand.

You are not in an ice cave. You are in the meat fridge at work. The hand is clasped tight over your mouth so your whimpering is muffled. The other hand fumbles with your small breasts over the top of the polka-dot starter bra your mum bought you because you are starting to blossom now. You can feel something hard pressing into where your thighs meet the crease in your arse. You know it will make it worse if you squirm but you want to get free. Then you get a chance because someone shouts at him from outside the fridge, his grip loosens and you dig your elbow into his bloated troll belly.

He grunts a troll grunt. He puts his hand around your neck and calls you a little bitch. But then you know it's over because she is shouting to him from the kitchen. He lumbers to the door and as he closes it he leans his face in and runs his tongue over his fat wet lips. The door bangs shut.

You can't cry you can't cry you can't cry because they will shout and send you home, and then what? If you yell Sandra will hear eventually and she will open the door from the outside and let you out and laugh at you for being scared of the dark and getting yourself stuck in the fridge again.

Was it as bad as the dream felt or was the dream just a collage from things the other girls had told you? No matter what you remember, it is nothing special, of course. Almost every girl you know has a troll to remind her that her body is not her own.

It was pouring today so I stayed cooped up inside. The cabin is cosy with the little fire going, the tapping on the roof and sides adding sound contours that make it feel particularly safe, so I felt better. Because I had the time I made the fire with sticks from my kindling pile. I am very proud of the fire. It took me about ten minutes to get smoke, then another five to get it going properly. I have guarded and fed it all day like a little pet. Kaczynski complained in his diary that he failed to consistently make fire without striking matches and that it annoyed him greatly. I am more authentic than Ted Kaczynski!

I did go out just to see how bad it was and got a headache from the hammering of icy raindrops on my crown. It was too heavy to see much and I got soaked through, so I will have to stay put until it slackens off. I have enough food to last and a bit of fish. Hopefully it will have stopped overnight, though.

I watched back and edited a lot of footage and it is coming together but in a way I am not quite sure about. Mostly when I watch things back they do not feel like I remember them. People seem to be very different to how they really seemed at the time. There is so much responsibility in putting the pieces of what has happened together to follow a story. And there is Rochelle, who will not fit into my story. And then there are the things that can't and do not say anything at all and lie vacant for my projections.

Am I pulling them out of the water like fish to look at? Like they are specimens and I am writing them into my field book? There is a gap between what they are and what I think they are and I am trying to talk about this gap with authority, declaring I know what I see and it is this.

I did a lot of reading. Then I did a video diary entry. Then I got bored and decided to search around the hut for hidden things. I had figured it must be at least fifty years old, maybe even one hundred. I had not bothered to check it properly for signatures like I had the tower, aside from a quick sweep. I felt sure I had missed something.

I checked all the obvious places again first, the walls around the cot, the desk with everything taken off it. Then I found them in a corner of the room. Now I have found them I do not know how I did not notice them before. It was not an obvious place, sure, and most are really faint, but there were enough of them. They are mostly names and dates, the earliest being 1929 and the most recent P Harris again, 1999. I counted seven authors of six signatures and five quotes. Some of the classics:

'Going to the mountains is going home' — John Muir

'I went to the woods because I wished to live deliberately, to front only the essential facts of life, and see if I could not learn what it had to teach, and not, when I came to die, discover that I had not lived' — Thoreau

I checked, out of curiosity, behind the fox head (there is also the compulsion to leave a mark that no one will ever notice). It just said Caroline, in very tiny print, with no date. It was the only obviously female name in here. Even where the names were ambiguous, the handwriting on the wall was all very masculine. What I mean by this is that maybe the men who wrote on the wall had learned to express themselves as men, to express their *man-sized* ideas in a handwriting that was reflective of how they held and thought of themselves.

Because they author these ideas like they *belonged* to them by virtue of being men. Thoreau and that bunch always talked, of course, in lofty terms of Man and He. In search of some inspirational wilderness quotes from women before I started the documentary, most to be found came from low-brow memoirs of the self-help kind and had to do with inner journeys rather than the outer objective Truths of the Mountain Men, and had titles like *The Single Woman: Life, Love and a Dash of Sass* or *Pink Boots and a Machete: My Journey from NFL Cheerleader to National Geographic Explorer.*

I wanted Caroline to know, if she ever came back, that I liked that she had hidden herself. I drew a little smiley face ☺ next to her name.

## MESSAGE IN A BOTTLE

INT. CABIN, AFTERNOON — *Erin is sat on the cot — daylight bleeds inside, casts light over dust motes — camera is hand-held — in shot are cabin cot, Erin from shoulders up, and window — it is raining heavily —*

**Erin:** So this morning I found something really interesting. After the autograph wall that I found yesterday. And the signature behind the fox head. I was sure there could be other more hidden things but I wasn't sure where else they could be. I was actually under the desk—

— *camera view turns towards the desk as Erin gets off the cot and directs the camera to it —*

**Erin:** As you can see, there isn't anything there

*— camera sweeps the underside of the desk —*

**Erin:** But. In checking under the desk I found something else. If you look here—

*— camera view turns to the floor — Erin is kneeling, her right knee moves against the floorboard, which gives — the opposite end of the board rises, around one inch — Erin fishes around underneath with her free hand —*

**Erin:** Oh. I can't do it one-handed

*— camera is placed on the floor —*

**Erin:** And underneath. I hadn't thought to check under the floor because I was sure there was just the foundations underneath there. But here, as you can see—

*— camera is picked up and view is directed towards the floor — the floorboard now removed and placed to the side — camera takes two seconds to focus in low light —*

**Erin:** Someone has dug out the ground underneath the floorboards. And they have left a little parcel

*— camera is now in focus — in the hole there is a package wrapped in tarpaulin, about the size of a shoebox — Erin takes the package out of the hole —*

**Erin:** Isn't this exciting? So I found this little package. And now I suppose I should open it

*— camera is placed on the desk with a view of the cot — Erin sits cross-legged on the cot with the package on her lap —*

**Erin:** It's like Christmas

*— she looks down at the package with her hands placed on top — pushes hair behind her ears —*

**Erin:** I'm kind of nervous. I hope it's not a letter bomb

*— she looks at the camera — pulls one corner of her mouth down in mock-nervousness —*

**Erin:** Okay, then

*— she starts to unwrap the parcel — carefully, particularly —*

**Erin:** I wonder how long it's been down there

*— having undone the parcel string and peeled away each corner of the tarpaulin she takes out a fabric bundle — she carefully unwraps the fabric bundle —*

**Erin** (ABSENTLY): I suppose they wanted to make sure it kept dry

*— inside the fabric bundle is a parcel wrapped in newspaper —*

**Erin** (ABSENTLY): It's like a game of pass the bloody parcel

*— she stops with a piece of the newspaper in her hand — studies it —*

**Erin** (ABSENTLY): Oh, I'll check afterwards

*— she lifts the objects from inside the paper one by one and lays them out on the cot very carefully —*

**Erin:** Okay, we have a roll of paper. A book. It's maybe a diary. A folded piece of paper. Some postcards from Alaska

*— she picks up the book and opens it —*

**Erin:** It's a diary. The first entry is dated the 14th of May 1986. It's signed Damon. Then inverted underneath. Nomad

*— she brings the book towards the camera and holds up the name, pointing with her forefinger — in spidery handwriting DAMON is written, then backwards underneath its mirror image —* ИOMAD —

**Erin:** I don't know if that's an alias or just a happy coincidence. Or a self-fulfilling prophecy

*— she sits back on the cot and picks up the scroll — unscrolls it —*

**Erin:** Okay. This is a manifesto. I won't go into it now. We'll look at it in detail later

*— she studies it for a second then turns it to face the camera, holding it closer for inspection — then she turns it around and considers it again —*

**Erin:** Some kind of Ted Kaczynski manifesto

*— she carefully rescrolls it and places it back on the cot — picks up the folded paper —*

**Erin:** And finally

*— she unfolds it and pauses, brow crumpling — studies it for seven seconds —*

**Erin** (ABSENTLY): Damn it. I should have known it. (REMEMBERING THE CAMERA) Erm. It's a map. Predictably

*— she frowns at it some more —*

**Erin:** It's better than my map (LAUGHING). Goddammit

*— she folds it pedantically and tucks it into the back of the diary — she places the diary back on the cot — she sits with her hands in her lap then distractedly places the newspaper over the top of the diary —*

**Erin:** That's exciting. What an exciting find

*— she looks directly at the camera, holds her gaze for four seconds — fidgets —*

**Erin:** I'll have to take a look at it all in more detail. Figure out this guy's story

*— she touches her face absently —*

**Erin:** Try and figure out if anyone found the package before

*— she twists her hair round a finger —*

**Erin** (ABSENTLY): Yeah

*— she stops twiddling her hair and stares into space, caught in a thought — five seconds — snaps out of it —*

**Erin** (SUDDENLY/BRIGHTLY): Anyway. Today is day three of the floods and the rain is still relentless

*— looks out of the window —*

**Erin:** Doesn't seem like it will subside very soon so no meat for Erin for a while. I'll have to get outside today, though, because I'm almost out of water. I'll wear my anorak. It will be nice to go outside. Yes

*— she sits for a few seconds looking out of the window then snaps to — approaches the camera —*

**Erin:** Okay. Over and out. (MUTTERS) That was stupid

*— she fumbles with the camera to cut —*

## CUT

## HOW THE MOUNTAIN GOT ITS NAME

I attempted a video diary entry and retook it about five times. None of them seemed right to me. I am thinking about how far I have come now and whether I am passing Leopold's test yet. I certainly feel more 'in tune' with the 'rhythms of life.' It is hard to talk about something so personal and unspecific. I was shooting a sequence on the map that was in the parcel. In the first cut I was saying that I had to burn this map too, like I did Stan's pocket map, had to burn it as quickly as I could before it embossed on my mind and corroded the claim of *pure invention* so that this place could still be mine. Then when I had the lighter to it I just could not do it. And the more I held it out with my thumb, scratching at the friction wheel, ready to light it, the more I looked at it. And the more I looked at it the more it embossed on my mind. Then the integrity was gone anyway so I figured I might as well not burn it. My thumb hurt from rubbing and rubbing the lighter without actually striking it.

So then I had to soliloquise about why I was not going to burn the map. But the map glared at me, making itself more and more familiar, and as I got madder at it I thought that I might still get rid of it like I did the other map, because I had seen that one too. Besides I could not just leave it, knowing it was so heavy. I mean like the heaviness you must feel when you find Roman vases in the dirt and you just know that they are not any old broken pottery because you can feel their *heaviness* from just looking. I had to acknowledge it, like holding a tiny funeral for a mouse that the cat brought in because it does not feel right to just let it be.

But Damon had made it and it was his time capsule and yet he would never know any better. And then again he left it here in the eighties and he could very well be planning on coming back for it one day. Maybe he really never meant anyone but himself to find it.

So I could not burn it. I had to put it back in the ground and pretend I never found it. I left out the diary and the manifesto for now because I need to study them. I do not think there is hypocrisy in this. He will never know I read the diary and the manifesto wants to be read and the map I could just try to forget.

A thing I did notice is that our maps are different. He marked different features on his to those I drew on mine. He marked some that I have not found, and some of mine were missing. I just have to be careful not to let seeing his infiltrate on my personal wilderness.

## I AM THAT I AM AND THE REST IS
## WOMEN & WILDERNESS

INT. CABIN, MORNING — *Erin is sat on the cot — camera is on desk opposite — in shot are cabin cot, Erin sat cross-legged, and the window — it is raining heavily still —*

**Erin:** I have been sat inside the cabin for five days now without leaving except to use the toilet. The rain is relentless. I have been thinking lots about what it's like to be alone for so long. It feels like right now the whole experiment is being intensified because I am not even outside and around nature. The only time I am solitary really is when I am inside alone. This is the biggest test

*— her voice is low and sleepy — she yawns —*

**Erin:** It's just me, myself and I

*— she frowns as if she does not know why she said it —*

**Erin:** Oh, that was stupid. Reshoot

*— she stares at the camera long enough so that she can cut out the first part in editing and begin talking as though she were just starting —*

**Erin:** It has been raining now for five days and I have been isolated inside the whole time. I don't have much stimulation in here apart from these guys, who are sort of helping

*— she nods to her pile of books —*

**Erin:** I can pretend we are in conversation. In here I don't have nature to make me feel small. I am surrounded only by all this male intellect. It is the only thing that stops me from disappearing. But it is maddening because their words are not mine. They keep reminding me that. The wilderness is not mine. And at the same time it is all I am. I keep thinking zone of middle dimension. I keep thinking, okay, Newton

*— her eyes keep darting to just next to the camera's eye — she touches her face and hair, as though she is looking in a mirror, checking reflection — the viewfinder of the camera is probably turned towards her —*

**Erin:** I am so wholly excluded from the communion. And without being outside all I have is these abstracted unattainable thoughts on nature. Why the fuck am I even reading this. URGH

*— she throws Emerson across the room —*

**Erin:** Am I doing it right? I need to get back outside

*— she pauses then exhales suddenly through nose — puts face into hands — sits still, rubbing her eyelids with her fingers —*

**Erin** (TO HERSELF): Maybe I can't do this. Will the spirit of the mountain disqualify me for wishing I just had someone female to talk to? Is a lone bird on a tree on a lonely mountain singing to itself? Oh, for fuck's sake. Reshoot

*— she rubs her face with both hands — slaps her cheeks — takes a deep breath — looks right into the camera —*

**Erin:** It's okay to not be content one hundred percent of the time. Right, mountain spirit? If it were easy then it wouldn't be hardship. And maybe it's right to feel lonely. I can do this. I am strong enough to do this. This is the hardest part. The rain will stop soon. The only time I am lonely is when I am inside too long. Besides. I am not lonely. I have the camera and my books

*— her resolute smile lingers and then fades —*

**Erin** (MUTTERING): Oh, I can't use that. This is useless

— *she gets up from the cot and reaches over for the camera* —

## CUT

## EMPTY THE TANKS!

I am confused about the postcards in Damon's parcel. The post-cards are written in Damon's handwriting but are addressed to different people at different addresses all across North America, Canada and Alaska. They are all dated September 1987 and are all of the same kind of sentiment. Damon is thanking people for their hospitality, help and friendship. He is telling them they are beautiful people with room for improvement. Then he is telling them they can improve by living for themselves. He is telling them to cast off their chains and live like he will live, purposefully and free. Then he ends with an ostentatious phrase about casting out into the unknown. He insinuates that they might never meet again.

I suppose this is what he would have liked to say to these peo-ple, as though they were parting words, but something stopped him. The strange thing is that the postcards are stamped and bent at the corners and marked like they have travelled. I think maybe he did more than one journey like this, and he brought them to the cabin with him as some kind of token.

It is still raining. Last night I had the epiphany to leave out one of the cooking pans to fill up with rainwater so I did not need to venture out to get water from the spring. The rain battered against the hood of my anorak in a way that was exhilarating, an overload of stimulation after endless days inside the muted dry. I ran about in it, yelping and laughing for a few minutes before retiring back inside like a fish that comes out from under its rock to dance a little in a flurry of excitement then catch itself and slink off back into the shadows. It was exhausting and after I wanted the stillness of the cabin again.

Inside I peeled off my anorak and my sodden leggings and hung them up next to the grate. Then I coaxed a fire and set myself on the cot in view of the pan through the window, with my books. I quickly forgot about the pan, though, and did not remember it until late afternoon, when my mouth was feeling suddenly dry. My clothes had dried and I was loath to get them wet again, so I took off my trousers to fetch the pan in just my anorak. It was brimming with water, with a couple of drowned insects for good measure. I picked these out and put the pot on top of the fire to boil.

I filled my canteen with the boiled water and set it to cool. Then I made a broth from the rest of the water with one of the flavour packets from the instant noodles. I curled up on the cot and wrapped myself in the blanket and my sleeping bag with a tin mug of the hot savoury water. I smelled must from the blanket, and savoury, and me. The little excursion earlier in the day had made me overwhelmingly sleepy. I fell into it and slept for the rest of the day and long into the evening.

I usually like to rise early and keep myself busy but with the rain I have been dead heavy all the time and dull and lethargic, but I wake in the middle of the night and I have an interlude of energy before falling back to sleep again. I use this time to read and write and draw, and wish the rain would stop so I could go night walking. I am dreaming lots again.

A thing I have noticed is that they are all in the present tense. As in I am not dreaming about things from before here, no memories or other people or anything. No one I know, at least. Kind of spectral figures. Familiar strangers.

# THE GOD PARTICLE, THE GOD TRICK

LOCATION: wooden cabin; Denali wilderness; Alaskan tundra; Alaska; Earth; 3rd planet of Sol; inner rim of Orion Arm; the Milky Way; the Local Group; Virgo Supercluster; The Universe; Everywhere Ever and All Over Again.

The tundra is always whistling. wwwwWWWWWhhhHHH-Hhhh. The tundra is empty. The tundra is partitioned by colour. There is the green-grey flat ground that I am on, the cabin, then the white-blue mountains. The mountains look like a backdrop. I feel like Truman Burbank.

If I sit still for long enough the whistling sounds like words. Big snowflake tumbleweed rolls just under my line of focused vision. I blink and it is gone.

If I sit still for long enough my eyes go blurry like a mirage. Like heat waves but cold, cold. It is hard to focus even when I blink hard.

Another sound starts behind the whistling. It sounds like a plane; I look around for one. Negative. It sounds like a person humming; I look around for a person. Negative. It sounds like bees. My hand tickles and there is a bee on it. Affirmative. The bee sits happy. I must be dreaming. The humming is louder.

In the shimmery mirage there is a dark shape coming closer. There is a figure in a cloak, furs, beads, skulls and with a staff. Her voice is very strange. I can't see the features of her face because of the bees, which swarm in a flat mask. As if her face has no shape; no pits, no curves, no nose. It is hard to tell where the sound comes out from. There is a vibration on her voice, as if she's speaking through a laryngophone, as if her voice emanates from all the tiny mouths of the bees in unison. It gives her what you might call an otherworldly aura. Almost techno-human. Like Professor Stephen Hawking. It is authorial.

Stephen Hawking has a daughter called Lucy and she grew up to be a writer. She wanted to inspire children to get excited about space and physics and all the things she grew up in awe of. She writes adventure books about a little boy called George who likes space. Isn't that frustrating?

She moves to sit by my side on my log, which does not budge under her, as though she is weightless. I look at her closely and, sure, she has this shimmering quality, buzzing and wavery and nearly not there, like a model of an atom spinning on its axis, just slow enough for you to see the falter, its constituent parts flickering visible. I reach out to touch her and can't seem to, her contours blurring as my hand gets close, but hovering just above I can feel her. A kind of soft quivering, a pulsating that feels like sound, low sirens in my temples. She draws in the dirt with the end of her staff. The gravelly sound makes me hungry. Like Coco Pops without milk. Her voice has an ungraspable familiarity to it; it is hard to concentrate on what she is saying because of her bee beard.

*The circle is the antithesis of the triangle, because the circle stands for cycles which are even and infinite. In the centre of a circle you are always the same distance from the edge.*

O

*The ghost of Adam Smith sits on a triangle that is held upright by the shoulders of his crawling subordinates. He is hoarding all the power, and as it grows exponentially, the growth of others is depleted. But as the others are depleted, they are harmed to the point of abandonment (the bees are the first to leave him). As such, he loses his sense of self, which depended on a sense of the others.*

So that is where the bees have gone. Around a week and a half has passed since I left Stan's. I cannot be completely sure because I put a bit of tape over the date and time on the laptop for now and I have spent a lot of time sleeping when I should be awake and waking when I should be asleep. I have been inventing people for company, to talk to and mitigate the loneliness. Are invented people a corruption of solitude?

I have bathed once in the stream in all this time, little splash washes on my smelliest parts now and then. I smell but I only notice this when I take off my underwear in the toilet shed. The rest of the time my smell is enveloped into me by my clothes. It worries me when I take off my underwear that I may attract bears.

My face itches a lot because I keep touching it; I keep touching it because I think I am growing a beard; I think I am growing a beard because of the itching. There is not a mirror and the camcorder is just illusive enough to make me think I can see hair.

From the bee-figure dream I can pinpoint exactly in my subconscious the fodder for it. Back in the visitors' centre at the entrance to Denali Park there were displays on all of the cultures indigenous to Alaska. I remember a diagram explaining the position of the individual in the Yupik Eskimo belief system in relation to the animals and plants it shared its home with, termed *Cosmological Reproductive Cycling*. In the diagram the human was part of a sort of energy transferral web, in the shape of a circle. It made me think at the time of a diagram we had in biology class, a food pyramid used to describe energy transferral in the animal kingdom. On the biggest pyramid and at the top sat the human, the unchallenged dominant omnivore at the top of the food chain.

Adam Smith casts·himself as the dominant creature of the triangle and food chain and propagates this as the natural order of things. He eats a mass of lesser creatures who have themselves eaten a mass of even lesser creatures who have been grazing on chicken nuggets and apathy because their natural food source is inaccessible to them (these are the crawling subordinates). All of their power accumulates in Adam Smith. He uses this as an economic analogy, substituting for food or energy wealth or money.

The triangle food pyramid is used to explain hierarchy in nature and justify Adam Smith's dominance. But it only looks that way because he said it does. The wolf does not sit on top of a pyramid. The wolf is dependent on the grass because when the grass dies the deer dies and when the deer thrives the wolf thrives and when the wolf overreaches the wolf is brought into check by its own hubris because the deer disappear and after a short period of thriving the wolf does too.

For the Yupik, like Naaja's Inuit, nothing alive died but was reborn, and this was honoured in hunting ritual so power could never be accumulated but only transferred.

*The orca and the wolf were seen as highly spiritual creatures that aided humans in hunting, and so offerings were made to both to maintain good relationships. The spirit that resided in each was interchangeable, in winter it was embodied in the wolf that brought the deer and in summer the orca that brought the walrus.*

*When an animal was killed as prey, it was returned to the wild to become complete again. To aid this, the bones of the carcass remained unbroken, and there was a farewell ritual where the animal would be entertained with drum music. If the animal was pleased with its treatment as a guest, it would return again in the future.*

I am surprised Stan could retain his survival-of-the-fittest worldview when spending so much time in the park centre. I suppose he must not pay too much attention to the plaques.

# THE WILD AS A PROJECT OF THE SELF

During the night the rain stopped! I woke up to its lack of noise. It took me a while to realise it had not stopped completely. The gentler rain was white noise. I fell to sleep again feeling looser.

The rain was slack still when I woke up and I decided to try some fishing. It has been days since I have eaten anything that is not beige and the urge to get outside was so great that I twitched with it.

*I think a boreal owl?*

Walking through the forest the rain was less dense still. It fell in fatter drops and at a different tempo to the rain as it hit the canopy above. The noise of rain inside the forest was both dulled and intensified, like a storm from underneath a high church roof. It was much more peaceful in the forest and I felt a stillness come over again for the first time in days.

I decided to try out on the lake in the tundra. I had been stupid to think I could just fish from the lake with my shoddy short rod. But lucky for me there was a rock that worked a bit like a jetty and let me sit with my short line in the deeper water. In the still water where the rod dripped, the beads skimmed on top for seconds like water beetles skating, before sinking.

It was luckily an okay spot. It took less than an hour to hook something and I wished I had a way to make the fish keep better so I could stock up and get all the death over in one go for a while. I stunned the fish against the rock jetty, trying to do it without thinking too much. A large ant struggled a tiny caterpillar that was twice its size over my rock and back to its queen. I attached the dead fish to the hook so I could walk it back without having to carry it in my hands. I wiped my hands on some damp grass with lake water to get rid of some of the sticky smell.

When I looked up I went stiff. On the opposite side of the lake there was a bear come out of nowhere while I was busy with the fish. A bloody big grizzly. I forgot my entire body and the rod fell out of my hands and the bear stilled too. It watched me watch it from my plinth on the rock, its fur flittering in the wind. It was close enough to see that but it was still small across the big lake. There was a potent unreality to it. It was still and mysterious in an accidental way and I felt very suddenly that something in me was going to be different from then on.

I put my hand on my chest to feel my heart beating vigorously but it was not. In fact I did not feel like I thought I would at all. Since I had got out to the cabin The Bear had existed like an aura, since before that even on the ice sheet, the Greenlandic tundra. It had felt conspicuous for not being there; lingering like a promise and quivering with anticipation and fear. And I had thought back then that it would feel like opening up, that I would see that Fire burning in its eyes and recognise myself in it. But instead after all there it was so suddenly. It looked so benign and abstract, an apparition. I wondered if perhaps it was.

*I want to see myself in you.*
*But we are very different.*

I felt like if I turned away it might disappear, and although some flight response was tugging me gently, telling me to get away, I did not want to turn my back on it. It seemed to be thinking the same of me. I started to think maybe we would be trapped like this forever, perpetually watching each other watching in wary fascination.

My blood tingled vigorously and I could feel it filling me up all the way to the tips of my fingers and toes, so that the sensation of my feet in my shoes felt like containment, like what it must feel like to be liquid and formless but held in shape, my hands like rubber gloves full of water. Like zero gravity. Like proprioception.

I put one foot behind the other on the rock, using my heel to feel out the stable parts, and climbed down off it without ever breaking contact with its eyes. I put down the rod in case it thought I was brandishing it. Then I started to tiptoe, desperately slow, closer towards it, following the lakeside. I was trying to move so slowly that it might not even notice. To get closer to it and really feel its presence. To commune.

I have never felt such an acute kind of instinctual consideration of what it is to not be alive. It became clear then that any nostalgia that we feel from *The Call of the Wild* is the pang of what we remember but do not have, from where we are before we go in search of it. It is all of the prospects of having life taken and of not being and of things that you can never possess or control or put into words. In that moment I forgot the anxiety of having a body, I forgot the need to possess it.

While I was thinking all this I had got a lot closer and I could feel my heart then where I could not before, throbbing in my throat like a pulsar. I was shaking badly from concentrating so hard on my stealth. The grizzly bear stared at me, transfixed. Unmoved and hypnotic stare. We were both fixed on each other in fear and desire or morbid fascination. Or none of that. Just purely under spell.

*But in that way I see me in you, in what I am not.*

Then it jerked its head. A sudden lurch snapping the thread that had formed between us. It peeled its black lips back to show its teeth and it jolted me to notice I was so close as to see its teeth clearly. It padded one front paw behind the other, walking its front legs backwards into itself, then using the weight of the rest of its body and jumping a little to bring its forelegs up and stand bipedal, unfolding to its full height and stature. Huge. Fuck.

I could see the matting of its fur where its underbelly was wet. It huffed through its nostrils, short, deep grunts.

*What am I doing what the fuck am I doing.*

Abruptly out of trance now. I suddenly see myself from right up above, as though looking down. I am small and it is big and the lake is huge blue glass beside us and the grass goes on on on around us and there is nowhere for cover.

I keep absolutely still and try to think. What did the pamphlet say what did the pamphlet say. Direct eye contact. Did it not say never to make — very dangerous. I avert my eyes, lower my head, still trying to see it. Keep one hundred feet between you. Was it one hundred? Five hundred? Maybe fifty. How far is fifty feet? Either way it is too late now. What else? Do not go without pepper spray. Well, that one's out. It said calm, monotone voice. Let it know you are human.

Hi bear. Nice bear. Gratey-shrill with fear. Be submissive. Shoulders down. Bow head. Respect respect, bowing like a Tibetan prostrating, bow-crawling a pilgrimage. Slowly slowly up the mountain. Back away slowly.

*Where the bloody hell am I?*

Rocks under heels making me unsteady. Cannot turn around cannot make it look like fleeing and initiate a chase. It does not come after me. It stands, watching me go. When I have reversed, undone my journey back where I started, let's not do that again, it lets itself fall limply to its feet. Thud.

And then it walks away. And I have to say that I did not see the Fire and that its eyes were vague from where I stood. It has nothing to give me apart from its just being and its bear-ness. Probably it will never think of me again and I will remember it always. But that is because the bear does not have sensibilities because it does not need them. It already knows all of this. I did not have the camera for any of this so as far as the documentary is concerned it did not happen. Which makes me think, funny, it was the most *happened to* that I have ever felt.


## SISTER

This morning the strangest thing happened. I was sat around in the cabin doing a video diary entry when my back started to tingle and the hairs on my neck and arms stood up, and I got the sure feeling that I was being watched. At first I put it down to being on the camera but then I felt I could feel its direction, as if it were coming from behind.

I turned very carefully, as though whoever it was would not notice me turning if it was just slow enough. Outside the window, just inside the trees and standing half beneath a shadow, a reindeer was stood still as anything, its legs so straight the wind could knock it over. It just stood there looking and I stared back at it through the window and it just went on like that, looking right at me and not flinching a muscle.

Now I know there are not many reindeer in this part of Alaska at this time of year but here was this reindeer looking at me with an intensity and persistence. I went outside to it to see if it would turn and run away from me because it was creeping me out just standing there. I needed to get closer to see it was real and solid and breathing. I walked slowly towards it and my blood clunked in my ears every step I got nearer because it really was not budging any. Then, as I got within around five metres, it suddenly huffed and took a step backwards. It came to as if from out of a trance and started to back away, baby-step by baby-step. Then it half-circled around me as if at the distance of a force field, and loped slowly out towards the tundra. The whole time it kept looking back at me warily.

But the strangest thing about it was that the reindeer came to me first in a dream. Last night I was outside just kind of staring at the forest moving in the wind, waving like water, at the pinkish tundra evergreens dotted like Christmas cake decorations, at the rust-red mountains glinting back the sun in streaks, the clouds behind their own snowy mountain range, just gently spinning round to get everything in panorama, when the figure appeared in front of me again.

*Child must have a comrade animal in order to be protected from the bad spirits.*

My head reeled a little from the spinning. I must have looked scared at talk of bad spirits.

*Not all spirits are bad. Most are good and watch over us. Besides, you will have the reindeer. I will find you one.*

*Who are the bad spirits?*

*The bad spirits are spirits without forms. Just spirits that are waiting to be in bodies again. They are not really bad. Just envious. They like to cause mischief to keep themselves occupied. Sometimes that mischief is death but really death only means to be made to change form again.*

I was incredulous.

*But I quite like my form.*

*And this is the tragedy of death. But it is a short-lived one.*

She dissolved back into the forest, then promptly reappeared leading a reindeer.

*This will be your reindeer. She is a herd mother so her imprint is very heavy.*

*Imprint?*

*All things have an imprint. It is the weight of the energy. Some are heavy and others are lighter.*

*What does it do?*

*It defines your potency. A heavier imprint leaves more of an effect. But an imprint can be positive or negative. If you have a heavier imprint you have a responsibility to be positive. But you must also remember that others with a weaker imprint are just as important but in different ways.*

The bees droned around her. They bustled over each other, to the very edges of her eyes. I thought I knew those eyes, like a word trapped behind the tonsils. I touched the reindeer. Its fur was soft and downy like a kitten's tummy and its skin hummed underneath with its charge.

*You can find imprint everywhere.*

Seeing the reindeer today brought it all back. What is going on here? Women are after all irrational and mystical, so maybe I was just being a girl about it? Would an actual real-life visitation feel any different to a hallucination anyway? If a hallucination is a work of your subconscious, it is already a message from another realm in a way. How do you tell the difference? *For human society I was obliged to conjure up the former occupants of these woods,* said Thoreau of the days real people did not pop into his cabin by the pond at Walden.

The reindeer kept on loping and looking and stopping from time to time to turn and stare back at the hut. I stayed out there shivering in my pyjamas, watching it go.


## HOW TO KILL AND DIE

After the reindeer incident the bee-figure keeps appearing to me in animal form. I will be walking through the woods and she will appear to me, for example as a brown ermine, springing from behind a tree so very suddenly there and sitting on her hind legs in a way that says *I am no mortal brown ermine.* I can always tell it is really her, sometimes by ways like this, as though me and the animal are communicating, and sometimes even when she chooses not to acknowledge me in this way, by signs from the physical world. I would call this other kind maybe an increase in *density*, like Roman-vase heaviness, for example the sudden pick-up of the wind when in the presence of the golden eagle, or a sudden stillness, or anything else that feels like it is hinting at significance.

I went far into the tundra today for more food. I saw another golden eagle, or the same golden eagle, and a gyrfalcon. I had been hungry for the taste of meat that was not fish and had to kill by my own hand again if I was ever to build up enough karma points to eat meat back at home. I thought about what she had said and it gave me motivation to take full responsibility for the transferral that maintains my own energy.

The clouds were moving fast in the direction I was walking and if I stood still with my head up to face them they would glide over and I would feel my belly go as if I were still moving too. The sun was hanging evening-low and its angle filled the clouds up with colour, so that they were pink in its face and purple in shadow and it was a big ball of orange, opaque enough to look at, leaking its hue onto the grass and making it orange too. The sky felt close and low like a projection inside a planetarium, the tundra wide and empty, and walking north as I was, they went on together uninterrupted until they disappeared behind the curve of the Earth, and it made me feel big and small to look at it all.

I did it like she says to. This time when I saw the hare I wanted, and I saw more of them because of the flat of the tundra, I considered my shot carefully and struck it in the hind. It had seen me and stood semi-wary, but I suppose it did not bolt because it was too unused to the sight of me to understand. It looked me in the eye before it took my bullet. I ran over to where it dropped to witness the magnitude of what I had done. It was still alive, like she said I should hope it would be. I picked up its warm limp body and held it up to face my face, and looked in at the life fading there. I poured some water from my bottle into its mouth so that it would not be thirsty. I shook from the sobs and tried to share in its suffering. And I am sure that its was much worse than mine, but it felt less like cheating to let it see me cry.

I told it I was sorry. I thanked it for giving me its body. And I made a promise to it that when the time came I would offer my body back to the Earth for it as nourishment and that I would be happy to do so. And in that moment, I knew it and I meant it and I felt the gravity of what it meant to say it.

## REMEMBERING THE *ANIMA MUNDI*

INT. CABIN — VIEW THROUGH WINDOW — *camera is in hand-held position: on cot facing out of the window — outside a reindeer is stood, grazing, very close to the window —*

**Erin** (EXCITEDLY): Look. Look, there it is again

*— the camera jerks with her hands and she moves to get a better view, cot squeaking — camera is steadied — focuses in on reindeer —*

**Erin:** I'm going to go out to her

*— view of camera scrambled, bed, ceiling, floor, as Erin clambers off the cot — floorboards — padding feet — pause — readjust — door —*

**Erin** (WHISPERING): Got to be really quiet and careful. Don't want to scare her

*— door is pushed open and outside light spills in — camera adjusts to light — camera moves around the door — reindeer in view from behind, about five metres distance — it can be heard huffing into the dirt as it tears the grass up — door creaks —*

**Erin** (WHISPERING): Shhhhhssh

*— reindeer suddenly picks up its head — turns to look directly at camera — bolts forward in surprise —*

**Erin:** Oh no oh no come back don't go

*— camera jolts side to side with her movement — jogging after it as it trots away into tree cover —*

**Erin:** Hahahaha

*— she stops running after it, watches it go — reindeer disappears into the black of the dense trees —*

## CUT

## WIKI HOW TO FIND YOUR POWER ANIMAL

Your power animal may come to you in a dream or meditation or in its actual physical form in waking life. Have you noticed unusual behaviour from a particular animal? Or do you keep encountering the same animal or the same animal species an amount that surprises you? Maybe you are noticing them regularly, as an image or as an object. Does the orca, for example, appear to you in the image form, emblazoned on everyday objects like T-shirts? Did you hear someone talking about going to watch Shamu at SeaWorld? Was *Free Willy* on when you turned on your television?

What animal intrigues and captivates you? What animal do you notice most, not only out in wild nature, but also in your everyday life as an image? If you feel attracted to an animal and it keeps appearing, in the physical world or in a dream, it may be a sign that the animal is seeking to reveal itself to you.

How does the animal make you feel? When you see the animal how does its presence make its impact on you? Do you feel its presence before you see it? What emotion does it evoke? Does it scare you? Does it elate you? Do the feeling and the apparitions/appearances coincide with particular situations in your life? Is there a sense of déjà vu? Do you feel about the animal as you feel about the situation?

The power animal could represent your feelings, or a situation that recurs in your mind, or a person or an event from your past, present or future.

If you answered mostly yes to the above in relation to a particular creature, then you have found your power animal! Learn to honour your power animal.

Another thing Sam said that I had never stopped to think about was that it is actually pretty offensive that suddenly young people on the internet want to know their 'power animal,' a New Age corruption of a particular native belief, through an online quiz. What I wanted to say back but didn't was that maybe aside from being appropriative and corruptive in its associations, this signifies a suppressed and lost desire for closer affinity with the animals. That rather than stealing a tradition because we think it sounds e n l i g h t e n e d, maybe there could be a more careful way to go about remembering a connection that was always there before?

It is hard to feel a connection with *any* animal in a spiritual way as a British person when the only animals you are surrounded by are domesticated cats, dogs, cows, sheep, horses and then symbols or images of animals. If symbols are mostly what we have to go on, is this uselessly inauthentic, just too far removed? A symbol of a symbol, not a direct one like a bear track in the mud? Do they lose their potency when you take them from an advert on television?

But if we are to feel affinity in order to care, which we must, then symbols are all we have to work with. And if we each held an animal in affinity, a comrade animal, wouldn't we care more about the continuation of its species? Maybe at birth we should all be given a comrade animal selected at random from a vast database. If you knew that a sea cucumber is an echinoderm from the class *Holothuroidea* and you were born into symbolic kinship with it, you would likely care more that it carried on slinking along the sea floor. You would feel the responsibility to help it along.

An animal's symbolic meaning can be as potent an acknowledgement of our shared invention of that symbol as the animal itself, and maybe more so. Ted Kaczynski made a comrade of the snowshoe rabbit. He called it Grandfather Rabbit. Whenever he shot a snowshoe rabbit he would say, 'Thank you, Grandfather Rabbit.' He would get a mystic desire to draw them. He drew and thought about them so much that he actually began to think like a rabbit.

## THE ATOMIC PRIESTHOOD

I am back on the old estate. As in most of suburbia there are always a lot of cats. Maybe every third house has a cat and almost all the rest have dogs. Only everyone is gathered around a fire pit that has been dug out of the concrete in the centre of our cul-de-sac. The limp little cat bodies are thrown into the pit because they are full of an invisible death.

There is a potion that has brewed itself from all the chemical run-offs, the Roundup and the Miracle Gro from every impossibly green lawn, trim as porn pubes, then the bleach from the sparkling toilet bowls, the suds of Fairy and Colgate, the nail varnish remover on cotton buds, the Dettol-soaked cloths. Carefully measured so as to be harmless alone but altogether in the cesspits under the roads forming new chemical combinations, transmutations, chance alchemies augmented by years of accumulation. Then pouring over the tarmac when drains fill up in rain, distributed as anomalies in the chain, distilled and distilled up and up, a fusion of the inorganic that leaves its mark as a *negative imprint* like she said, malignant and unseen, the tick that sucks the mouse dry.

But no one knows where the invisible death comes from because they can't see it so all the dead cats must be burned to save the live ones. Some of the afflicted cats, the ones still alive but coughing, are also thrown onto the fire. Children are kept inside.

The voice comes from beside me, and I recognise it immediately, without the humming mediation. It is the voice that I had in my head the whole time I read *Silent Spring*, scrapped together from a brief interview Larus showed us; undeviatingly calm and certain, a little drawling, with a trail of whistle to the end of every word. She holds a staff in her right hand; the tiny bird skulls and shells go clack-clack-clack. A few singular bees crawl about the lichen of her skin. 'Cats, who so meticulously groom their coats and lick their paws, seemed to be most affected.'

'It's you, I knew it was you!' But she says nothing.

We stand and watch as the last of the cats disappear into the flames. Some of the owners are weeping. Other cats watch from behind closed windows. The air smells that horrible smell, the one the adults would not answer for when you asked as a child, when all the pigs and cows had foot and mouth, and the significance makes you retch now. People file away back to their houses.

'In central Java so many were killed that the price of a cat more than doubled.'

I don't know where Java is but I know it is far away. I wonder if the Javanese burned their cats too, to keep their problems atomised. Treating the maladies, treating the maladies like a very rational physician.

Then I woke up. The fact that the light inside was moving might have infiltrated my dream and brought about the fires. It was darker, but still light with the midnight sun, a dusky twilight. Shadows toned up and down and across the floorboards. My first thoughts on waking: *The world is burning down! The coloured lights of nuclear holocaust!*

What she has been saying about negative imprints and energy; we are a very potent species, we have a very heavy imprint. I think about what Larus said about aliens leaving messages in our DNA and, well, we have already left our own messages in the earth at Hiroshima. We made rockets to go to the moon and look at ourselves. But the technology that built the rockets to go to the moon was adapted from the same technology that the atom bomb was made from. Nuclear radiation is the negative imprint left by our glorious inventions. We did it! We made something to give us immortal remembrance!

What is the message of this, our most enduring time capsule? Its content is senseless, it is a messageless symbol, a dead language. But even where a message fails, the time capsule itself still conveys an intent. It is a pointing finger, you just can't see at what it points. What is the prerequisite for intent? Just a self-conscious marking? With the Wow! Signal they were looking for a pattern repeated enough for it to seem unlikely to be a coincidental and natural occurrence. In his whale graphs Larus was looking for the frequency with which certain distinct data occurred. Maybe these graphs could not be used to interpret our waste depository sites because we use pictorial symbols rather than language as language is one more degree of symbolism removed. But the pattern and symmetry and frequency of the pictorial symbols should also suggest *intent*.

So the symbols at the waste depository sites would have to be something that can't occur naturally like giant sculptures, rock carvings, detailed pictograms. Something with the human stink about it (patterns suggest a maker). But if you don't know what is the human stink, then maybe you will not smell it (there are patterns and symmetry in nature and these have already been used to argue for a teleological proof of god, which I know to be misleading).

The occurrence of the waste depository sites would be infrequent, making them anomalies, and suggesting unnatural origin, unlike signs that are said to point to intelligent design, which are everywhere, so the intent would be recognised, and would colonise and corrupt the epistemological wilderness of the future. It says without saying SO THAT WE MAY LIVE INTO YOURS. Any attempt to share meaning and a message with the future will probably fail but what probably will not fail is this meaningless scribble. It is a desire that manifests itself a lot in our culture, the desire to leave a mark; graffiti in a bathroom stall, vandalism, a signature: all a defiance of time. We have sown our signature into the soil. We have survived time.

*And what is your message?*

The light shapes shifted only slightly, it was their vague wave of intensity that had woken me up. As my eyes came to, their change in colour, at the shadow's borders, dancing around the edges, rendered the billows of light like a petrol rainbow.

The T-shirt I had tucked into the window to keep the light out was clinging on by one sleeve where the stitching bunched the fabric, like it does sometimes when the wind makes the old latches slide down a little.

After having only seen the northern lights in time-lapse that is how I thought they moved. Licking the sky like a green flame. In real time they hardly move at all. Serves me right for knowing a natural phenomenon only by watching it on the internet. It jarred me, I had to move to check I was not having a sort of stroke and seeing everything in slow motion; a momentary lapse like climbing the last stair that is not there. They moved, but not in big winding ribbons, more rapid little flames within big ribbons that moved more slowly. There were different states of focus; a school of fish that ribbon like a sea serpent.

Eskimos think the lights are the spirits of the animals they hunted. Beluga whales, deer and seals. Native Americans from Wisconsin think that the lights are *manabai'wok*, giants who are the spirit form of great hunters and fishermen. Other natives see them as the spirits of ancestors, and all interpret them as a benevolent force. And in a way they are all right, given metaphoric licence. The lights are the physical manifestation of a magnetic field that deflects high-energy solar radiation, protecting life on Earth. The lights are particles that have made it through where the magnetic field is weaker at the poles, and collide with gas particles.

Cultures see in the constellation of stars things that feature in their vernacular of images. Carl Sagan said that when the ancient Egyptians saw the Big Dipper they saw a horse carrying a man leaning back followed by a hippo with a crocodile on its back. What will people of the future see in the nuclear trefoil? It looks a little like a peace sign, or an X-marking-the-spot.

In the narrative of conception the egg is the conquest, but in a photomicrographic image of sperm cells meeting an egg, what really looks like the most 'powerful' on a comparison of constructed scales of significance? Why do we talk of sex in terms of penetration, rather than a cave mouth swallowing? What is our own significance against the vastness of space?

Take something vague like the lights and make it into something very specific depending on your myths. We are all saying the same thing in different ways. But that is just it; a vernacular. Aliens who find our time capsules would not share any kind of vernacular with we who are under the anthropological umbrella of 'Life on Earth,' so Larus is wrong to be looking for pi in space. The Human Interference Task Force were wrong to try to find universal symbols.

Ah, Larus. The northern lights are super-rare in the Alaskan summer. I thought I must have still been sleeping. But then I remembered like an echo what he had said, that there was going to be a magnetic supercharge this year. He said that the sun's activity goes in cycles that peak every eleven years, and that this year is the eleventh. I forgot everything for a second and got an urge to talk to him and tell him. He would have liked to know.

In a way I am starting to feel a little bit better about the betrayal, because the flaws it gives him free me from his tether. He taught me a lot, but he is still quite blinded by his man-vision. John Lilly did not treat the dolphins with the reverence he preached they deserved, he was a hypocrite and he brought a lot of discredit to the study of cetaceans. But that can't undermine the few really pertinent things he also said about other-than-human consciousness. Larus and his ulterior motive do not make everything that I *did* learn from him null. Because imagine if we took the personal lives of great thinkers as their oeuvre. Sure, we should hate them for it, but if we *ignored* all of the wife-beaters, all of the wife-silencers, all of the wife-killers, wouldn't we have some gaping holes in history?

## HOW MUSHROOMS CAN SAVE THE WORLD

My comrade reindeer came back again. I know for sure it is real now because I have pinched myself when I have seen it and I have filmed it on camera and watched it back several times over just to make sure. I find it very strange that the reindeer is always alone. This is not the usual behaviour of a reindeer, and this fact makes me think it really is my comrade. But then, this is the part that cannot be theoretically tested. The reindeer could just be a lost and lonely reindeer.

It has not tried to talk to me or tell my future like she said it might. But I do not know if maybe I am looking too hard and thinking too literally. Like looking too hard with my actual physical eyes instead of looking more indirectly with my third eye, which really only means feminine perspective, as in admitting there is not one truth, there are many narratives, there are many names for mountains, and by taking on the perspective of the reindeer I will actually see myself and my future. It is simple and rational, like how Jung said that you can predict the future if you just know how the present has evolved out of the past.


## THE VANITY OF MODERN EXISTENCE

INT. CABIN, SUNLIGHT — *Erin on cot, camera on desk opposite — in shot are cabin cot, Erin and the window, legs draped over edge of cot, her hands stiffly under the diary as if at a lectern — she looks up from it and directly at the camera — there is something unsettling in the way her eyes look — wide, imploring/haunted —*

**Erin:** 'KACZYNSKI IS GOD' is scrawled in capitals on the title page of the diary. I have read the first half. Like the title suggests. Damon is pretty much Kaczynski

*— she looks down at the diary and pauses with a hand hovering*

*over her bookmarks, little scraps of paper — she picks the first and carefully turns to its page — pages are stiff from years sat pressed together —*

**Erin:** So like here he says

*— she takes a breath —*

Once upon a time there was a land covered with pristine virgin wilderness. Where colossal trees soared over lavish mountainsides and rivers ran crazy and free through deserts. Where eagles wheeled and beavers beavered at their dams and people lived in concord with bare nature. Achieving everything they needed to achieve by the day, using only rocks. Bones and timber. Padding softly on the Earth and living to full personal potential. In a peaceful state of anarchy

*— she looks back at the camera —*

**Erin:** Which is lifted right out of Kaczynski. And then this

*— she turns to another page —*

That summer there were too many people around my old cabin so I decided I needed some peace. I hear there are handlebars and viewing plateaus specifically plateaued for viewing at Yosemite now. They think that wildness can be put in a box and looked at. John Muir was a douchebag

**Erin:** Saturation again. Damon must have been in another cabin somewhere a bit less remote before he came to this one. Kaczynski did that too. He got upset when some bulldozers tore down his favourite thinking spot and that's what sent him further out into the wilderness and into madness and made him send the letter bombs

*— she sits looking at the diary in her hands with slumped shoulders — she looks back at the camera —*

**Erin** (QUIETLY): It's really fucking sad if you think about it

*— then she smiles weakly, turning to another page —*

**Erin:** And then this. Before the forgetting existence was a mosaic of beauty. It is the iron fist of technology that has smashed that to smithereens. And we are the shards. Each just a remnant of this beautiful mosaic. Discordant from our true nature

*— she stares at the page — looks up —*

**Erin:** And it's all very hyperbolic but I get it

*— she turns to another page —*

Technological society is a leech on the soul. Existentialism is its result. Primitive man had a challenging existence. He had to fight off predators and other men and hunt and kill. He was raw and fully alive. He was not safe from failure but he was not hopeless to all of his threats. He could act on them. Modern man is under constant threat by things he has no power to control. Nuclear weapons. Pollution. Carcinogens. Our environment is already radically altered from its natural state. Soon man will be as radically different as his modern environment

**Erin:** He man he. Of course. But he goes into this more. He says that

*— she turns to another bookmark —*

Nature is not a feminist. Nature is ruled by chaos and competition. Strength and cunning. Nature made a human creature that must fill the roles of care and duty to offspring. So that the species may flourish. They are weaker and domestically minded. This obviously makes them social beings and so more suited to civilisation. This is why the mountains are not peppered with women. They will be more cumbersome during the revolution and will also fare worse. But of course they will be necessary after the revolution. So we must take care to recruit them

*— she frowns down at the diary — makes a kind of 'huuumph' sound — bounces the diary a little in her hands, absently — chews*

*the inside of her lip — she turns to another bookmark — the pages stick together — she peels them apart —*

The enemy is the machine. We should not make enemies of ourselves

*— she looks back to the camera, bouncing the diary in her hands again — the stiff pages hardly move —*

**Erin:** You can see the way his philosophy develops. He starts going then into how the revolution should work and what his idea of utopia after will be like. All the time going back to this idea of freedom freedom freedom, which he always writes in capitals. He wants to destroy everything institutional and symbolic. Factories, of course, but also hospitals. And libraries. And he says there will be many casualties. He says that death and chaos are the sacrifice needed. That freedom and dignity are more valuable than a life free of pain. That to die fighting for survival is more fulfilling than a life void of purpose

*— she is absorbed in her trail of thought — she does not notice the book in her hands — her hands play with it absently — apparently she does not notice because she does not treat it with the delicate reverence she did before —*

**Erin:** And then if you follow his logic. And you end up with this post-technological society. Then doesn't feminism have what it wants anyway? Because if like I believe there is no natural way of being. And patriarchy is just scaffolding. Then does taking down the scaffolding not solve the problem?

*— the diary slips from her hands and lands on the floor face down — a page is dislodged and slips across the floor with the gust the book's landing made — Erin looks reproachfully at the piece of paper — she bends and reaches to pick it up, gathers the diary as she does — she sits back on the cot and looks at the paper, places the diary besides her — then she unfolds the piece of paper — her lips move silently as she begins to read —*

*— her face caves in on itself — she brings her hand to her mouth and the other begins shaking — she lets out a whine that is broken and animalistic —*

*— then her eyes dart suddenly to an area behind the camera and to the left — she brings away her hand as though to talk — her face has a receptivity to it now, like it is in the act of communication, all parts expressive in a way that had not been in evidence to the inanimate camera — as though there is someone in the room with her whom she is addressing —*

**Erin:** He... He killed himself

*— and then, shaking her head desolately —*

**Erin:** I don't. Don't know

*— in the background, through the window looking out into the trees that get denser and denser until they are forest, a dark shape comes forward from the obscurity — it is small because it is in the distance, it would be easy to miss — Erin slowly shakes her head at the point behind the camera with her mouth a big 'O' — eyes are drawn to it because it is sudden movement in a previously inert space — in contrast to the space around it it becomes clear — a large animal with long spindly legs —*

*— Erin's expression droops and her eyes slip diagonally down to the camera — she blinks at it then slowly rises, slowly, like her body is almost too heavy to lift — she leans across the floor and reaches out —*

## CUT

# WEST, WEST, WEST,
# DESTINY, DESTINY, DESTINY

After I read it I went a bit dizzy like I had to sit down and get moving acutely at the same time. I got the fear/adrenaline that perhaps a rabbit feels being run into the ground by a fox; a chemical consolation prize for its oncoming doom. And there must be one, a payoff, I think, otherwise the rabbit would just lie down and let the fox take it, not prolong its own suffering. There must be a small part to the death chase that feels good.

I packed up my bag to move back out to the fire tower. Damon's quest and the distance he went on it had put my own feeble experiment into perspective; in contrast a glorified camping trip. He too saw the hypocrisy of the Mountain Man but he actually followed through on it with frenzied sincerity. A distance so far and so absolute as to never come back. In fact the *only* absolute solitude.

An Event Horizon is a place in space-time and events beyond this point can't reach an observer who is outside of them. It is a point of no return and on the other side of this point the gravitational pull turns so intense that escape is impossible. This is a black hole.

Here in the cabin there is always looming the possibility that Stan will come to find me. This is reason enough to leave for somewhere more authentically *distant*. And I shall not take my map. A map is a corrupting thing, an imposition on the wilderness it tames, translates to the symbolic. And it is a mapping for others to follow, like Thoreau mapped for others to follow him on his *philosophical* terrain but by talking about it he took away its agency, its pure wildness. Because pure wildness is the absence of words, is self-willed. Damon found this out and had to give up all of his words.

I cannot take the camera because it is more than the documentary now. Documenting too throws a quadrant on a thing, pins a thing down like a specimen for dissection. You cannot document a wilderness because that undoes its wildness, its being apart and for itself, and now I understand this. To document is to litter, to litter photographs of the tundra in the tundra behind you. And besides, it diminishes the directness of the experience, which becomes once removed via a superficial lens of viewing. Can you even have a feminist documentary on wilderness? Can you even have a word for wilderness? Do the Eskimos and the Inuits have one?

It is like Sam told me; the categorising of indigenous people is a colonial pursuit that controls their identity with words. Like in the Indian Act. It is a way to distinguish in white law who gets status or non-status, who gets what.

We map them out, draw out their boundaries, like when I entered Denali Park or you enter any park and there is a visitors' centre roping off the inside from the outside, nature from non-nature. Gender is another act of division, deciding who gets what admirable qualities. There are no Mountain Women because the Mountain Man will not call her Mountain Woman. The Mercury 13 were ready for space flight, but NASA wasn't ready to call them astronauts. (Side note: Athabaskans had a matrilineal society before rights were given to their men in white law.)

All along I have been catching butterflies, pinning them in a glass case and putting a name to them: my own name. I had thought it so innocent, the calling of things by their real names. The good truth of speciesism; helping me to see difference. But it is not, it pins the animal to a system that pretends to be truth, static and mechanical, it reduces the luminous and the complex. This makes the thing, the animal, lose its deeper truth. William Blake the poet got upset at Newton and the Enlightenment scientists for 'Unweaving the Rainbow.' I have been trying so hard to put it into words but I have been struggling because it can never really be worded without making its immediacy dissipate. I have been unweaving rainbows.

I set fire to the pile of man books like I did the animal guts, because I do not want The Bear to smell them either. In words they keep the wilderness from me. I am sick of their authority. I am sick of their exclusion, their air of expertise, their colonial intent. I am sick of their wording that which should not be worded. Maybe we need some gaping holes in history! I hate them! And I hate them all the more for being so hypocritical, with Damon so painfully true to himself!

I watch the guts crackle but the books do not light because I threw them on whole in anger and the flames lick at them but do not take hold and snuffle and die. Are they fucking immortal? I pick them up one by one and tear the pages from them, reignite the flames, feed them in gently. They curl to black in my fingers, page by page.

But I have to do something with this, running away like a little squirrel who takes a strange object to its dray, and what to do with it when I have it there? A voyage that leaves everybody else behind. A voyage to see the moon's second face.

Mike Collins was the astronaut left behind to see to things in the command module while Buzz Aldrin and Neil Armstrong walked on the moon. He drifted for a day in a hunk of metal that he had little control over, alone in the dizzy void, velvety infinity making him sick with perspective or lack of, no anchor for his soul and a brain telling him that whatever he thinks he can see he is probably still falling. And when he got to the dark side of the moon and he could not see Earth anymore, he lost radio contact with Houston for forty-eight minutes.

*Not since Adam has any human known such solitude*, the loneliest man at the beginning of the world or in the world or out of it. Only, Mike Collins says he did not feel loneliness but awareness, satisfaction and exultation. The most crystalline and private solitude. Oh, Eve, why did you have to show up and tamper with the clarity?

We always had a preoccupation with the moon as this symbol of a philosophical island. A man is an island on the moon. It is so far away it is definitive exile. Is that Cain on the moon? Is he lonely? Is he drunk?

The moon has not been an island since Apollo, or it is an island like Crusoe's but after the footprint. Someone already flew up and touched it and saw it from all sides and figured out there are no green men and no cheese. A solitude to be felt by no one since Adam and now Mike Collins.

And yet it could always have been purer still. If Buzz Aldrin and Neil Armstrong had died like they easily might have, and Collins had to do a return journey to Earth on his own, first the dark face then the burden and relief of being the survivor, the only one to escape the shipwreck, returned without the heroes, empty-handed. But how pure would have been the level of solitude on that return? Does that thought corrupt it? Like it could always go deeper still? Like smashing the atom of solipsism to find out it does smash and it is actually made of weird squiggly things.

In Chinese mythology there is a woman on the moon and she has a whole band of moon rabbits for company. I felt spacey as I left the cabin, but much less heavy than when I walked out here. A flock of geese made a 'V' in the sky. This is called a skein.

## NOW COMES GOOD SAILING MOOSE INDIAN

I stayed up all day and part of the night reading Damon's journal to its end, only leaving the tower a couple of times to pee and just to stretch my cramping legs. I was sore all over from just sitting still, and so exhausted from crying and reading that I fell into a nightmare sleep that I could not pull myself out of until late this morning. The diary does not elaborate on how he chose to do it. It only suggests that he would not ever be found.

Damon is hanging by the neck from a tree, its branch groaning against the pull of his body, but it groans less and less with his diminished mass. The bears and the wolves found him before the ranger, like he planned. His legs are torn away where the lower-standing creatures have managed to reach, from his waist down, a hula skirt made of strands like earthworms, which wriggle as the torso sways. It takes a big bear to stand on its hind legs and wrench the forlorn body to the ground, where the lower-standing creatures wait with yelps and warbles that sound like ecstasy and pain at once. They feast on his body, frenzied but harmonious, creatures great and small.

*Humankind has been the biggest leech on this planet. No creature has ever dominated so unanimously or pervasively.*

It had crossed my mind that maybe his suicide was faked so that he could truly cast off all ties and live in his wilderness with no one ever coming after him. To be dead and mourned as the most unconditional form of liberation. But reading the diary, and especially towards its end, he writes so convincingly about how it feels to follow the deduction of his philosophy all the way to its conclusion, and know there is no way back, that I really have to believe he was there.

*We are heading for collapse. Eventually the fortress we built will cave in on itself. But not until everything outside of it has been absorbed into it, remodelled in its image. Not until we have corrupted everything that is beautiful and whole and pure.*

He talks and talks about how there is this innate thing, this selfishness in us, and that no matter our good intentions it always overrides. And it gets me thinking about the parallel on a macrocosmic scale. That really, if there is no changing the course of our 'advancement' and its inevitable conclusion, why even struggle against it? Maybe we should meet it running, we should just run at death and the death of civilisation yelling and flailing like Damon did. The planet could regenerate with new interpretations of life, like after the dinosaurs or all the sea creatures in the Silurian period or everything in the Great Dying in the Permian period when 96 percent of life forms perished and the 4 percent that did not went on to become all life as we know it now.

And if at that end of it, when all the glittery dust motes settle and the black mushrooms start to metabolise the fallout, if there is nothing left that could contemplate our loss, then is nothing really lost? Even those with the capacity to *feel*, would they even care? Would the dolphins be sad to see us go if any of them survived?

The Doomsday Clock is a clock whose time is agreed upon by a group from the *Bulletin of the Atomic Scientists*. Midnight represents the apocalypse. The clock indicates the planet's vulnerability to apocalypse from human-made existential risks, their main concerns being nuclear weapons and climate change.

Nuclear contaminates time and future wildness and will outlive us as a time capsule. Climate change permeates the now, every fibre of being on the surface of the planet touched and corrupted by it, even if only by the colour change of its cast shadow. Human-made change is already written into every little bit of wilderness.

No part of the planet will be untouched. Not the deepest ocean trench, not the never-seen portion of Siberian forest, not the unknown and unnamed underwater cave or the blind crabs living in it. All will bear our dirty fingerprints. We have left our negative imprint everywhere. And the first and worst felt of the human species losing their identity and culture will be the Eskimo and Inuit, who did very little to bring it about.

The rocks will testify against us to the future, speaking of us as geomorphic agents.

The Mountain Men are dead now. All purity has been proved untrue. Alaska is owned privately, by natives, or is federal land. Can a wilderness ever be wild if it is owned? Does the wilderness reserved lose its self-will, its wildness? The human stink is everywhere, the smell is enough to almost paralyse me and at the same time frenzy, make me want to limp-run away, run towards, a cliff-lemming suicide tendency.

The clock has recently been set at three minutes to midnight, the closest it has been since the Cold War. In a press release, when they moved the clock hand, the scientists said *the probability for global catastrophe is very high.*

They sat around in a board meeting with other minds representing the frontiers of scientific knowledge, sitting around with dozens of Nobel laureates agreeing on that conclusion and feeling the full weight of its implications. How do the people building the way we know the world manage to stagger on with the weight on their shoulders so heavy?

*There are just too many people on this finite planet now. I can only dream that there will be some virus, some superbug, a disaster, an earthquake along the fault lines of civilisation. Something to restore equilibrium.*

*And yet one cannot orchestrate this. One cannot inflict this philosophy onto others and remain sincere. Kaczynski got this wrong. For to be a human being is to be part of humankind. And to be part of humankind is to be in the ranks of the enemy. And so what is to be done? What can an individual do but quit the army that fights for a cause he does not believe in? He cannot hurt his brothers in arms whose only fault is their ignorance.*

He is right and Kaczynski was wrong and even Thoreau was inauthentic. Thoreau's writing was a time capsule and with it he colonised his wildness. It is to write intent everywhere, to sow it around like bad seeds. Wilderness is an absence of these seeds, or more than absence — the inexistence of them. A dead Damon is wilderness. Even more absolute wilderness is a Damon never born.

In the opinion of Stephen Hawking if we can just cling on for long enough to wait for the technology that will take us to space, we will come out okay. We can bugger off to Mars and live happily ever after. A select group of us on even finiter finite resources. As though moving the problem elsewhere could solve the problem. But we can't escape the problem when it is inside us, plaited through us, inextricable.

After all I have said and thought about his diary and the parcel, I really have to reassess because they were not left there as his intention. And without intent they can't really be said to be his time capsule. More an archaeology of him. There is no ego in an accidental archaeology.

The postcards were an obvious giveaway. I feel stupid for not having clocked it at all before. Of course he would not have sent them all and then collected them back. Somebody else had collected them for him, and along with his diary, brought them to his holy place as a little shrine.

*It pains me to be here at the edge but I would fail my beliefs if I were not to do this. Is this not really the meaning of life and everything? Is it not the end of the quest, to have found your own truth and really lived by it? I feel fulfilled.*

From what is said in the diary I think what must have happened is he left a letter for his family, presumably inside the cabin with a postal address to which it should be sent, for the next person who found it, or for the search party sent out for him.

He believed in something so hard that it undid him and he loved it so much he had to give it up. Maybe in part so he could not see it diminish (gouge out eyes, see less suffering). A lover's suicide before the fervour subsides and a death in innocence before the debasement and a perfectly embalmed and beautiful corpse.

He came to the wilderness in the first place to claim his freedom and then found the only thing he could do to be true was to renounce it. He took his own life to repent for *our* sins, like Jesus minus the wide-open arms and the preaching and the son-of-god complex.

There is a sad kind of beauty in it, like a deep blue bruise that came from nowhere and you want it to go away but then again you don't because you like how it makes you feel sad to look at it, and more real to touch it and hurt. And in his last days of life he must have felt so free finally of the burden, once he had made up his mind, so cathartically pure. So free of the burden of being because he had decided to do the one and only true thing he could do to live by what he believed in. He had found his truth.

I want to try to conjure what he did near the end so that I can try to live it too. If he went wandering, where he went wandering. From the window of the tower the mountains sit pink blue grey behind the trees, always chameleon to the sky. Was he drawn to them, sat impassive and anchored and true, did he climb to the top to see the world he had let go of, the entire world over?

He will not ever know that there was a girl from a small town in middle England to know and understand the sacrifice he made, because he did not want it to be known. What he wanted was an act of nothingness.

And I feel a little fear at the danger of my quest now. I am a little scared at the intensity of the ache and camaraderie I feel for this man I never knew. I find myself thinking by proxy about how I would do it, hypothetically, if I wanted to do it in the most sincere and poignant way.

What it would need: personal significance and the least

amount of suffering and the fewest traces left behind. A desire to be eaten back up by the Earth, to dissolve back into the quantum soup that you came from with the smallest smidgen or trace. Rocks on your feet to join Rachel Carson under the water and nourish the fish kingdom.

But what does personal significance matter if the act's sole purpose is to deny completely your individuality? The one thing I have to lay down to offer is me, bye-bye, me, bye-bye. But then, if you are going to underwrite your life with that one act, and no one else is ever to know about the circumstances of it anyway, you might as well allow yourself poetic justice, right?

Did Rachel Carson choose not to intervene in her cancer to underwrite her whole life's work forever? Or did the universe perceive so much *charge* in her as a pinnacle figure in her sphere of existence that it attached this significance to her dying?

And the burning question: how do I go back from here? When I can see it so painfully wither to touch, and when just by my presence everything is undone? I am not alone here, there is something I bring with me. My bad seeds, and this place so easily inoculated.

Alfred Worden of Apollo 15 wrote a poem about the moon that went: *she is forever moving just out of reach and I sail on/never touching, only watching and wanting to know.*

Alfred Worden wanted to stalk, wanted to get his sticky fingers on that coy temptress, wanted to word the moon. I think of my map and my documentary and all of my lists, my collecting. Because the map is not just not the territory, it is also something rather sinister.

When we draw a map we are sewing our signature into it. When we map we divide and parcel. When we divide the forms of life in taxonomy and name them in our image, we set ourselves outside, omniscient. We structure our difference; we say, we are the only animals that name and order the other animals, the rest of them just exist. But how do we know the dolphins are not swimming around shouting 'coral' at coral in sonar?

And naming the animals and knowing the animals, it did not make us look after them better. It is another way for each 'namer' to survive time. Our separateness allowed us to bring everything to the brink of mass extinction, to say, oh well, we can do without them.

I might have learned to don a fraud penis to go to Scott's Antarctica, but why would I want to now that I know what that entails? What Thilda was saying when she said you don't need a penis between your legs is that you don't need one there to make you a good *coloniser*, but why would I want to be a coloniser at all?

My documentary is a sinister and selfish one, a fraud penis. That is just it. There is a point of footage specifically that I watched back where Rochelle said, 'The freedom to roam free like a white man.'

I am wearing a big heavy robe and walking around and there is a line of faceless people trailing behind me and they are all dressed in white tunics. I am at the head of a glorious procession: roll up, follow me, throw off your imaginary shackles, the world is your oyster! Quit your job, sell your stuff, you can conquer the world, life is too short for regrets! They follow me everywhere in a long winding file like ants, my followers. There are so many of them. When we walk through grass the grass gets trampled to a dirt-dry path. When we walk through snow there are only sludge dirt tracks left after. When we walk through the deserts there are wagon tracks in the red sand.

The trail has been opened, stomp stomp stomp. Best-guarded travel secrets, too good not to share! Secluded beaches, untouched forests, pristine crystal mountain streams! And despite the lack of authenticity there are those that come to seek it anyway. In trying to find something authentic of their own they leave a well-worn trail behind.

My own time capsule, my documentary, my baby, like President Carter's baby sent into space to colonise the wilderness of the future. The reason Damon's legacy is different to Chris McCandless's is that there was no time capsule sent out by or for Damon. This is the tragedy of Chris McCandless, because it was not him who wrote a book and made a film and brought the crowds to his wilderness. If I were to make one with the documentary then Damon too would become a mecca, and that would undermine his entire point. And mine.

I guess I knew deep down but I could not admit it to myself because it was my baby and no one thinks their own baby is ugly. And it gave me purpose-propulsion-direction in striking out and living vividly when I had none. And I did not want to kill my baby.

For the Eskimos secrecy holds potency and is essential in the continuum of magic. For example, if a hunter were to witness a singing animal, and the animal were an omen of good hunting in that area, the hunter could not tell other people of his or her discovery because this would make the magic lose its power.

Inside the forest where the trees are densest and the air is damp with exhumed gases condensing like inside closed windows, Damon had dug himself a hole. He got rid of the spade once the hole was dug, took it away from the grave so as not to leave a marker. Then he buried himself to the shoulders with dirt. His right arm stays outside to bury the other with. It is not perfect but it is the best he could do on his own. He knew enough botany to know which of the plants are poisonous.

Weeks later a whole ecosystem of microbes has made good work of his meat and tendrils of plants are redirecting his nitrogen to their leaves and ants march off, shards of him on their backs. Wasps have made a nest of his brain, they enter and leave through his nostrils and his eye sockets and the gateway to his soul becomes a wasp flyway. The buzzing and humming and pulsating are the sounds of rage and passion, of nature claiming back her flesh voraciously. It is exactly as he wanted.

## SEEKING BUT NEVER QUITE FINDING

I am too confused and upset to reason over it anymore, so I go for a walk. When I jump-turn down from the last rung of the ladder there it is, stock still as always. I have never seen it that far from the tundra, never. And right at that instant I hate the bloody thing, for being so illusive and taunting me so, and how fucking dare it appear with nothing to say when it knows I am struggling.

I yell at it. I bend for a stone and throw it at it. It is a pathetic throw, it bounces on the ground to the side of it and the reindeer flinches and sidesteps, eyeing me warily.

I yell at it some more, shouting, go on, then, go. Then sob.

But it doesn't. It does not move. It stands just grazing a little for minutes on end with me just watching and sniffling snot onto my sleeve.

And then I think to myself that multiple exposures to coincidence accumulate into destiny. It *must* have something to show me, I only have to try my very hardest to follow it this time. Why else would it keep coming back and standing so persistently? It is ready to speak to me.

Sometimes it runs so then I run, only I can't run too far until I get a stitch, but then it slows too, as though waiting for me to catch up.

Hours of this through the forest finds us out on the tundra and by the river, where it cuts deep against the banks before it becomes braided with sandbanks further down. The sun is in the centre of the sky. The insects come up from the grass in little clouds. The reindeer lopes into the river without even stopping for a thought.

It only takes it around ten seconds to make it across, being moved at a diagonal by the water only slightly because it is gliding so fast, then it struggles a little out the other side, its bandy legs tremoring slightly, a forlorn old man trying to lift himself off the floor with crutches. When it has heaved itself out, it turns to face me. There it stands, shakes itself down, and looks at me. It lowers its head and snorts.

So I hold my breath and jump in before I can think any better. The water is cold as hell, from running off the mountain after sitting around as ice up there. It is much harder to swim when your ears and mouth are full of ice water that makes your brain freeze and there are sirens in your ears and the water in your mouth makes you gasp and choke. And the sudden and real shock from the water brings me rapidly into the reality of the situation. For all of ten seconds I am flailing in the water in panic, being dragged along and not much able to sort myself out.

Flapping my arms down to bring my body up, I try to turn my head to where the reindeer had been but I cannot see it. Obviously it is not going to jump in for me, we are not about to have one of those inter-species rescue moments of empathy and connection. My comrade reindeer has renounced its one job, and I lose all hope.

I have thoughts like *I had better think about my life in retrospect* like you are supposed to and remember the time I found an injured squirrel and fed it water from a syringe and wrapped it in socks in a cardboard box but it died in the night. I wonder if my mum will feel a psychic maternal twinge, stop stirring her tea and drop the spoon. I see her ears prick up like Beethoven the St Bernard dog from the film franchise, when the little girl falls in the swimming pool ten blocks away. Thinking about things like this I feel so far away and apart as though I am in another life altogether, having a look through the eyes of some girl called Erin.

And in an instant I realise it is the first time I have really thought about elsewhere since being here. And in an instant I see everything all at once. 'It was in this state that I experienced "myself" as melded and intertwined with hundreds of billions of other beings in a thin sheet of consciousness that was distributed around the galaxy. A *membrain*,' said John Lilly from his isolation tank.

Every time I go under the water and screw my eyes shut hard I see shifting shapes behind my eyelids like in a lava lamp, and when I emerge, the sun bursts through for my having been starved momentarily and therefore malnourished and more susceptible to its intensity.

But then the adrenaline kicks in and my body takes over and being the rational one, manages to get me right and make me swim with my head up. My rucksack has the dry-bag inside, which is full of air along with all my valuables and is buoyant so keeps me from going too far under. I had the foresight to pack it in case I got caught in the rain. I am heavy with all the water in my boots and it crosses my mind to take them off to stop them dragging me down. But I cannot stay out here without shoes. I honestly think in that moment that I actually would rather die than give up and go home without having found out whatever it is I am trying to find out.

The crew of Apollo 13 did not get to land on the moon. An oxygen tank exploded and they had to abort their landing, spending almost a week in space trying not to die. They had limited power, only enough to propel themselves around the moon back towards Earth then float on unaided, hoping they would hit the exact angle they needed so as not to skim off the atmosphere like a flat pebble off a placid lake. They essentially had to catapult themselves and hope for the best while steadily running out of oxygen and freezing.

While I am gulping water I wonder if they thought about making a suicide mission to the moon instead. With sudden clarity, as if seeing the moth that had been camouflaged against the tree's bark, I get it. Looking down on the surface as they circled around, this place that they had seen as their life's pinnacle, and everything built up to that promise of standing on the moon's face, basking in majesty and in singularity; it might have seemed worth abandoning living for. To end at the crescendo.

But for whatever reason they chose to try to go back, even at the risk of miscalculating and veering off into the void. They said, 'Let's go home,' and the whole world stopped turning to wait to see them tearing through the roof of the sky. It is strange how it is framed as what could have been the loneliest death in history. Not a death in solitude for the envy of Mike Collins and Adam.

The difference is the element of choice, of *intent*. It is not a casting out with purpose but a getting lost. It is the difference between solitude and loneliness. Newton's ball was lonely because he drew it, the ball did not will itself there. And like Newton's ball a woman's body like Rachel Carson's body is not her own to choose to keep in chastity or solitude.

Marianne Moore said that solitude is the cure for loneliness, which was very crafty of her, and perhaps my trip's whole mantra. She was saying take your lonely body and reclaim it as your own, think it solitude!

But drowning is hardly reclamation. That is why I do not want to let the river take me, or give up my shoes. After clambering onto the grassy bank, I lie panting on my back, trying to get steady, watching the clouds pass overhead in indifference. The mosquitoes are quick to jump on me like carrion. I am too tired to swat them away and get bitten to a pin-cushion through the fabric on my forearms.

It is a long walk back because I was dragged downriver quite fast, and my body is lead-heavy and stiff from cold. I fall over in the mud that goes slick when the rain starts pouring. I have to laugh at the sky opening up minutes after I start walking. I could wade my way back up the river and end up drier than I am. I go despondently back to the cabin and not the tower because in the cabin I can make a fire.

It takes me into the evening to get myself there and then it is all I can do to make the little fire in the grate to try to get warm by, because once I stop moving my body will not really do what I want it to. I just about peel off all my clothes and shake them out at the door, then place them on various surfaces and protrusions next to the fire. I lay down a makeshift rug and dry myself with my scanty micro-towel, not allowing myself the blanket until the fire has properly dried my skin off. My hair is matted with river bits.

The panic starts when I notice that my feet are blue, like really blue, and it dawns on me that I have not yet stopped shaking. I remember reading a survival manual that went into the stages of hypothermia. The first stage that signals the onset of the severe and death-causing kind of hypothermia is called *Paradoxical Undressing*, where a person's brain tells them wrongly that they are really warm, so that they take all their clothes off and seek out snow to roll around in. I try to decide if I feel warm or cold, and if my undressing could be classed as paradoxical. It is hard to tell when you feel so cold and yet your limbs are very definitely burning.

The survival handbook also said things about delirium, and the final stage to look out for has a sinister name; it is called *Terminal Burrowing*. When a dog can feel death coming it takes itself somewhere quiet and solitary to die if it can. The final stage of hypothermia triggers the same response; the afflicted will look for a small and enclosed space to curl up in.

*I am just going outside and may be some time* is what Lawrence Oates said, perhaps as a prelude to burrowing. Some German researchers decided that this is an automatic process triggered in the brain which sends us into a primitive mode that thinks up burrowing as a protection behaviour, the same trigger that sends animals into hibernation. So it is possible Lawrence Oates did not have cryogenics in mind. He could have instead been undone to the most basic level of his humanity (benefit of the doubt should be put into practice here, in fairness).

It hits me that Damon's odyssey to this cabin was an elaborate Terminal Burrowing, was a dog's death. After the onset of the burrowing mode it is already too late. It would not have been possible for him to change his mind.

I figure that as long as I am aware of this final stage and avoid it, I will not end up dead in a hollow. Just have to stay warm, warm. I scramble to put as many layers on as possible. I tell myself, even if you feel hot leave those clothes on. How hard can it be to stay dressed? I consider maybe tying my hands together to stop this, then think better of it. I settle for attaching a little note with a paperclip to the zip on my ski jacket. The note says 'paradoxical undressing'; I hope that this will suffice to remind me to stay dressed. I put my hands in my pockets because they are making me anxious with how dead-looking they are, skin like tracing paper and all the veins blue crayon.

I feel so very tired. But sleep is hibernation, hibernation is burrowing, so sleep could not be a good idea. I try to think of ways to stop from sleeping. I so badly want to lie in the cot but instead I sit upright on the chair, so that if I slump I might fall off and wake.


## MUCOUS MEMBRANE LINING THE GUT CAVITY OF A MARINE WORM LIVING IN THE VENT GASES ON A FAULT BETWEEN CONTINENTAL PLATES

*How do I find a way back and do I even want to?*
In the visitors' centre were relics and photographs, each attractive in some visceral way that made a magpie of me.

Sometimes an object appears before you and seems to fit itself into your chronology like a fusing cell.

There were eerie masks with grimaces and rectangular grins, on animal and people faces. The masks were worn for rituals and then destroyed directly after. They were an immediately physical way to don an identity for the expression of something particular and temporary. An uttering of varying identities.

When the Eskimos gave a name to a matured spirit, after the danger of childhood had passed and the spirit of the young person was thought to be well and truly lodged inside, the name given was always the name of the last departed person, because

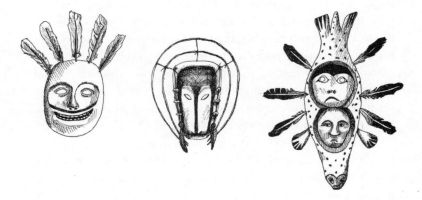

the spirits were thought to transmigrate through the generations. Young children were brought up in mind of the gender of the last person to have their ancestral name, and then usually reverted to roles based on their biological sex when they reached puberty. They have a very rudimentary taxonomy — animals have names so that they can talk about them but are not separated into families in such detail, are not unwoven. A person could don a mask and become any gender, any life form. Transmigration allows them to do away with taxonomy; a queering of the animals like their queering of gender that is really a way to acknowledge *symbiotic association*; like Lynn Margulis said, we cannot live apart from each other.

And then along came the white Christian missionaries! They reorganised their society, imposing patrilineal names and social customs. They undermined the Eskimo women's respected positions. They saw this animism as evidence that the Eskimos worshipped bad and ungodly spirits, that they needed to be saved from the burden of their devil worship and impure customs. In the missionaries' myth, women were blamed for the mortality of Man, for even daring to eat an apple, which stood metaphorically for their knowledge or heaviness (myths are so easily inverted). Men were ambassadors for the people now; the missionaries' one male god told them to go forth and fill the world and subdue it. To rule over the fish in the sea and the birds in the sky and everything in between. This god said SEW YOUR SIGNATURES INTO THEIR NAMES. Adam named the animals, and in so doing, he thought himself apart.

The stewarding approach to the natural world took the Eskimos outside of their circle and tried to make their thinking linear. The missionaries made them speak a language which divides everything into opposites, and pitches each against the other and categorises them good or bad, masculine or feminine. In this language the differences between each opposing pair justify the subjugation of one to the other. Better is determined by what is associated with masculine: rational, civilised, intellectual and strong, so anything that connotes these categories holds value. Worse is the opposites: natural, primitive, spiritual and all their associates. Masculine is better just because masculine is better. This is not a reflection of reality but a structuring of it. A breaking apart and stacking of what could otherwise be fluid and fluctuating, but languidly.

Once you divide things into constituent parts you can stack them and you can subdue some parts with others, and this way those doing the building can sit on the top. The missionaries had already trialled this technique in Europe. Casting shamans or strong female figures as demon worshippers and witches scared people into thinking that women who deviated from their new subordinate function were evil and bad. In a theft of body, women were burned at the stake for practising birth control and midwifery. We were enclosed at the same time the commons were enclosed. And women feel connection to what came before even if only because they are made to feel more vividly what has been lost or kept from them.

Like the animals were atomised by species and set apart from Adam, the physical world was stable and geometric and absolute. But now this myth is being undermined with a new one. Science is our rational way of seeing and knowing. We have been looking very hard, very closely, with new aids to vision. Now a new science is falsifying our apartness. A queer science of approximations and non-objectivity. Things are not absolute Mountain Men either/or. Another book that Larus gave me was *The Tao of Physics*. It told me that when Niels Bohr the physicist was knighted (Order of the Elephant) in Denmark in 1947 he had to choose a coat of arms and for it he chose the t'ai-chi symbol, the yin-yang, and that his inscription read 'opposites are complementary.'

Bohr said that dualisms — is it a particle or a wave? — do not describe exactly the true nature of things, but that the interplay between the two poles brings us closer to their reality, because everything is always both things at once depending on how you are looking. He said that 'only the totality of the phenomena exhausts the possible information about the objects.' Much like objectivity in naming animals or peoples does not describe exactly, leaves something diminished.

I think about Rochelle and all the words I can never find for her. I think instead of finding many, many *almost* true words for her. Then it all ties together in my head so suddenly, coming to shape like the image that emerges with just one missing puzzle piece and abruptly you know exactly how it will be. Now science, quantum physics, is our ally in the war against patriarchy because it says you can't ever touch the atom of another thing, Alfred Worden, not really; there will always be a force between the electrons of you and it which repel each other on an unfathomably small level. Nothing is solid. Can you feel the hollowness of things as you touch them?

Rochelle is a little to me like the moon is to Alfred Worden. She does not want to be spoken of. I did not know if the best way round her was to omit her from the documentary completely. I did not know before why I could not just be a man about it. Just say it like I think it and possess it when the whole reason I set out was to make this documentary just to prove I could.

In the quantum realm this is called the Observer Effect. Your measuring of a thing alters the thing itself. The very act of measuring forces the universe to make a decision at random from a bunch of probabilities. When we measure, the probabilities become a single actuality and this is called *a collapse of the wave function*.

*This* is the reason I did not know what I wanted my documentary to say. I can't talk about Rochelle without talking about my own subjective observation of her. I do not want to collapse her wave function and so I just should not talk about her at all. And the same of this place, this whole experience.

Maybe 'a feminist documentary on wilderness' is a semantic impossibility. A woman knows the burn of the power and impact of eyes on skin, she knows the observer effect, she feels herself behind the eyes when a man does not because a man does not know the burn, never has his vantage as detached observer brought into question.

The instant you speak about the thing or you try to pin it down it slips from your hands like soap. The thing can't be pincered. Matter is a particle and a wave all at once. Both aspects are valid, it just depends on how you look at the matter. And the problem with symbols like words in place of things is that as time passes, like matter in entropy, a symbol will move away from the source at accelerating speed. The markers for nuclear waste sites are never truth, even before the language dies.

Now she is again vivid and present, so fully formed I could walk over and actually touch her if only I could muster the willpower to move. We are at the bottom of an ocean or maybe the moon, because the space is dark and heavy, the sand or surface is chalky-looking and grey, and in front of me is what I took at first to be an astronaut. It is Rachel Carson, without her shaman disguise this time, like an astronaut in her old diver's suit. It is loud with bees, she is humming and nodding along to the bees but I can't see where the bee noise comes from until I get near to her and realise that I have found the bees: they are inside the fish bowl of her diving suit.

Her voice has a new strange quality to it, as though it were song. It was always her voice in many guises, many mouths to help carry it along. Many layers all at once instead of one pulse. How do I explain it? As though the air moves with it, as though when she speaks the trees rustle and a hundred birds sing with her and the air blows leaves across the room, only the windows are shut and everything is still, no pages rustle on the desk, but I feel it in my temples, this vibration. She was a witness for them and they now a witness for her, reanimating her. Like her bees, tiny mouths in unison. And if it comes from inside my head, her thoughts, my thoughts, what does it matter? I am contaminated.

*Why is my reindeer trying to kill me?*
*Why would you think that?*

*Because it led me into the river, and I nearly drowned, and now I*
*don't know if I am awake or asleep or dead or what. My hands and*
*feet are blue and my head is filled through the ears with ice water.*
   *It was not trying to kill you. It was trying to show you something.*
*Then why would it go where it knew I could not follow?*
*Precisely.*

I stare at the ceiling some. She goes shimmery, shimmery in
the corner of my vision. My head starts to fizz, like it actually
starts to fizz as though it is full of fizzy pop. The ceiling spins
a vortex. It goes round in a swirl like a galaxy. Like the shape
of a galaxy that is also the shape of a hurricane and a shell,
it is a recurring shape, a pattern repeated throughout nature,
also found in the ratio of your uterus. What does it mean? The
Golden Ratio. It is a cosmic constant. It might make up space-
time itself. I think I am fainting.


## ALL THAT IS SOLID MELTS INTO AIR

Waking up I was cold and confused. For a whole five seconds I
took in the sound of the hammering rain, smells of damp wood
and glowing ash, with dust in my nostrils and grit on my face,
and had no idea where I was. I lifted up my head and figured my
position on the floor of the cabin, next to the fire, and registered
that I must have been unconscious. I rubbed the dirt from the
floorboards off my face. The bites on my forearms itched and
my skin and my scalp especially tickled with the hundred tiny
bits of plant and animal from the river. Where I scratched grime
collected under my nails.

   My head throbbed and was heavy to lift like it had taken in the
water. Memories of the river came back to me and I laughed in
the sudden appreciation that I was still alive. But then as quickly
I felt stupid and vulnerable and vastly under-prepared. Apart
from being gluey with cold and maybe some mental scars in the

form of future dreams of cold dark rushing water I did not have much to show for my nearly-death. But so easily I could have been another stupid kid Stan's uncle had to fish out the river with a wooden pole and wire noose. I coaxed the fire up again to heat some coffee.

And now I am back everything is okay again. As in I am a normal colour if a little pale and my fingers are their usual dexterous selves. But I can feel her now like anti-matter. I can feel her lack like an invisible density.

I like the way the plaques talk about the beliefs of the Eskimos like they are truth, because they are. They are narratives as science is a narrative and is both belief and truth also. Animist or mystical, i.e. non-linear, non-absolutist, 'truths' and knowledge are reduced to the feminine, seen as inferior, irrational, a cloud system knitted into being, induction over deduction. This is pitted against the masculine Mountain Man's absolute foundational Truths. But a feminine mystic knows it is lying to say 'I know that Truth' when you can't. That it is more accurate and honest to say that opposites are complementary. It does not matter if she is real or not. I am a mystic because owning a vagina is mystical.

What next? There is one more thing, a small envelope with Damon's name on. I hesitated over it for a while because I thought I knew what might be in it and it felt just that little bit more intrusive. But then I reasoned I had gone through with it so far I might as well see the whole thing to its end. So I read the letter that his mother left when she built her shrine for him, all the things she wanted to say to him but could not because he was dead.

*My son, my parasitic twin.*

I stare up at the cobwebbed ceiling and feel hollow at the futility of it all. His mother's voice reminds me of mine and now I miss her terribly. I feel a whole new size of emptiness, it amazes me I even have the processing space for all these feelings.

For the very first time appreciating that I am like a Russian doll she made inside her as every baby girl is to its mother, each a little like the preceding but different, with the potential to birth another if she wishes, and my mum has watched me grow, warily, into her mannerisms and her image and then away from them, until eventually I abandon her and become less her and more myself. And this is a transmigration and I carry many shards of her with me always, as she does me.

And all her hopes and dreams and expectations for me are something that I am leaving behind, but to her they will always be there. And she had a mother that she came out of and that woman I hardly even knew but I am sure had similar sorts of feelings, because that is what can happen when you give something so many parts of yourself. This is a contamination also, and you can't be mindful of it and still find an intact apartness. Even in death you are still felt in tremors. Even Damon's purest act was not entirely pure, because he left his negative imprint with his mother.

I feel a change has come because even a few months ago I would have found these thoughts unacceptably sentimental. I am not sure if I am crying on my cabin bed and missing my mum because I am a girl and I was never going to be able to hack this odyssey of solitude for that reason, if it was always biologically determined, or if I have figured out truths about my life by my own will.

And they are all laughing, all of the Mountain Men of history laughing and chanting DARWIN WAS RIGHT, WE TOLD YOU SO, WE TOLD YOU SO, their voices echoed by the mountains, giving them a god-like veracity, and for them I have no answer. Did I cast out or did I just get lost and does it matter either way?

# THE THIN VENEER

I can't get to sleep tonight although I am exhausted. Not from the wakefulness that has kept me up often here; when I get that I can be content just reading or writing or toying with thoughts, because I know it does not matter too much when I do or do not sleep what with the days being all wrong anyway.

This time I can't sleep from a feeling; that the sky is too big and the space between it and me is heavy like deep water; the deeper down you swim the more pressure there is pushing you down and up at the same time, and the more I think about how far there is between me and the sky the more my head feels the same pressure on it. And the space between me and the road, me and Fairbanks, me and every place underneath a big red arrow stretching from here all the way round the world and back again like on some old public service animation where I go black and white and zoom out and out until the tower is just a speck on a cartoon image of the world and the arrow makes a noise as it elongates like 'vrrrraaaaawm' going up in pitch with onomatopoeic tautness.

For almost all the times I have slept in my life until these weeks, that is around 6,935 sleeps, I have been comforted by the thought that in the room next to me are my parents sleeping, in the houses next to me are my neighbours sleeping, in the town around us people are sleeping, in fact the whole of England is sleeping and the Australians are keeping the world running by doing the day shift.

Sleeping with someone does things to your trust. As in by sleeping in close proximity to other people you are making your-self your most vulnerable for them, and maybe the proximity of trust could extend to all the people asleep in all the houses around you. It is a thing I am very aware of lacking right now.

But if I concentrate I can invert the deep pressure feeling, can make it feel safe and still and like the space is filled with

Styrofoam. Because sometimes when I lie in the centre of sub-urbia falling asleep I have other thoughts. That lying down en masse to sleep makes you gravely vulnerable, a whole flock of sitting ducks, and it is then that I start to think in particular about nuclear dawn.

Everyone still and asleep and so much trust being channelled around, seeping out of pores and windows as a gaseous thread and into nostrils and mouths connecting them like string on a tin-can phone. And no one is thinking to look at the sky where an object is getting closer and closer silently. And then it happens and at ground zero most people do not even know any better because they are vaporised before the electrical signals even reach their brain to tell them so, but maybe some come to for just an instant of absurdity, to be confronted with a helix of colour and pain while their soul or their energy or whatever it is departs and then that is it, snuffed out, nothing.

To feel like I am in a box of Styrofoam here is to feel like safety-in-singularity. It is to not be afraid of all the crazy shit that I badly wanted away from, that affects me for being part of a macrocosmic world, that I do not conceive the complexity of because here I am in a world of my own, all on my own.

Really suddenly, like the clunk of a clock's first chime, this makes me feel deeply sad. A night bird makes a noise outside and a small rodent probably scurries away from it and a shadow passes the gaping windows and the trees are hushing and maybe back home everything could already be blown away. My head throbs and my teeth will not fit together properly. If I try to keep them slightly apart they feel like magnets yearning for each other.

I could be the last person on Earth, or I could be the last person in my vicinity with any hope of ever finding the other last people in their vicinities, all of us running around frustratingly like little bugs that are lost and you want to yell at them 'IT'S RIGHT THERE' until you think about it and actually they are worlds away from the place you plucked them out of, from their perspective, which means the same thing anyway when you have no way of knowing any better.

And I realise if it is all gone I want to be gone with it. I want to throw myself onto the sand like a dolphin embracing death on the beach with its family by dehydration and the suffocation of its own chest crushing its lungs under the pressure of gravity. I want to be blown up in the big stupid mess that it is. I do not want to be a Born Survivor.

I could take my phone from the bottom of my bag, just try to call Mum, just to check the world is still there. We do not even have to talk. I could just get her on the phone just to hear her say, 'Erin?' then hang up and turn it off again. Just to hear the sound of her alive and speaking.

It must be around midnight at home. She is probably asleep. Although she is my mother so there must be that thread connecting us, although we might not be so consciously aware of it. Like mother bonds and sister bonds and dolphin bonds. Like we are *spooky action at a distance*. And it is not New Agey if you are thinking analytically Jungian. Girls are just a little more aware of the secret power of bonds because being connected to them is part of being woman. Jung's anima was a lady, not because the anima has a vagina but because she is an archetype we all agreed on.

And besides we observe something like it in other animals. A connection to something that is not what you would call *direct* experience. Like water buffalo in Thailand that looked out to sea half an hour before the 2004 tsunami hit, and just bellowed like mermaids with conch shells, and ran for higher ground, with villagers scrambling after.

There's a suggestion we could make an early warning system for natural disasters based on this sense, a hotline people can call if their pets freak out. This data gets logged and if enough pets are freaking out in a particular area then the hotline sends out the warning and everyone runs for the hills. And even if it is only because the animals can 'hear' seismic activity in a literal sense, isn't it the same thing really? Isn't telepathy just listening to another plane of 'sound'?

I fish for the phone from the bottom of the bag. I move into the beam of the dusky light from a slither of the window that is uncovered. In my head I say her name over and over and I imagine her face and I imagine her where she might be, her present, maybe awake on her back in bed and listening to the rhythm of Dad's breathing. I press the button to turn it on.

I imagine her face twitch. She sits up in bed then looks at Dad to see if she woke him. She rubs her eyes then goes still, straining to hear. She slowly swings her legs out of the bed and slides herself off and moves towards the cabinet that has her phone on. It is really dark so she goes slowly, feeling with her feet and hands before bringing her body forward.

I clench my toes to try to squeeze some of the warm blood into them. I stare at the phone really hard. Another animal outside makes a sudden whooping noise and I flinch. It powers on but no signal. I wait ten seconds then twenty, staring at the gap where the bars should be, willing them to come. Of course there is no signal in the Alaskan tundra.

I exhale heavily and deflate. Then I turn the phone off, return it to the rucksack and crawl back into my sleeping bag. The bag is still a bit warm from my body before. I spend a few minutes fidgeting, imagining the friction of skin on fabric making heat like lots of little sticks and fires.

On the ceiling there is a spider that always has at least three carcases wrapped in mummy bundles on its silvery web. I have noticed that it rotates them, that its oldest kill is always the one it chooses to eat and then it is usually replaced and the next-oldest is eaten. I admire the spider's diligent forward planning. The spider is always preparing for the future even though it consistently gets new things to eat. The spider knows that the world can always change in an instant; that the future is not to be counted on. It lives in a very delicate microcosm that can be blown away also, by a gust of wind, but that does not stop it weaving.

## THE FALCON CANNOT HEAR THE FALCONER

Back at the tower and I am preparing for the final voyage. Like Ishmael in his spiritual malaise, casting out into the ocean to escape it all or else end it for good. Because that is the only thing for it, to give yourself up to the waves. And of course I am holding out for a coffin raft yet.

On my way to the tower I came across a sign. It could not have been more imbued with meaning if it had been written for a film, or more climactically timed, or perhaps I am weaving everything into a myth of myself. My reindeer is dead.

Some of the flesh had been stripped or pecked off but the flies were still in the process of infesting and their maggots had not hatched yet. It could have been brought down by wolves the very day it forsook me in the river. It sat warm in the sun and all around it smelled sickly, the buzz and the smell making the air dense so that I felt it way before I saw it. The antlers sat perfectly on the eyeless head that grinned mockingly, jaw chattering, laughing to itself like it was some macabre joke, leading me on all along when really it had nothing for me.

As if to say, ah, how easy it is to die. Just like that, so blunt and final and so very, very dead, a dead end and no clues or directions left behind. Whatever it was I was expecting the reindeer to tell me it very definitely was not going to tell it now. Its silence was corporeal and absolute.

No companion, no comrade and no project to give me purpose and nothing to guide me, just my naked self. And with it power in a way; I am real and vulnerable; there is no one watching over me; I am a self-willed woman.

I have never seen death so up close before. It was different to the hares, and the difference is not just scale. I would say it is familiarity and the fact that I imbued it with significance. Like in nature documentaries when David Attenborough puts a personified spin on things and you end up rooting for the baby tapir and then it goes and gets killed by a jaguar and it is not just the circle of life because David Attenborough went and made it personal. This is more than that still.

I did not even see the body of our first dog when he got put to sleep because I was ushered out of the room to sit on my own in the waiting room, surrounded by sympathetic-looking people with their sympathetic pets all whimpering along with ten-year-old me until my parents came out carrying just the worn brown dog collar. That had been death to me; just a dog collar without the dog in it. And this was it in concrete; the abrupt end to mystery and innocence that I had hitherto in life mostly evaded. And then I knew that the only thing that I had left now was to climb that mountain and see what Damon saw from up there.

I have been looking at the highest point of the range nearest to me. The ones behind look like they might be bigger and somewhere out there is Denali, the biggest of all, but the one I have been watching is tall and has snow on the very top and the clouds obscure it sometimes so that it looks like Olympus with its feet in the clouds and Olympus is plenty momentous enough for me. It just calls to me. If Damon went from here then I am sure that is the place he went to.

From its snow and the clouds I know it must be around two thousand metres. I remember reading in the park centre that the snowline starts at one and a half thousand metres. Two thousand metres is twice the size of Snowdon but it is still not high enough for altitude sickness. That is how tame the British peaks are. I climbed Snowdon and that took us five hours. So I am hoping I can do it in two, maybe three days. That is one day getting as high as I can, to just under the snowline if possible, then sleeping for the night. Then the next day I can head out with perhaps enough time to summit, and failing that spend one night in the snow and cold. Then the descent should take me no time.

I have test-walked to the lower slopes to judge how long it should take. South-west for around five miles the forest stays dense until reaching the slopes of the mountains when it starts to thin. I walked up high enough to see way out over the forest, to where it mottled out on to the tundra, and the braided river which glinted back the blue-silver sky, spread across the sediment like veins of mercury. On the mountainside above, the trees stopped and scree wound like lightning scars through the smoky green and purple skirting. Life waned up the mountainside and the peak was white and dead and here the crows had their kingdom.

Lower down where the plants clung still, bleached shapes poised spectral, luminous in the glare from the white sun. There were Dall sheep; they looked happy on the mountain and elegantly strange. I walked west across the ridge below the sheep until the afternoon, watching the colours change as the cloud ran its textures under the sun like a shadow puppet.

I have rationed everything exactly and I have pared my rucksack down to the barest essentials so that there is not even a spare tampon of extra weight. I have just enough food to summit over the two days or two sleeps before coming back down, depending on hunger, but right now I have no appetite whatsoever so perhaps I will stay longer. I have sticks and a piece of tarp and some cable ties with which to construct some kind of shelter. If the rain comes again it will be miserable but there is nothing to be done about that. *But please, spirit of the mountain, please don't let it rain.*

# THE ABSTRACT WILD

We do not use mountains as metaphors for challenges for no good reason. It serves me right for being stupidly under-prepared for this and life and everything. Halfway through the day I left off wading through the snaring purple carpet of alpine tundra vegetation to hit scree and from then on I was stuck in a laborious cycle of climbing tentatively twenty metres or so only to slip back ten. I felt like Sisyphus without a boulder or the lustful in Dante's inferno, doomed to swirl around in a stormy circle for eternity. Maybe if I kept on I would come across Damon's soul too, both of us so lustful and hungry for *something* that we were doomed to keep after it forever on this scree-skelter. That he just fell and died on his way to the top; that ironically he did not even get to make his one statement because the universe made it for him. But then that could have been his perfect death; willingly dead but not by his own hand, which means he did not have to feel bad about being selfish and breaking his mother's heart (although it would still be broken because she would not know any better, I suppose).

Each slip on scree I would fall on my knees shaking and weak and too terrified to move in case I slid further. Where I had to sit to get everything back under control I would sit facing upwards, not really looking around me because I was looking at the ground to centre myself and so as not to trip up, and not wanting to look at everything below me until I was at the very top. I wanted this to be a grand revealing, velvet curtains drawn until the finale and for the finale to be one of those moments in life that needs a soundtrack with a loud and euphoric chorus followed by a quiet and melancholic bridge in a new key.

I kept at this for hours, slipping and crying and crawling and just lying where the scree left me on my side, gasping and sweating, sometimes laughing at how stupid and futile a figure I had made myself in each moment and in general, ready to give up only to get a second wind and an angry burst that would propel me upwards like a turbo boost on Mario Kart.

And then I got into a rhythm with it, perfecting the amount of pressure to put into each footstep to stop from upsetting the loose rocks. And once I had this it got easier again. I had gashed my knees up terribly and I had cuts all over my hands that smarted when I moved my fingers or when the salt from my own sweat got into them and they were full of grit but they felt good. Like the pain and difficulty made it more worth it. Like wanting to come out of the wreckage with a visible wound, wanting an impact with some tangible effect. Something to show for it all.

I came across some of the mountain sheep and they sprang off away from me, barely dislodging a pebble, then turned to look back as if to say, you, trunk-legged creature, are not made for here, before loping on. They really are ridiculous animals to look at until you realise that being wrapped in cotton wool makes falling on a mountain like falling over in a spacesuit in zero gravity; inconsequential. That rather than clouds with legs they are ingenious inventions of nature.

The wind would come very suddenly and with such force that it could knock me off balance so I found myself bracing for this, flinching for it like a bad puppy to a raised hand. It would scream like a Tolkien wraith when it came and rattle me so that the best I could do was to get close to the ground and stay down. One time doing this I came face to face with a delicate yellow flower struggling to grow, isolated and friendless and I cried a little for it all alone on the crag and no way of knowing how by its loneliness it was diminished.

I kept on going with the snowline as my carrot until I let myself stop around one hundred metres below on a little forgiving plateau. As soon as I got to the mental place of 'I will stop here' my legs gave way and my knees were further damaged but I did not even feel it because the relief of a resting point was so great and it felt so good to be horizontal with the promise of a long interlude.

After a little nap I drank deeply from my water, leaving just enough to see me over in the morning, before I got to the snow-line and could refill from melting the snow. Then I went about making my tent, forcing the sticks into the ground with difficulty and pegging the tarp on two sides so that it made a humble pentahedron, open at both ends. I tried to angle it so that the wind went over and not through it, but this made the sides whip back and forth.

I must have been walking for over ten hours. The light dimmed after what felt like not much time, just enough time for me to sit about recuperating and to warm up my meagre dinner on the propane. It was bitterly cold once the sun had dipped, even though it did not ever disappear completely. There was still the vague idea of sunshine, the sun hovering somewhere nearby, but the wind undermined it ruthlessly.

I tried to sleep but the wind blew just so and rattled the tarp, which rattled the pebbles in a motion like a Mexican wave all around the perimeter, and this made it sound as though there was someone or something scuttling around outside, making circles around me. I would poke my head out and be reassured, then it would happen again a little later and I would think come on now, Erin, we have been through this numerous times, then, no, there really does sound like there is something, best go check, oh, no, all clear, okay, cool, time to sleep, but what was that? That wailing? Is it Damon, has he come for me? Like this so many times that I gave up and just went outside to sit sentry for myself and put the propane back on even though I needed it for cooking tomorrow because I was just so cold even with the ski jacket and there was not a scrap of wood to be found for a campfire.

But there I was alone and enduring and from outside my own head to any observer of course it would seem like I could do this as well as any man. I was ticking all the boxes and besides, Jack London's men all had dogs and a dog is an invaluable asset in that scenario.

A dog like Buck, who gleams with the magnificence that inspired a cult to bask in him. It is the ghost of Buck that remains in Big Mountain gold country — Alaska, the Yukon, the wilds of North America. But anywhere can have its own Big Mountain Country. The philosophy of the cult can be transplanted onto any place and translated into any language. Russians have their own breed of Mountain Men from the days they tried to colonise Alaska. They called them *promyshlenniki*.

Buck sits by my side exuding pride and vitality and power and kingliness because he knows he is king of the dogs. But he is a dog and a dog is not a person. Jack London never meant to say that men should act like dogs, at least not so literally.

*He must master or be mastered; while to show mercy was a weakness. Mercy did not exist in the primordial life. It was misunderstood for fear, and such misunderstandings made for death. Kill or be killed, eat or be eaten, was the law; and this mandate, down out of the depths of Time, he obeyed.*

Okay, this primordial thing is in us all. But the call that came from the wild was specifically addressed to you, a dog. Dogs can regress back into the wild because they are just tame wolves. Big dogs are anyway. Specifically wolfy-looking dogs. You were a dog running round catching and killing and living by tenacity. There is no Neolithic man running round howling in the woods. Jack London only spent one bloody winter in the Klondike! And the call that brought him there was a siren song; it was a promise of gold, and a little house in the big woods on the banks of Plum Creek by the shores of a silver lake on the prairie.

*To be a MAN was to write MAN in large capitals on my heart. I played what I conceived to be a MAN'S game, this future was interminable. I could see myself only raging through life without end like one of Nietzsche's blond beasts, lustfully roving and conquering by sheer superiority and strength.*

Jack London wrote *Call of the Wild* when he was young and healthy and full of his own electricity. It is easy to be an individualist when you are a winner and you are too caught up in glory to think about how the losers fare, or how your conquest undoes the very thing that drew you out there.

There is not enough bounty for everyone to claim a piece, so for Big Mountain to keep on working it had to be understood that Man has no obligation to the happiness of anyone but himself. That to have the *right* to pursue happiness was to be free, even if free was only to be forever in *pursuit*.

This is what the Mountain Man was born from. A healthy white man's ideal. What Ted Kaczynski does not acknowledge or maybe realise is that he is his own worst enemy; it is this rampant freedom to pursue which propagates the Machine. It is as though Ayn Rand wrote both their bibles.

Jack London was remembered only as a writer of macho survival stories for boys. A *fascist*. It was just that one story! What about the story he wrote about the woman who gets Thoreau? The voice he gave to class struggles? So maybe you were his young ego but you were not his only one.

He was in a bad place, you know that. His father had disowned him a second time. He quit Berkeley and ran to the Klondike because he was *forced* to be an individualist. But he realised something in the wild. He realised in its contrast how lacking he was. It is different for you, Buck, because you are a dog. They just cling to you, Buck, Stan and all these boys. They want a strict moral code. Something to believe in. Primordial truth. Sad, unhappy, suggestible people reading the works of sad, unhappy writers and taking their words as gospel.

They cannot take his oeuvre for its transgressions, his

corrupted values; Wolf House, all those bedrooms. They want a noble truth, purity from their gods, and so they choose to hear you. You outlive him as a negative imprint, a Voyager he later regretted sending.

But you are just a dog. An imaginary dog at that. All your *masculinity*, it is a literary embellishment. Most wolf packs are headed by a male and a female breeding pair, remember, who rule together in equality, don't forget.

The dog is unnervingly blank. As though he feels indifference towards his creator now that he has his own life outside of him. Then the Call sounds from up out of the belly of the forest and Buck pricks up his ears to it. He rises and lopes to the limit of my night vision, turning with a look of contemptuous pity. He pads into the night to answer the Call and he will keep on answering as long as the Call sounds or until the paradigm shifts, because he is not *quite* immortal and it is this that will end his reign.

And after all, only the mountain has lived long enough to listen objectively to the howl of the wolf. Aldo Leopold said that. But man says I am civilised, and the rest is woman and wilderness. So what is woman? Is she where the symbols aren't? Woman is wilderness, if she is man's unwordable other. Woman is closer to the mountain and the wolf than man even if only because he put her there. Therefore, woman can listen better than man, if not as well as the mountain, to the real howl of the wolf.

# MY MOUNTAIN MY MOON

## WHATEVER PARTICLE OF THAT SPIRIT
## IS IN ME

I hardly slept and I was exhausted but this felt right, to struggle the last part as a disciple of asceticism after Thoreau's own heart, like a monk head-butting the ground to nirvana. Like how they say that if something was easy it would not be a challenge and if something is not a challenge then it is not meaningful; so make every day a struggle and lo! you will feel the richer for it, like all those who struggle in poverty are really the richest and most meaningful people in the world, god smiles down on their suffering and they feel the radiance of his smile on their sunburnt backs.

I kept on thinking I was about to summit when looking up I would see the ground stop and sky behind it, but each time I got there I would be faced with another slope to climb. I learned not to be tricked in this way so that eventually when I reached the genuine last slope I was dubious, like yeah, right, that old hat, so that when I *did* clamber over and see the final point, stood alone and jaunty with an actual landscape beneath it, not just another mosaic of rocks, I felt like I had been hit in the stomach with a football.

I said no no don't look yet not just yet get to the very top first so that you can drink it all in savour every last drop of it. So I took my rucksack off to make things easier and I kept my eyes down until I could not find a higher place to be. I settled down into my crossed legs and let myself look the whole place over and squealed like a proud eagle.

It was stupidly windy so that my hair unwrapped itself from my hairband and made little Medusa-snakes of itself, licking me in the eyeballs. I scraped it back, making an Alice band of my hands and using them as a sun visor also. The sun was almost unbearable so high up and with no cloud cover, but it made my vision heavenly bright and ecstatic. The clouds were thin and wispy and some stalked underneath me, motionless but transitory; still, ephemeral jellyfish taken by the current.

I felt giddy from the sheer euphoria of it all and also from vertigo at being so high and the world so tiny. I could see everything, my whole map over for what it really is. I mean, I could not see the cabin per se but I could see its vicinity, the place where the trees wound between me and it. But I could see my tower or I fancied I could just about, a spire amongst the deep green spruce of the taiga, and the tundra to the right of it spilling on, multifaceted and textured and connoting so many things at once; fat salmons, a clutch of speckled blue eggs, the ripe and gravid feeling of harvest-time and the hazy nostalgia that distance gives to space as time does to memory.

There is so much colour, even on the bare mountains so much colour. They are rust and lilac and ochre and pink, all hues of deep contrast, the bright sun bits too bright to look at almost and the shadows so deep they look dimensional like mouths to deep caves. Each piece of contrasting colour is like its own object, can be taken alone like pieces of a paint-by-numbers, but take a step back and they come together and make something breathtakingly complete. If I am right in my bearings then they call these the Polychrome Mountains.

My Olympus, my castle in the sky, and down below my queendom all poured out. I feel good and full, brimming, like a fountain all full up and pouring over, like melting. And if Damon did come up here it is hard to imagine how he could climb back down and go through with it, renounce all this beauty. I feel accomplished. It is the feeling that I did it, all of this; they have not succeeded in keeping it from me.

But then, directly after, following it through the door like a fast black cat, the feeling of *did what exactly?*

A sudden pang of something when I realise I can see the road, far away but definite, barely visible yet I can feel it like an animal does a scent trail, an invisible ribbon through its terrain. A mixture of things, first like being Simba in *The Lion King* when Mufasa tells him *everything that the light touches* and beyond is the shadowy place, the road my perimeter of light. But also a vague kind of yearning, a sharp little tug.

The light starts to dim and the mountain's shadow gets longer. He could not very well have stayed up here forever, not alive anyway. So perhaps for someone in his state of mind it would be perfectly logical for this place to be the end of the story. After going to the moon some of the moonwalkers could not come to terms with the feeling of its climax, all of life after dulled in its light, made ugly under the scrutiny of this spotlight that would not leave them.

As the sun moves from off the peak the wind picks up, stinging and pulling at the skin of my face and arms, sore with sunburn. My lips are chapped and hard and my nose raw to touch. I take the ski jacket from around my waist and curl into it. I am suddenly and crushingly tired, with sunstroke maybe, and it becomes perfectly sensible to just stay put here, just curl up to sleep on myself, a tired eagle on its lonely scarp, its nose tucked under its own wing.


## A DECLARATION FOR THE RIGHT OF CETACEANS

Damon and the Mountain Men, like old scientists, were searching for an absolute and true reality. They went about it by dissection, peeling it back in search of its kernel of truth, a foundation to build up from. The Greeks saw it in the Euclidean geometry they found recurring in nature. From the solid geometry of three dimensions Newton constructed a constant description of the world in his classical mechanics. The fourth dimension was uniform time, which flowed smoothly. Matter was full: indestructible particles moving through space, the void. From these separate unquestioned planes knowledge could be built deductively and a uniform map of matter and life could be built.

But then along came Einstein and said we must forget the Lapse of Time. He said Newton's planes do not work on Newton's planes, you can draw a square but space is really like a balloon not a flat plane, and you can't draw a perfect square on a balloon.

It is considered very old and pagan yet new and post-Enlightenment to think of ourselves as not masters or stewards but members of the universe. We forgot this in the first place because Descartes would cut open dogs and when they would scream he would say *ignore the screams, they are merely the creakings of a machine*, and we ignored them.

They blasted the atom at the Large Hadron Collider and instead of the kernel of this atom they found a house of mirrors and in the middle a weird shaman sat cross-legged with a gong, who told them *everything is everything and nothing all at once* enigmatically, but what did they expect, looking for a kernel inside a kernel when by definition a kernel's kernel is a tautology?

The Mountain Men went looking in nature, as in outside of human (human Man), but this is a false dichotomy. They did not see that nature was what they threw at it. Somewhere in Texas there is a mountain and at its summit there is built a steel pyramid (I marked time, remember me), glittering back at the sky, and I think this object stands very well for Mountain Men everywhere.

You can't break the world into independent existing units. Particles can't even be said to exist in definite positions, they only show *tendencies to exist*. Probability, not certainty, is the fundamental feature of atomic reality, so the Mountain Man was doomed to fail. This is Heisenberg's Uncertainty Principle and it forbids perfect knowledge. The new science says that it is only a web of approximations, it is an idealisation sometimes useful from a practical point of view like demographics of populations, or the construction of an identity.

Once he had figured it out Einstein thought of the implications of this and said *it was as if the ground had been pulled out from under one, with no firm foundation to be seen anywhere, upon which one could have built*. Science had seemingly been undermined if the whole point was to find the very solid absolute foundational true description of everything.

But Thoreau anticipated Einstein when he said *if you have built castles in the air, your work need not be lost; that is where they should be. Now put the foundations under them*, as though they were talking through time, saying, hey, so there is no such thing as the absolute after all! And absolute wild, absolute solitude; there is an absolutely pure form of neither!

And Thoreau said to Einstein that men making speeches (meaning scientists), they are banded together, *one leaning on another and all together on nothing; as the Hindoos made the world rest on an elephant, and the elephant on a tortoise*. He said, I will tell you what is at the centre of the atom without even looking: just shitloads of tortoises! But, he said, it does not matter because the atoms together make the wood I chop to build a fire.

Thoreau was as imperfect as the rest of us, always seeking truth although he knew he could never find it. He still spoilt the magic of the mythically bottomless lake at Walden, by measuring it to its bottom standing on its centre while it froze over, and writing out the measurements so everyone would know it was *he* who had solved its mystery.

Subatomic science asks us to take what we can observe and fill in the gaps, intuitive like mysticism because it is just an abstraction of reality and we have to use instruments to pick it apart, we have no direct experience of it. In a similar way a mythical or spiritual belief system that is less restricted by deductive logic can get closer to the truth of the thing by admitting there is not one truth: there are many. Maybe my mum saying she does not think about space is really pretty enlightened.

Future civilisations might excavate the Large Hadron Collider from out of the ground when we are gone and try to interpret it like we do the Tarot, as a divination method that taps into archetypes we created. And in a way this is all it is.

## BECAUSE IT IS MY HEART

I slept part of the night out on the peak, but it was too cold without the sun and I woke up. I had to crawl back down to my pack and get out everything warm to wrap up in. I did not get to greet the morning on the peak but now I know what it is like to wake up inside a cloud, and how many people can say that? The light got brighter at around 4 a.m. and I woke up to wonder if I had maybe died and gone to heaven. But the cloud passed, I took food from my bag and chewed it, looking at the landscape coming up all pink and new like a fresh layer of paint, and I decided not to move from off the ridge until I had found a conclusive reason to. All of my bones ached.

And as the sun came up I ached more to look at it. Nothing had moved but it looked different again and was permeated with feeling. We do not have a very good or specific word for the feeling of it but I suppose we tentatively call it *love*. A feeling can't be mapped to a word without changing the feeling. I could exhaust the possibilities of descriptions, but to get the closest without ever actually touching is all science and words can do.

Everything is beyond the touch of language. Why even bother to tell stories if language is so vacant?

When you are a very young child you do not understand that there are things outside of yourself, but as you begin to grow you start to feel sad or happy or affected by seemingly irrelevant things like the explosion of rockets or the size of the ocean or the contour of hills.

Everything looks happy and good in pink golden light but the beauty has sadness and sometimes this is difficult to distinguish from sadness itself and I wish I could have told Damon this. There is acute love for the thing then realising that one day one way or another it will leave you or you will leave it or the light will change, but the magnitude of this hurt is itself something that adds to the beauty. You let it enter: permeation, contamination, not-alone-ness, shared knowing of this beauty. You grow with it like inosculation, and the sadness comes in knowing that it is so other to you, that it is like tree branches growing first together and then apart. We need this acute sad feeling to make us care about the preservation of otherness. Perhaps then the feeling is more accurately *the love of sad beauty*. Or nostalgia that has not happened yet.

Then in the distance cutting across the hue between the ground and blue the speed and effortlessness in its wings. I would know it anywhere from the way it writes itself in the sky. Peregrine. I knew that they lived here but in all my looking I had not found one. And there it was, for me and not for me. My knowing of it is not possessive; I know it in reverence. Not looking at it from below as I am used to, but eye-to-eye, I can see the world like it does, and to see with it is a mighty privilege.

What I see at that moment holds so much significance for me personally even though it means nothing really and nothing at all to the peregrine, but when I remember it all, this is how it will be capsulated; in this single image, pinky golden and perfect but impermanent and sad, but with all the promise of a new day and a new chapter in my time and I will order it as such in retrospect in my own narrative.

I want to tell Damon that this is it, this is exactly it or as close as we could come. It is the feeling of space-time in and out of you and connecting you to all of it and none of it. To be able to look down from a mountain and feel sad is the whole point. Damon renounced all of this because it was the one thing that was his to give up but the thing he gave up was the point in itself and the point does not still stand without him. His little death meant nothing to the mountain and it all goes on despite him. There is no wilderness when we are gone. It needs us and our words outside it like proprioception, to define its contours, the same as we need it. And from the realisation onwards, we can adapt and new synapses can be found.

And when I looked at the road this time I felt something different to the taint and diminishment of before. When I looked at the road I felt very small and I remembered Stan saying his bit about girls being social inherently, innately, by nature, like it is in our geometry. The tug I felt when I looked at it was of a thread in the fabric, a tendril through me and it. But that tug is the reminder that you were attached all along. A tug does not mean I failed to leave properly; I could never really leave. None of us, not even Mountain Men, can ever really leave.

I stayed put for most of the day, steadily brimming up with purpose. But I was also brimming up with urine from drinking the snow melted with the propane. My appetite was building back up and what little was left of the food was back down on the plateau. I considered briefly weeing up there just to be practical, but it conjured the image of a dog leaving its scent. I thought I would not want all the smelling animals that might come up there to think that of me, even if none ever did, probably just the crows went there and they can't smell. Besides all of this I did not want to do that to the mountain.

I took a last long look, blinking my eyes like they were shutters and I was capturing still photographs of this scene to file away in the far crevices of my mind, the special self-defining crevices that stay secure and well preserved and accessible for life. Then I climbed down, set off to the place below the snowline and got there before dark, in time to make my tent up again and pee in privacy from whatever behind a rock, and heat up the last of the food.

## ALL MY LIFE NOW APPEARS TO BE ONE HAPPY MOMENT

Trudging down the mountain was much easier than up because the scree that was a hindrance before became an ally and I got to the bottom in half the time. When I reached the timberline I turned to look up at the mountain from its most imposing angle before I was under the tree cover and could not see it anymore.

Behind it in the pale blue sky the moon was full and almost exactly above the peak but skewed just a little, as if it was being floated there, as if it was a Malteser the mountain was blowing to hover over its mouth. The moon was a very pale white blue disk, only just not the colour of the sky. I had not seen it while I was up there, but I suppose it must have been behind me all along.

The mountain and the moon sat across from each other like telegraph hills, and I imagined I could light up a beacon on the mountain and the lady with the rabbits up on the moon would look down and see a small flare burst out of her image of Earth, an iridescent badge on the black felt of infinity.

From a mountain vast cities are pinpricks of light and from the moon they are tinier still. Follow it back further still, this image, of Earth in space getting smaller and smaller the further away you get, speeding much faster than the speed of light away after the Voyagers, but the stars behind Earth do not seem to move at all because they are already so far away, their constellations still look exactly the same as they do on Earth. You have to get about thirty-six light years away past Arcturus, which the Inuits call 'The First Ones,' and only then do they start to merge into each other, and by this time you can't see Earth at all.

Earth looks insignificant in the vastness of space, as everything does from far away. But we don't live far away and can only imagine what this looks like because we made some very clever machinery that can change our viewpoints. New viewpoints give new perspectives. That is what astronauts mean when they get the Overview Effect. From very nearby in the grand scheme of things Earth really looks perfect.

Larus told me that when NASA were working on ways to detect life on Mars for the Viking programme they called James Lovelock, maverick scientist and inventor from England, to California to come help them. Lovelock told NASA they need not send a spacecraft to Mars because he could tell from the atmosphere that there would be no life there because Mars' atmosphere was at chemical equilibrium and lacked the dynamism of Earth's atmosphere. This got Lovelock thinking about life altering its atmosphere and that is how he got on to the Gaia Hypothesis, which he wrote with Lynn Margulis, the symbiosis lady.

They were interested that the sun's radioactive output had increased over aeons of time but that Earth had not heated up in turn. They postulated that Earth as a whole was self-regulating to maintain this stability, that all of life and non-life were part of one single 'organism' of sorts. All parts of the biota worked together to regulate the biosphere, the hydrosphere, the atmosphere, etc., and everything on Earth had evolved reciprocally with the end of keeping the planet stable and optimum for all life. This worked through a cybernetic feedback system that meant that things always fluctuate around the optimum, like a thermostat which changes its output dependent on its reading to maintain a relatively stable, but never perfect, temperature. This was homeostasis.

Lovelock decided that without biodiversity we might not just be lonely, we might actually not have a liveable and breathable climate and atmosphere, that as we upset the balance, the planet will get more hostile to us.

In *Timaeus* Plato said our planet was alive and the rivers and lava were its circulatory system. From the eighteenth century onwards there were a few geologists and geochemists who posited that the biosphere could affect the geology and chemistry of its surroundings but they were pretty much ignored. The German Romantic Schelling would talk about Earth like it was alive and the American Transcendentalists Emerson and then Thoreau, they read Schelling.

This started a tradition that birthed John Muir, father of the American national parks, Jack London, who was in the Bohemian Club with John Muir, and Aldo Leopold, who pioneered environmental ethics. It also inspired the Beats, Jack Kerouac calling himself an 'urban Thoreau' and going by 'Jack' instead of his given name 'Jean-Louis,' after London, and then the Beats led on to the counterculture of the sixties and John C. Lilly of dolphin tank fame, who hung out with the Beats. Rudolf Steiner also read Schelling, and it was William Golding who was friends with Lovelock and gave him the name of *Gaia* for his idea and put him on to Steiner. So really Lovelock was a product of a long tradition and his and Lynn Margulis's ideas took off because they were compatible with the post-space race *zeitgeist*.

*Metempsychosis.* That is what the Ancient Greeks called the transmigration of souls, similar to what the Inuit believe in. $E=mc2$ is the famous equation by Einstein and what it means is that the amount of energy in a particle is equal to its mass times the speed of light squared, and what this means is that the Inuits are right again. It means that energy and mass or matter are interchangeable. It means that matter can be transformed into other forms of energy. When Lovelock channels Plato, this is metempsychosis of sorts. Rachel Carson has gotten into me by metempsychosis, which is also like the homeostatic process that Lovelock called *feedback*.

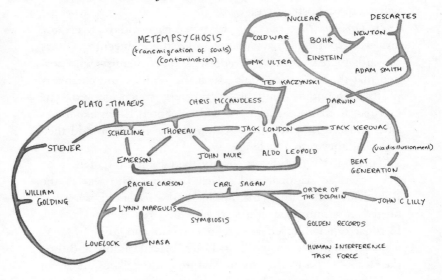

Homeostasis is also how we maintain a stable identity. We as individuals build from and into a shared image of ourselves. There are tendrils that anchor us to an adaptive and receptive way of knowing and being, building a view from a body, my body.

When we die we usually get an epitaph. Inuits in Greenland do not write words on the headstones of their dead, because they know an epitaph traps an identity and undermines its freedom to transmigrate.

Ideas and words are metempsychosis, are the weaving of the tapestry, are love for the mountain, are the deep relation between past, present, near and far, are the consciousness between us.

Newton's ball was never alone: it was cocooned by the fabric of space-time. Solitude is an illusion but so is loneliness and it was Emerson himself who said, 'We see the world piece by piece, as the sun, the moon, the animal, the tree; but the whole, of which these are shining parts, is the soul.'

I think of it, rather than a unanimous whole that underlies everything, more like a collaging of shards all patched up like a quilt, overlapping like a Venn diagram on a Venn diagram on a Venn diagram.

Lilly, Kerouac, Sagan, Einstein, Newton, none of them was unblemished by patriarchy but we had to have them all to get us to where we are now. We had to get to the moon with Apollo so that we could look back at ourselves like this. I had to come out here and follow Damon and get lost enough to realise that's what I was, so that I could find my way again. We had to have Descartes and his dualisms even though they are atomising and not real and identify the self with an isolated ego that exists inside a body like a cage, and this inner fragmentation mirrors the fragmentation of Newton's world of matter outside as a void within which separate objects and events happen all alone, forever lonely, so that we could have Einstein and the rockets that could take us up there to look at ourselves and see the seams of this, to use the moon like a mirror, like children or parrots recognising their reflection for the very first time.

These are our new visions, the macro and also the micro, the seeing for the first time and knowing and loving the microscopic creatures in our guts that we could not live without. And it is because we can look so closely and see things inside things and look so far away and see things outside our solar system that we can realise the arbitrariness of our distinctions. Our myopia undone.

The moon is our mountain. The Hubble telescope is finding higher mountains still. We had to get up there to look down with the eyes of Gaia (another useful myth), so that we could see how to mend our fragmentation, see that Earth self-regulates to keep everything in balance, as if we were allowed to get clever enough to get sad looking at mountains for Gaia to be able to see herself and think, bloody hell, isn't that good. Be good now.

This sudden new knowing of deep connection is a new Copernican Revolution. It's just that, as with the first Copernican Revolution, we do not quite know it yet, it is still filtering into us, we are in the process of many incremental viewpoint changes, so many and so quickly that we don't have time to keep up. It will take decades for them to diffuse, but we are in the process of realising our new position and responsibilities as *members* rather than *stewards*.

And this dawning comes right at our make-or-break moment. In 1870 the novelist Wilkie Collins predicted 'the discovery one of these days of a destructive agent so terrible that war shall mean annihilation and men's fears will force them to keep the peace'; and in 1951, just as he prophesised, the hydrogen bomb was invented, 2,500 times more powerful than the bomb that destroyed and is still in the process of destroying Hiroshima.

The rocket technology that got us to the moon was originally created in mind of annihilation, and you can follow the creation of the atom bomb deductively to its logical and predictable conclusion, unravel unravel until you get to here, the singularity.

Millennial anxiety is anxiety about this annihilation aimed back at us in abstract, about things so far out of our control as to be seemingly self-perpetuating, is why we frantically mark time, time-capsulise. It is not an innate impulse but a situational one. What annihilation threatens is this web we have spent so long building and our means of transmigration and our sense of self. And Damon felt this anxiety and he gave up his identity because of it, by self-annihilation.

The concept of nuclear deterrent is *your castle cannot go on existing after ours is gone*. Nuclear is the power to wipe out a civilisation (including a future one), to blow up its centre, destroy its institutions, its means of preservation, its universities and its libraries, like Kaczynski wanted rid of. The threat is against our ideologies. In this way the colonisation of space and the veneer of 'survival of the species' mask the real agenda, 'survival of the nation.' It is the threat of inexistence and the retaliation of blowing away the web of everything of the other (but now we know that to do so is to destroy small parts of ourselves too).

I used to think it very strange that the Nepalis did not try to climb all the way to the top of Everest, even though they obviously had the skill to climb because Tenzing Norgay must have been a skilled mountaineer before Edmund Hillary showed up, and so must lots of other Sherpas. But when they looked up at Everest in awe they did not think, 'I am going to conquer that mountain,' they thought, 'Ah, Chomolungma, goddess mother of the world,' and respected it and felt awe for it but no inclination to go about debasing it. Like presuming that there can't be intelligent life on other planets or they would have made themselves known to us by now. Maybe they are already observing us, but they do not feel any drive to make themselves known to us.

Edmund Hillary the mountaineer climbed Everest because it was there. Astronaut Gene Cernan of Apollos 10 and 17, when asked why he thought we went to the moon, said *because it's there*. When Tenzing Norgay the Sherpa got to the top of Everest he got on his knees, buried some biscuits in offering and prayed to the goddess of the mountain for disturbing her. We should have gone to the moon like Tenzing Norgay.

Maybe this really is the point in the age where everything changes, a rewriting of myths, a sort of coming-of-age in the human narrative. Remember that everyone mocked Copernicus at first when he said that maybe Earth did not sit at the centre of the universe, hey, guys, maybe it does not all revolve around us. Which is what Lovelock and Margulis were saying too.

These ideas do not instantaneously propagate. They resonate only once a situation occurs that prompts their germination.

They are little seeds we carry with us through life and which remain inert until the perfect conditions arise.

All these thoughts kept me busy for the hours and hours that I walked back. I had to stop to rest up and take off my shoes and let my blisters fill up so I could pop them. I fell asleep under a tree with my shoes off and slumped against it.

## STRANGE MATTERS DARK MATTERS

It is peaceful, with the forest humming from everything busily making the most of the time before the rains come again. The sky is milky with a benevolent cloud, and the eagles are capitalising on the vantage before they can't see again. They hang under the cloud like mobiles.

I have spent an inordinate amount of time just looking.

Standing at the open windows of the tower and looking out at all the stuff just gathered beneath me for contemplation. You can't see a lot from the fire tower and a lot can't see you, the trees grown tall around through its years of disuse.

Before you might have seen it from all over. Only from the mountain could you see everything.

But what I can see is still a lot. I can see the ocean of trees and I can see on and on to its edge. Boreal forest, the world's lungs. Sometimes in the morning a mist hangs over like smudged chalk and it strikes you vividly that this is it breathing. Like the vapour you exhale on a cold day but a whole atmosphere respired. I drink it in deeply through my nostrils, all the newest oxygen all for me. I can see the river winding through to meet the tundra, or just about, I see it glinting in slithers. Over the millennia of that river's course it will have snaked side to side, the trees clambering up or falling with the soil torn from under their feet. And the trees growing, dying, falling, rotting, each to feed another in its place.

And inside the forest the light spills green through the leaves as if through coloured film so that the light is green on my arms and on my face. The smell of spruce, and the spruce needles making the floor spongy like a play mat, dry and comfortable so that you can lie down on it to breathe it all in stronger.

I just listen. Can you hear the sound of the forest breathing? Underneath the ground is the forest's brain. Can you hear it thinking, ticking away? Tiny threads of mycelium one cell thick branch out like neurons and link up to form a living network underneath the forest, miles long. The mycelium connects to trees' roots, giving them a larger surface area and a higher absorption of nutrients and minerals, then breaks down with enzymes it excretes and reabsorbs from the soil, and in return the trees give it metabolised carbohydrates, the fruits of photosynthesis.

The tendrils of the mycelium are synapses and through them information travels. The mycelium is thinking and what it is thinking about is the health of the life around it. It is conscious and responsive to changes in its environment. It is planning for the long-term health of its environment.

Mycelium has inherited Earth several times over. It always surges after mass extinctions because it can metabolise and recycle the debris. It makes life-sustaining soil out of this debris, and so lays the ground for other life to follow, initiating the ecosystems that will diversify its food chain. Is it self-interested or is it just lonely? You can't really say. Loneliness is a kind of self-interest anyway.

Mycelium is a half-being, an in-between shape-shifter. It looks like a plant but it breathes out carbon dioxide. It comes from the kingdom *Eukarya*, from which we branched hundreds of millions of years ago. Mycelia are more animal than plant really. But they bridge the kingdoms like diplomatic interpreters. They translate between organisms and their environments.

And mycelium is a shaman, a seer into the spirit world, or into death. It turns the inorganic into organic, can dismantle chains that otherwise tangle, smoothing the mess that might upset its system by processing pollutants and radiation. There are no clear polarities for mycelium, no life or death, no organic or non-organic, but inextricable interconnectedness. It is the dark matter of the organic world.

Everything we know and can see is called baryonic matter and this is made up of the atom. Dark matter does not emit or absorb light but we have to assume it exists until the Large Hadron Collider tells us so for sure because there is something that we can't see exerting gravity on baryonic matter. We can't ever see it, this strange dark thing, but computer simulations of what it might look like if visible show it as a web that interweaves with baryonic matter like a connective tissue between the infinite everything. Literally everything in this tangled web like sliding spaghetti. I am a strand being pulled through other strands of spaghetti, only the spaghetti is not a strand, it is an infinitely long tangle, a snake swallowing itself. The very fabric of being denies solitude!

The web-like pattern of dark matter is an archetype found anywhere information is organised. It is the same shape you see in diagrams of mycelium, neurons, of the internet and the universe. So is mycelium a kind of brain and is the universe conscious? All of the above are governed by the laws of physics, and this pattern recurs simply because it is the optimum way to organise and share information.

Mushrooms are the fruits of the network under the forest; the mycelium is the root system to colonies of mushrooms. Mushrooms at Fukushima are growing out of the contaminated forest. They are hyper-accumulating the radioactive waste out of the soil. They can be picked, burned, and the ash can be put into glass. And then the radiation is only as difficult to dispose of as all the other nuclear waste we have bottled up. Perhaps the universe wants to help us to help ourselves. Perhaps it leaves us clues. The particular shape of the cloud from a nuclear blast is a dome on a column. A mushroom.

And so Sylvia Plath was being especially clever when she chose mushrooms as her vehicle for inheriting the Earth. Mushrooms offer the chance of renewal. And the wilderness can always be renewed if we only stop sending Voyagers into it. The wilderness can be given back to itself. New Zealand has given the legal status of personhood to Te Urewera National Park and the Whanganui River and its tributaries, which means they now have all of the rights and autonomy that a person does and cannot be exploited and are not owned.

As I lie on the forest floor, an ant or some small fast thing runs across my face and onto my lip and it tickles but I do not want to brush it off in case it gets crushed. I let it carry on making a planet of my face, running all directions, acknowledging its contours and using the information to paint itself a picture of my terrain, like the rover on Mars, like me here in Denali.

# HOW TO SAY GOODBYE

## SOLASTALGIA

So really why am I out here and what am I looking for? I am looking for something that is lost and kept from me but I do not quite know what it is. When I find it I know it will be broken and that I need to fix it but I don't know how to do that either. What I want right now is to be able to go back in time and talk to a younger lost me and tell her some things that I *have* found out.

You are sixteen years old and you are confused and lost and numb. You do not know your body or yourself and you mediate them through a little pill that you think is doing you good, reshaping you to fit in a world that will not otherwise accommodate you. You are told at the same time that it is yours now finally; you are lucky to be a modern woman. But it feels otherwise.

How do you feel about the place you call home? Crumbled industrial spaces, shiny new mega-stores, rivers yellow at the lips like disease with Coke-can flotsam, no space to be alone so that you can even know what it is to be together. You feel about it like you feel about your body, as though forces from outside are keeping you apart from it. You are helpless to possess it and you don't understand that others have no right to. What is this homesickness?

Every time you switch on the news you are overwhelmed by the weight of the bad in the world. You cry because you feel so helpless about it. A whole aboriginal community is put on antidepressants because they are suffering from PTSD. They are suffering from PTSD because there was an oil spill off the coast of British Columbia and the oil washed up and it killed everything that was beautiful in their home. You think this is the saddest thing in the world. How big is home? How atomised? How atomised are you?

It makes sense that you are a little psychotic and sad. You have got raging hormones and fake ones too and you are living in a shattered world. If your body is not yours to put in the wilderness, then without choice you can only ever feel lonely; unhomely; displaced. And you have been trained, socialised into mega-empathy like a dolphin is. That is not to say you feel it more because you are closer to it by virtue of some innate characteristic. But you feel it a little when a whole forest on the other side of the world is felled, or when another animal becomes extinct, because you see a shard of your lost self in it.

To know yourself you need to know what you are not the same as, but there are shards of you everywhere. According to Greenlandic Inuits, you have many souls. As many as seven. The souls are tiny people scattered through your body. The tiny people are shards of bigger people that can be found in pieces, in places outside of you.

You are made up of webs of relation which are always in the process of reconfiguration, but it is when you tear away too quickly and too much that you uproot, like a plant can be transplanted if you are gentle and slow but if you rip it up and put it in a place that is hostile, it withers. Like the placing of a child into foster care or the extinction of animals; it is then that there is homesickness and there are fewer shards of a lost self to be found.

Likewise as part of the web you can feel its reverberations, and you can feel how everything you do too warps the fabric in some small way. You have to be aware of these reverberations. You have to be aware of the placement of your body, your specific viewpoint, your Observer Effect. To begin healing is to realise this and to make amends and to remember.

Sam said you should not just go off in search of something better for yourself. He said water protectors are living in a camp at Standing Rock where they want to stop an oil pipe being built through sacred land. And they must feel the most hopeless feeling of the panic of loss, but they will not just take themselves off alone somewhere quieter to be in peace and converse with their ego. They will stay and try to resist what is a corruption to the very core of their being, even if their resistance can only end in failure. *Sam, I am so sorry I did not see it.*

And how it must have seemed to him, my project of staking a claim to solitude and autonomy, trying to emulate the Mountain Men while at the same time there are other women being violently reminded of their lack of even more. It is all a game to you, he must have thought. I saw his resentment as a man-shackle, a reminder of myself as a dragged-around woman, and thought I was casting this off by ignoring him. I have been emulating and my whole journey has been compliance. I can Buck as well as any man, but now I understand it better, why would I want to be like them, the Mountain Men?

So this morning I have to say goodbye to the tower and the ghosts of P Harris and Johnston Wills and the wolves, leaving the spider to its flies, taking the little wooden boat from the side of the ship, used for getting to the island back to the main ship again.

And probably I will never come back here. And probably nobody will for a long time. I am pulling myself back from deep space and into orbit, feeling sad and happy like the moonwalkers.

I have slept all those nights alone and far away, and I have proved to myself that I can be the kind of person who does those things and there is nothing in my biology stopping me. The documentary as proof never mattered. Maybe that is all but it feels enough, to know that if I wanted to I could be the kind of person who can handle it, that my character is strong enough to endure itself alone as a Mountain Man.

Even if at first it was terrifying and I thought maybe I could not do it and my nerves were so wound up that I had to act to myself, act to the part of me that was shit scared and lonely and in a continual feeling of fight or flight.

But the fight half-fought and in the end it overcame and it won. And this is the hugeness of my small voyage. Something has been stretched in me that makes the general elastic of my life more malleable and I will be able to always feel and notice this new plasticity.

Thoreau decided that as important as it was to be alone in his cabin he still did not want or need to do it forever. No matter how Walden reads he still went back to Concord. Chris McCandless decided this too if his diary is anything to go by; he just died accidentally before he could do anything about it.

## THE KNOWING SELF IS PARTIAL

When I got back to the cabin I crawled into the cot and slept for a whole day. I was so tired I felt like I might never be able to move again, but eventually hunger got me up, I made some rice with salt and ate it and then slept for some hours more. When I woke up I decided what was to be done with my time capsule.

I gathered together Damon's things neatly and reparcelled them in the tarp, then I put them back beneath the floorboards and left them exactly as I found them. And I hope hard that no one else ever finds them and that, if they do, they believe they are the only person to have found them, and that they are a woman (or Eskimo) too, because everyone knows girls are well versed at keeping secrets.

I laid everything out on the floor and sat cross-legged looking over it: the camera, my diary, the laptop, my notes. The collection felt like a snowshoe hare without a soul inside, an empty vessel. Now that I can't use it for what it was for, what I wanted it to be, a feminist Golden Record, because there can be no such thing.

And then one of those last days I walked out onto the tundra in the evening when the sun was unusually orange like an extremely orange egg yolk, the kind of orange yolk that you know is full of goodness, and it spilt across the tundra making everything yolky and big. And on the tundra right behind the cabin, as if I had felt them and the inclination to go outside came to me because of this, there was an entire herd of reindeer just stood about together, munching on tundra grass and being reindeer.

And in that moment it occurred to me that my reindeer did not die because it was not my reindeer at all. It had always been this herd; it had been one after another crossing my path, the scouts to the herd, the forerunners preceding the main migration.

And I thought to myself, *that* is the point of reindeer, *that* is what she meant by my reindeer telling me my future. My reindeer tells me that I cannot follow it; it is the proprioception I need to know myself. Thoreau again: 'We need to witness our own limits transgressed, and some life pasturing freely where we never wander.'

The reindeer tells me that my future is the linear continuity of whatever I build it from because I build and then preserve my own history. It is never complete or completely true but I have to hold on to things that relate to an idea of myself and what I am doing; my cloud castle. It is important to have a story. And this, my history, can be encapsulated in my time capsule. There is pushing a time capsule into the stratosphere and there is the utter negation of symbols, annihilating completely. Somewhere in between I know there is something meaningful. It is what I do with the time capsule, its intent, and not the time capsule itself, that matters.

*Do you know the difference between a caribou and a reindeer?*

*No, I do not.*

*A caribou is larger and more slender and part of a wild herd. A reindeer is semi-wild but it has been domesticated. They are the same species. Reindeer were domesticated in Eurasia over 2000 years ago, then brought to Alaska by colonisers as food, in 1892, as part of the Reindeer Project, created to replace whale meat in the diet of indigenous peoples. The colonisers thought that the geography of the land would prevent the domesticated reindeer leaving to join the caribou herds. In 1997, all of the reindeer joined the Western Artic Caribou Herd and disappeared.*

*How tenacious.*

*Some may have already spread via Inuit tribes who share a cultural history with tribes of Eurasia, over in Siberia.*

*Oh.*

*But does all that make them any less potent?*

*I guess we all came from somewhere.*

I felt the pulse of the whole great herd of caribou, calf mothers and babies and, yes, some males as well, stood out on the tundra making Dali-shadows in the molten bask of the sun. And I knew that it did not have to be a particular reindeer guarding me like an angel and it did not have to talk to me and tell me my future because there is enough magic in seeing a whole herd of anything just being, just being apart and for themselves.

This is it, the point of complexity and otherness and the thing that I needed to take away and the thing worth saving and the reason to not bugger off to Mars and the reason Damon should have stayed alive. I think I am ready to talk to Damon now. I think I have decided what I need to say.

Damon, I have been unravelling, unravelling, to try to get to where you were at, and I came undone, I was scared I might go all the way too and end as a tangled mess of unravelling. I followed your philosophy all the way to its genesis, like the deduction that led to the atom bomb. Of this unravelling and of the atom bomb you would say let it happen, let it all unravel and go up in nuclear flames, it's sad but it's for the best, the world is better off without us. But I have come so far. I thought there must be a reason to save something of it if I can. To let it all go is to lose too much. And I found a reason. Because it can all be written differently, we can change the direction of the story.

*Nothing is lost with no one there to miss it, you said that.*

Stay with me. The complexity of our symbols distinguishes us from all the other creatures (as it stands right now) and you think that from the symbols emanates the bad thing, the thing that propels us towards catastrophe. And perhaps it does right now, but I do not think it is inherent in the symbols. Yes, our language is dichotomising, but for now it is the only one we have to work with. The Enlightenment taxonomers wanted to possess and to control the natural world and they sewed their signatures into the names. Yes, as with the Earthrise photo we can lose the directness of the thing to symbolism, but shared meaning is potent too. We need our symbols so that we can feel the love of sad beauty. If the mountain had no symbolic meaning it would just be a chunk of rock. If I did not know the difference between a kestrel and a buzzard it would be easier to forget them both. Naming can be reverence and not possession.

Narratives are important. Narratives can be dangerous. The trick is to be critical, to always be trying to choose the right and good one. To be critical of your view from what body, to what limit. There would be no love of sad beauty without us. There would not be anything worth dying for without beauty.

Well, there might be some love of sad beauty without us but not felt by anything potent and influential enough to do any-thing about it apart from feel sad and in love. For example, the pack rat collects objects that interest it and it stores them all in its midden. Middens are considered by palaeo-ecologists to be reliable time capsules of natural life of millennia ago. And the bowerbird, when it builds a nest, gives its nest a yard and yard ornaments made from beetles' wings and orchids and things. It might be to attract a mate but the bowerbird's beautiful objects have to exist otherwise the world would be too easy to let go of. What do bowerbirds and pack rats mean by their collecting? Are these creatures saying, 'I too am in the appreciation of beauty club,' and at the base of it they are just as scared of being alone as the rest of us?

We need to realise that our categories are illusions, but we also need to be able to name the tiny things, the microscopic creatures that live inside us, we have to name them because how could we know them if we did not name them and how could we love them if we did not know them? We need to be able to find a place in the continuum to point at and say 'me.'

Wilderness as a static boundary keeps humans out of nature, as though we are still two sides of a dichotomy when we are not. But it is also useful to stop from saturation, the unbalance of the system from too many Mountain Men. Thoreau wanted full libertarian 'freedom,' like Buck the dog, but men are more destructive than dogs, which would leave wildness to fend for itself against many Mountain Men with guns and pickaxes, which it can't. The 'self-willed man' stakes his claim to freedom while taking no care over anybody else's.

This regulation does not take away the wildness. The plants and animals do not even think of it. You can call the mountain Mount McKinley but the Athabaskans will still call it Deenaalee. And wildness allows for renewal. Like the flux of Inuit identity, the wild is not static. The tamed can be feral can be wild again.

The categorisation of indigenous peoples was a colonial endeavour in the first place, an awarding of status and non-status. They mostly had no written language before white people arrived. But there is empowerment where communities can self-identify. Eskimo language is being written down, in order to preserve it, in order that young Eskimos can relearn the language that underpins their culture. They need a taxonomy of self to know themselves. The plaque in the visitors' centre has a hopeful message of regeneration. It says that modern ethnically Eskimo and Athabaskan people are reclaiming and reviving their languages and cultures.

Once you realise the thing that would be missing when all is lost, you have a responsibility to it, to the future. Because transmigration is a really beautiful concept and if you understand how potent it is you have a responsibility to help it carry on. Like the difference between a dead Damon and a Damon never born. You feel it too. You must have left your diary somewhere your mother could find it.

The yearning of lack and the panic of saturation are part of what sent me, but to try to shrug them off is to shake off the shackles of responsibility that are at the same time ribbons of meaning. It is important to have a story for yourself, in order to be in love with the world. And it is the love we feel when we look at the mountain which could save it. Maybe women are made more prone to loneliness, but is this a bad thing? We will be lonely without the plants and the animals and we feel their loss more acutely. There is no purity so there is always the possibility for renewal. Like mother goddess renewal, not like a male god of beginnings and ends.

*Stop being so New Agey.*

*Why don't you try not being so literal?*

# A LETTER FOR THE UNABOMBER

Ms Erin Miller
Cabin in the Wilderness
Denali Wilderness
Alaska

Ted Kaczynski 04475–046
USP FLORENCE ADMAX
U.S. PENITENTIARY
PO BOX 8500
FLORENCE, CO 81226

Dear Mr Kaczynski,

I am a girl writing to you from a cabin in the wilderness. I have read your manifesto while here from beginning to end because instead of taking for granted that everybody who said you were just a crazy person was right, I wanted to understand why you set off the bombs, for myself. I am a big fan of your work; your understanding of the technological system and your predictions for the future of humanity echo worries that I have myself. You are right that this reckless and unsustainable system is causing climate change. But I have come to the conclusion that you take these things so far as to void them, and have actually given more ammunition to the system you despise. I think you need to know this because yours is a dangerous logic and while you spout it others are living and dying by it.

I know what happened to you at Berkeley and I am sorry that you can't help that it made you the way you are. You are not wholly to blame for your legacy but I can't resurrect Thoreau to chide him, or Charles Darwin or Adam Smith, and evidently each has an influence on and on in infinite regress. But you are alive and with living disciples and you have a responsibility for your words while they are still mutable. You could be the last link in a chain that unravels from itself.

I am sure you get lots of letters, both fan mail and hate mail alike, but I wanted to ensure that you received the thoughtful perspective of a woman because I feel your philosophy would benefit from this greatly. I know you do not like girls and especially not feminists, or the English, so I am addressing you as a fellow member of the human race, specifically one who is uneasy about the future of humanity under the current technological regime. It worries me also to think that the time may come where there is complete discord between humans and nature. It terrifies me that our civilisation seems to think that we could exist happily as the sole inhabitants of a barren planet. This is not the way I want things to go either. However, I do not think that this outcome is an inevitable progression from where we are now, only a possible one. And I do not think your revolution of individualists who will destroy the system then return to life in the wilderness as loners or in small clans is a fair or just or helpful cause.

I did some math. I am not very good at math like you are but roughly I think I worked something out. So Earth has about 57,500,000 square miles of dry land and not all of it is habitable, but if you take away the 23 percent of mountains and 33 percent of desert which totals 32,200,000 square miles you are left with 25,300,000 square miles. Now divide this between the 7,107,663,700 (give or take a few) people on Earth circa 2013, and remember this is also rough, but just for the sake of argument then $25,300,000 \div 7,107,663,700 = 0.00355953813$ square miles, or 9,219.2 square metres. 9,219.2 square metres per person, which is just a little larger than a football pitch. Enough room for your cabin but not for the woods or much land to grow things and generally be self-sufficient, even with each individual farming their own plot and trading with neighbours, even with some grouping together in order to farm animals. There is still not enough room to avoid the rest of humanity or to be immersed in nature because all the cabins would disrupt the grazing and migration land of animals and also many trees would have to be cut down for all the logs. Also by estimates, the amount of land that would be needed to support a hunter-gatherer lifestyle far outweighs the amount of land available per head currently (only enough land to support around 100 million hunter-gatherers).

I am sure you would argue that population would not be an issue because after the revolution and subsequent fall of technology many drones would starve to death without the system to feed or medicate them. But here I think you underestimate people's resourcefulness. Surely those with sense would not just curl up and die but loot the cities of their resources, and when these are spent they will drive their SUVs into your wilderness and shoot your wildlife with their machine-made rifles to feed their children, who cannot be fed by the system because of the revolution. Another danger is that the elite would monopolise the remaining resources due to their power and the availability they already have the upper hand on, and would therefore be the ones not to perish, leaving them with a foundation from which to build back up and become monolithic (they already have exclusive billionaire underground bunkers set up for the apocalypse in Germany somewhere). This for me is immoral, and very easy for you to say from your privileged position. Not everyone can have access to the freedom you condemn them for snubbing.

Maybe I am biased because my tiny female brain is 40 percent social, but the way I see it, the biggest threat to the freedom of each individual is the patriarchal hierarchical structure of society and the waning of its resources, which puts strain on those at the bottom and is mostly caused by those at the top. I weigh this threat as the one which affects the most people, rather than that which weighs most heavily on certain individuals (i.e. you).

A predominant concern for us both is population density, because the denser it gets, the more restricted becomes the individual's freedom. Therefore your dismissal of the feminist and gay movements is a fatal flaw as their success is key to a social reform that could curb or decrease indiscriminate population growth.

Generally liberating poor people, liberating women, getting oppressed women into the workplace, or educating them on the options available to them and providing them with the means, could reduce reproduction. Around the world nearly 40 percent of pregnancies are unintended. Around 350 million women in developing countries did not want their last child or do not want another, but they do not have access to information or services to help them. This means deconstructing patriarchy so that women can take control of their bodies. The deconstruction would also mean that the sole pressure is not on the woman when it comes to child-rearing. Equally shared roles between parents and even communal care would relieve this. The current paradigm does not want communal care because it means the child is not moulded in the image of its parents and is therefore not time-capsulised.

I think one of the sentiments that underpins this problem, perhaps the most significant sentiment, is actually the individualism that you advocate. A more collectivist sentiment would encourage alternative ways of fulfilling the desire to nurture, without feeling the need to immortalise the self in genes, and lead to an increase in adoption of children.

The concept of metempsychosis is a beautiful thing, and I think that once it is embraced the need for biological children will seem outmoded, we will think like the Inuits and name our children in plural. Every person around you gives and takes from the fabric of you. This is spiritual and intellectual more than it is biological. It is how men have been doing it throughout time.

You can't just spay people; you have to remind them that our shards don't migrate with specificity of genes in mind.

But anyway, population is not everything; it is the individualist consumer mentality of the developed world that causes more emissions than the 'overpopulated' developing world. This can be reformed into a free and equal society based on cooperation and voluntary contribution from all for the good of everyone, which is the fairest way to liberate, spreading freedom as opposed to consolidating it. The technological system can be used to help reform, spreading the message and reminding the people that we are WORLD CITIZENS. Our skill for invention is not the issue, but the way that we are directing our skills. Scientific research and technology are vital in bringing basic rights and freedoms to such a large population. It is scientific research and technology that have given us an understanding of deep time and therefore of our future generations ahead. It is scientific invention that got us far enough to stop and consider ourselves.

This individualism is tied up in your invocation of FREEDOM. Your kind of freedom still requires a dualistic philosophy for it to be maintained. Searching for absolutes in nature builds just another dualistic metanarrative, one of good vs. evil and pure vs. impure. This kind of freedom is the philosophical driving force behind the Machine. You are worried about the subjugation of human nature, but see, essential human nature does not exist.

The thing that has been bugging me all this time is the influence of the idea of natural law in the arguments of the Mountain Men. Although I could just argue now that science or natural law is just a bunch of stories, I wanted to meet you on your own territory, so I have come up with some scientific proofs against the argument of the Mountain Men that civilisation is unnatural and women just biologically suck:

There is the evolutionary case of sexual dimorphism. Although I could just invoke Lynn Margulis and her whole argument for origins and cooperation over competition, I want to be specific. In our close relatives of the ape family, males have much more pronounced canines than do females (apart from bonobos, a matriarchal species). In the bones of our long-dead predecessors it has been noted that males had much more pronounced canines, which shrank and shrank until they are as they are now, in no way divergent between the sexes.

One theory is that this is because females, when selecting a mate, selected social and sharing males, reducing the evolutionary need for big old canines. The theory is that this is because there was not much or maybe any division of labour between the sexes, we all hunt-gathered, and likely took our meat from scavenging. Sexual specialisation probably came very late in human evolution, as late as the dawn of agriculture, the so-called Neolithic Revolution 12,500 years ago.

The Palaeolithic came before the Neolithic and had a very vast time span of around 2.5 million years. It has only been 12,500 years since the dawn of agriculture, and the birth of the 'modern human.' The Palaeolithic world and way of being stayed static for all that time. They obviously had the formula for being human just right then, before things started to change.

The birdman with the boner painting in the caves at Lascaux is dated to the Upper Palaeolithic, the last division before the Neolithic and the birthing of behavioural modernity. Behavioural modernity is characterised by abstract thinking, planning depth and symbolic behaviour like art and ornamentation. So the birdman was painted at a time of upheaval and the caves are a time capsule of this period.

The message fails time, no one can agree on what the birdman means, but that does not matter. We are allowed to interpret it for our purpose like the palaeo-ecologist interprets the pack rat's midden (narrative licence). So here goes:

I could, for example, say that the birdman is aroused by the dominance that at this point in history he had begun to exert on the natural world. The yak thing represents the natural world. Perhaps that is an enlarged vulva hanging below her abdomen, representing femininity. Lots of art from this time features the female body, so called Venus figures. As though at the time the people revered the female body as a life-giving deity. Perhaps what the painting represents is the rise of patriarchy, at the cusp of two opposing paradigms. But the bull is knocking the birdman down. Perhaps what it says is matriarchy WILL PERSEVERE!!!

My point is that I believe there is no proof that competition and dominance are essential and innate features of the human being. The subjugation of women is not necessarily an essential fact of life.

More facts (or speculations). Dopamine is the neurotransmitter associated with risk-taking and therefore adventure. It gives us a reward hit when we accomplish a task. The more risk involved in the task, the bigger the hit. A reason not everyone wants to be a Mountain Man could be that some people make less dopamine than others. Dopamine is associated with the left side of the brain while serotonin is associated with the right. As a general trend men are associated more with the left side of the brain and women with the right.

Dopamine is associated more with antisocial personality disorders and serotonin with borderline personality disorders. A person with antisocial personality disorder lacks empathy for other people while a borderline personality disorder feels like empathy you can't control, boundary issues making it difficult to share another's pain without feeling it too much as your own (the process of osmosis until the saturation point is reached).

These are very general trends. There are more Mountain Men than Mountain Women. But a siphon movement can only start when an outside pressure has been added. A dead hand is an undesirable and persisting influence. And if you pour liquid into a mould to set it will set in the shape of the mould. Learned behaviour has been proved to actually change genetic make-up, so even biological sex is in a process of transformation always.

The evolutionary biologists say that maybe the dopamine in the brain was the thing that sent us out of Africa. Maybe it is the chemical of species proliferation. Maybe it made me leave home. Maybe it sent the Apollo astronauts to the moon.

But could be it is not quite an innate and natural impulse like that and the real reason is that NASA were very selective about who could join Apollo. Some psychologist did a personality assessment of all the Apollo astronauts and concluded that they were all 'Type A.' A Type A personality is very competitive, rational, ambitious, you could say glory-hungry and selfish. And this could have to do, the psychologist said, with the fact that they were all the eldest sibling or the only son, and had patriarchal military-type fathers (remember the original desert solitude-seeking nature solace Mountain Man with the most famous absent father, our Lord Jesus Christ).

And women can be Type A too, but maybe it would be better if people stopped being Type A altogether, or if we at least stopped letting Type As do all the important and influential stuff. And if Type A is still the type that provides the most astronauts, then the space colonies are not going to be much fun, are they?

The 'primitive' necessarily gets meaning from the contrast of civilisation. And besides, you did not ever manage to shrug off civilisation. You worshipped mathematics as absolute. But mathematics puts another false map on the world, which pretends to be a territory but is really just another map, same as the others.

It is a thing we invented based on spatial allegories coming from our bodies and their interaction with the outside. There are different mathematics and they are inconsistent with each other, but are perfect systems. They are not real or true in your absolutist sense, so they went against your project of wilderness. It is the belief in this reduction that drives your Machine and you do not even see it.

My main point is we are at a place in time now where we can be reflective. It may have been almost inevitable that our symbols would do this to us, but now we have the reflectiveness to be critical of them. But we need our symbols in order to be able to talk and think about ourselves. And to change the paradigm.

Aldo Leopold said, 'a thing is right when it tends to preserve the integrity, stability and beauty of the biotic community. It is wrong when it tends otherwise.' And I think this is a philosophy to live by. Our challenge is to remember that we are a part of this biotic community, and once we have remembered, to act accordingly.

In a way you are right for wanting to emulate 'primitive' cultures. Indigenous cultures generally are more partnership-oriented and feminine. But let us not also forget that they were not perfect; Palaeolithic man may have wiped out the woolly mammoth and some Native Americans used to run whole herds of buffalo off cliff-sides even though they weren't going to eat them all. And neither is the natural world a perfect system to emulate; Inuit get annoyed at orcas for killing so many seals just for the fun of it. But you are wrong to say there is a right-just-objective way and it is the old way, the law of the wild. There is no ahistorical way of being. If you burned all the libraries how would you have 'known' nature without the naturalists?

We can learn from the past but also need to adapt to the future. Women are, in our society, simultaneously social and maternal, crazy and wild. The relationship we need with the natural is one that is feminine. Admitting this and ending the unfair and ungrounded exclusion of women from your philosophy of wilderness is an important step in deconstruction. I am leaving my cabin now, but it is because I have got everything I need. I have got what you were trying to keep from me.

The Machine is perpetuated by us and we are inextricable from it. We need to change the collective conscious to change the direction of the Machine. You are not an isolated ego. Even you, the hermit, exist in relation to your polar antithesis, society. We find ourselves in relationship to the other. When we do not, complexity is lost and we are diminished selves.

I know of a pipe that you made for a friend on which you hand-carved the words 'Mountain Men are always free.' Mountain Men shun society, yet their solitude relies on the continuation of the system to contain the rest of humanity and leave room for their wilderness. You cannot escape the fact that you are a human being and wherever you go others will want to follow. Scythes cutting through thickets.

On a final note, I know of some people who you might like to get in touch with. They are called the Voluntary Human Extinction Movement. With your fame I am sure you could rally to their cause by hunger-striking to death in prison. I have a friend who followed your logic and did exactly this. He was much braver and sincere to himself than you have been with your letter bombs. You could honour his life better by admitting your faults of logic.

Reform over revolution.
Down with patriarchy,
Erin Miller (QUEEN OF THE WILD)

## THE CLITORIS IS A DIRECT LINE
## TO THE MATRIX

Rachel Carson says it is finally time to lay her to rest. She has taught me what there was to learn. I lay her down in a long wooden canoe. This is so I can set her out, flowing back to the sea to commune with the whales. I set the canoe on fire. I have to set it on fire to fumigate her spirit. This is to try to get rid of some of the imprints the dead leave once the spirit has dissipated. She explains that, more and more, it is impossible to fumigate entirely. Left behind the body is always a fine powder, unnervingly green. It is a lifetime's accumulation of polychlorinated biphenyl and endocrine disruptors and bisphenol-A from the liver (the chains that cannot be dismantled). These cannot transmigrate into the spiritual realm, but they can't be reabsorbed back into the natural world either like the ashes can. They remain in the physical realm as a negative imprint.

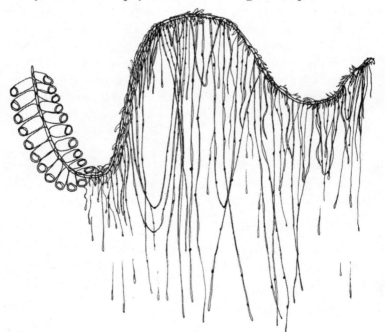

(But there is also the positive charge and that stays too because ideas can't be set on fire. I feel shards of it slide into me, like chakra disks that do not hurt.)

As the canoe glides across the ocean it burns up and gets less and less until nothing is left. Then the soul is completely free to transmigrate. Part of the soul slips into the ocean because that is where it wants to be. This soul attaches to a siphonophore, an odd creature that looks like a jellyfish so that sometimes it is mistakenly identified as one.

But these creatures are really a unity of tiny cellular creatures, simultaneously individual and collective and multicellular. Each member of the colony has a different function towards benefiting the organism as a whole. No member could survive independent of the others that do the things that it can't. They are genetically the same and they live and die as one. And all are connected to a stem and to a circulatory system, and they develop from the same embryo, like sprouting a Siamese twin from your side again and again and again.

(But then, what with global warming and the acidification of the oceans, lots of the sea creatures will die and she will have to transmigrate again. Where will all the souls accumulate when there are not the billions of small creatures and no room for more big and potent ones? What havoc will they play, waiting for a body?)

## WHAT BOOK IS THIS THAT
## REFUSES TO END?

When the Helios 2 probe launched in 1976 it was the fastest spacecraft ever built, its top speed reaching 157,000 miles per hour. Proxima Centauri is our nearest star and it is 24 trillion miles away. If Helios 2 were to head directly for Proxima Centauri at its top speed it would take 17,000 years to reach it;

17,000 years is a span equivalent to the one that separates modern-day humans from Cro-Magnon cave painters. If Voyager 1 were to travel the same distance it would take it 74,000 years; 74,000 years ago early Palaeolithic people were almost killed off by a supervolcano that erupted in Indonesia and spread ash around the whole planet.

On and on the little spaceship goes. So far in time it is thirty-seven years away. The year Voyager 1 launched was 1977. That year there were eleven major plane crashes, Harvey Milk became the first openly gay elected official in the US, American man Roy Sullivan got struck by lightning for the seventh time, Spain had its first democratic election since Franco, Queen Elizabeth II opened the parliaments of Australia and New Zealand, the Bucharest earthquake killed 1,500 people, Jimmy Carter became the thirty-ninth president of America, Gary Gilmore from Utah was the first person to be executed after the death penalty was reintroduced in America, Hamida Djandoubi was the last person to be executed by guillotine in France, smallpox was eradicated, Elvis Presley died, optical fibre was first used to carry telephone signals, and the Big Ear radio telescope, which would eventually be taken down to make way for a golf course, picked up its famous Wow! Signal from deep space. This was on August the fifteenth, twenty-one days before Voyager 1 was launched.

The year I was born was 1993, the year of the Velvet Divorce, and when guys from the IRA perpetrated one of the biggest robberies in US history and set off a lot of bombs, the year the Chemical Weapons Convention was signed, Bill Clinton became president, Russians mounted the first art exhibition in space and no one went to see it, Kim Campbell became the first female prime minister of Canada and resigned the same year, a van bomb killed six at the World Trade Center, there was the Great Blizzard of 1993 on the East Coast of the US, South Africa abandoned its nuclear weapons programme, the US Air Force let women fly war planes, a Unabomber bomb injured a computer scientist at Yale, a floating chapel sank and killed 266 people, the nineteenth G7 summit was held, the public were allowed into Buckingham Palace for the very first time, China undertook a nuclear test and it ended a worldwide moratorium, the European Union was established, *A Brief History of Time* became the longest-lasting bestseller, and Freya Stark, Deke Slayton of the Mercury programme and William Golding all died.

Written into the Big Bang theory are Cosmological Horizons. These horizons mark the limit of our Observable Universe. The Observable Universe has a spherical distribution with an observer at its centre. Events outside this radius have not had time for their light to reach the observer yet and never will. The Cosmological Horizon is the shady border to the furthest point the observer can retrieve information from. Likewise, light emitted by the observer might not ever catch up to distant and exponentially receding objects in an expanding universe. This is the Future Horizon, and events which are past here the observer can have no influence on. Every single point in the universe can be the centre of a different Observable Universe and parts of all can overlap.

I will start my journey home a voyager called back like a well-trained falcon. Only there is no calling back the actual Voyagers; they will keep on going if we like it or not. Voyager 1 could go on travelling forever and ever into the wild yonder on its own velocity. And Voyager 1 is its own central observer, it can leave our Observable Universe and enter a new one of its own.

Voyager 1 is our time capsule into another universe. It might be that no one who ever finds it will understand what it means. But they would likely understand that it has *intent*, and even though the intention fails it is the drive behind the *intent* that will live on, sinisterly, like the twitch of the almost-dead baddie at the end of the horror film.

The Voyagers are relics of a time when people thought

missions to space held integrity and wonder. But the next big missions to space will be commercial ones because the public are bored now. The moon is awe-sapped enough that we do not mind mining it. And when the miners have opened the emigrant trails we might colonise our brand-new *tabula rasa*. Space X wants to launch missions to mine minerals from space and create the world's first trillionaires. Virgin Galactic will take a bunch of rich and famous people to the moon. On board the inaugural flight will be James Lovelock. Either he had a change of heart in old age or he is going along as a suicide bomber.

And then if the Curiosity rover were to find a pictogram, or a bipedal vertebrate fossilised on Mars, or the archaeological remains of a complex civilisation, then it would mean that life had appeared elsewhere in another Cambrian Explosion, and that life is probably quite good at forming complex life elsewhere too. But it would also mean that it is not so great at making life whose destiny is to propagate apart from the other life that binds it. It could be a premonition. A terrible fossil lizard to the Victorians. Or a cautionary symbol.

There is maybe one small redeeming thing, because the thing about horizons is you are never any closer to them. That is just the nature of horizons. Even Voyager 1 can never catch up with the future, and after billions of years I suppose it must disintegrate or something and that will be it, us out in a little plume, a little puff, but whether it does or not there will *always* be another horizon and there will *always* be epistemological wilderness just beyond it.

Once I had everything packed away in the cabin, the board replaced under the desk and the items exactly as they were when I came, all was ready for a layer of dust to settle again. The dust is made of particles of me now. It is also made of the particles of other things: pollen, spores, space rocks, spiders, wood from the cabin itself. Dust seems a nice legacy to leave behind. I did not even fumigate my litter in the fire. Instead I put it all in a plastic bag and carried it with me out of the wilderness, because to leave the plastic particles in the air from the burning to me seemed too much a desecration.

Could be I was always on it but I began my long journey home. When I left the cabin, my cabin, I pulled the door shut quietly as though to not disturb the dust as I left, like I could have come and gone on that very first day and just left silently while the cabin slept and it never even noticed me. I turned around to look at it when I had got a little away, alone and small and heavy and dawny in the 4 a.m. morning light, and took a picture which I shall keep always but show no one.

I really hate goodbyes. I think goodbye when it is a forever goodbye is the saddest and most beautiful word. It is a contraction of god-be-with-you, which is touching because even without a god what you are saying all at once is 'I hope that the shining light that guides you whatever it is is always with you and you don't ever lose your way or yourself and we won't ever meet again now but I want for you to always be safe and happy.'

It is saying you will be apart from me now but a shard of you will always remain. Another part of me will go with you, because we are always taking and giving shards from each other and you always lose a part of yourself when you say a forever goodbye. You lose the person they make you. Fear of this loss sometimes drives people to isolation, but this in itself is a tenfold loss. I will always carry Damon with me as a shard, like shrapnel.

We are perpetual motion and change, but there is something that endures and it changes, but gradually enough that some of it endures. You would not be able to know yourself, at least only a little and only sometimes, without this enduring thing. It is maybe 'I do really hope the light is always with you even if the light can't be said to be unchanging but whatever your new light is I hope there is one and I will always hope it will be with you still.'

Because it is the light that will guide you onwards to the next thing. If there is not this enduring thing, this kind of gravitational force, then we can lose our way completely and forget that carrying on and not losing the way as much as possible is the whole game. The light is a baton and life is the race and goodbye is the passing of the baton but you have to keep on running and keep on passing that baton but each time you pass it you actually swap it, someone gives you a new one.

That we can feel sad at this motion and this parting and feel a genuine want that although this thing or this person will go on in its own way without you, that it does so with this light even though you can never know it really, this is a beautiful thing. I bawled my eyes out as I walked away as I am in the habit of doing when I feel the pass of the baton occur.

The only astronaut to admit to crying on the moon was Alan Shepard of Mercury and Apollo 14, and this is just proof that they sent the wrong people to the moon because it is good to cry. Crying is the most honest way of saying (and better than with corrupting words), hey, outside world and other beings, I feel you being there.


## A LETTER TO MY FUTURE SELF

Dear Erin of the future,

This all seems glaringly obvious to you now, but perhaps you will have forgotten some things. I want you to remember how you got there. That is why I decided it was okay to keep some of the project in Eskimo secret because that way the only person I can colonise is you and that is actually a desirable thing (I like to be consistent). It is to shout I EXIST, which is not a conceited thing to do if you only shout it in your own face.

Almost anything or any method of information transfer when intended for the future can be termed at one time or another a time capsule. So this written thing is a time capsule. Maybe all written words are time capsules. Virginia Woolf said of writing, *arrange whatever pieces come your way*, which sounds like time-capsule curation to me. Not collection as possession but a collection like that of the reverent bowerbird. So here it is, an affirmation of me, for you.

The Eskimo and the Inuit, known as Twospirit people, they know that genders are arbitrary because anyone can embody them, but they still use them to describe themselves. Identity and words are important for narrative. Scientific theories are only approximations to the true nature of things but sometimes the error is tiny enough for them to be pretty useful.

Like Newton's world of solid bodies moving through empty space as an analogy for the realm of everyday life called the zone of middle dimensions. In the zone of middle dimensions you feel the effect of the apple that hits you on the head. It is not much use to tell Newton that the apple does not hit one's head, not really.

I am not a singular organism but an amalgamation of organisms. I am the elected voice of this amalgamation, for the life inside my life and the mites in my eyelashes. In taxonomy we separate things to make it easier to talk about difference. Taxonomy is a masculine language that dichotomises, like gender is a masculine language, structuring hierarchies. A colonising language; taxonomy is the colonisation of the natural world, but it is pretty useful because it helps you to tell the difference between *goosetongue* and *arrowgrass* and not die.

And if I am a woman I am a historically situated and contextual woman, but I am a woman all the same. And it only matters that in popular opinion I have been more social and permeable and collectivist and can identify more with trees and animals than a man can. But physics now says that everything is permeable. My feminisation was training in the interrelation of Earth systems.

Lovelock gave Earth a feminine (historically defined) name because he valued the feminine (historically defined) characteristics of renewal, life-giving/-destroying and cooperation. History dictated that women understand more about empathy, starting with training in the home and 'mother' bonds. If women are better trained in empathy, then maybe women are a little more in love with the world.

The universe is perpetual motion and change but you can take a step back to where it comes into sharp focus as you look at it. Consciousness is integral to theories of matter because it is consciousness that creates the whole observation that changes the course of the universe, even if only in a very tiny way. It took a long time for things to get this complex and tangled and each of us is woven into this tangle inextricably.

Because it is densely tangled the web does not change very quickly or drastically, and in this way it gives the illusion of stability. When the speed of change is accelerated to an extent that it is a pace too fast for adaption, it gets very suddenly to a place where nothing is recognisable. Examples of this are mass extinctions, nuclear annihilation, or the loss of an indigenous culture. I call this danger *velocity*.

When they talk about space they still talk in terms of 'nature' or 'wilderness' like the Inuit don't have a word for, because the only way to talk about a thing is to pin it down and quantify it. It has to be outside you in language. Otherwise science can't work. But Bohr said this is just a trick and that the properties of an atomic object can only be understood in relation to the object's interaction with the observer and that you can't talk about nature without talking about yourself. And it works the other way too, in inverse.

This whole time I have been looking so hard through binoculars that I have not even noticed that I am looking through binoculars, which are a pretty nifty thing to have, or that they have been hurting my eye where I have pressed them against it. And I have been looking so hard through binoculars at what looks so far away that I have not seen what was right in front of me. It is all very well and good to build a castle, but you have to make sure not to build it *on top of people*, and I could have crushed a few people.

Another thing Thoreau said about foundations is *we have not to lay the foundation of our houses in the ashes of a former civilization*; here he meant literal houses and this is why he liked America, Land of the Free, more than Europe, where there were many civilisations under houses. The ambassador of American wilderness conveniently forgets his own impurity; he has still built his on top of a whole lot of native people.

Around me the cabin is still, quiet and dusty. Everything sits in its place as it has since the beginning, familiar and inexplicable. I feel how a swallow must feel getting the sudden inclination of the east, one day looking around itself and suddenly, nope, dislocated. It is all void of purpose now. The weather is turning, the berries are dropping, the gnats are dying off. The east, that is the place to be. The swallow can't pinpoint when its purpose changed but it did and now everything has something different about it and it has to leave for home.

And its place and its nest and the time it spent there do not feel wasted or failed or empty because that is not the way it works for birds. And none of it matters for me either, all that time and all that work, it is not wasted but changed, stretched. It has fulfilled its purpose and the pieces of it do not fit together anymore.

Like a reptile trying to shrug on the jacket of its old self to realise that it no longer fits. Only reptiles are not sentimental and do not keep their old skins in the dresser drawer with the other miscellaneous special things, but we do our baby teeth and that is part of what makes us human. Maybe you still have the baby teeth in the little silver box with the fairy on it or maybe you lost them.

Somewhere in a parallel universe out east where summer is winter and winter is summer, it is winter and the swallows have already flown, and right now a swallow is pecking on a reptile's discarded skin.

Enclosed in all of this are the maps, some pictures and drawings, the raw bits of film, my (our) diary. Because although I know my map is not this place, the map remembers an important place even though it only exists in the realm of my mind. Just because it can't tell anyone else anything useful does not deny its significance to me (and you). That is the whole point of keeping postcards, right?

I would like to leave an epitaph because I think you will find it funny still, as I do now. It is a poem by a man called Stephen Crane. It goes:

*I saw a man pursuing the horizon;*
*Round and round they sped.*
*I was disturbed at this;*
*I accosted the man.*
*'It is futile,' I said,*
*'You can never—'*

*'You lie,' he cried,*
*And ran on.*

From Erin in the cabin in our wilderness,
Denali,
Alaska,
Earth

# ACKNOWLEDGEMENTS

I can't give enough thanks to Jack Underwood for telling me to carry on in the early days, to Harriet Moore for ceaseless support and tender critique, to Nick Sheerin for caring editorial guidance, to all my friends, but especially Claire Liddiard, Hatty Nestor and Zina Sarris, to the Sarris family for allowing me space in their house to write, and to Mum, Dad, Nan and J. J. x

I would also like to express gratitude to the following writers who allowed me to draw on their words and work in this novel.

The lines of dialogue attributed to Rachel Carson on pages 48, 57, 230 and 231 and the chapter title 'THE CHEMICAL WAR ON THE GYPSY MOTH' are taken from *Silent Spring* by Rachel Carson (copyright © 1962 by Rachel L. Carson, renewed 1990 by Roger Christie) and are reprinted by permission of Frances Collin, Trustee.

The quotation from Sylvia Plath's journals on page 91 is taken from *The Unabridged Journals of Sylvia Plath* ed. Karen V. Kukil (Penguin Random House, 2000).

The quotation from Ted Kaczynski on page 82 is taken from *Technological Slavery: The Collected Writings of Theodore J. Kaczynski* (Feral House, 2010).

The line 'the earth is an indian thing' on page 121 is from *On the Road* by Jack Kerouac, copyright © 1955, 1957, by John Sampas, Literary Representative, the Estate of Stella Sampas Kerouac; John Lash, Executor of the Estate of Jan Kerouac; Nancy Bump; and Anthony M. Sampas. Used by permission of

The chapter title 'THE CLITORIS IS A DIRECT LINE TO THE MATRIX' is taken from a billboard created by artist collective VNS Matrix.

The chapter title 'WHAT BOOK IS THIS THAT REFUSES TO END?' is taken from Anna Tsing's *The Mushroom at the End of the World: On the Possibility of Life in Capitalist Ruins* (Anna Lowenhaupt Tsing, Princeton University Press, 2015).

# Two Dollar Radio
## Books too loud to Ignore

**ALSO AVAILABLE** Here are some other titles you might want to dig into.

### AWAY! AWAY! NOVEL BY **JANA BEŇOVÁ**
### TRANSLATED BY **JANET LIVINGSTONE**

⇢ **Winner of the European Union Prize for Literature**

← "Beňová's short, fast novels are a revolution against normality."
—Austrian Broadcasting Corporation, ORF

WITH MAGNETIC, SPARKLING PROSE, Beňová delivers a lively mosaic that ruminates on human relationships, our greatest fears and desires.

### THE DEEPER THE WATER THE UGLIER THE FISH NOVEL BY **KATYA APEKINA**

← "Brilliantly structured... refreshingly original, and the writing is nothing short of gorgeous. It's a stunningly accomplished book." —NPR

POWERFULLY CAPTURES THE QUIET TORMENT of two sisters craving the attention of a parent they can't, and shouldn't, have to themselves.

### THE BLURRY YEARS NOVEL BY **ELEANOR KRISEMAN**

← "Kriseman's is a new voice to celebrate."
—*Publishers Weekly*

THE BLURRY YEARS IS A POWERFUL and unorthodox coming-of-age story from an assured new literary voice, featuring a stirringly twisted mother-daughter relationship, set against the sleazy, vividly-drawn backdrop of late-seventies and early-eighties Florida.

### THE UNDERNEATH NOVEL BY **MELANIE FINN**

← "*The Underneath* is an excellent thriller." —*Star Tribune*

THE UNDERNEATH IS AN INTELLIGENT and considerate exploration of violence—both personal and social—and whether violence may ever be justified. With the assurance and grace of her acclaimed novel *The Gloaming*, Melanie Finn returns with a precisely layered and tense new literary thriller.

## *Thank you for supporting independent culture!*
### Feel good about yourself.

# Books to read!

## PALACES NOVEL BY SIMON JACOBS

← *"Palaces* is robust, both current and clairvoyant… With a pitch-perfect portrayal of the punk scene and idiosyncratic, meaty characters, this is a wonderful novel that takes no prisoners." —*Foreword Reviews*, starred review

WITH INCISIVE PRECISION and a cool detachment, Simon Jacobs has crafted a surreal and spellbinding first novel of horror and intrigue.

## THEY CAN'T KILL US UNTIL THEY KILL US ESSAYS BY HANIF ABDURRAQIB

→ **Best Books 2017:** NPR, *Buzzfeed, Paste Magazine, Esquire, Chicago Tribune, Vol. 1 Brooklyn, CBC* (Canada), *Stereogum, National Post* (Canada), *Entropy, Heavy, Book Riot, Chicago Review of Books* (November), *The Los Angeles Review, Michigan Daily*

← "Funny, painful, precise, desperate, and loving throughout. Not a day has sounded the same since I read him." —Greil Marcus, *Village Voice*

## WHITE DIALOGUES STORIES BENNETT SIMS

← "Anyone who admires such pyrotechnics of language will find 21st-century echoes of Edgar Allan Poe in Sims' portraits of paranoia and delusion, with their zodiacal narrowing and the maddening tungsten spin of their narratives." —*New York Times Book Review*

IN THESE ELEVEN STORIES, Sims moves from slow-burn psychological horror to playful comedy, bringing us into the minds of people who are haunted by their environments, obsessions, and doubts.

## FOUND AUDIO NOVEL BY N.J. CAMPBELL

← "[A] mysterious work of metafiction… dizzying, arresting and defiantly bold." —*Chicago Tribune*

← "This strange little book, full of momentum, intrigue, and weighty ideas to mull over, is a bona fide literary page-turner." —*Publishers Weekly*, "Best Summer Books, 2017"

## SEEING PEOPLE OFF NOVEL BY JANA BEŇOVÁ
## TRANSLATED BY JANET LIVINGSTONE

→ **Winner of the European Union Prize for Literature**

← "A fascinating novel. Fans of inward-looking post-modernists like Clarice Lispector will find much to admire." —NPR

A KALEIDOSCOPIC, POETIC, AND DARKLY FUNNY portrait of a young couple navigating post-socialist Slovakia.

# Books to read!

Now available at **TWODOLLARRADIO.com** or your favorite bookseller.

## THE DROP EDGE OF YONDER
### NOVEL BY **RUDOLPH WURLITZER**

← "One of the most interesting voices in American fiction."
—*Rolling Stone*

**AN EPIC ADVENTURE** that explores the truth and temptations of the American myth, revealing one of America's most transcendant writers at the top of his form.

## THE VINE THAT ATE THE SOUTH
### NOVEL BY **J.D. WILKES**

← "Undeniably one of the smartest, most original Southern Gothic novels to come along in years." —NPR

**WITH THE ENERGY AND UNIQUE VISION** that established him as a celebrated musician, Wilkes here is an accomplished storyteller on a Homeric voyage that strikes at the heart of American mythology.

## SIRENS MEMOIR BY **JOSHUA MOHR**

⇢ **A Best of 2017** —*San Francisco Chronicle*

← "Raw-edged and whippet-thin, *Sirens* swings from tales of bawdy addiction to charged moments of a father struggling to stay clean."
—*Los Angeles Times*

**WITH VULNERABILITY, GRIT, AND HARD-WON HUMOR,** Mohr returns with his first book-length work of non-fiction, a raw and big-hearted chronicle of substance abuse, relapse, and family compassion.

## THE GLOAMING NOVEL BY **MELANIE FINN**

⇢ *New York Times* **Notable Book of 2016**

← "Deeply satisfying." —*New York Times Book Review*

**AFTER AN ACCIDENT LEAVES** her estranged in a Swiss town, Pilgrim Jones absconds to east Africa, settling in a Tanzanian outpost where she can't shake the unsettling feeling that she's being followed.

## THE INCANTATIONS OF DANIEL JOHNSTON
### GRAPHIC NOVEL BY **RICARDO CAVOLO**
### WRITTEN BY **SCOTT MCCLANAHAN**

← "Wholly unexpected, grotesque, and poignant." —*The FADER*

**RENOWNED ARTIST RICARDO CAVOLO** and Scott McClanahan combine talents in this dazzling, eye-popping graphic biography of artist and musician Daniel Johnston.

# Books to read!

Now available at **TWODOLLARRADIO.com** or your favorite bookseller.

---

## THE REACTIVE NOVEL BY **MASANDE NTSHANGA**

← "Often teems with a beauty that seems to carry on in front of its glue-huffing wasters despite themselves." —*Slate*

A CLEAR-EYED, COMPASSIONATE ACCOUNT of a young HIV+ man grappling with the sudden death of his brother in South Africa.

---

## SQUARE WAVE NOVEL BY **MARK DE SILVA**

← "Compelling and horrifying." —*Chicago Tribune*

A GRAND NOVEL OF ideas and compelling crime mystery, about security states past and present, weather modification science, micro-tonal music, and imperial influences.

---

## NOT DARK YET NOVEL BY **BERIT ELLINGSEN**

← "Fascinating, surreal, gorgeously written."
—*BuzzFeed*

ON THE VERGE OF a self-inflicted apocalypse, a former military sniper is enlisted by a former lover for an eco-terrorist action that threatens the quiet life he built for himself in the mountains.

---

## THE GLACIER NOVEL BY **JEFF WOOD**

← "Gorgeously and urgently written."
—*Library Journal*, starred review

FOLLOWING A CATERER AT a convention center, a surveyor residing in a storage unit, and the masses lining up for an Event on the horizon, *The Glacier* is a poetic rendering of the pre-apocalypse.

---

## HAINTS STAY NOVEL BY **COLIN WINNETTE**

← "In his astonishing portrait of American violence, Colin Winnette makes use of the Western genre to stunning effect." —*Los Angeles Times*

HAINTS STAY IS A NEW Acid Western in the tradition of Rudolph Wurlitzer, *Meek's Cutoff*, and Jim Jarmusch's *Dead Man*: meaning it is brutal, surreal, and possesses an unsettling humor.

# Books to read!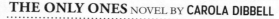

Now available at **TWODOLLARRADIO.com** or your favorite bookseller.

## THE ONLY ONES NOVEL BY **CAROLA DIBBELL**

→ **Best Books 2015:** *Washington Post*; O, *The Oprah Magazine*; NPR

← "Breathtaking." —NPR

INEZ WANDERS A POST-PANDEMIC world immune to disease. Her life is altered when a grief-stricken mother that hired her to provide genetic material backs out, leaving Inez with the product: a baby girl.

## BINARY STAR NOVEL BY **SARAH GERARD**

→ *Los Angeles Times* Book Prize Finalist

→ **Best Books 2015:** *BuzzFeed*, *Vanity Fair*, NPR

← "Rhythmic, hallucinatory, yet vivid as crystal." —NPR

AN ELEGIAC, INTENSE PORTRAIT of two young lovers as they battle their personal afflictions while on a road trip across the U.S.

## THE ABSOLUTION OF ROBERTO ACESTES LAING NOVEL BY **NICHOLAS ROMBES**

← "Kafka directed by David Lynch doesn't even come close." —*3:AM Magazine*

A RARE-FILM LIBRARIAN mysteriously burned his entire stockpile of film canisters and disappeared. Years later, a journalist tracks the forgotten man down to a motel on the fringe of the Wisconsin wilds.

## ANCIENT OCEANS OF CENTRAL KENTUCKY NOVEL BY **DAVID CONNERLEY NAHM**

→ **Best Books 2014:** NPR, *Flavorwire*

← "Wonderful. Deeply suspenseful." —NPR

LEAH IS HAUNTED BY the disappearance of her brother Jacob. When a mysterious man shows up, claiming to be Jacob, Leah is wrenched back to childhood.

## CRYSTAL EATERS NOVEL BY **SHANE JONES**

← "[Jones is] something of a millennial Richard Brautigan." —*Nylon*

REMY IS A YOUNG GIRL living in a town that believes in crystal count. When her mother becomes sick, she sets out to accomplish what no one else has, and increase her mother's crystal count.

5-19

o read!

TWODOLLARRADIO.com or your favorite bookseller.

## THE ORANGE EATS CREEPS
NOVEL BY **GRACE KRILANOVICH**

→ **National Book Foundation '5 Under 35' Award**

← "Breathless, scary, and like nothing I've ever read." —NPR

A RUNAWAY SEARCHES FOR her disappeared foster sister along the "Highway That Eats People" haunted by a serial killer named Dactyl.

## RADIO IRIS NOVEL BY **ANNE-MARIE KINNEY**

← "[*Radio Iris*] has a dramatic otherworldly payoff that is unexpected and triumphant."
—*New York Times Book Review*, Editors' Choice

RADIO IRIS IS THE STORY OF Iris Finch, a socially awkward daydreamer with a job as the receptionist/personal assistant to an eccentric and increasingly absent businessman.

## HOW TO GET INTO THE TWIN PALMS
NOVEL BY **KAROLINA WACLAWIAK**

← "Reinvents the immigration story." —*New York Times Book Review*

ANYA IS A YOUNG WOMAN living in a Russian neighborhood in L.A., torn between her parents' Polish heritage and trying to assimilate in the U.S. She decides instead to try and assimilate in her Russian community, embodied by the nightclub, the Twin Palms.

## MIRA CORPORA NOVEL BY **JEFF JACKSON**

→ *Los Angeles Times* **Book Prize Finalist**

← "A piercing howl of a book." —*Slate*

A COMING OF AGE story for people who hate coming of age stories, featuring a colony of outcast children, teenage oracles, amusement parks haunted by gibbons, and mysterious cassette tapes.

## CRAPALACHIA MEMOIR BY **SCOTT MCCLANAHAN**

→ **Best Books 2013:** *The Millions, Flavorwire, Time Out Chicago*

← "Aims to lasso the moon." —*New York Times Book Review*

A PORTRAIT OF MCCLANAHAN'S formative years, coming of age in rural West Virginia, during a stretch of time where he was deeply influenced by his Grandma Ruby and Uncle Nathan, who suffered from cerebral palsy.